The Return Of The Earth
Mother Series: Book 2

DESCENDANTS OF THE FIRST

PRAISE FOR
THE RETURN OF THE EARTH
MOTHER SERIES

'A powerhouse of fantasy, myth, and Black sisterhood. The storytelling is lush and the tight plotting kept me on the edge of my seat.'

Kalynn Bayron, bestselling author of 'Cinderella Is Dead' and 'This Poison Heart'

'Descendants of the First is a delight of a sequel. With an expansively beautiful world at stake and an intricate system of magic with myth, this is a fantasy that charges full steam ahead.'

Chloe Gong, New York Times-bestselling author of 'These Violent Delights'

'The characters are so compelling. I am in awe of Amayo's imagination.'

Lian Hearn, bestselling author of the Otori series

'Something special. Excellent writing, brilliant book.'

Dorothy Koomson, internatonally bestselling, multi-award-winning novelist

'The story takes a gentle hold of you but then tightens its grip firmly until you can't drop the book.'

Five Books

'From a rich and deep culture, Amayo weaves a world of literary magic.'

Buzzfeed

'A compelling story.'

BookRiot

DESCENDANTS OF THE FIRST

BY RENI K AMAYO

ONWE

ONWE

First published in Great Britain in 2021 by Onwe Press Ltd

This hardback edition was first published in 2021

Printed and bounded by Clays Printers (UK) Ltd.

A CIP catalogue record for this book is available from the British Library.

eBook ISBN 978-1-9160429-7-1
Hardback ISBN 978-1-9160429-6-4

FSC
www.fsc.org
MIX
Paper from
responsible sources
FSC® C018072

www.onwe.co | @weareonwe

To my sisters.

You mean far more than I can ever find the words to say.

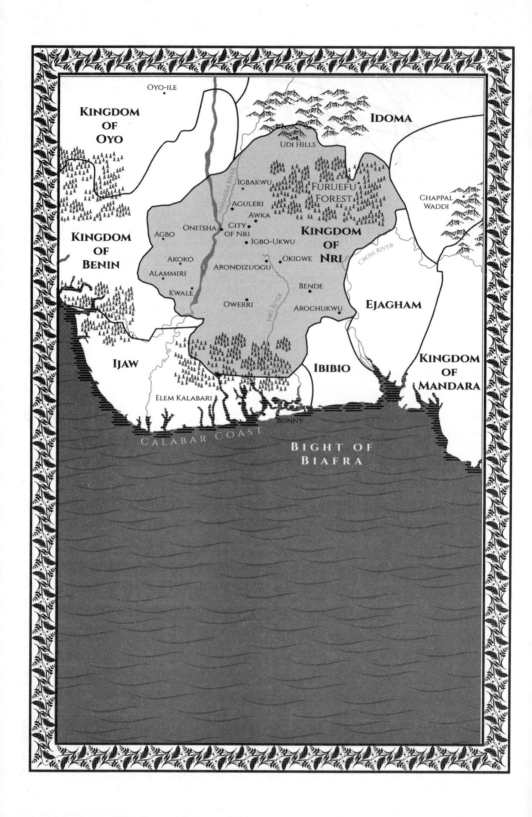

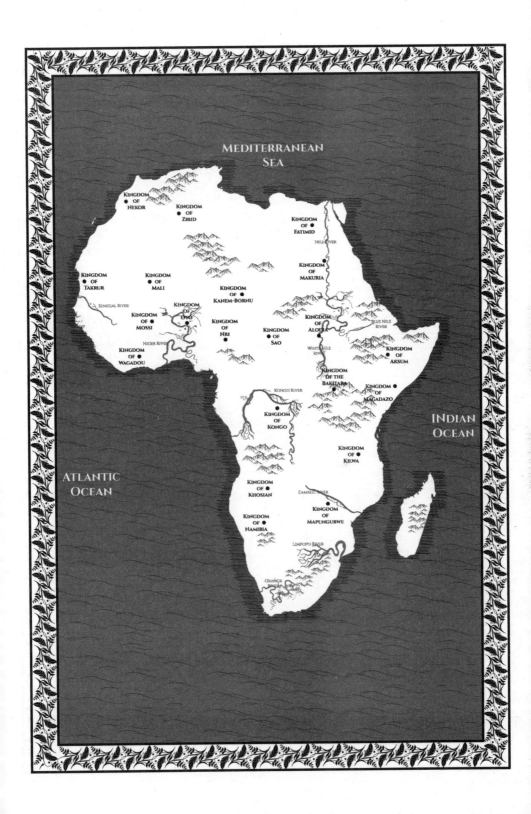

MEDITERRANEAN
SEA

KINGDOM
OF
NEKOR

KINGDOM
OF
ZIRID

KINGDOM
OF
FATIMID

NILE RIVER

KINGDOM
OF
MAKURIA

KINGDOM
OF
TAKRUR

KINGDOM
OF
MALI

KINGDOM
OF
KANEM-BORNU

SENEGAL RIVER

KINGDOM
OF
OYO

KINGDOM
OF
MOSSI

KINGDOM
OF
NRI

KINGDOM
OF
SAO

KINGDOM
OF
ALODIA

BLUE NILE
RIVER

KINGDOM
OF
WAGADOU

NIGER RIVER

WHITE NILE
RIVER

KINGDOM
OF
AKSUM

KINGDOM
OF THE
BAKITARA

KONGO RIVER

KINGDOM
OF
MAGADAZO

VLR

KINGDOM
OF
KONGO

INDIAN
OCEAN

KINGDOM
OF
KILWA

ATLANTIC
OCEAN

KINGDOM
OF
KHOSIAN

KINGDOM
OF
NAMIBIA

ZAMBEZI RIVER

KINGDOM
OF
MAPUNGUBWE

LIMPOPO RIVER

ORANGE
RIVER

THE TRIALS TO ALA

Nsibidi of Soul

Trial: She has seen her inner God

Igbo translation: Chi

Nsibidi of Ground

Trial: She has spoken to the earth

Igbo translation: Àlà

Nsbidi of Air

Trial: She has been carried by the air

Igbo translation: Ikuku

Nsbidi of Love

Trial: She has given herself for another

Igbo translation: Ihunaya

Nsbidi of Death

Trial: She has taken breath

Igbo translation: Ọnwu

Nsibidi of Life

Trial: She has created breath

Igbo translation: Ndụ

Nsibidi of Creation

Trial: She has moulded beauty

Igbo translation: Okike

Nsibidi of Peace

Trial: She has found freedom

Igbo translation: Udo

Nsibidi of Ala

Trial: She has returned

Igbo translation: Ala

PROLOGUE

Urukpuru

A sigh escaped Nwamara's lips as her claws sank into snow for the first time in de-cades. The bird-woman hadn't realised how much she had missed the biting cold against her warmed skin. It provided a little respite from the heaviness tugging at her chest, drawing her to memories of a different time. A different world.

The sun kissed the floating land; its light rays beamed off the clouds that bordered the sky city's edge. Urukpuru, the wonder in the sky. Nwamara let the snow fall through her claws. She didn't understand this new world. It had no gods. It had no Mother. Yet, it had *something*. A whisper of magic in the air. She stretched out her wings. Whatever it was, it had changed her. Though the thought was not sad, it filled her eyes with tears. They fell, wet and fat, melting the frost that had formed on her cheeks.

'Nwanne-nwanyi Nwamara?' Nene said. 'What is the matter?' Her auburn feathers had sprung up, and her thin body tremored.

Nwamara's jaw stiffened. It wasn't the first time that Nene had forgotten to use the human tongue. How many times must she lecture the little nnunu? When would Nene finally understand that, if she hoped to survive what was coming, she *had* to practise. The bird-woman cowered under Nwamara's glare, a sight that made her chest squeeze. *What will we do with you?*

'Here,' she said gently in the human tongue, stretching her wing out to the gnarled bunch of vines before them. This was it. This was what had called her the day that Ochichiri, the Eze, the ruler of the Kingdom, had returned to dust. That day she had woken up with the gift of flight. That day everything had changed. Nwamara regarded the dried entanglement of vines and she waited.

When it finally began to move, Nwamara had been coated with frost. She glanced at Nene, her reddish-brown feathers lost beneath a blanket of snow. How long had they been waiting for? Nwamara couldn't tell. As the vines sprang to life before her, lurching out this way and that like a sprawling babe, she realised that it didn't matter.

Her heart lodged in her throat as the taste of death sprouted into her beak. Was that what she had been called for? Her end. Her return to dust? Wasn't that what had happened to Ketandu? The nnunu had been called to the sea, only for it to claim her last breath. Nwamara's heart raced at the thought.

'What will be, will be,' she sang, as a glow broke through the vines. *No.* Her heart stopped. 'It can't be.' The words choked out of her tight throat as her head spun. She might have stumbled, had she been on her feet, but her wings kept her steady. *It can't be.*

From the corner of her eyes, she could see Nene reach out for crystals of onyx and cloud nestled within the living vine. Nwamara let out a hiss as she slapped the bird-woman's claw away. Was she blind or had she lost all form of sense?

'Nwamara,' Nene spluttered, clutching at her wing as she blinked back fresh tears.

'Nwanne-nwanyi Nene, you nearly surrendered yourself to dust. Open your eyes and *look* at what you had been quick to grasp.'

Nene's beak parted as she looked down cautiously. Soon enough, the crease on her forehead smoothed as her eyes widened. 'Àlà and Ikuku,' she gasped.

Nwamara's chest tightened at their names. Àlà and Ikuku: lost parts of the Mother's scattered crystal. Through the crystal's glare, she could see them now, as clearly as she could see the snow. The Twins. The Daughters of Nri.

'They must evoke them,' Nwamara breathed along with the song forming in her head; it resonated with a frequency that clutched at her throat. The song of Truth. Nwamara doubled over as she clawed for the air that had been knocked out of her. She had only heard that song once in her centuries of living. Before the god's departure. Before Eze Ochichiri started his blood-soaked reign. A shiver escaped Nwamara and the world began to tremble.

Nwamara tugged Nene's wing and pulled her up as a gush of blue liquid bled from beneath the vines. A river of sapphire formed like a serpent slithering through the land. Even from her height, hot steam pressed against her cheeks.

'A curse,' Nene breathed. 'They will bring forth a curse.'

'Or salvation,' Nwamara said gently. 'Either way, what will be, will be.'

CHAPTER 1
THE ỌNWỤ MARK

City of Nri

Olu's stomach turned as a thin line of crimson formed across his palm. Years spent in battle left him numb to the sight of blood, so why should such a small cut affect him so?

'Ozo,' the amoosu said, her right hand beckoning to him, but it was the left that had held his attention. It held a bloodstained daga and a time-worn iko. As Olu peered closer, he could see that she was trembling. She was afraid.

Olu tended to have that effect on people. Perhaps it was his stature. He stood heads taller than most, his muscles had been beat strong with training, and on his face he wore a scar from a fight he seldom had the stomach to speak of. He knew he could be fearsome on the best of days. He tried and failed to relax the rigidness in his body. This was not the best of days.

He attempted to read the woman but, like most amoosus, her face was veiled by a cascade of seashells. Long chains pooled against a flat disk that hung at her neck and extended out over her shoulders.

'Ozo, you need to squeeze,' she said, as she drew closer, pausing at every step as though he were seconds from leaping at her.

He couldn't deny that he wanted to. He wanted to knock her away and bolt out of the Edemede. He felt suffocated under the weight of its curved beige walls, lined

1

with thick woven materials, which whispered of the countless evils they had seen.

'Ozo?'

Olu's nose flared at her persistence but he did as she asked. What choice did he have? The girl could not die.

'It's hard the first time,' General Ikenna said from beside him.

Olu bristled. Was that what Ikenna thought the problem was? The newness of the hellish practice? He sucked in his rage and let out a cool sigh before allowing his gaze to fall on Ikenna – the grandson of the lord of war relations, Obi Somto.

Though they were peers, having started their duty at the same time, Ikenna's blood had propelled him to a height unattainable for Olu. As the next in line to succeed his uncle, Ozo Okoro, as Head General of the Eze's army, Ikenna had power; that is why Olu had gone to him, his oldest friend, and asked for help.

He had known that Ikenna would ask for something in return; he always did. Olu just hadn't imagined it would be something so *depraved*. He should have refused him. In truth, he should have pummelled him. But then the girl … Olu took a deep breath and cracked his neck.

'This is unnecessary,' Olu said, his voice more biting than he would have liked. He fought to settle his growing rage as he watched a mocking frown on Ikenna's thin lips.

'Unnecessary?' Ikenna repeated. 'Yes, I suppose it is unnecessary to go against my grandfather's wishes and break twins out of the Towers – twins, who, according to you, *killed* the Eze.'

Olu's head snapped towards the amoosu woman, who immediately looked down to her feet. He felt a sting in his palm. His fingers dug into the fresh wound as he turned back to Ikenna.

'Never. *Never.* Say. Those. Words. Again.' Olu forced the blows his arms wanted to deliver into words. Now was not the time for action. If he acted, he would kill. If he killed, he would not be able to free the girl.

The girls, he corrected as he thought back to the one they had found with Sinai. His stomach tightened at the memory of the girl who wore Sinai's face. The girl who had torn the earth apart almost a sun-cycle ago when she had witnessed her village being ransacked by the Eze's men. His men.

It didn't make sense for her to be *here*. Nor did it make sense for the girls to still be alive upon their discovery in Eze Ochichiri's quarters. The Eze's law was clear on the matter of twins; they should have been killed on sight. Instead, they were apprehended, and reports of flying chairs and winds that cracked the walls clung to the guards' quivering lips. The whispers had instilled fear in Obi Somto. It was that fear that had kept the girls alive.

Now, all that stood between the girls and death was time. Time for Obi Somto to realise that the Eze was dead and the responsibility of those girls rested solely on his shoulders. Olu had no doubt that when that time came, Obi Somto would burn the city of Nri down if it meant vanquishing them.

Olu cut a glare at Ikenna. No one, outside the two of them, should have known about the Eze's death. He turned to the amoosu. Would he have to kill her now? He glanced at her neck, slender as a branch of rosewood. Snapping her head should be easy enough. Yet the thought left a sour taste in his mouth. *Damn Ikenna.*

'I gave you my word,' Olu said carefully. 'I will do whatever you ask if you could help me free those girls. An Ọbara oath is not necessary.'

'Your word is *nice*—' Ikenna started as he drew the daga across his palm before holding it over the iko; a chill ran down Olu's spine as he watched Ikenna's blood mix with his '—but sadly I've been betrayed enough times to know that I can't rely on anyone's word, not even a man with your reputation. Freeing those girls means severing ties. Important ties. I would be a fool to do that on your *word*,' he said, handing the iko back to the woman.

'I want —' Olu started. He was stopped by a blood-curdling scream from the amoosu's wide-open mouth. He grasped on the hilt of his abara sword as his body sprung into action but it would have no effect on the danger, which seemed to be buried within the blood-filled iko. Beneath the white shell headcover, the amoosu wore a tortured expression.

'You can't do this,' she whispered, the crow seashells clanging as she shook her head. Olu lowered his abara sword. It simmered green with its deadly enchantment as he put it back in its sleeve. The fear in her voice made the hairs on his arms stand up. 'You can't, you can't, no you can't.'

'Are you broken?' Ikenna demanded. His voice remained steady but Olu had glimpsed fear within his slit eyes.

'Look,' the woman said, thrusting the iko towards Ikenna, 'it bears the mgbanwe … and … and … the ọnwụ mark. Death. It means change, it means death, so much death. Yes, yes, the Kingdom will find a new ruler – you, Ozo Ikenna, you will rule, but-but the Kingdom … death will come over it, as relentless as wildfire.'

'I will be the Eze?' Ikenna said, his voice thick with emotion.

Olu frowned. Was that all he'd gleaned from her premonition? 'Death,' he said firmly. 'She sees death.'

'Why wouldn't she?' Ikenna scoffed. 'We're changing a kingdom. For every mark of change, there is a price. Of course, there will be those that will die. Think of what happened when Eze Ochichiri took power.'

Olu looked at Ikenna as though for the first time. The hunger behind the man's eyes made him want to turn away. 'Ikenna.'

He jutted his chin forward. 'Who else if not me? My dear grandfather? Gods, can you imagine that? *Eze Somto?* Or better yet Nri's golden lord, *Eze* Akunna?'

Olu held his glare but he couldn't ignore the pang of defeat at his chest. As lords of war and finance, Obi Somto and Obi Akunna were the most powerful Obis, the natural contenders for the empty throne. They were also soullessly cruel.

'Olu, we have a chance here for *real* change.'

Despite himself, Olu shook his head at the thought of innocent bloodshed; nothing could be *worth* that.

Ikenna's eyes narrowed. 'I have no other reason for keeping those murderous *curses* alive. If you don't go through with this, I will not help and your precious twins will burn.'

Olu's jaw clamped at the thought of Sinai engulfed in flames. 'The world needs them,' he said gruffly. 'Ikenna, friend, you must believe me.'

'No. It is you who must believe when I say that the Kingdom needs *me*.'

Olu turned to the amoosu woman. He could feel her silent pleading. She wanted him to refuse. She was begging him to refuse. Dread sank into his stomach as he looked at her trembling hands over the blood-filled iko. He stretched his sore hand, reopening the thinly crusted wound. The scent of Sinai hung around him. A memory of a time when she was safe in his arms. The girl must live.

'Proceed.'

CHAPTER 2
CURSED ONES

Furuefu forest

Shimmering honey nudged Sinai awake. She groaned, shifting away from what could only be another morning in the Furuefu forest. Sleep: all she wanted was sleep. She folded her arm over her head and tried to nestle back into the darkness, but the forest was relentless. A cacophony of bird whistles and rustling thundered about her, and the breeze filtered through her coarse hair.

'Eurgh,' she murmured as her mind sprang into action. It had been the same every morning since their escape from the city of Nri. Faces she didn't recognise flashed through her mind, the smell of smoke and charred flesh filled her nostrils, then … Olu.

His emerald gaze lingered as she opened her eyes to the new day. The thought of him brought a frown to her face. Olu. A soldier in the Eze's army. Her friend, once her protector. Now her shame.

Snap.

The air thinned as Sinai stared down from the tree she'd slept in. All she could see was the morning mist. She bit her lip. That sound was a twig, which meant Naala was leaving without her. Again.

Sinai sighed as she clambered down. Her movements were even clumsier than usual as thoughts of having to spend another day searching for Naala clanged against her head.

'Wai—' Sinai started, halting her cry as she came face-to-face with Naala, the girl that she had met in the palace three moon-cycles ago. The girl that looked almost exactly like her. The girl that felt like family … a concept that Sinai had never fully known in the cold palace that had raised her.

'Sinai, you know I can't wait for you to sleep in,' Naala said.

Sinai hadn't expected a warm reception, not since their escape from the palace, but it seemed this morning Naala was feeling particularly distant. *Sleep in?* Sinai thought, glancing back at the peach horizon. The sun had barely broken through.

'Don't give me that look—' Naala sighed, pressing her fingers into her eyes '— we've been through this – I can't afford to waste any more time. With every delay, they are getting further away.'

They. Sinai didn't really know who *they* were, though *they* now determined every moment of her waking hours. All Sinai knew was that *they* had all survived the Eze's village attacks and Naala owed them her life.

Moments before they'd fled the city, Olu had gasped, 'The Amaghi,' as vines that Naala had sprang to life had tightened across his neck. The Amaghi, the secret people who had rescued Naala's lost companions. Only a trusted few knew of them; Olu, it seemed, was one of the few. Even so, it hadn't been easy for Naala to ask Olu that. It was the only thing she had said to him that hadn't been curses, or threats to kill him, or 'murderer'. She had screamed that word at him several times, her voice laced with venom. Sinai was certain that Naala would have killed Olu had she not stood in her way … a gesture that had torn this distance between them.

'I am ready to go,' Sinai insisted, ignoring the ache radiating from her blistered feet.

Naala raised her eyebrows; her lips were tense as though she were restraining a smile.

'What?' Sinai asked hesitantly.

'Your hammock.'

Sinai's cheeks flamed in the moist air. The hammock. How could she have forgotten the stupid hammock … *again*.

'Oh, yes. Well, I meant – I *will* be ready *soon*, as soon as I get it down. Just please don't—' The words dried at the tip of Sinai's mouth; the hairs on the back of her neck lifted.

Something wasn't right.

A cold chill ran down her spine. A warning rang through her body. Something was following them. Something thirsting for blood. Something—

'Sinai,' Naala snapped; her eyebrows were pulled together. 'You think we're being followed again?' Her dark eyes roamed over Sinai's face intently. 'Listen to me, there is *nothing* out there.'

There had been a time when Naala had taken her claims seriously but, after one too many fruitless searches, she had started to get annoyed. Now, it seemed, she was concerned. Sinai released the breath she had been holding. She would have preferred Naala's annoyance. The pitying look in Naala's eye made her feel crazy. She wasn't crazy. There was something—

'Abomination!' a voice rang from behind her. She turned and buckled at the sight of four men standing in front of an ibu elephant with spears jutting towards the girls. She could feel the heat emitting from the green enchanted metal. *Abara metal*, she thought, as her stomach dropped.

'Cursed ones,' another man snarled. Behind them, the ibu elephant lazily drew up its trunk. Its body was caked with white mud that flaked around the dead animals, spices and baskets draped at either side of its belly.

Traders, Sinai thought. Her gaze shifted to a large basket with thick, curved red oak frames, tied securely with a dark rope. She felt power as black as night stirring within her.

There was something breathing in that basket.

Sinai squinted as a pair of small hands, several shades darker than wood, clutched at the bars before shifting out of sight. *A child?* It was not uncommon to hear of traders taking trips to the rural villages to grab peasants that they would sell into servitude in the larger cities. But whoever was in that basket couldn't have lived more than five years. Sinai's heart ached at the thought and a light breeze began to clear the morning mist.

'You don't want to do this,' Naala warned. Sparks of gold danced across her eyes but they came to a stop when one of the men jabbed at her with his enchanted spear. A strangled cry escaped her gritted teeth. 'Blast it!' she roared, her eyes ablaze, as a thin crimson line began to form on her arm.

Writhing pain singed at Sinai's untouched arm. It tasted of abara metal. It clutched at her throat and blinded her before it began to cool. A shiver ran down her spine. The pain was not hers yet she had felt it all the same.

It had first happened when they had been taken out of the Towers on Olu's command. Sinai had expected to feel relief upon seeing him, but, instead, bloodthirst had coursed through her. Thick and relentless. Naala's thoughts, Naala's pains, had bored their way into her skin as though they had belonged to her. As though it had been *her* village that Olu had torn through with his abara sword on the Eze's command. Sinai drew a breath as she pushed the memory aside. *Not now.*

'Not a word, abumoonu,' the man said, his eyes glued on the two girls as he hissed at his companions, 'How much will they fetch for?'

'Fetch for? Death is all that they can fetch! Look at them … twins, *anu ofia*!' one man cursed. His thick hair fell in fat rolls that obscured his eyes as they jumped erratically between the two of them.

'We need to kill them,' another said. His still, coal eyes sent a chill running down Sinai's back.

'Eh-he,' the other agreed, 'it's the only way we can be saved!'

The man who had struck Naala cackled. 'Bah, that is nonsense! I've come across my fair share of so-called *cursed* twins and they're just like you and me – weaker, in fact – and the city will pay a hell of a lot more for their heads.'

Sweat formed on Sinai's brow as she threw a glance at Naala. She was studying them. Her fists opened and closed, preparing for action. Sinai's heart clambered against her chest.

A voice boomed in her head: *What do you have to be afraid of? Was it not you who killed the Eze?* It sounded almost like Meekulu Kaurandua, the palace cook who had saved Sinai in more ways than one. The woman whose blood still stained Sinai's palms.

Sinai steadied herself. She *had* defeated Eze Ochichiri, the godkiller himself. She and Naala had killed him with a power that Sinai had yet to make sense of. Like Naala, it felt familiar and yet remained a mystery; it stood in the background of her existence, lurking around her, dark and distant.

That would no longer suit; she needed to wield it *now*. Sinai tugged at the power. Her heart hammered and her palms moistened from the effort, yet the power felt as aloof as ever.

Something shifted.

Naala's eyes dazzled gold as the vines sprang to life, wrapping around the ankles of each of the men and pulling until they came crashing to the ground.

Sinai gaped at the entangled men.

'Don't just stand there!' Naala cried over their violent shouts. 'Run!'

Run? Run. Sinai pulled at her heavy legs but, before she could make much headway, a thought clutched at her. She plunged to the ground. Her heart pounded as spots of black mist, speckled gold, grew at her periphery.

'Get up!' Naala cried, jerking at her arm. 'Run!' Sinai felt something wet hit her palm. She looked up to find lines of blood trickling down from Naala's wound. 'Move!'

'We can't,' Sinai breathed as she looked back to the elephant. It had buckled back from fright and let out a brass trumpet sound. 'The child!'

'The child?' Naala exclaimed, the whites of her eyes growing as she followed Sinai's gaze to the basket and then back to the men who had struggled back to their feet. 'Blast it!' Her hands came to her head. 'Think, think, think.'

Naala paused, her neck curving as she looked up to the skies. Bursts of gold erupted from her eyes as more tree vines slithered down to the ground, wrapping around the ankles, torso and arms of each of the men.

'Witch! Abumoonu! Witch!' they cried before the tangled vines brought them to a muffled silence. Naala breathed heavily through clenched teeth as the vines lifted the grappling men to the top of the trees where they hung cocooned.

Sinai jolted at the wet sound of snapped vines as they fought their way out. Naala wasted no time. Thick branches tore off the trees before knocking each of their heads until they settled.

'That won't keep them long,' Naala breathed. 'Let's get the child. We have to go.'

Sinai sucked in a deep breath, shaking off the feeling that would come over her after witnessing Naala's many feats … the feeling that she had no use at all.

The elephant's wrinkled hazel eyes followed her as she approached before it turned to graze. Sinai let out a slow breath as she reached the basket before unlatching its rusty hook. It was a girl. Her thick hair had been pulled into two puffs, far larger than her small head.

'Ndewo,' Sinai said gently, her heart aching at the girl's trembling frame. She was younger than Sinai had initially thought and Naala's performance was sure to have frightened her. The little one shifted forward and hesitantly peered out of the basket.

'Why is she locked up like this?' Naala murmured as she came over.

'She's their capture,' Sinai said, as Naala's lips pulled to a frown. 'Servants are an invaluable *commodity* in the palace, especially if they are trained from childhood. It's not uncommon for people from the squalors to sell their own children, as a means to survive. Some were snatched from their village and sold into servitude or … the *akwuna* house.'

Naala's lip tightened before her eyes met the trembling girl. Her face softened. 'Ndewo, little one.' She crossed her palm across her chest and extended it to the girl, performing the greeting in Nri. 'Where are you from?'

The girl crawled out to the edge of the basket and returned the gesture with a smile.

'Twins,' she whispered.

Sinai paused and looked at Naala. 'Oh …' she murmured. Of course, the sight of the both of them must be terrifying, especially to a child. Twins, cursed beings that wore the same face.

'Like Isiawele and Isioma?' the girl beamed.

'Who?' Sinai asked.

'Like Isiawele and Isioma?' The girl shrugged as she let her legs swing out of the basket. 'Well … *are* you good like Isiawele and Isioma or bad like them?' she said, pointing up at the men.

'We're not like them,' Naala said quickly. 'We want to help you.'

The girl paused as she inspected Naala's face before her eyes lit up.

'Can you take me back home now, please?'

'Where is home?'

'Siwunmi. You can take me there?' the girl said as she swayed slightly on the open basket door.

'Siwunmi?' Naala murmured. 'That is quite far away.' Shadows formed over her face as she weighed something in her head. *The Amaghi*, Sinai thought.

'Oh, it is far?' the girl huffed as her bottom lip trembled. 'I should never, never have picked them.'

'Picked what?'

The girl sniffed as she ran her hands across the bars. She gulped to settle her voice. 'I was picking licky-licky when the bad men took me.'

'Picking what?' Sinai murmured.

'She means the fruit, icheku.' Naala smiled distantly. 'I used to get in quite a bit of trouble picking icheku too. What's your name?'

'Ginika,' the girl replied, and Naala's face fell.

Sinai opened her mouth to ask Naala what was wrong but the other girl's face hardened. She knew that look; she could ask all she wanted but Naala wasn't going to say a word on the subject.

'Gini?' Naala said eventually. Her voice was thick but her eyes dry as she blinked back at the girl. 'Let's get you home.'

*

Sinai felt like a mule. Her back ached, her feet were wet with blood and her lungs were beaten raw.

'Hurry up, Sinai,' Naala hollered. Worse than that, she was an ineffectual mule. Even with Gini's tiny hand in hers, Naala still marched poles ahead. *What do they give to people in these villages?* This couldn't be natural.

Though Naala and her were similar in size, there was a power to Naala's body that she lacked. Where Sinai was soft and supple, Naala was lean and strong; her body ran with slight lines and curves of muscles that Sinai had never seen on her own body. Gini, however, was but a child; how could her legs keep up where Sinai's failed?

'I know,' Sinai mumbled, pondering, not for the first time, why she was even there. She had initially told herself that it was the guilt. When she had stood between Naala and Olu, she had seen something break in the girl's eyes. Something Sinai desperately wanted to get back. She wanted to help Naala find her friends but soon into the journey Sinai had started to feel like a burden. She was far slower than Naala and had no idea how to navigate the forest. Naala was constantly teaching her and, despite her explanations, Sinai somehow managed to get things a little bit wrong. Soon she had to admit to herself that she wasn't here to support; she was here because she had nowhere else to go.

'My legs hurt,' Gini sighed. *Oh, thank heavens,* Sinai thought as Naala stopped to look down at the girl.

'We're almost there, but do you want to have a break? Perhaps eat some food?' Naala asked as she shifted the boar that they had taken from the bandits' possessions off from her shoulders, and placed it on the plush ground. The girl nodded, jumping up and down in excitement.

'Food it is,' she chuckled.

'Food it is,' Sinai repeated as she watched Naala pull out a flint daga and scraps of uchie tree bark from her satchel.

'Do you want me to help skin the meat?' the little girl asked as she circled Naala's legs.

'*You* know how?' Sinai exclaimed. Naala inspected Gini with one eyebrow raised. The girl nodded and Sinai felt her stomach twist. Sinai's culinary training consisted solely of watching her food be served, a fact that filled her with shame every time she watched Naala prepare their food.

'Then sure.' Naala shrugged, pulling out another daga and handing it over to the girl. Naala's head shook slightly as a wide grin formed on her lips. Sinai watched both of them kneeling down and working away at the boar; she bit at her bottom lip as she tried to find something to do with her hands.

'I'll grab some water,' she announced after a few lost minutes had gone by.

Naala nodded. 'That's a good idea—' she looked up '—there should be a river not too far from here. Just head towards the north west. Be sure to pick the mmiri pods; don't try to drink the river—'

'Water. Yes, I remember,' Sinai said. She had remembered. Contrary to Naala's beliefs, she did know things. Just not as much as she needed to.

Naala studied her carefully. 'Do you need me to show you the way?'

'No,' Sinai replied quickly as she shifted from Naala's piercing gaze. 'I know, head north.'

'North west.' Naala sighed, getting up to her feet. Sinai's cheeks burned.

'Yes, that's what I meant,' she insisted, gesturing for Naala to sit back down. 'You were the one that said we didn't have time. You carry on with the food. I'll get the water.' Sinai headed into the forest before Naala could utter another word.

*

She was lost. Heavens, help her, she was *lost*. How could she have—

'Water,' Sinai murmured, as she caught flashes of blue between the tree bark. 'Water!' she exclaimed, before pushing herself forward until she found herself on the bank. A wide lake dazzled before her, shimmering in shades of cyan. Blue-green ripples glistened in the afternoon sun. Clusters of mmiri pods sprouted alongside ninebark shrubs and witch hazel but it was the river itself that stole her attention.

Sinai could picture herself swimming in the liquid dream.

'No,' she muttered to herself as she tried to shake away the taste of the cool water against her skin. She was so sore, so filthy, but she had to … she had to what? Watch Naala and Gini cook? The thought of standing in their camp, watching them at work whilst she twiddled her thumbs, pricked against her skin.

Sinai tugged at the vines that held her shoes together. Surely she could have a little dip in the water? She loosened her torn skirt until all she was left in was the wrappers that she tied around her waist and chest. Even if she spent twenty minutes dipping, she'd be back before they'd finished. She'd be more refreshed; perhaps she'd even walk faster after soothing her feet.

She double knotted her garments hastily before drawing her feet towards the water and letting it kiss her toe.

A cool fresh sensation ran through her and Sinai grinned with delight. Her worries and stresses all seemed to melt away as she moved deeper into the river. She watched as a bale of large turtles drifted curiously towards her, their eyes drooped and lazy as their paddled arms swept through the water. Sinai didn't want to frighten them. She waded slowly through the river, clenching her stomach as the cool water crept up her body, glossing her dark skin. She smiled as the large turtles began to circle around her; their glazed, hardened shells sparkled in the sun like quartz. Sinai sank her body deep into the water before lifting her feet up and turning on her back. The cool water held her head steady as her face bathed in the glory of the sun. She hadn't felt so relaxed in moon-cycles. She allowed her mind to wander to thoughts of beautiful skies and a belly full of warm rich food.

Feed.

The word sprang into her mind and she gasped audibly as she plummeted into the water before bursting back up. She spluttered as stray droplets found their way to the back of her throat. When she finally managed to open her eyes, she saw the last of the turtles scuttling away deep into the river, blending smoothly with the darkness that lay beneath. Sinai's heartbeat pounded against her temple as she looked around.

That thought hadn't been her own. Yet it had left her feeling drained and disorientated, with a burning desire to feel blood and broken bones crunching in her mouth. Her stomach heaved at the thought.

She paused as she watched the flurry of trees that sloped over the river. She squinted as she saw something, a slither of silver light rippling beneath the leaves. Her stomach dipped. That was it. She knew it as clearly as she knew her own name. It hadn't been in her head; *that was it.* The thing that had been following them; not the traders, not the wind but this … this *beast.*

Naala and Gini.

Sinai flinched at the thought of them. She had to get to them. She needed to warn them. She pushed herself forward, and her heart came to a painful stop as she realised that something was holding her steady in place.

CHAPTER 3
THE FIRST DAUGHTER OF OYO

City of Nri

'Are you sure it's safe?' Ebun said quietly, as they approached the crystallised gates of the Oroma room.

Ina regarded her coolly, resisting the urge to strike the cowering girl. *It's not her fault,* she told herself. *She's right to be afraid.* Her friend – *their* friend – Lebechi had died just a few days prior.

Lebechi's death had been so sudden, so unexpected. Worse still was her family; their eyes had darkened with sorrow and *something* else, something too terrible to be said. Ebun was right to be afraid; however, there was no excuse for being complacent.

'Just wait here for me,' Ina muttered before throwing a look at the girl. 'But,' she began, her voice low and serious, 'if you hear *anything* untoward, scream for help then fetch me.'

Ebun gave a slow nod but she didn't meet her eyes. Ina's lips curled as she watched Ebun clutch at her forearm absentmindedly. She didn't trust Ebun – she was weak – but who else did she have?

Ina took a deep breath as she entered the Oroma quarters. She felt for the rim of the small daga she had hidden in the folds of her garments. Noblewomen were not permitted to bear weapons, especially not ones wielded from the enchanted abara metal. She had paid heavily for an enchanted daga in the black market, and she would pay double if she was caught with it. But that meant little to her. Ina had promised herself a while ago that she would die before being placed under anyone else's control. Not since Chief O— Chief Oj—

Ina shook his name out of her head vigorously and squeezed her eyes shut. Every time she thought of him, her body rang with a sense of powerlessness, a loss of control that tore at her skin. She breathed out as she pictured Asilia, the Eze's ferocious lion, tearing the slime of a man to shreds on Sinai's command. Slowly, she felt her sense of self returning back to her, and she was able to breathe. She opened her eyes.

'Blast it,' Ina cursed. The mirrored plates that walled the room spat out pale beams of light from the ọkụs hanging at its corners, leaving no doubt that the room was empty. She shouldn't curse. It was beneath her. A foul and common practice and yet … 'Blast it,' she sighed. He was late.

Ina stormed past the grand columns, adorned with clear sparkling quartz, slowing as she reached the sundial in the end of the room. The minuscule circular ọkụ light threw a shadow over the flat end of the golden cone. Ina's lips stiffened further as she read the time. He should have been here minutes ago. She loathed waiting.

'Ndewo, Lolo Ina,' a deep voice said behind her, and Ina had to stop herself from screaming. A haze of fear brushed over her skin and she reached for her daga, jabbing it towards the owner of the voice.

'Ina,' Olu said with his hands up. His emerald eyes fixed on the small weapon. 'Sorry, I didn't mean to startle you.'

Ina stared back at him. Her breathing was sharp and her heart pounding. She let the sickly feeling of fear wash over her but she didn't move. Tears pricked at the corner of her eyes.

'Ina,' Olu repeated softly.

She blinked and let her hands fall back to her side, squeezing them in an attempt to stop the shaking. She hated her fear. She hated remembering its cause. Most of all, she hated the blasted pity bleeding into Olu's eyes.

'Are you okay?' Olu asked as she returned the daga into the pouch in her garment.

'You shouldn't have scared me,' she said briskly, 'hiding behind pillars like some sort of snake. It is not a fetching trait.'

'I'll try to keep that in mind,' he said softly. He fought away the smile tugging at his lips.

Ina responded to his efforts with a scowl. She noticed dark circles hung around his eyes and a dullness sitting beneath his dark-bronzed skin. Her scowl faltered. *When was the last time he slept?* she wondered.

'What's going on, Olu?' Ina said. That question had been on her mind every day since Sinai had left for the Eze's quarters near on three moon-cycles ago. She had never returned and something had *changed* in the palace. Ina knew the change was connected to Lebechi's death, the Eze's disappearance, even Sinai; she just didn't know how. She *needed* to know how. It was the only way to ensure that she could survive it.

Olu's rigid stance suddenly relaxed into a deep sigh. 'The Eze is dead.'

Ina took a step back as though someone had pushed her. She blinked, trying desperately to keep her face composed.

'Impossible,' she breathed, watching him intently for signs of lies or madness.

'He's gone and everything has … changed.'

Ina recalled the increased military effort, the hidden meetings and the recent demureness of Lolo Akuada, the wife of the head of war.

'Obi Somto is preparing to take over?'

Olu's eyes widened before he lowered them. His jaw clenched as he straightened his posture.

'Obi Somto is dead, as is Head General Okoro.'

Ina let out a short sound that would have resembled a laugh if it hadn't been so sad. None of this was funny, yet something about the ridiculousness of it all filled her with frivolous energy.

'So they're all clambering for the Eze's seat,' she whispered. 'This will bring a war to Nri.' She squeezed the rim of her daga.

'It won't get to war. Once General Ikenna has secured a strong position within the Obis then—'

'General Ikenna? That brute? *He* wants to take the position too? He wants to be *Eze*?'

'He's not a brute,' Olu said quietly, almost to himself. 'Yes, he may need moulding but that will come with age. He's still a young man. He cares for this Kingdom and wants it to be great. It's time for new blood.'

'Caring is the minimal requirement for a leader,' Ina retorted. 'It is certainly not the determining factor.' She shook her head. 'Ikenna is too brash, too desperate for power, any fool can see that he would do ...' She looked up at Olu. 'It was him. He killed Obi Somto and the Head General.'

Olu tensed.

'His own *grandfather*? His uncle?' Ina said, bringing her hand up to her mouth. Nausea settled in the pit of her stomach. She was struck with the sudden urge to run, to flee before she too was dragged down by the madness infecting the Kingdom of Nri.

Olu's green eyes glazed over coldly. 'It was necessary,' he said flatly. 'With the Eze gone, Obi Somto and his military prowess ... he would have overwhelmed us, taken over the city. Somto and Head General Okoro championed the Eze's cruelty; they enjoyed it. Do you know what type of man you have to be, to be the hand of the Eze, the overseer of all his cruel deeds and *enjoy* it? He had to act.'

Ina narrowed her gaze. 'Do you truly believe that, Olu?'

His eyes fluttered as a wave of exhaustion washed over him.

'I have to,' he said.

Ina frowned. His skin was so dull, his eyes tired and she could see little veins pulsing around his forehead. An image of Nkoli came to mind; a silly woman who had taken an Ọbara oath years ago to get out of her deepening debts. She had looked like this.

'Surely not,' she murmured. A lump formed at her throat. The Ọbara oath was a curse, a disease that crippled all that took it. Olu was a man, an infuriating one at that, but she liked him. He did not deserve to have his life tied to an oath in such a way.

'What have you done?' she whispered, her eyes pricking before she blinked away furiously.

He gave her a hard look before looking back at the ground. 'I had to get her out of here,' he said quietly.

'Who?' she spat as heat steamed from her head. How could he be so *stupid?* Nothing, no one, could justify this.

'And Ikenna is not a bad man – it was not … it's not as bad as it may seem.'

'Get *who* out of here?' Ina said through gritted teeth.

He looked back at her pleadingly and suddenly it clicked.

'Sinai?' she breathed. Sinai had gone to see the Eze, and now he was dead. 'Was she involved?'

'I don't know the details, but all I know is that she would have died had she stayed. The only way to get her out was through Ikenna and the only way Ikenna would let her out was if I swore my allegiance to him.'

As his words rushed over her, licks of anger scorched against her skin.

'Fool,' Ina spat, her face warm with fury.

'Ina.'

'No—' she shook her head '—there could have been another way. Why did you not consult *me?*' she raged, catching herself before her itching palm made contact with his face. 'You've thrown away your life!'

'She needed to leave.'

Ina sighed in frustration. She saw the hope brimming in his eyes and she knew that there was no saving him. He didn't even know what he had done, and by the time he did, it would be too late. Ina felt a thick lump forming in her throat and she threw her head back, sniffing back her tears before turning back to her old friend. 'And so do I,' she said quietly. 'I'm going back home – back to Oyo, immediately. I will not stay here while you people tear this land apart. If the Eze is dead then I have no tie to this kingdom.'

Olu looked back at her. 'Ina.'

'No, I will *not* give this city my life,' she said forcefully. The memory came quicker than she could stop it. Chief Ojo's wine-soaked breath against her skin. His weight squeezing out the breath in her lungs. Ina shook her head furiously. 'It's already taken too much.'

'They won't let you go,' Olu said, and Ina held on to a crystal column to steady herself. 'Whether the Eze is dead or alive, you are still the daughter of the king that rules Oyo. Whoever seeks power will need to keep Oyo on their side, which means…'

'They'll need to keep me,' Ina murmured, her voice breaking as she shut her eyes and clenched her trembling hands.

'Oyo was once my home too,' Olu said, 'I consider you kin. I will protect you.'

Ina's eyes flew open and looked back at him sternly. 'How? You can't even protect yourself,' she snapped. Her heart twisted. She had caught the hurt on Olu's face before he had the chance to mask it. Ina opened her mouth to say something but the words wouldn't come out. What else was there to say? Ina shook her head and walked out of the room.

She opened the door to find Ebun lounging idly in the corridor. Fury slammed into her body. She wanted to shake her and scream; even with Lebechi gone, the girl didn't understand. She still had no idea what was coming for them. In truth, neither did Ina, but she knew that she didn't want to find out.

Ina clapped her hands at her before thundering down the hall, only pausing when something caught her eye. She drew closer to the open window and watched a huddle of nnunu women gathered on the grounds below. She had never seen them gathered like that before. They usually sang in solitude through the city of Nri, begging to gather enough gold shells to gain favour to fly again. Her stomach dipped in fright. *Were they whispering?* She frowned. Nnunu women couldn't *talk?*

Ina squinted as she saw some of their feet hovering over the ground.

'Are they … fl—' Ebun started before she caught Ina's glare.

'Let's go,' Ina said calmly, though her heart slammed against her chest. Ebun had seen it too. She couldn't have imagined it. *They could fly.* She looked across the palace she had called home since she was three years old. It had never felt more like a prison. She needed to get out of here, and somehow the nnunu women were her way out.

CHAPTER 4
SHADES OF CYAN

Furuefu forest

It clutched at her throat. A fiery thirst that held her firmly in place. Sinai's arms slapped against the cold river. She needed to leave. It was coming. She needed to warn—

Be still.

Sinai's body slackened with relief as the dryness clutching at her throat loosened. A woman drew towards her and Sinai was struck breathless. She had heard tales of ancient creatures, embodiments of a person's soul, a person's chi. They were said to be the purest of creatures, a guiding light. Is this what the woman was? A saviour from the beast that lurked deep in the forest? She must be. The fear Sinai had felt had slipped away and only joy was left.

As she pulled closer, she could see the woman's head was submerged in the water up until the bridge of her nose. Her pitch-black eyes flashed with bursts of blue and green, as though she had captured the river itself within them. She lifted her head slightly; revealing a string of pearls that ran across her face just above the tip of her nose. They seemed to be embedded in her deep brown skin. Her thick hair hung to the sides of her face.

The woman drifted backwards and the thirst returned, worse than before, slicing through her throat with inexorable force. Sinai sprang forward but, each time she did, the woman drew further and further back, pulling Sinai deeper into the lake. The woman began to sink low into the waters, and Sinai joined her, letting the water swallow her whole.

The lake darkened into a deep black, save for the woman's pearls. They glowed so bright that the light seemed to coat her entire frame. All Sinai could see, all there was, was her. The woman paused and swivelled to face Sinai with a black blanket of hair encircling her. A smile formed on her full lips, tinged dark red, the colour of dried blood. White circles of light danced around her arms, her bare chest and torso, which extended into a long tail. As Sinai watched her, a memory began to bloom in her clouded mind. She had seen this woman before, or a statue of her, a lifetime ago. *Mami Wata*, the thought sprang in her mind.

The Mami Wata's eyes bulged before she shot towards Sinai, her flashing eyes rummaging over Sinai's face.

You can speak? a rich voice sprayed in Sinai's mind.

Yes, I can? Sinai thought back, a little confused, as the Mami Wata peered at her. Ice ran down Sinai's back when the Mami Wata's long fingers wrapped around her chin.

Interesting. The Mami Wata pulled back as she swivelled her arms around.

Sinai pushed against the rippling water as a large bubble formed. The Mami Wata placed her blood-red lips on the thin ball and it drifted towards Sinai. She pulled away as it approached her mouth but it planted itself just over her nose and below her chin. Sinai took a deep breath and her lungs filled with air. Strange; she hadn't known that she had been holding her breath for all that time. She looked up at the Mami Wata.

Thank you, she thought, as the Mami Wata encircled her, her long tail wrapping around Sinai's flailing legs. Sinai numbed at the cooling touch.

You look human, the Mami Wata voiced. *I've not known a human to speak to my kind like so.* The Mami Wata sniffed at her. *Your kind speaks not with words but with emotions*, she noted as she took Sinai's head in her hand, tilting her head as her eyes flashed. *No. Not human. A mmo, perhaps?*

Not human? Sinai murmured, shaking her head free as a chill crept up her neck. The memory of the Eze crumbling before her eyes slammed into her mind. Of course she knew she wasn't *normal*. It wasn't normal that she could hold the Mother's Crystal without turning to dust. It wasn't normal that she had used it to kill the Eze. She knew this and yet the idea of not being human disturbed her.

What was that? The Mami Wata's voice pierced through Sinai, her chilling fingers clutching at her chin. *Show that again.*

Sinai grimaced as the memory of her last encounter with Eze ran through her mind.

Impossible. The Mami Wata's grasp tightened, her eyes flashing blue. Finally she released Sinai from her grip, but her flashing eyes were widened as they fixed on her. *You are a Descendant of the First? It is impossible.*

Sinai's muscles tensed as the Mami Wata bore into her. She shuddered as a cold, slippery tail drew the hair away from her face.

Yet, here you are. Possible. Her eyes flashed as her tail traced Sinai's face. *There is another that wears your face. Another that holds your blood.* Her flashing eyes had grown wild.

An odd sound tore through Sinai's mind. It sounded like pipes and chimes contorting deep within the Mami Wata's throat. *Amuru ha abuo. The Children Born of Both.*

Though she said it at nothing more than a whisper, the phrase rang through Sinai's head; it seemed to vibrate through the river itself. Sinai flinched at its echo.

Show me more, the Mami Wata roared and Sinai felt a burning sensation against her temples as memories stormed through her head. The Eze's outstretched arm as he crumpled into dust, the crystal in Naala and Sinai's hands, its blood-red glow before the crystal settled back to green.

Chínēkè! Sinai winced as the Mami Wata's booming voice crashed into the sides of her head. *So, the Children Born of Both have evoked the Chi Crystal? This is why I have re-awoken?*

The what? Sinai thought as a shiver ran down her spine.

The Chi Crystal. You have evoked the Chi Crystal. The Mami Wata frowned as she regarded Sinai's face. *You don't know?* Her eyes darkened and a bitter smile swept over her blood-red lips. *Do you know of this, at least?: 'The chicken says that it is those who are knowledgeable who go to war with clubs'.*

Sinai was too afraid to shake her head. The Mami Wata's nose flared. *The fates have given me a true dilemma.*

Sinai swallowed. *A dilemma?*

If I help you to do something you don't understand, we will all end up in ruin. So says the proverb.

Help me with what?

The Mami Wata raised one hand to her temples and rubbed. *What do you know of the Njem?*

Sinai looked at her blankly.

The Mami Wata's eyes narrowed and she bared her teeth. *You evoked the Chi Crystal and you know nothing of Njem?*

I didn't evok—

Silence— Sinai's throat tightened so hard she flew her hand towards it *—and listen.* An image of the Mother's Crystal filled Sinai's mind. It sat nestled within Naala and Sinai's hands, shifting from green to red to green again. *When you evoked the crystal, you marked the first stage of the Njem. The gods and beasts alike have been awakened and so the transformation begins. Now you must finish what you started.*

The Mami Wata's words sat on her mind, heavy and garbled. *I don't … know what you mean. I don't know how …*

This is true. A painful truth. The Mami Wata pulled closer to her, her eyes now as black as coal. *The kingdom will burn for it, if you let it.*

The kingdom will burn? Nausea crept up Sinai's throat. Sinai had never felt so small in her life. So lost.

Yes. This kingdom will burn if I leave you ignorant as you are now. The kingdom will also burn if I tell you too much and force you on a path that you don't understand.

Sinai shook her head in protest.

It is done, the Mami Wata voiced. *In starting Njem, you have entered us into a state of chaos, a state that only the Earth Mother can still.* The Mami Wata's eyes flashed green.

The Earth Mother is dead, Sinai thought, as her throat tightened.

Yes, but you, Amuru ha abuo, are not. You have evoked the first crystal so you must evoke the second and in so doing open a portal to a great evil.

No.

You no longer have a choice in that matter; your choice lies solely with the third crystal. What you choose will either destroy the Kingdom or save it.

The Mami Wata's words tore at Sinai's flesh. *What choice?*

Why, there are many. Many choices and many truths. Right now, the truth you seek will lead to peril. You seek the truth that is the least painful. I can taste it, a common sickness in your kind. The Mami Wata examined Sinai's face. *Only one truth marks the difference between defeat and victory, the one hidden beneath the illusion. The painful truth.*

The Mami Wata's words weaved in and out of Sinai's mind. Tangled and unclear. *I … I'm sorry. I don't understand.*

I know, but you need to, and fast. Otherwise …

Sinai clutched at her head as heat tore through her brain, leaving her with the taste of blood in her mouth and the scent of smoke lodged in her throat.

You need to tell me more. Sinai jerked forward feverishly.

So you can have us all destroyed? The Mami Wata's voice was so low, so cutting; Sinai grimaced. *I should kill you now; what difference would it make? It is clear that you cannot do what you must do to prevent our demise.*

If you could just tel—

Silence! There are things that one does not learn simply by being told. The Mami Wata frowned. *You must learn for yourself; that is the only way.* Her eyes flashed blue as a chilling sensation ran down Sinai's spine. *Shatter the illusion and seek the truth. It is the only way that we all have a chance,* the Mami Wata murmured as she drew her tail towards the crystallized air bubble. Sinai flinched as it burst.

When she opened her eyes, the Mami Wata was gone. Sinai's limbs stretched out aimlessly in the water. She couldn't breathe. She looked up. Her stomach plunged when she saw how far the surface was. *No,* she mouthed, as she hurled her body through the thick water. Sinai's chest burned for air as she propelled her body upwards. No matter how hard she pushed, she was no closer to the surface. Her arms were too heavy. The world's edges began to darken. Sinai tried to call upon her power but, like the river's surface, it felt impossibly far.

Sinai started to drift downwards, the weight of the world pulling her back towards its core. The darkness at the edges of her eyes spread until all she could see was the black.

Something hard tugged at her hand.

She was floating upwards.

Pressure slammed against her chest.

Sinai suddenly felt the urge to cough. When she did, she retched out bouts of river water as her eyes blurred in the sun. She blinked and coughed, spluttering on the muddy riverbank before collapsing under the weight of her body.

Naala's face hovered above her, her eyes black with murderous rage.

'What the hell are you playing at?'

CHAPTER 5
THE BLESSING OF TWINS

Siwunmi, Furuefu forest

Naala's knees bounced as she threw a glance over at Sinai. The girl's face glowed under the floating ọkụ lights that lined the rust-coloured streets of Siwunmi. Sinai sat tall and elegant, incongruous with the small, sand-coloured ụlọs that surrounded her.

'Aunty tied the bad man up with-with his feet and hung him upside down, like this,' Gini proclaimed, jumping out of her mother's arms. 'Then we lost the other aunty in the river, or was that before?'

Naala shifted as she too recalled what had occurred at the river. She had just finished skinning the last of the boar when she had heard Sinai's voice thundering through her head. An explosive pain had clutched at her heart, so tight she could scarcely breathe. Naala hadn't stopped to think. She had scooped up Gini and dashed through the forest. The girl had thought it a game but there was nothing funny about reaching that deathly still river; knowing, somehow, that Sinai lay trapped within. Naala had placed the little one on the shore before breaking into the river. That's where she found her. Her eyes closed and skin greyed as she sank into the black waters. Naala's heart twisted at the memory.

Sinai's face broke into a shy smile, as small as it was it ran up her face, flushing her with a warm glow. No one would be able to tell that just one izu prior she had been thrashing on a riverbank blabbering frantically about beasts and lost gods. What other secrets lay beneath her calm exterior? After moon-cycles spent with the girl, Naala still had no idea what to make of her.

'Is that so?' boomed one of Gini's many grand-uncles, his wrinkled eyes brimming with tears and the same unbridled joy plastered on the rest of her family as they listened attentively to the chattering child. Naala's throat tightened. Gini reminded her so much of her old friend who had shared her name. The friend that Naala had dragged into her many mischiefs and would-be-adventures. The friend she had failed to save.

Gini wasn't the only one who felt familiar. There was something about Siwunmi itself, the village buried deep in the forest; it was as though Naala could blink and find herself back home in Igbakwu. She watched the air move in and out of the child's chest and the bright life sparking in her eyes, and wished the same for her dear old friend.

'Thank you, thank you once more for saving my little one,' Gini's mother gushed at Sinai and Naala as she pulled the girl back into her arms.

A subtle movement caught Naala's attention. Sinai was wringing her hand over her own wrist. It was so out of place against her otherwise graceful frame. *She's nervous*, Naala mused. It always struck her as odd when she noticed that. By all rights, Sinai should be the most confident person here. She was of the noble class. Her akwete cloth, alone, torn to strips as it was, would still fetch more than all the homes in Gini's village. It wasn't just her wealth. It was the way she held herself, so still and centred. So unlike Naala's boisterous demeanour. How many times had her grandmother scowled at Naala to stay still, to be more delicate with her movement?

'You're like the jaguar, Naala, always moving this way and that. A woman should be calm like the sea, deep with emotions that never reach the surface, not wild as you are,' her grandmother would chastise.

'The sea is not so calm; there are many broken boats that can attest to that,' Naala would tease. She wondered what her grandmother would say if she had seen Sinai.

Naala glanced away as her mind began to churn. What *would* her grandmother say about the girl who looked so much like her? Their resemblance was by far the biggest mystery that Naala had ever encountered and yet the thought of solving it made her sick. She did have questions, but she also had answers. Dark theories forming in the deep of the mind. Theories that would have made her grandmother weep.

'Ndewo.' Gini's father cut through her thoughts as he brought his crossed hands across his chest and extended them to the group, rising to the customary welcome.

The trees rustled in the night's warm breeze, infusing the smell of the food with lush leaves and dark woody scents. It really did feel like home. Something else lay beneath the night's scents. Vanilla pods and pine. The scent that haunted her nearly every day in Furuefu. The scent of Eni. The boy who had found her, stranded in the forest, after her village's attack. The boy who she couldn't seem to get out of her mind. As always, she looked around, half-expecting to see his probing, dark eyes watching over her. Her palms moistened. *Where are you?*

'Oya, let me pass, Nna is about to start the welcome ceremony,' Uju, Gini's older sister, said as she steadied a straw basket full of steaming, soft-boiled yams on her head before setting them on the ground.

Their father chuckled at the disturbance, his laugh as big as homely as him. 'It seems we have come to that special time where we *truly* welcome our guests.' He looked down on the kola nuts, again placing his right hand in the wooden efere. 'When the kola nut reaches home, it will tell where it came from. Whatever good he is looking for, he will see it.' He then placed the efere at his feet, where it brushed against the bright, thin garments that draped over him in a long robe.

'I am Maduforo, son of Uzochi and Ada, born in Obodo. My wife is Chiasoka and she was born also in Obodo,' he said as he broke the kola nuts into smaller pieces with his hands. He looked up and passed the efere to Naala, nodding as she brought a piece of kola to her mouth.

'I am Esinaala, granddaughter of Ugoulo, raised in Igbakwu.' Naala bit into the kola nut, its bitter taste filling her with nostalgia. She passed the efere to Sinai and waited for a response that didn't come.

Sinai's eyes grew wide. Slight tremors shook the efere of kola nuts nestled in her hands. Sinai opened her mouth slightly before throwing a darting glance at Naala.

Something cold squeezed at Naala's stomach. Sinai needed help.

Naala's palm itched as she resisted the urge to take the kola nut from Sinai and do it herself. A frown spread across her face as she realised that if she were to do that, besides her name, Naala would have little else to say about the other girl.

'I am Sinai,' she said eventually, her voice thick but steadier than Naala would have thought. '... Sinaikuku,' she added, 'daughter of ... well, they call me an efuola ... born in – raised in the palace of Nri,' she said, before casting her eyes down and passing the efere along.

A shudder reached the nape of Naala's neck. *Efuola? So Sinai was considered illegitimate.*

'So you mean you two are not born of the same mother?' Gini's mother suddenly said, and the gathering quieted. Chiasoka's eyes scanned the two girls warmly, her expression so open and earnest that her question almost didn't seem intrusive.

It hit Naala in the chest all the same.

'No,' Naala said. It came out much harder than she had wanted it to. She looked up and tried to smile but she just couldn't get the corners of her lips to rise. 'We just met,' she added, hoping to smooth things over, but try as she did, she couldn't remove the cold edge from her tone.

'Yes, it remains a mystery,' Sinai added breezily. The lightness that Naala had tried and failed to exude hung effortlessly over the girl.

Naala looked down despondently at the achicha ede on her efere. *Focus on the food,* she willed, as she brought it to her mouth.

'Yes, I see,' Chiasoka said thoughtfully, 'but isn't it strange that you—' she bent her head towards Naala '—also do not know the woman that birthed you?'

Naala blinked back at Chiasoka. She didn't want to discuss this any more.

'No,' she bit carefully. Naala had rarely thought of the woman who had birthed her. The woman who had also abandoned her on the foot of her grandmother's doorstep. Having come face to face with Sinai, the thought of the woman made Naala sick. 'But I do know the woman that birthed her; I know her brother too, and, through them, I knew her,' she said finally. As she spoke, she pictured her grandmother, her uncles and aunties. She'd never noticed how similar they all had looked. They had the same high forehead, the same oval lips, their warmed

31

wood skin shades lighter than her deep brown. Naala had never looked like anyone before. Until she had met Sinai. She shook the thoughts out of her head before they had the chance to clasp her throat.

'Well, then perhaps she had two of you?' Maduforo suggested, nodding along with his wife as Naala's felt her heartbeat thumping against ears.

No! she roared in her mind.

'I don't think so—' Naala frowned '—my grandmother would have told me.' *Please stop talking about this.*

'Maybe she didn't know?' Chiasoka offered.

'No.'

'She might have—'

'Only a madwoman would do such a thing,' Naala snapped before she could stop herself. 'I was not born of a madwoman.'

Chiasoka flinched before casting her eyes down. Naala noticed a tremor across the older woman's chin. She had clearly said too much. A heaviness settled on her chest. It didn't seem to matter how hard she *tried,* she couldn't seem to escape that *look.* She had seen it on the faces in her village countless times: a look of dismay.

'Or a woman without a choice,' Chiasoka offered quietly and Ugu moved over to sit by her mother, resting her head on the old woman's shoulders.

Naala frowned. She was missing something.

Maduforo cleared his throat awkwardly.

'This must seem very strange to you.' He smiled. 'It's just our village is … blessed.'

'That's one way to put it,' Ugu muttered.

'Your father is right. We are blessed, very blessed, no matter what the law says,' Chiasoka said, her expression warming from the closeness of her family.

'I don't understand,' Sinai said as Naala caught Ugu exchanging sharp looks with both of her parents. *They're hiding something.* All around her similar glances were thrown to and fro. *Something big.*

'Leave it,' Ugu said to her mother.

'You are very beautiful girls,' Chiasoka said, 'with kind eyes.'

'Mother, I said—'

'Ugu,' her father warned sharply before pointing towards Naala and Sinai, '*look* at them. We are all in the same boat,' he said calmly. 'This village has been blessed,' he continued, 'blessed with twins. In nearly every family, we have at least one set; my wife alone has birthed three identical sets.'

Naala frowned. Twins? The word left a bitter taste in her mouth. She shifted slightly as she looked around at the villagers. Yes, some of them looked alike, but none of them had the same face. Her frown deepened.

'I …' Sinai started, equally confused, though she couldn't seem to find the right words.

'Where are they?' Naala interjected. 'The twins.'

'We have a sister village.'

'Father,' Ugu pressed.

'Ugu, know your place,' he said swiftly, his nostrils flaring with irritation, an expression that she had not previously seen on him. 'We have a sister village on the other side of Furuefu. That's the great thing about this mighty forest: it is hard to navigate, and, as such, it is easy to hide within it. The patrols cannot be as robust as they are in the open settlements.' He leaned in slightly. 'Some years they even forget to collect their taxes—' he offered a ruthless grin '—that's why we settled here; there is scope to protect things from the gaze of those that wish to tear it down. We split up all the twins, Isiawele, and Kaima, and Tobenna,' he said, pointing to the two boys and one girl, 'their twins reside there. We try to swap them over every year or so.'

'I usually stay with our tribe up in the north,' Isiawele blurted, and as he spoke a blob of achicha ede dropped on his navy garment. He glanced over at Ugu apologetically, and Naala couldn't help but smile. His garment was adorned with little elephants sewed onto the material; no doubt his older sister had been the one to embroider it. Naala had done the same for her little cousins.

'If you think that anyone here is going to wash that for you before you go back to the north tribe tomorrow, you have another thing coming,' Ugu chided. 'Next time, eat with your mouth closed.'

'I had no choice,' Chiasoka announced. Thin tears had wet her long eyelashes. 'It wasn't easy … and if things had been … I had to protect my children. Being a mother is … not easy.'

Ugu shook her head. 'Enough of this,' she said, before turning over to the girls. 'Since you know all of *our* secrets, how about you tell us yours?'

'We don't have secrets,' Sinai said a little too quickly.

Naala groaned internally as Ugu raised her brows, a grin quickly replacing her scowl.

Fortunately, Gini diverted the conversation before she had to. The child sprang away from her father and tugged at Naala.

'Ask about the Amaghị?' she whispered loudly in her ear.

Naala beamed back at the little one. She had kept the girl entertained during their journey with stories of her lost friends, and the girl was convinced that her father would know of their whereabouts. 'Nna knows *everything*,' she had exclaimed.

Naala looked back at Maduforo quizzingly. There *was* something wise about the man; perhaps the small girl was right. Heavens knew she needed help.

It had been far easier to find Siwunmi than it had been to find the Amaghị's settlement. Though she had similarly never been to either. Since Naala was small, she had an uncanny sense of direction. It was as though the earth spoke to her in a language she couldn't quite describe. She had started to attribute it to the same power that had allowed her to move things with her mind. It had been infallible; that is, until she had tried to find the Amaghị.

'I am looking for a secret society,' Naala said carefully, her palms moistening as she scanned the village for answers. She was struck once again by *his* scent and her heart quickened, '… called the Amaghị. If anyone knows where we can find them, it would be appreciated.' Naala held her breath.

'Hmph.' Maduforo sighed. 'I'm sorry but I've never heard of such a settlement, and we make it our business to know of all the settlements within Furuefu.'

Her heart squeezed to half its size and something bitter hit the back of her throat. It had been foolish to hope.

'Amaghị,' someone suddenly murmured, and Naala looked up to see a lean man with a lopsided grin. 'Amaghị, Amaghị, Amaghị,' he repeated as he stood up, stroking his dense beard ironically. His eyes, coated with thick black lashes, sparked as though he had caught on to a joke. 'I recognise that name.'

'Sure you do, Ifeanyi,' Maduforo said, winking as Naala instinctively rolled her eyes. 'The people from Igbakwu are straight-forward, truthful, but our people ... well, we are known for our *stories*. The majority of them elaborated, especially to impress pretty girls.'

'Impress pretty – cah,' the man scoffed, flinging the air with his hand. 'If I am *impressive* it is purely by accident and never by design.' Ifeanyi brazenly made a space for himself between Naala and Sinai.

He looked over at both of them, a playful grin on his lips that grew into a chuckle as Naala's nostrils flared. There was something sickly sweet about his nature. She wanted nothing more than to shove him away, but something stopped her. Despite herself, there was a part of her that wondered. What if this fool did know where her friends were? Where Eni was? The thought of seeing Eni again made her stomach light. She needed to know that he was safe. She needed to be close to him again; close enough to feel the heat from his body, his breath against her skin. *What's wrong with me?* Naala thought as she steadied herself, pushing aside her fanciful thoughts. *Focus.*

'But in all honesty,' he continued, placing a hand on his heart, 'I did hear something on my travels.'

'On your romps, you mean,' Ugu muttered drily, as Ifeanyi flicked his hands up in protest.

'No, no, no – I do not *romp*,' he said, shooting her a warning glare, 'but I did come across a woman.'

'Here we go.' Ugu scoffed.

'A *woman*,' he stressed, warding off Ugu, 'who mentioned the Amaghị, right? A secret society that uses brown –no, black hamerkops?' He paused with a grin as he noted the jolt that had ran through Naala's body. 'Ahh you see, I'm not talking rubbish, eh,' he jeered.

'Go on,' Naala said through gritted teeth. Her heart thundered impatiently as she dug her fingers into the warm soil to stop herself from shaking the man. *Where are they?!*

'Only if you flash me a smile,' he teased.

Naala squeezed her hands into fists. *Don't make me slap you, please don't make me slap you.*

'I think you should be *careful* with how you proceed,' Sinai warned him lightly.

He grinned back at her and Naala sighed. *I'm going to slap you. You're really going to make me slap you?*

'Fine, fine,' he said with a smile, before entering a prolonged pause. Naala took in a deep breath before narrowing her eyes. 'She *said* that they are up in the North,' he finally said. Naala waited for him to say more, but it seemed as though he was done. He rested on his toned arms. A smug expression plastered over his face.

'The North? That's it?' Naala prodded.

'Yes, that's what she said,' he said. 'So,' he added, flicking his eyes between the two of them, 'can I get thank-you pecks from the beautiful non-twin twins?' He lifted himself off from his arms so that he could pat both of their lips and tap it against his cheeks.

Naala stared back at him, frozen in place. The remnants of his fingers on her lips sent her into a blind rage. She grabbed a handful of his hair as he held his hand up in protest.

'How about a slap?' she muttered as Ugu and Maduforo broke out into similar deep belly-laughs.

'Okay, okay,' he said as she slowly released him, 'so a smile then?' he said, jolting up before Naala could make contact with his face. He chuckled as he turned back to face them and Naala seriously considered running up to strike him; her only deterrent was she was sure he would make a run for it. She refused to give him the satisfaction of having her chase him. 'What is this animosity? I told you where they were,' he chuckled.

'The North?' she repeated frustratingly.

'Yeah – the lady said it's up, up up up, so the North,' he concluded.

'The North of where? Furuefu?' she asked, as her mind turned over his words. 'I mean, that can't be, we entered the forest from the North.' Had she missed something? 'Are you sure?' she added, eyeing him curiously. Could he be lying? As slimy as he seemed, he also seemed somewhat sincere.

'Yup,' he replied.

Naala frowned. *North?*

CHAPTER 6
THE WILL OF THE PEOPLE

Furuefu forest

Sinai was not awake. She could tell by the misty haze that coated the air around her. She felt a tug at the pit of her stomach. She recognised this place … she recognised its high walls patterned with gold dust, its marbled floor and pristine decor.

The palace, she thought, heart pounding. *I'm back in the palace.* In a room – no, not a room, a hall – and she was walking. No, she was running.

Sinai paused, her chest tight from activity. A loud banging erupted from the distant gates of the palace. The empty hall filled with people. Their mouths open as wide as their eyes as they dashed around her screaming. Smoke wafted through the air and she could hear the roar of fire.

'They are coming, the bụrụ-ọnụ are coming!'

Sinai's heart pounded as she followed someone up a flight of stairs. Blood-curdling cries echoed below. She stopped at the top of the stairs but it was nothing more than a room. Her breathing quickened as she turned back to the stairs. Whatever was coming was approaching fast. She knew with absolute certainty that death would follow their encounter.

Everything went deathly still.

She found that she missed the loud screams. The silence was far worse. Ice crept up her chest. She tried to squeeze the air out of her lungs but it remained lodged in her throat.

She closed her eyes as something thundered below her. She wanted nothing more than to disappear.

It was only when the crisp night's air grazed against her cheeks that she sprang her eyes open. She was outside. Walking the dead streets of Nri alone. At every corner, she was met with charred bodies stacked and discarded on the floor.

The kingdom will burn. The Mami Wata's voice echoed in her ear and she crashed to her knees.

Movement halted her sobs. Sinai looked up and caught sight of a small boy. His eyes and chest covered in sparkling red dust.

'Was it you?' she whispered in horror.

'No,' the boy replied, 'it was the will of the people.'

*

'What are you doing?!' Naala blurted.

Sinai's eyes flew open. Was she still in the palace? A muddle of greens, browns and blues separated out of a blur and Naala's face formed; her eyebrows were knitted together and the bottom of her lips were sprung open. No, she was in Siwunmi. Siwunmi? Hadn't they left the village days ago to go north? *Up, up, up.*

She was up. Up in one of Furuefu's many trees. Only, something was wrong. A flutter ran across her stomach and her heart bobbed up to her throat. Sinai looked down at the empty air between her and the distant hard ground. She wasn't in a tree at all; she was hanging up in the *air.* Her heart thudded painfully as she began to lose height.

Naala thrust out a hand, which Sinai clutched. A scream tore through her throat when she realised that rather than Naala holding her up, Sinai was going to drag them down towards the forest floor.

Sinai landed with a thud. A sharp pain ran through the right side of her body, but for the most part, it seemed as though she was intact. Gingerly, Sinai tugged her arm free from the pile of powdered soil that Naala must have conjured to soften their fall. Naala didn't move. She sat still, her eyes blinking to the heavens. Sinai reached out to her, but she swotted her arm away.

'Sorry,' Sinai said, avoiding Naala's burning glare as she tugged at her throbbing arm. Naala's gaze hovered at Sinai's palm. Sinai looked down, afraid it had been distorted, but all she saw was the gold symbol that had been etched in her palm after she had held the Mother's Crystal. She knew Naala had a similar one on her left palm, identical save for its colour, which was a jet black.

A frown pulled on Naala's lips. 'Are you okay?' she asked, and Sinai dropped her arm.

'Yes,' she replied quickly before the memory of the dream she had came to mind. They were getting worse, less abstract and more real. Ever since her encounter with the Mami Wata, the danger that she had felt in the shadows of her mind was now front and centre. She couldn't see past it, and yet she couldn't seem to convey it to Naala in such a way where she would understand. She needed her to understand. Sinai wet her lips as her heartbeat thundered loudly in her ears.

'I really think we need to talk about what the Mami Wata said.'

Naala's face fell. 'So, you still think that encounter was real?' Her words stung.

'Yes, Naala, it was real. It was real,' Sinai said forcefully, before pressing her lips together. Sinai didn't want to admit it but she could feel the cold clasp of doubt clutching at her resolve. *It had been real, hadn't it?*

'We searched,' Naala said, 'for hours, and nothing … you were under the water for a long time. Have you at least *considered* that it might not be real? You have to admit, your imagination, your dreams – they are often … intense. Couldn't it be one of them?'

Sinai considered Naala's words and something forceful turned within her. *No.* She'd seen what she'd seen. Sinai knew the difference between a dream and reality. She knew it.

'I didn't know you were listening,' she said, to which Naala shrugged. Of course she was listening. Naala was always listening, always watching, her mind constantly churning. So why couldn't she see this? 'But I'm sure it's … I'm certain it's *different*.'

'We checked,' Naala repeated.

'I understand, but it's a Mami Wata. They are very *powerful* beings. It's hard to describe but they really do lure you in. Although over time, I did feel my own autonomy coming, but by then I was too engrossed in the story do anything about it.'

'The story?'

'Yes, the—'

'About *beasts* and *gods*?' Naala sighed. 'Can you hear how this sounds?'

'I saw something,' Sinai said hurriedly, 'before I went into the water, it wasn't an animal it was something else – a beast.'

'A beast—' Naala sighed '—do you have any idea how many people spot *beasts* in the rustling winds or dust? The forest is known to play tricks on the mind and these tricks are turned into stories, and some of them feel real, but at the end it's just folklore.'

'Isn't that what your village said before the Eze's army came to slaug—' Sinai stopped herself as a dark look spread over Naala's face. They hadn't discussed this before. She hadn't told Naala how she had felt her rage, seen the memory of her friends and family hacked to pieces, the anger she had felt that they didn't listen to her pleas. 'I'm sorry but it's real, and, just like before, the consequences of not listening could be—'

'You knew?' Naala snapped. All Sinai could do was blink back at her. 'You *knew* what he had done. You knew how he butchered ... and you protected *him*?' her words were thick through her clenched teeth.

Heat ran up Sinai's back. *Olu, it always went back to Olu.*

'Not everything is ...' Sinai tried carefully. Her eyes had begun to stung. 'Sometimes people – things – aren't what you think. Sometimes there's more to them than meets the eye.'

'Profound,' Naala said roughly.

'Someone I trusted dearly – she trusted him, despite his actions. You don't know what the palace is like; you don't know what the Eze was like, he inspired the worst—'

'Oh, don't even,' Naala scoffed. 'The Eze was awful, but he's not the only guilty party here.' Naala ran her fingers through her braids violently as she squeezed her eyes shut. She let out a cry of frustration before storming away.

Sinai's heart sank but she didn't follow her. In truth, she was too scared to.

Naala paused her retreat before turning to face Sinai. 'And that is such *rubbish* – the Eze *inspired* him to kill? Do you know what type of person gets inspired to kill? I would rather die than kill innocent people at the whim of a madman, and if I did, I wouldn't expect forgiveness from my victims.'

Sinai felt exhausted. Why couldn't she make her *see*? She would never see, and she didn't even know the worst of it. If Naala ever found out what she had done during their last moments in the city of Nri, Sinai had no doubt that their already strained relationship would be irreparable. 'It's just not that simp—' she started weakly as Naala threw her hands up in the air.

'Simple?' Naala raged as she paced up and down. She stopped and turned on her heels. 'I want you to go,' she said as a slight tremor shook the earth.

It felt like a punch in the gut. Sinai was surprised, proud even, that she didn't double over. 'Fine,' she said quietly, as her hair slapped against her face. She hadn't noticed how wild the winds had grown. 'I didn't mean that, it's not fine,' she confessed, shaking her head as Naala watched her stone-faced. 'You don't mean that either.' *Did you?*

'Oh, but I did,' Naala retorted. Another gut punch. Sinai's lip tightened but then she saw something flicker in Naala's eyes. Was that regret?

'You don't mean that,' Sinai repeated. 'If you did, you would have abandoned me ages ago.'

'No.'

'You caught me on my fall right now.'

'So?' Naala scoffed. 'I don't *want* you to die, I don't want a lot of people to die, but that doesn't mean I want them following me around like a lost dog.'

'I see, now I'm the one that's lost,' Sinai said. The words tumbled out of her mouth before she could catch them. Sweat plastered against the nape of her neck. A dog, she had called her a *dog*?

'Excuse me?'

'It's quite clear that you have no idea where we are going,' Sinai snapped and Naala blinked back furiously.

'If I didn't have you pausing for breaks every five minutes or fixing your hair or your endless chatter, perhaps I could concentrate and find them,' Naala said. 'And so what if I'm lost? At least I have a reason for being here; you're just along for the ride.'

Sinai's teeth were clenched so tight her jaw began to hurt. She wanted to hurt. She wanted to kill.

Feed.

Her heart stopped and her mouth grew too dry to swallow. *It's here,* she thought desperately. Her mouth was open but she couldn't seem to find the words. Tears pricked at her eyes. The beast was here and they were going to die.

Naala stopped and threw her hands once again into the air in defeat.

'There's no need to take it so personally,' she said; her voice seemed muffled under the ringing in Sinai's head.

Run! something screamed within her, but her voice was buried deep in layers of fear.

'Okay, I'm sorry – I know I shouldn't have said that,' Naala said hurriedly, 'I just—'

Run!

Sinai shook her head. 'It's here.' Her voice was thick with tears.

'What?'

'The beast from the lake.'

'The Mami Wata?' Naala asked, her eyes locked on Sinai. There was something different in her eyes. Understanding. *She understands the danger.*

'N-no ... worse,' Sinai said as her eyes widened.

Feed!

'Can't you hear that?' Sinai hissed as Naala looked around.

Naala turned around, breathing slowly as she inspected the landscape, but she shook her head.

'I don't see ... ?' Naala started.

Feed! It was close. Closer than it had ever been and it needed blood.

'Run!' Sinai screamed at the top of her lungs, grabbing hold of Naala's hand – as a loud inhuman screech cut through the forest and tore through her skull.

CHAPTER 7
THE CRACKED TREE

Furuefu forest

The beast stalking them was quick and large. She could hear it thundering towards them, cracking trees as it sought out its prey. Hot adrenaline surged through Naala's body, invigorating her every move. She could feel the Black and Gold realm stirring within her. The power built up within her until she finally let it go.

A ball of earth rummaged through the forest and hoisted the two girls up, adding more speed to their flee. Thin branches spiked with leaves slapped against Naala's skin. She threw her hands up in defence as, frantically, they sped through the forest on the boulder. Her mind raced ahead of her. *Focus*, she tried to tell herself, *you need to focus to survive. You have to survive.*

Sinai drew her hands up and expelled a blast of wind; the curved stream of air acted as a barrier to the upcoming branches. Naala took a quick breath as her thoughts began to settle. She craned her neck to get a better idea about what they were running away from. What they might need to face.

Her heart dove into her stomach as she saw a huge reptile-like beast almost as high as the trees. Its long neck stretched out far, and it stood firm on four legs. Its translucent skin bore no signs of damage as it knocked about the forest. Rainbow veins spread across its entire body and its beady eyes were as clear as the forest mist. The beast squeezed them shut, as it stretched out its long, pole-like arms, revealing a set of thin, tattered wings.

Its tremendous frame hunted through the forest, knocking down the trees as though they were thatching grass. Naala's mind spun. She couldn't process what was happening. Another blood-curdling screech ripped through the air and she felt her chest vibrate.

'No!' Sinai screamed beside her as a giant sequoia tree began to sway before them.

Naala gasped as she watched ahead in terror.

The boulder couldn't stop; if it did, they would be trapped with the beast. If they weren't fast enough, they would be crushed. Naala decided before she could think. She took a deep breath and the earth boulder accelerated. She seized at the Black and Gold realm feverishly. Her throat was sore as a painful scream tore from her lungs. *Faster! Faster!* They were approaching the creaking giant and she still didn't know if they would make it. *Faster!* Her teeth gritted to near breaking point as they entered the shadow of the mammoth tree. *Faster!*

She was fast, but not fast enough.

Boom!

Darkness collapsed over Naala and Sinai. Naala let out a ragged breath, shaking as she patted her head, shocked that she was still alive. She turned to Sinai, who placed her hand out on the willowy bark wood that surrounded them. Naala looked around the strange circular dome. *We're inside the tree*, she thought as the dense smell of splintered timber and moist soil filled her nostrils. She let out a laugh that turned into a violent cough. Tears pricked at her eyes as she tried to contain the sound.

A sharp noise caused her to snap her head around. Naala held her breath as she heard a scratching noise against the bark. Something was digging them out. Naala's heart pounded; she watched in horror as something tugged at the thinned slabs of wood that coated their protective dome. She blinked as normal-sized hands began to scrape through the top of the dome. *It wasn't the beast,* she exhaled before her heart suddenly stopped. They weren't hands that were digging them out. They were claws. Naala pressed herself against the other end of the dome.

What is happening?

Before she could think, a stream of light exploded into the small dome and two strange beings peered into the hole. Their faces were a bizarre combination of a woman and a bird. The creatures were tall, perhaps even slightly taller than her. Their eyes were huge and round, yet there was something strangely human about them. A strip of red skin wrapped around their round eyes like a band and a flat beak protruded at the bottom of their face. The glossy black feathers that extended over their bodies shook as they drew out their claws in a beckoning gesture. Naala glanced over at Sinai; the girl seemed shocked, but not afraid.

'Take my hand,' one of the creatures said, its voice airy and ethereal, as though it had an oja flute embedded in its throat.

Before Naala could respond, Sinai had extended her arm and was being pulled up by the strange bird-woman. Naala clambered out after her, brushing off the assistance of the odd creatures, as she hauled herself up.

Once she was out of the dome, the creatures gestured to their feathered backs.

'Get on back, or you die. Painful, terrible death,' they said, songful.

Naala and Sinai exchanged a short look, broken up by another piercing screech. Naala found herself clambering onto the bird-like creature's back before letting out a throat-scratching scream as they soared up into the azure-blue sky.

CHAPTER 8
URUKPURU

Urukpuru

Cold air bit at the tip of Sinai's nose and smacked against her cheeks. Terror and excitement raged through her body as she clutched onto the nnunu woman's feathers. She was riding through the sky on a nnunu … a *nnunu* of all things!

They swooped higher and higher, soaring through the clouds until they settled into a glide. The wispy clouds that had once seemed to graze heaven itself were drifting slowly by her, planting cold, wet speckles of rain on her face as they flew through the sky.

Thin slithers of fear sliced through Sinai. It didn't belong to her. *Naala*. Her head was buried deep in the nnunu's feathers, her body rigid and shaking with fear. Naala, who dominated the forest grounds, seemed almost contradictory in the blue skies.

Sinai's heart ached before spots of black mist formed in her periphery. Could her powers help? There was nothing to stop her from trying. Sinai drew a breath, and tugged at the power, feeling it flesh through her body. The air began to stream around Naala, as she willed it to press against her, in what Sinai hoped would provide a cushion to hold in her courage. It worked. Sinai could feel the fear subsiding.

Until something explosive hit against her chest.

The nnunu faltered under Sinai's jerked movement. She couldn't believe it. There was *something* floating in the sky. A structure of some sort, consisting of three mammoth lumps of land with flat circular surfaces suspended in the air. *How is this possible?*

Sinai squinted ahead. The largest mass was positioned high and centre; the other two were smaller and sat below the large one, at either of its sides, creating an almost triangular shape. A crystal-like structure protruded from the centre of the biggest landmass. The surface of the two other structures seemed mostly bare, glistening in a similar fashion to a clear lake reflecting beams of light on a sunny day.

The nnunu woman picked up her speed and a bolt of terror crashed through Sinai. *That* was where the bird-women were taking them? She almost pulled away but in the end the fear of the hard crunch of the ground kept her steady.

As they drew nearer, Sinai noted clumps of crystals scattered indiscriminately across the horizon, coated in white glistening powder. Streams of thin, wispy light varying from blue to white fell over the land like waterfalls, and a blue serpentine river spiralled through the entirety of the land before burying itself within an unusual structure that looked like two rows of ivory, branchless trees bending to one another as they formed a tunnel.

She drew her breath and squeezed her eyes shut as they landed with a soft plop on the crisp floor. Bitter cold tore through her body causing her to shake violently. She jumped back in horror as strange curls of smoke escaped her mouth; the more she breathed, the more smoke came out of her mouth and nostrils. The same thing was happening to Naala and the nnunu women.

'W-what is this p-place?' she breathed, her words broken up by her chattering teeth. She looked around the cold, bare land. The land was coated in white powder, and she could now see little shrubs growing every which way across the horizon. Sinai hugged her arms.

'Ndewo, amụrụ ha abụọ,' the bird-women said as they crossed their black wings across their chest and brought the palms of their claws towards her.

There was something disorientating about these nnunu women. In all her life she had never seen a nnunu woman greet anyone before, nor had she heard them speak and certainly not *fly*. Even as she regarded them, they seemed *different*. Longer than she remembered, lean and almost regal, so unlike the huddled and bowed nnunus in the palace of Nri. *Were they even nnunus?* she pondered, before her mind settled on what they had said.

'Amụrụ ha abụọ?' she repeated. That was the same term that the Mami Wata had used to describe her. The Children Born of Both. Did the nnunus also know of the curse that was approaching the Kingdom?

'Yes, yes, yes,' chirped the bird-woman with specks of brown feathers embedded in her black coat. 'Cold?' she added, cocking her head to the side.

'What?' Sinai replied, confused.

'Too cold,' the other bird-woman said.

'Need feathers,' the brown-speckled nnunu woman chittered.

'Yes – but what did you say? What do know of the amụrụ ha abụọ?' she insisted as they nodded along.

'Need feathers, yes, yes, yes,' they said in unison before bracing for flight and shooting up into the air.

'Oh! Oh – no! No, please!' Sinai called as they hung suspended in the sky.

'Amụrụ ha abụọ needs feathers,' they sang, 'Amụrụ ha abụọ needs feathers.'

'No!' Sinai screamed as they soared away. It was a scream that shook her entire body. A scream born of the biting cold and the shattering fear that coursed through her. A scream that spoke of her frustration at the nnunu's sudden departure, and with them the information that she so desperately sought.

CHAPTER 9
IMEDA

Furuefu forest

'What ...' Sinai whimpered '... w-w-hat are we going to do?' She turned to face Naala, who looked far worse for wear. 'Are you all right?'

Naala glimpsed back at her with heavy eyelids, her skin dulled and her full lips pressed together as she struggled to steady herself against one of the jutting crystals. She nodded as she pressed her free palm across her eyes, squeezing slightly before attempting to stand up. She ended up doubling over after a few short staggering moments. Sinai took a step forward, but Naala put one hand up, signalling for her to stay back.

'Are you sure?' Sinai murmured hesitantly. Naala just shook her head slowly before pausing and turning behind the crystal cluster where she retched her guts out. Sinai winced before turning around to give the girl some privacy. 'Do you need anything?' she called as Naala continued to heave behind her.

'N-no,' Naala managed to say before returning to her retching.

What are we going to do? Sinai thought soberly as she looked around at the vast land. She couldn't see anything except the shards of crystals and bony shrubs along the endless skyline. She gazed ahead at the horizon; the sun was as white as the moon, dazzling with streams of brilliant light. She had never seen it like this before; in fact, she had never *seen* the sun at all; she was usually forced to flinch away from its blinding brightness, but now it stood clear to her, as though it were nothing more than a ball. She observed the streams of light that washed over the land.

'The eye of the sun,' she murmured to herself as an image struck into her head like lightning. '*Urukpuru?*' she said as she looked around. 'Urukpuru!' she exclaimed, her mind racing back to the legends of the old gods that she had heard at the palace festivals.

They would tell stories about wild beasts, temperamental gods and one particular story about a majestic city in the sky, Urukpuru, the land that Anyanwu, the fire goddess, had called home. The city was said to be lit aflame with blue fire that burned eternally within the ...

'Crystals,' Sinai recalled; as she bent over to touch the protruding crystal at her side, she used her numb fingers to brush away the wet powder that coated it. She stood astounded as she watched a pale-blue light flicker within the heart of the crystal. 'It's real?' she added under her breath before breaking out into a laugh. 'Of course it is!'

'What are you shouting about?' Naala muttered as she walked slowly over to Sinai. Save for the slight sheen on her deep-brown forehead, she looked like her usual self again.

'Are you okay?' Sinai asked as Naala waved her hands offhandedly.

'I'm f-fine,' she muttered, shivering slightly as she looked around; the focus had returned to her face. 'I'm c-cold. This place is ... unnatural.' Her brows came together tensely. 'We need to f-find a way out. Now.'

'It's Uruk-kpuru?' Sinai said.

'It's c-cold,' Naala retorted.

Sinai swept her eyes across the barren land. It was cold; too cold. The type of cold that settled into bones. The type of cold that felt like death. They wouldn't survive too long without help.

'What is Urukpuru?' Naala asked.

'It's Anyanwu's sky city,' she replied as Naala scanned the horizon, her dark eyes darting this way and that.

Naala peered closely at the flickering blue light within the crystal. She sighed as she straightened back up, her forehead crimped in thought. 'Perhaps if we head to the river,' she mumbled, mostly to herself.

Sinai recalled the serpentine river she had seen as they'd entered the sky city, and the strange ivory structure that housed it. Doubts played in her mind. Did Naala really think it was safe to venture off? What if they ended up finding more than they bargained for?

'It's the only place of note in this land,' Naala said, shrugging as though she had read her thoughts.

Sinai nodded. It was true; the river would most likely provide their first clue for escaping. That is, if escaping was even possible. She shivered. She didn't know if it was from the cold or her nerves.

'How do we get there?' Sinai said, looking around; every corner looked exactly the same.

'We go that way,' Naala said firmly, pointing over to the left.

'Oh,' Sinai replied, looking over at Naala quizzingly. 'The tug?'

Sinai watched as a reluctant smile found its way on Naala's mouth. 'No, I saw it as we entered.'

Sinai frowned. 'How? You had your eyes c-closed,' Sinai muttered to herself. *How on earth could she have seen that when I had my eyes wide open and I'm still unaware?*

'I did, but the air—' she stopped as her gaze softened '—it really helped. Thank you.'

Sinai was taken aback. She hadn't anticipated that Naala would have known it was her who had steadied her with the air. Her chest tightened; she felt strangely exposed.

'Oh, that's okay,' she said quickly.

'And sorry.'

'For what?'

'For not believing you about the beast.'

Sinai didn't know what to say. She had so many words pounding through her mind. She wanted to speak to Naala about the Mami Wata, the fate of the Kingdom, the fact that they were *twins*, the shameful thing she had done before they left the palace. She opened her mouth, not knowing what would tumble out first, but the frown that spread across Naala's face stopped her in her tracks.

'What will that beast do to the forest?' Naala said, her voice thick with emotion, and Sinai blinked.

Siwunmi, she thought, and memories of their time with the warm villagers slammed against her chest. The thought of the village being ravaged by that beast made her queasy.

'We need to get out of here, we need to help them,' Naala said before storming off, leaving Sinai scrambling to catch up.

*

Sinai and Naala huddled close as they treaded through the cold land. Ice seeped into their shivering bodies.

'So those creatures are b-b-ird women? The n-nnunus in the city?' Naala suddenly asked as she on clutched tighter to Sinai's arms.

'Yes,' Sinai replied, her face tight and numb.

'I've never come ac-ccross one before but I've always wanted to hear them sing – wait, are you getting warmer?' Naala beamed, her gaze fixed on something ahead. When Sinai followed it, her chest flushed with adrenaline. The river. It lay before them, bright and topaz blue, so dense it looked more like ink than water. A light mist steamed above it.

'I am ... do you think it's the river?' Sinai could feel her excitement dulling with every word. They'd found the river; now what? The emptiness of the sky city hadn't subsided; if anything it had grown. How would they make it off this floating city? How would they save Siwunmi?

Naala scrunched her face. 'Where to go,' she muttered, before her brow relaxed. 'When we approached the land, the structure was to the left of us.' She demonstrated with her hands. 'So we need to keep to the left.'

'Sure,' Sinai murmured, though she had no clue what Naala was talking about.

'What do you suppose is in this river?' Naala asked.

A smile crept over Sinai's stinging face, now that she did know. She looked down at the dense, blue liquid. Its colour was far too dense to be water. 'It must be the Imeda river ...'

'Imeda?' Naala muttered, drawing closer to it and bringing two fingers to its smooth surface.

'Wait!' Sinai called and Naala halted.

'For what?'

'It's the Imeda river!'

'Okay?'

'It's cursed,' she said as Naala drew away from it. 'Bluer than blue ...' She looked around before spotting a little bush covered in the wet powder. She walked over to it and tugged at it until a few brown twigs with hard, green leaves came off in her hand, and returned to the water, flinging them in. As soon as they touched its surface, they sizzled loudly. Foam began to gather around them and the leaves singed into nothing as the bark peeled before their eyes, until all that was left were bone-white twigs.

'Ah,' Naala murmured, clutching and then unclutching the hand that she would have dipped into the river. 'We stick to the riverbank, then. It looks like it'll be a long walk.' Naala's brows pinched together. Sinai didn't have to ask to know what she was thinking of, it was the same thought running through her mind: Siwunmi, were they running out of time? 'I need a distraction,' Naala announced as she jumped over a patch of teal-stained wetlands, 'tell me about the myth.'

'Okay,' Sinai said, her throat drying at the thought of performing. 'I mean, I'll try to do my best to tell it *right*, but I warn you, it will never be like when I heard it at Ákúkó-álá. The palace festivals are *something*. The flame tamers create such dazzling scenes with the ọkụ light as the orator tells the tale, and I ... I certainly can't do any voices.'

'I didn't realise that they told such stories at the palace. I'd always assumed it was all about the army or ... the Eze,' Naala said. 'I thought myths were forbidden?'

'Well, it wasn't typical,' Sinai said carefully. 'Most of the stories *were* about him, but every now and again, in a little show of defiance, someone did something ... well, atypical.' Sinai's stomach twisted as she recalled the fate of the storyteller. 'Ozo Iben,' she added quietly.

She had always liked him, with his smile almost as bright as his eccentric garments. Unlike the other storytellers in the palace, his stories had always had a *heart*. They had been either stomach-clenching funny or sobbingly sad. 'We didn't see him after that story. It was a shame, he was ... kind,' she added soberly.

'What was his story?' Naala asked.

'Ahh, yes, well, he said that Anyanwu built this city using three wild seeds blessed by the Earth Mother. They say she wanted a home close to the sun but still within the earth. She resided here with her family.'

'The anwu people?' Naala interjected.

'Yes. They were special,' Sinai said as they walked along the blue lake. '*Elite*, as Ozo Iben had described them. They started off as us but over time their bodies transformed from flesh and bone to light and fire.'

'Really?' Naala mused.

'So the legends say,' Sinai murmured as she stepped over a puddle. 'Anyway, one day Anyanwu fell in love with a human. She brought him here but he did not belong. He was not a god and it seemed he didn't have what was needed to complete an anwu transformation. He grew paranoid and bitter.'

Naala shook her head. 'I think I know where this is going,' she said. 'We had a similar situation in my village: Chizu and Sofu. Of course, when I tried to warn Sofu, I was called *divisive*.' She tutted.

Sinai chuckled lightly. She enjoyed when Naala commented on her village, though it also made her wary; so often it had led to a sad, reproachful look in the other girl's eyes.

'Well, someone should have warned Anyanwu,' Sinai continued quickly. 'They say that the human, driven by madness, consulted Amadioha, and the thunder god gave him a ball of lightning that he instructed the man to put in Anyanwu's favourite river. The thunder ball made the river bluer than blue and, as the fire goddess bathed, it weakened her.'

'Oh,' Naala said thoughtfully.

'It gets worse. While the goddess was weakened, Amadioha was able to corrupt the anwu with a jikọọ.'

'A what?'

'I don't know what it is *exactly*, but from what Ozo Iben said, it seemed to be some sort of curse. A curse that took away their will, and surrendered their control to the thunder god. He made them do terrible things. They destroyed the sky city and, well, *themselves.*'

'That's awful.'

'Yes,' Sinai murmured. A heavy feeling settled into her chest as she thought of the lives that had been lost on this land. The lost faces she imagined morphed into the ones she had seen in Siwunmi. Sinai shivered before continuing. 'When the fire goddess regained her strength, she tried to cleanse her people of the jikọọ with her flames, but something was wrong; she was broken. So instead of cleansing them, her flames destroyed the whole city and everyone in it.'

'Oof.' Naala sighed before turning to Sinai. 'Do you think it's true?'

Sinai shrugged as she glanced around the mystical land. 'If you told me a week ago, I would have said no; now I don't know what's real any more.'

'How do you suppose we do this?' Naala said, looking ahead.

Sinai followed her gaze to the tunnel structure ahead of them. She could see details of the pearly white trees. They were thin with slashes of grey folds in the creases; as they bent over in a bow, their branches clung to each other creating a dark cave. Sinai's heart sank as she noticed that there was no separation between the river and the trees; the blue liquid sloshed at the base of their trunks. There was no way for them to enter the tunnel without them going through the river. Sinai gazed into the deep black; nothing moved, no sound flowed through, but she was certain that something was lurking within.

'Do you think it's safe?'

'No,' Naala replied as Sinai looked across the barren land. She agreed with Naala's assessment, but what else were they to do?

'Okay,' Naala said eventually, 'we can't get through to the tunnel without wading through the cursed water, we can't enter … unless …' Something bright shone behind the blacks of her eyes. 'Can you command the air?' she asked, turning to Sinai.

'Yes,' Sinai replied hesitantly.

'Do you think you can use it to allow us to walk through the water – keep it away from us somehow with the—'

'Air, yes,' Sinai interrupted as Naala's plan flourished in her mind.

Her heart pounded as she felt for the power that hung about her. She felt it slowly sink into her skin, washing her with a sense of completeness. Sinai felt the movement of the air bend under the instruction of her fingertips. Sinai raised her hands and a sudden gust of wind blew through the river, cutting out a path wide enough for the both of them. Sinai was pleased to find that the river wasn't too deep; it would come up to their thighs at the most.

'Good,' Naala murmured, before turning to Sinai cautiously. 'You think you can hold it?'

'Yup,' Sinai replied. 'It's no more taxing than remembering to hold on to a string,' Sinai explained.

'Okay,' Naala said as she took a deep breath before stepping into the exposed river floor carefully. She stopped with a jolt.

'What is it?' Sinai cried out as Naala turned around slowly, a smile spreading over her face.

'It's really warm!' she declared.

Sinai let go of a breath before returning Naala's smile. She carefully stepped into the cleared river and almost cried as the heat kissed against her sore skin. It wasn't long before Naala was hurrying her along.

Darkness engulfed them as they walked through the tunnel of trees, halted only by the steamy blue glow of the cursed river. A sickening sense ran through Sinai as she noticed something moving at the corner of her eyes.

'You see them too,' Naala said as she peered curiously at the strange creatures swimming in the parted lake. They looked like bright-coloured fish skeletons, no bigger than her forearm. While they seemed to have no flesh, they moved around animatedly, undeniably full of life. Sinai couldn't tear her gaze away from the creatures.

'Can you hear that?' Naala suddenly whispered, pulling Sinai out of her thoughts.

'Music,' they whispered in unison. It was a beautiful sound; harrowing and haunting, yet light and beautiful. It sounded through the cave in the same windy tone that the nnunus had spoken with. Naala gestured for Sinai to move closer to her, and as she did, Sinai noticed the river's end. The blue inky water fanned out into a series of puddles over gravel and rocks. Sinai used the air to clean out their path. They hopped from one rock to another until they came to a short strip of dry land bordered by a wall of aqua glass, with a crusted hole at its centre.

The girls hung at the shadowed sides of the large opening. The rim of the huge gap looked as though someone had smashed through the glass before collecting all the tiny fragments and clumping them back together in small, clustered heaps that glistened in the glow of the distant river.

At the other side of the wall, a flock of nnunu women danced and sang vigorously. Sinai felt her heart pound as she watched them. Thin vines, embedded in the aqua glass, lit up with their song. The vines ran through the glass and into the walls until they came together at a source in the centre of the room. They sang louder and louder and the silver light continued to brighten. The room grew brighter, drawing Sinai closer.

Touch.

Sinai gasped. She felt a strong pull towards the lit vines. It was the same pull that she had felt in the Obi's court so long ago. The same pull that had compelled her to touch the Mother's Crystal. The nnunu's song reached fever pitch.

Touch.

Sinai needed to touch the vine. She drew her fingers towards it but, before she could make contact, Naala grabbed her hand tightly. Her widened eyes blinked back at her rapidly.

'What's wrong, Sinai? What's happening to you?' Naala questioned.

Sinai looked down at the girl's clasp on her hand.

Touch.

She drew up her left hand and a burst of air slammed Naala against the wall of the tunnel. Before she could scramble back up to her feet, Sinai placed her finger on the vine and the world before her broke away.

A man entered a small hut. His face was handsome, warm and terribly sad. She recognised the man though she had never seen him before. Something in his eyes, the corners of his mouth reminded her of—

Naala broke her way into the vision. Her face contorted as she pushed through Sinai's pulsing air buffer.

'Stop this,' she struggled, 'the river! You're making the river rise!'

Before Sinai could reply she was facing the man once again.

He was looking at something behind her. Sinai followed his gaze to see a woman sitting calmly on a cushion. She wore layers of white cloth; her entire body was covered. A hood cast shadows over her face, but Sinai could still see her pale skin.

Lolo Obioma? *she thought in shock, before a gleam caught her eye. On the Lolo's chest lay a necklace with nine engravings, one of which was filled with an emerald crystal. The Earth Mother's Crystal?*

'Thank you for welcoming me to your village, Chief Obifune,' she said. 'I'm so sorry to hear about your wife's departure.'

The man, Obifune, didn't say anything but his eyes squinted at the mention of his wife. Sinai hoped that someone would embrace the sorrowful man but the room remained cool, and soon the raw emotion behind his eyes had hardened to granite.

'I've come to bless your daughter,' the woman announced.

Obifune looked back at her sternly. 'That's so kind of you but she is asleep.' Just as he said that a cry emitted from the room. His body became rigid and the skin bunched around his eyes. One of the village women rushed into the hut, bowing apologetically, before dashing to tend to the crying child.

'Just in time,' the woman said, grinning. 'Obifune, I know you are aware that I am a representative from Eze Ochichiri. We are connected in spirit, mind and soon—' she rested her gloved palms over her stomach '—in blood. A blessing from me is one of the highest honours in the Kingdom. It would be absurd for anyone to turn it down; one might need to question as to why.'

Obifune looked back at her, his body calming as he gestured to the village woman who hung silently in the shadows to bring the child closer. He took the child into his arms tenderly as the woman drew herself up from the ground and walked over to the restless child. She watched the baby heedfully before raising her hands to take the child. Obifune did not look at her or ease his grip; rather he tensed his body, his eyes gazing down at the cooing infant.

'Chief,' the village woman pleaded, and the pressure in the room suddenly eased as Obifune's body slackened. He allowed the sheathed woman to take his child. His eyes remained fixed on the baby as the woman began to speak in a tongue that Sinai didn't recognise; the emerald crystal blushed slightly as the woman rocked to and fro.

'She's a special child,' the woman said eventually before returning her to Obifune. 'Will you be sending her to the palace? She could do well for herself there.'

Sinai watched Obifune's jaw clench but he looked back at the woman with dull eyes.

'No.'

'A child needs a mother,' the woman said, glancing at the village woman hanging at the door. A mother of her own class. And as I understand, you have no sisters, no women left from you or your wife's blood.'

'She is needed here. They will lead our people,' Obifune said firmly.

'You have selected her husband?' the woman murmured, a smile playing on her lips.

'What?'

'You said they will lead, I assume you mean her and her husband,' she added as Obifune looked back at her, allowing a short, contemptuous smile to flash across his face.

'Slip of the tongue.' He shrugged.

'Of course.' The woman laughed, before stepping closer to him, stroking the baby's face with her gloved fingers. 'I would be careful about such slips, Obifune,' she said darkly. 'These are not the days of the past – women do not lead, not any more.'

Obifune smiled tightly back. 'Of course. I'm sorry we won't be able to have you here for much longer; the sun is coming down and, as you noted, I do not have any women from my blood to host you comfortably.'

'Yes, I should be going,' the woman murmured slowly. 'It was a true pleasure, Obifune,' she said before adding, 'Ndewo,' placing her crossed gloved hands on her chest before bringing her palms towards him.

'Ndewo,' he replied, bowing his head towards her, his hands firmly clasped on the sleeping child as he left the room.

The woman watched the door silently.

'Well?' she said out loud.

'It has to be them,' a man said, and Sinai turned around to see the faceless man from her dream.

The woman held onto her pendant. 'They are exquisite,' she murmured to herself, as she brought out a leather-cased parchment from her garments. It was a dark-red colour and bore a Nsibidi symbol, a square with three dashed lines at its left and at its right a circle with a line cut through the middle.

Blood? Sinai thought to herself.

'So, do we … kill them?' the faceless man said nervously, as the woman wrote vigorously on the parchment.

'No,' she muttered as she lifted her head and slipped the parchment back into her garment, 'we

control them. That is the way we ensure we win.'

'Control them?' the man said, confused. 'You want to stay here under Obifune's gaze?'

'Don't be simple. Obifune cannot live.'

The man looked out the window, 'He seems ... good.'

'Yes,' the woman said curtly, 'but if we really want to do this, if we want to somehow save this world, we must do that which is difficult. I like him, I do, but he will never let them go whilst he is still alive. What must be done, must be done.'

*

Sinai gasped as she released her hand from the vine. Naala's eyes narrowed in burning anger. Horror crept up her spine as she turned to see what stood before her. The river had engorged itself, reaching the top of the tree tunnel; the only thing that stood between its curse and the girls was the airstream that Sinai was unknowingly using to keep it back.

'Oh, heavens,' Sinai murmured.

'Bring the river down,' Naala seethed as Sinai's heart hammered in her chest.

'I-I don't know how,' Sinai stammered. She didn't even know if she could hold the engulfed river for much longer; she felt it push voraciously against her air shield.

'You have to!' Naala growled; her eyes shone bright gold and her teeth gritted.

Sinai could see small sticks snapping at the sides of the tunnel. They would do nothing to help; surely Naala could do *more*.

Sinai tried to keep her concentration, but a sharp sound from Naala stole it away.

'What?' she asked, sneaking a look behind her. Sinai caught sight of the flock of nnunu women floating at the entrance of the aqua glass and an inaudible sound escaped her throat.

'Sinai!' Naala called as the blue river began to flow towards them.

She had released her hold.

Claws tugged at her hand and she found herself flung through the air. She hit the ground with a thud, opening her eyes just in time to see the glass door sealed shut, the blue liquid slamming against it.

'You've finally come,' a musical voice said.

CHAPTER 10
THE HEALER

Furuefu forest

'Of course, *I'll* be staying with the nakombse,' Lolo Nwanyi said, tucking a stray braid back into its place. Chisi smiled brightly at the noblewoman though she had no idea what the Lolo was talking about. She didn't dare ask.

She folded another one of Lolo Nwanyi's garments, turning her head slightly to the other woman, lest she complain that Chisi was ignoring her. Since Meekulu Kaurandua's passing, Chisi had been transferred to wait on the Akunna family. She spent her days washing garments, changing akwa sheets and running errands. She hated every second of it.

Tiptoeing around the Lolo Nwanyi's feelings was perhaps the most tiresome aspect of all. She should have been done with her akwa duties by now, but the Lolo was in the mood to talk, and so Chisi *had* to be in the mood to listen.

'Their nobles aren't like the nobles in Nri,' Lolo Nwanyi continued, her hand still fiddling her braid. She wore her hair in an intricate pattern, plaited down at the front with three medium-sized braided loops crowning her head. As she tilted, the gold chains intertwined in her hair rattled. 'The nakombse dress as though every day is a festival,' she said pointedly as Chisi nodded. 'You should see their cotton robes. You know they are experts in design? They say that any woman who wears one of their red robes is destined to find the truest of loves,' she squealed before snapping up abruptly. Her door had burst open.

Chisi's mouth dried as the head of the Akunna family, Lolo Nwanyi's father, entered her quarters. Obi Akunna walked through the room with rows of gold plates clamped around his white dreadlocks, tied neatly at the nape of his neck. He had always reminded Chisi of a scorpion. He was not loud and brash like other predators. He didn't need to be. After all, he oversaw Nri's finances, making him the richest and most powerful man in the city, second only to the Eze. No, he took his victims discreetly. He would allow them to get comfortable before he delivered a paralysing sting. Chisi shivered at the expression on his face. His thick eyebrows were settled into a look of disdain.

'Ndewo, Nna,' Lolo Nwanyi said, placing her crossed palms on her chest and extending her palms towards her father.

Chisi dropped her work and imitated the girl, adding a slight bow to her greeting.

'Ndewo, daughter,' he said.

Lolo Nwanyi flinched. Chisi didn't blame her; he always said the word daughter as though it were an insult. The noblewoman recovered quickly, plastering a smile over her tight face.

He looked over the room, and though he hadn't glanced once at Chisi, she couldn't help feeling as though she was also being watched.

'You needn't have come to fetch me, Nna? As you can see, I am ready,' she squeaked, her bright feverish eyes studying his every move. Her father blinked back at her.

'And where do you think you're going?' he said coldly. Chisi took note of his demeanour, and she threw a glance at Lolo Nwanyi, her stomach twisting as Lolo Nwanyi flinched back, her eyebrows pulled together. Chisi could sense a quarrel forming in the air, and in the Akunna family, such quarrels always ended with blood.

Chisi picked up her empty basket. Lolo Nwanyi wouldn't notice that she hadn't changed the akwa sheets. Chisi would come back later in the day to finish her room, hopefully once the girl had departed for her trip. Even if she received backlash for leaving the sheets unchanged, it couldn't be worse than staying.

Chisi edged towards the door, but Obi Akunna stood firmly in her way. Her stomach flipped as she stood dumb before him. She tried again to move past the man and he looked down at her with a glare that caused her to scuttle back to the walls.

'To the Kingdom of Mossi?' Lolo Nwanyi said weakly as she lifted her eyes to him, her hands fluttered as though she didn't know what to do with them. 'Remember? We discussed it *moon-cycles* ago.'

'I *remember* telling you to mind your brother,' Obi Akunna said, his voice a low growl.

'What?' Lolo Nwanyi choked, 'Mind my ... ? Nna, I have. I've been watching Ndub—'

'Lies,' he hissed, as a vein throbbed at his temple.

Chisi's limbs numbed at the outburst. Her heart ached as she caught glimpses of the door behind the Obi.

'Nna,' the Lolo gasped, and her bottom lip trembled as tears misted in her onyx eyes.

'And now you *dare* to speak to me of the Kingdom of Mossi?'

'Nna, I—'

'Have you really no shame? Unwed as you are. You, of all my children, should be grovelling for your place in this family. Rectifying your failure to provide a grandson. You dare request *anything* from me when you left your brother for the dogs?' His words were no higher than a hiss and yet his neck bulged under their strain. His eyes were blackened with rage.

Tears pricked in Chisi's eyes. She blinked them away as she wiped her clammy palms on her garment. She had never seen Obi Akunna like this. She didn't want to see any more.

Lolo Nwanyi's head sprang up to look at him.

'Nna—' her face remained tight, though it was now wet with the tears she had fought to contain '—must we discuss this *now*?'

He scoffed at the comment, glancing for the first time at Chisi.

She held her breath.

'Oh? So you *do* have shame?'

Lolo Nwanyi straightened her head. 'I—' she sucked in a breath '—I accept my failures, Nna, but I beg you to recall that I have *had* many proposals, more than my peers, from *good* men and you – well, you have refused them all.'

'Good men?' Obi Akunna jeered. 'Which one of those low-rankers were worthy to father *my* grandson?'

'Father, that's … that's not my fault.'

'Is it not? Then whose fault is it?' he said, stalking towards her. He brought his hand to her face and wiped at her wet cheek.

Chisi could see the Lolo trembling under his touch.

'If the bee does not go to the flower, then the flower *must* be soiled,' he murmured as she stepped back. Fresh tears sprang to her narrowed eyes, her lips slack and trembling.

'I am *not* soiled,' she spat, her bottom lip hanging in shock.

'Yes, you are! You are soiled, daughter, and you are reckless! A witch who has murdered her own brother,' Obi Akunna boomed as Lolo Nwanyi shook her head, her fingers clawing at her once perfect hair.

'Ndubuaku is not dead,' she cried manically. 'Please, I've done all that you've asked, let me go,' she sobbed violently.

Her father's nose wrinkled as though he had caught a whiff of something awful.

Chisi's heart bled for the woman. Lolo Nwanyi was difficult, yes, but what else could she be, growing up in a family of vipers? Thoughtlessly, she reached for the woman's hand. Before she could grasp on to it, Lolo Nwanyi snatched her hand away, glaring at Chisi, her eyes red and venomous. Chisi backed away from her, stumbling towards the door as she bowed clumsily. Before she could open it, the door swung open.

Obi Akunna's son, Ozo Ndubuaku, stood before her. The boy's eyes were dulled and darkened with a drained, tired expression. Chisi felt as though she had seen it on someone else before, perhaps several people.

Behind him trailed a man she had never laid eyes on. He looked down on her hungrily. Shadows appeared over his face as though he were wearing a headpiece. He wasn't. This man didn't even have any hair. His head stood bald, coated in the same fawn-brown skin that extended over his face.

Chisi blinked back at him as fear crept up her spine. Not the jumpy fear that nobles inspired, but a fear that clutched at her throat like death itself.

'And where is this little pet going in such a fright?' the man said as he heaved Ozo Ndubuaku into the room, closing the door behind him. 'Obi Akunna, you awful man, what did you do to the girl?'

Chisi's heart thundered.

She was dead.

Obi Akunna would surely kill her for inspiring such a comment. Meekulu Kaurandua had burned for far less. Her vision blurred with tears.

'I don't have patience for your games, Healer Agymah,' Obi Akunna said coldly, and Chisi darted her gaze back to the healer.

It was strange. This man did not look anything like one of the palace healers, who usually wore red cloth tied at their shoulders, grand feather headpieces and their right eye coated with white paint. This man stood before her in tattered grey garments, his head bare and his fingertips black.

He grinned manically before sniffing the air around her. His movements were sharp and swift. Chisi jumped back as the grin spread across his face.

'A useful pet, I see. She stays,' he said briskly. It almost sounded like a *demand*. Chisi couldn't stay. Not here, not like this. She trembled at the thought of defiance but she had to *try*.

'O-ozo,' Chisi stammered, 'I'm on akwa sheet duty.'

'Exactly, and it doesn't look like you're finished with Lolo Nwanyi's,' he stated matter-of-factly, pointing at her basket still full of fresh fur and dried lavender.

'I...' she started, nervously turning to Obi Akunna who glowered at her with a force that made her chest tighten. 'Y-yes,' she stammered before shuffling through the room, avoiding the nobleman's murderous glare.

As she passed through the archway into the Lolo's sleeping room, Chisi let out a steady breath. When she opened her eyes she was fuelled with hot energy. She would finish the chore the quickest she had ever done and then she would be free to leave. There was something unholy in the air, and if she stayed long enough she knew it would claim her.

'Take a good look, Nwanyi, look at what you've done to your own brother,' she heard Obi Akunna say as she dropped the woven basket in the corner of the room.

'I haven't done any—'

'Silence!' Obi Akunna said. 'I told you to watch him. I told all of you to be *careful*,' he said.

Chisi could hear heavy footsteps stomping around the room. Chisi gave a sideways glance through the archway.

'Father, I'm sorry, I didn't realise,' the boy pleaded, his shoulders curved forward and his hands limp at his sides.

'You signed away my legacy without *realising*,' Obi Akunna hissed; the edge to his voice made Chisi nervous.

Her hands quivered as she drew the heavy fur from the nest and placed it on the basket lid, drawing out the thinner linen material from the basket and spreading it onto the large gleaming gold nest.

'I don't understand,' Lolo Nwanyi said, her voice barely a whisper through the archway.

'Shall I enlighten you, *Lolo*?' the healer said, a smirk unfurling on his lips. There was a look in his eyes, devoid of all emotion. His gaze flashed to Chisi and heat stabbed at her cheeks as she turned away. Her moist fingers fumbled with the sheets as an ugly laugh rang through the archway.

Rather than call her out, he continued to explain. 'As you *should* know, General Ikenna is seeking Eze Ochichiri's empty seat. Though his bloodline is weak, the little spittle of a man is gaining power through a series of calculated deaths and Obara curses. Your sweet, dear brother unknowingly entered an Obara curse with the man, tying his life, and your father's bloodline, to his cause.'

A stillness shook the room. Chisi dared to glance through the archway though her hands trembled at the effort. She knew little of the Obara oaths, but she knew they were a great evil best left unspoken.

'Oh, look how blank she looks,' the healer sneered as something glittered in his squinted eyes; his smile was hard and unforgiving. 'Must I spell it out? Very well, Ikenna has your father's manhood firmly in his iron gr—'

'Silence!' Obi Akunna roared. Though his body remained deathly still, the rough skin around his jaw quaked at the effort. 'I will not be controlled.' His dark eyes turned distant and cold.

'We can find a way,' Lolo Nwanyi said quickly, 'we can fight this.'

'*You* have done enough!' Obi Akunna spat. 'You sat there musing over your travels when you should have been watching him. I *trusted* you with that task.'

'Nwanyi is not to blame,' the boy piped, 'the responsibility is mine and mine alone.'

'*You?*' his father sneered. 'You who is so feeble of mind? You who stands cursed by the blood of your witch of a mother? You have never understood, but Nwanyi, Nwanyi does. She *always* understands and that is why she left you to your devices. She did this on purpose, and you're too much of a fool to see. She will have her son take the position that by all rights sits with you, imbecile that you are.'

'Nna,' Lolo Nwanyi whimpered, her face fixed in a pained stare, 'I swear—'

'Be silent! You failed me, daughter, and his blood is on your hands.'

'We can find a way,' Lolo Nwanyi cried. 'Ndubuaku can *say* that you pledge your allegiance, but we don't *have* to follow through.'

A bitter laugh cut through the room. 'What a strange way to view blood,' the healer mocked, 'as something that can be manoeuvred by your frivolous lies. There is *no* way around it. If your father does not act in allegiance to Ikenna, the oath will claim your brother's blood from his body, suck it out until he's nothing but skin and bones, and a curse will be released on your bloodline. If you try to kill Ikenna, the oath will claim your brother. If you try to run, the curse will claim your brother. If you—'

'Stop!' Lolo Nwanyi cried. 'Nna, who is this man? Why must we listen to him? For all we know he could be a heretic, spewing lies to get us to twist to Ikenna's will.'

'I am your only way out, pet,' the healer growled as he stalked towards her, his chin pressed to his neck and his eyes filled with hate. 'If Obi Akunna so wishes.'

'Nna?' Lolo Nwanyi stammered.

'My only son,' Obi Akunna said in a hoarse voice, 'I was so pleased when you came into the earth. Five wives and only one of them bore me a son. That day was glorious. That was the day that I *knew* I had someone to hand my Ofo stick to, a new and better me,' he murmured.

'Nna,' the boy snivelled, his top lip wet with slime, his throat-lump bobbing up and down.

'And look at you. A disgrace,' he spat. 'A serpent that would have *them* lord your life over me. You offered yourself as their beating stick to make me bend to that low-born's will.'

'Nna, please just—' Lolo Nwanyi cried.

'Impossible,' Obi Akunna roared.

'Nna—'

'Kill him,' he said, and the room threw up into uproar. Chisi's heart thudded as she watched Lolo Nwanyi dash in front of her brother.

'No!' she shrieked, clutching as thick, red shadows tore out of the healer. They curled over him until he disappeared. In his place a strange firefly hovered, its crimson glow spread across the room. Lolo Nwanyi whipped her head to and fro, swatting at the insect but it found its way to Ndubuaku's neck.

Obi Akunna snatched Lolo Nwanyi away from her brother, who had begun to convulse, clutching at his neck before he tumbled to the ground.

'Ndubuaku!' Lolo Nwanyi shrieked; her eyes were red slits and her head was thrown back as she struggled in her father's arms. He held on to her tightly but her cries found her way to Chisi, piercing through the servant girl until she too drew tears.

The boy's body shrivelled before her eyes until he was nothing more than bone and hardened skin. Chisi turned and retched into the akwa basket. Her body shook furiously as she backed back into the cornered room.

'Nwanyi,' she heard Obi Akunna say ruthlessly, 'Nwanyi, open your eyes this instant.'

'Please,' she heard the Lolo whisper, 'I can't. Please, Nna, I can't.'

'Nwanyimeole!' Obi Akunna demanded and a whimpered response ensued. 'Take a good look at what *you* have done to your brother. A good look at what your incompetence breeds. You have lost me a son. If you do not bear me a worthy grandson from the *finest* stock, Nwanyimeole, and *fast*, a far worse fate will fall on your head. Do you understand me?'

Chisi screamed silently into her hands as a strangled cry ran through the room.

'Get out of my sight,' Obi Akunna said tiredly, and Chisi heard the door slam after a series of scrambling footsteps. Her heartbeat pounded in her ears as she drew closer to the archway. *How am I to leave?* she thought as she stole glances into the room. The monstrous Healer Agymah was back in his human form.

'Unfortunate, but necessary,' he noted, before turning to leave.

'Wait,' Obi Akunna called, his voice thin and wispy.

'I am not one of your servants, *Obi*. You awoke me and so I answered your call; count yourself lucky that this is where it ends between you and I.'

'My son … my son's death is not a repayment,' Obi Akunna struggled.

'Is it not? Well, how about we add your life to the mix, the life I've chosen to graciously spare,' the healer bowed mockingly.

'I want revenge,' Obi Akunna demanded, his voice regaining its usual prowess. 'I want Ikenna's head.'

'Ikenna has shrouded himself with amoosus who protect him with Ọbara magic. My *talents* are useless against him now. Get an assassin, if you will. Poison him, crush his head; you can certainly pay for it.'

'No,' Obi Akunna said sharply, 'he is guarded by the entire army, by Olu – that man is … I tried. Over and over again until … he got my boy – he got my boy to stop me from trying.'

'You have Nri's wealth at your fingertips. I'm sure you can figure out a way.'

'*ɛyɛ sɛ wo yɛ*. I demand it!' Obi Akunna said.

Chisi's forehead furrowed. She didn't understand the language but the healer certainly did. His eyes darkened with rage.

'You dare use that against me?'

'Not against you, *Adze*. I'm simply staking my claim on what is due to me for re-awakening you.'

'Once I complete your order, you will no longer be protected,' the healer snarled. 'You would reckon with my wrath?'

Obi Akunna shrugged. 'He killed my son. For that he must die. There is nothing else. I know the cost.'

'So be it,' the healer said. Red shadows started to emerge from his chest once again. Before Chisi could scream, the healer was in front of her; he grabbed at her underarms and lifted her to her feet before dragging her back into the main room by her neck.

'Please, I won't say any—' Chisi pleaded as his dark eyes began to mist red. A cold chill soared up from her feet and ran through her whole body. She couldn't move.

'Do you know what allows me to possess your kind?' the healer said, his head tipped to its side as he peered at Chisi.

Obi Akunna didn't respond, his gaze remaining fixed on what remained of his son.

'It is Eriri Uhie,' the demon healer continued. 'It flows through all of your human bodies. Imbedded in your blood. It is what gives you your *fight*. What drove you to request the death of your son. What pushes you towards survival. It is gritty, raw, the thread of your passion. It fuels your darkest thoughts and most selfish desires. It's intoxicating by nature, and yet it is also *pure*.' The healer's eyes ran hungrily over Chisi, his mouth parted to reveal teeth as sharp as a jaguar's. Chisi's eyes burned as the tears she wanted to let fall sat frozen in her eye ducts. 'With it I can control each one of you.' He flicked his finger and Chisi's left arm sprang up to the sky; he flicked his finger again and she spun around to Obi Akunna, who had turned to see the performance. Her teeth bit at him as a snarl that didn't belong to her escaped her mouth. 'Imagine what could be done if I could possess thousands,' the healer said.

'An army,' Obi Akunna murmured wistfully.

The healer let out a cold laugh, 'Not any army. *The bụrụ-ọnụ.*'

'Do it,' Obi Akunna demanded. 'And be sure to deliver me his head.'

'*Do it,*' the healer mimicked. 'I will, as soon as you grab three thousand oranges in your left hand.' Obi Akunna frowned as the healer chuckled to himself. 'Your request is stupid. I alone cannot *do it.*'

Chisi felt her body pull towards the monstrous man and once again he sniffed the air around her. 'But this little pet has come into contact with someone *special*. Real contact. They've spoken, and formed a tie. This person will bring forth a pit of chaos – and with that,' he added, 'I can do *anything*.'

'You can get the bụrụ-ọnụ?'

'Once that pit is open, there's no bounds to what could be done,' the healer snarled. 'But in the meantime, I'll need blood.' He took out a heart-shaped glass bottle with golden symbols etched into its face, filled with a dark red substance, before turning to Chisi. 'Take this and place three drops of it into the well at midnight,' he said before bringing his mouth to her neck.

Chisi felt sharp pricks against her frozen skin before she began to stumble under the weight of a growing heaviness pressing against her head.

'She is fit for the task?' Obi Akunna said.

'With my venom coursing through her veins, she's fit for anything,' Chisi heard him reply as everything turned to black.

CHAPTER 11
NINE BREAKS

Urukpuru

Naala leapt up from the floor, ignoring the ache at the side of her body. Her eyes darted around the room catching every whisper of movement. The bird-women returned her gaze with wide-eyed interest. Large unblinking eyes met her gaze, coated with a strip of red skin extended from ear to ear.

Beside her, Sinai peeled herself up from the ground. Her movements were slow and lumbered, as though they had time to spare. *Get up!* she wanted to hiss but she had no time to chastise. She needed to concentrate. At any point they cou— Naala jolted as they began to advance.

'Stay back!' she ordered, flicking her gaze to branches of chalky wood that domed the room.

'You've come,' they sang as she implored for the Black and Gold realm. Though she felt the power coursing through her veins, only a flurry of pale wood dust trickled through the air. The sight of which caused another spur in the bird-women, their long willowy bodies inching closer. Naala's chest hollowed as she jerked her head around the room. They were surrounded.

The bird-women stood in silence for a while until a low beautiful hum began to echo through the chambers, musical whispers scattered across the room,

'You've come.'

'You've come.'

'You've come.'

As they spoke, something in the centre of the room began to shine brightly. Naala could see that it was a crystal cluster; one side was a dark onyx, the other a clouded white.

'I saw something – a vision,' Sinai whispered. She was finally up on her feet.

Naala pressed her lips together tightly but it was no use. The words came rushing out before she could stop them. 'Did you see an escape from the situation that _you've_ put us in?' Sinai's expression faltered but Naala paid her no mind. They didn't have time for any of this. Every second wasted meant more time for the beast to destroy Siwunmi. Naala couldn't let that happen. Not again. Her gaze darted up to the pale wood that, try as she might, she couldn't move. _Blast it._

'Esinaala and Sinaikuku,' a voice sounded, and Naala's throat tightened. She looked ahead to see the nnunu women parting as the bird-woman who had spoken moved towards them. Her feathers were pitch black, not glossy like the other nnunus but a deep and smooth matte texture, save for their tips, which shone in brilliant gold.

'Ndewo,' she murmured, crossing her feathered arms over her chest and extending the palms of her claws towards them, 'I am Nwamara and I'm so happy you found us,' she said, her eyes shining with wonder.

'So happy.'

'So happy.'

'So happy,' the nnunus whispered in unison.

'Yes,' Nwamara murmured, as she circled them, her eyes bright and watchful, 'Nonye and Nene were so excited to tell us about your arrival that it seems they forgot to bring you along.' She glanced over at two nnunus over to her left, who had dropped their chins to their chests.

'Alas, everything turned out right in the end. One might think this was how it was always meant to be,' she said excitedly, throwing them a wink.

'Meant to be,' they chirped, clapping excitedly.

Naala stepped back as the nnunu inspected them, 'Look! Not one bite on you, how lucky you are! Between us two, the Aido-Hwedo is most distressed.'

The Aido-Hwedo? Naala repeated internally as old stories of the fabled beast came to mind. The rainbow serpent from the Kingdom of Dahomey? *That* was who they had nearly faced? Naala shivered as she recalled the echoes of its piercing scream.

'Distressed?' Naala scoffed, 'yeah, we know.' The nnunu's eyes brightened.

'You do, yes, yes. As you must know too, when one is distressed, one can act blindly. A blind Aido-Hwedo is a terrible one indeed. Why, you two might have lost one of your spirally limbs, or worse, entered the deep sleep.'

'Sleeping is the worst of those two?' Naala asked, wrinkling her brow.

'Of course,' the nnunu woman exclaimed, 'if you had been asleep, then we would have never found you and you would have died in the cold, your bodies so ill-equipped for … well, nearly everything.'

'She has a point,' Sinai murmured as Naala forced the air out of her nose.

'Yes, but if *we* hadn't found you, we would have met the same fate anyway,' Naala insisted.

'Exactly! You did find us, so the Aido-Hwedo could not have bitten you. You two are very much awake,' she said, smiling, before scrunching her face and inspecting them further. 'Aren't you?' she asked curiously, her eyebrows raised and her beak upturned.

Naala blinked back at the nnunu. 'Awake? *Yes*, we are very much awake,' she said before catching Sinai's distant look. *At least, I am*, she thought bitterly.

'Sorry – can I just ask, what is that?' Sinai whispered distractedly as Naala swotted the bird-woman away.

Naala followed her gaze to the illuminated crystals at the centre of the room. Her throat tightened. It hit her all at once. An undeniable pull. A call to surrender *everything*. She recognised the urge; it was the same that had allowed her to abandon her friends and run off to Eze Ochichiri's quarters. A frown spread across her mouth; when she turned to Sinai, it deepened further. Sinai's eyes were bright with wonder. Naala's teeth clenched. Hadn't she done enough?

Nwamara smiled back at her with delight. 'It is the Àlà and the Ikuku crystals,' she said with a knowing nod, as though it would mean something to them.

'The what?' Naala regretted asking almost as soon as the words left her mouth. Not for the first time, her curiosity had got the best of her.

'Why, the Mother's Crystal, of course.'

Naala and Sinai glanced at each other briefly. That was *not* the Earth Mother's Crystal. They knew this. Above all else, they knew this.

'You must be mistaken,' Naala blurted.

'I must be?' Nwamara smiled, her large eyes brightening.

'Sorry,' Sinai interjected, 'but yes, you see, *that* is not the Mother's Crystal. The crystal is green and it is with—' Sinai stopped herself before blinking ferociously '—is … somewhere … lost, we suppose. We had it, we held it and that's not it … right?' Sinai turned to Naala.

It was not the first time Sinai had become skittish about the crystal. When she had first noticed it, Naala had still been reeling from her encounter with that green-eyed murderer. Her eyes narrowed in a thought that the bird-women all too quickly stole.

The howl was frantic and piercing. Naala clutched at her ears. 'What is going on?!' she cried over the noise, ducking at the swooping nnunus.

Her heart was still drumming through her ears long after they had settled at Nwamara's raised feathered arms. She lowered them gently. 'It is fascinating to watch how your minds work,' Nwamara chirped. She drew closer, clasping their wrists with her claws. Naala tugged away but the willowy bird-woman was surprisingly strong. A cold sweat trickled down Naala's spine.

Nwamara paid her no mind; instead, she turned their wrists to expose two symbols that lay embedded at either side of their hands. Naala stilled. She had first seen the mark when she had touched the Mother's Crystal a lifetime ago, the strange black symbol had found its way to her skin and try as she might, she couldn't get it off.

'Chi,' the nnunu woman whispered before letting their hands go and looking at them eagerly.

'Chi?' Naala repeated as she held onto her wrist.

'You say that you encountered the Mother's Crystal, and while that is not false, it is not entirely true. You girls, you Children Born of Both, encountered *part* of the crystal; the Chi part.'

Naala frowned. 'The Chi part? No, we touched the Ndụ Crystal, the Mother's

Crystal, not the Chi Crystal.' Naala had never even heard of a Chi Crystal. There had only ever been one crystal and yet … she turned to the gleaming stones as goose pimples ran up her arms. She couldn't deny that it did feel *familiar*.

The nnunu blinked back at her before breaking into a hearty laugh as she clutched at her stomach. 'The Ndụ Crystal? Oh, you humans, you do tickle me. S*trange* creatures, are they not? They see through such tiny lenses.' Nwamara wiped away a tear as she settled into thought. 'I do wonder why you humans glamorised that part so, Ndụ – Life. It has only ever been but *one* part of the Mother's Crystal, one part of the Mother's heart, and yet it seems to be the only part that your species can truly accept. Curious beings.'

'But the Eze said—'

At the mention of his name the nnunus began to make spitting sounds. A pained expression crossed their beaked faces.

'Will we now bother with what *the Eze* said? The man was a …' Nwamara started before snorting in frustration. 'What is the word?' she murmured, looking around the room and letting out a whistle noise. One of the other nnunus stepped forward, whistling back at her eagerly. Nwamara paused, pressing down the corners of her beak in thought. 'Yes, I believe that is it.' She turned on her heels. 'Fool, the Eze was a fool; he did not understand what he was doing let alone what he possessed.' Nwamara gestured to a group of bird-women who had excitedly huddled together, folding over one another until they formed a ball. 'But we did.'

'What are they doing?' Sinai murmured.

Naala's gaze was unblinking. She had no idea.

'Amadioha,' Nwamara said, pointing to a nnunu woman with sand-coloured feathers, who excitedly flew forward, 'the corrupted god of thunder and justice went to the Earth Mother's sanctum with his followers and tried to take Mother's Crystal.' A small group of bird-women began to follow the beige nnunu who had begun to head towards the huddle, their chests puffed out and their faces etched in seriousness.

'Oh, are they performing?!' Sinai exclaimed, slapping her knee.

Naala stared ahead; she had never seen anything *performed* before. That was for the city. She despised the growing excitement bubbling in her stomach.

'When Amadioha found the crystal, he did something ... unspeakable. Something so terrible that it shattered the crystal into nine different pieces scattered across the Kingdom,' Nwamara said, as the huddled group flew up into a frenzy before settling into nine individual balls, two of which clung close together. Naala edged closer. 'The break shattered a connection with the magical realm and Amadioha was no more. One of his followers, Eze Ochichiri, found one of the remaining pieces and he used it to rule the Kingdom of Nri.'

'Is this true?'

'Of course it is,' Nwamara said, nodding, as she gestured towards the glimmering crystal clump in the centre of the room. 'These are two parts of the Mother's broken crystal, Àlà and Ikuku.'

'Can you feel it?' Sinai whispered as Naala glared at the gleam within the bird-women's eyes.

Naala frowned. 'You want something from us?'

'Yes.' Nwamara smiled. 'I want you to finish what you started.'

'We didn't start anything,' Naala said quickly, fearing what would follow, her chest tightening as she pulled away from the lure of the crystals.

'You evoked the Chi Crystal. You awoke the Aido-Hwedo. You awoke the Descendants, us and many more. Now you must evoke Àlà and Ikuku, then you must find the others and evoke them too, for you are *Amuru ha abuo*, Children Born of Both, and such is your birthright.'

Naala felt a lump in her throat. Her mind swirled at all the things she *must* do. She must find her friends, she must subdue the beast, she must protect Siwunmi, and now she must *evoke* crystals.

Naala watched the vines feeding out of the crystals flash with fresh light. Her mind played over Sinai's face as she grasped at those very vines, her eyes glazed over in a trance as she unwittingly brought up the cursed river. She had no control.

'No,' she murmured.

'No? Naala, can't you *feel* it? It feels ... *right*,' Sinai started to protest.

Naala rubbed at her brow. 'Wasn't it you who said that this will bring a great evil into the world?'

'What? I didn't say a thing!'

'Yes, you did – at the riverbank. Isn't this exactly what your Mami Wata predicted? You said it on the bank. You spoke of evoking crystals and unleashing a great evil. You spoke of the end of the Kingdom.' Naala's heart quickened as she spoke. Ramblings that had been nonsensical to her mere days ago were now real enough to touch.

Eni. She could feel him again as though he were right beside her, his breath warming her neck. The end of the Kingdom. How could the Kingdom end without her seeing him again?

'You said you didn't believe me,' Sinai murmured distantly.

'That was before I was chased by a flying beast, taken to a city in the sky and kidnapped by bird-women.'

Sinai frowned and turned to Nwamara who stood watching the both of them amusedly.

'She's right.' Sinai conceded though her gaze lingered on the crystals as she spoke. 'I *was* told that evoking the crystals would unleash a great evil into the world but is that – is that true?'

'It is,' Nwamara stated blankly.

'It is?' Naala repeated, feeling a warmth spread across her cheeks. Pulling further away from the crystals.

'Yes, evoking the crystals will reopen the pit of Eriri Uhie. A mighty evil,' Nwamara said with a shudder.

Naala gaped back at her as mounting pressure pressed against her temples. 'Then why would you encourage us to do such a thing?!' she hissed, pulling away from the group and back to the glass wall. The topaz river slapped against its rigid surface. There was nowhere to run, nowhere to turn.

'Because it must be done, of course,' Nwamara insisted.

Naala almost choked as she swivelled around. 'You *want* us to unleash this evil?' Her heart pounded so furiously it hurt. The blasted walls seemed to be closing in on her. She drew upon her powers once again and a mist of dust expelled through the air, scratching at the back of Naala's throat. 'Blast it.'

'I want you to pass through the stages of Njem and it begins with chaos, but there is no need to fear, for on the other side lies balance.'

'Balance?' Sinai repeated wide-eyed.

'No,' Naala said firmly.

'The Mami Wata also said it was inevitable – that because we evoked the first crystal, we will evoke the second and the third. If we do this now, perhaps we can settle the Aido-Hwedo?' Sinai looked over to the nnunu woman to confirm. Nwamara nodded. '… and can't you *feel* it? It feels right—'

'Sinai! Please, *control* yourself. How many evil acts has the world seen because someone somewhere thought it felt *right*? I will not unleash evil into the world because I can.'

'*You* will not unleash it. It will be unleashed,' Nwamara said. 'You have no control over this; what will be will be. Whether you act or not the evil will be released, the only part you do control is how it will end. If you are deliberate, if you follow the divine path, then you will end with balance. You will end with the return of the Earth Mother.'

Nwamara's words sliced through Naala. Fatigue settled on her, pulling down her tense shoulders. She closed her eyes and breathed. Her heart raced. All she could do was breathe, and as she did the scent of vanilla and spiced pine drifted around her. Her eyes sprang open; instead of Eni's piercing gaze, she was met with Nwamara's large eyes.

'The Amaghi,' Naala said quietly. 'We go to the Amaghi.'

'The Amaghi?' Sinai blinked. 'Listen, I understand that they are your friends and of course you should find them but … Naala, this is *the Kingdom* we're talking about.'

'Exactly,' Naala replied, 'this is the Kingdom. We can't *evoke* things without understanding *all* of our options. We can't repeat the same mistake. The Amaghi have more than my friends; they have the knowledge we so clearly lack. They knew about the Eze's attacks, they knew about the Black and Gold realm, about the whereabouts of the Mother's Crystals. They know this,' she said determinedly. 'We will go back to the forest and we find them.'

'Amaghi …'

'Amaghi …'

'Amaghi …'

'Oh,' Sinai said quietly, before proceeding to open and close her mouth.

'Say it,' Naala said impatiently.

'Siwunmi. The beast … the Aido-Hwedo …' Sinai didn't finish her sentence. She didn't need to.

Naala's heart stopped as the thought of the village destroyed by the beast tore through her mind. Pricks clawed up her neck.

'You want to go to the Aido-Hwedo or the Amaghị?' Nwamara posed, tilting her head to the side. 'I must tell you, both are wrong. The Aido-Hwedo is tired and Amaghị are strange.'

'Tired?' Naala repeated.

'Yes, you saw the rampage; the Aido-Hwedo was distressed and now he must sleep.' Nwamara rattled as Naala looked up, her heart creeped up her chest.

'The Aido-Hwedo is asleep? For how long?'

'I'd wager he won't wake for at least five days.'

'Five days,' Naala repeated as a fog cleared through her mind. 'Five days gives us time to go to the Amaghị; it gives us time to learn how to defeat the beast before it can touch Siwunmi.'

'You don't need time, you need to ev—'

'Nwamara,' Naala interrupted, determined not to waste a second of the time they had been granted. 'We need to go to the forest; we need to find the Amaghị.'

'If you seek the Amaghị, you won't find them in the forest,' Nwamara announced.

'You know where they are?' Sinai gasped.

Naala held her breath.

'Yes,' Nwamara chirped, 'though I advise against visiting them. They use *strange* magic.' Her face scrunched as she shook her head vigorously.

'You know where they are?' Naala breathed shakily and Nwamara nodded.

'Of course,' she said, and Naala felt as though she would burst. Moon-cycles, she had been searching for … moon-cycles.

'Where?' Sinai asked.

Nwamara blinked back at them. 'Urukpuru.'

Naala's heart stopped. 'Here?' she replied in a strangled whisper. *Up, up, up.* 'That's why I couldn't feel it. It wasn't on the ground.' Her eyes pricked with tears that she blinked away as fast as they could come. *I'm so close.* 'You must take us there,' Naala insisted.

A twinkle emerged in Nwamara's eye. 'No.'

Naala's chest tingled as the weight of the bird-woman's word pressed against it. 'Please, please take us to them.' She clenched her hands into fists in a hope of stopping the shaking. *She was so close.*

Sinai added gently, 'We've travelled so far.'

'Evoke the crystal and then we show you the Amaghị.'

'No,' Naala spat, her blood running hot at the nerve the nnunu displayed, 'we can't *evoke* the crystal. We don't know what that could bring, and even if we did, we don't exactly know how.'

'Of course you do, you've done it,' Nwamara insisted.

'We just held it and it – it killed a man!'

Nwamara cocked her head. 'Okay,' she said slowly. 'You kill and then the crystal is evoked?'

'I don't know, yes … maybe?' Naala replied, defeated.

'Okay, so you kill and we evoke the crystal,' Nwamara exclaimed as the bird-women burst into a sudden excitement, singing joyfully.

'No,' Sinai said sharply.

'Yes! You can kill me, and then the crystal is evoked.'

'No! No one dies – we've had enough of that,' Naala exclaimed. The bird-woman inspected her closely.

'You are sad?' she asked.

Naala opened her mouth to protest but nothing came out.

'Okay – find the Amaghị, *then* activate the crystal?'

Naala hesitated. She could lie. How easy would it be to agree to what she would never do? What she could never do. She looked into the bird-woman's bright eyes and let go of a breath. She couldn't do that and now she would never see Eni again. 'I can't promise that,' she said thickly. 'I can only promise to do whatever is best for the Kingdom.'

Nwamara stared at her quizzingly before letting out a soft whistle.

The nnunu women began to chime a bright, clear song; it resonated through the cave, bouncing around the walls in high and low pitches. Naala looked around as the light at the centre of the room grew brighter. She took a cautious step backwards as something vibrated through the room, creating spirals of dust thrown up in the air. She sprang her hands over her head at the sound of a crashing crack. Instead of the cascade of wooden shards she had expected, a stream of blue water began to pour from the ceiling and circle around the iron structure that housed the crystals. The nnunus suddenly fell silent, their last shrill note echoing through the room.

'Time will,' an eerie voice suddenly sounded.

Naala looked around the room aghast; she didn't know where it had come from.

'Birth,' the voice breathed.

'Hope back to the earth.'

The voice hopped around the room in strange intervals and echoes.

The light stopped and the echo quietened into nothing. Naala looked back at Nwamara.

'It is a deal,' the bird-woman said with a twinkle in her eye. 'Let's go to the Amaghị!'

Naala looked back at her; she had been waiting for this for moon-cycles now, so why could she taste cold dread at the back of her throat?

CHAPTER 12
THE BOWED MAN

Urukpuru

Sinai let out a chilling scream as they approached the bunched, pale wooden ceiling at quickening speed. She squeezed her eyes shut, bracing for impact, but all she felt was a cold kiss of air.

Hesitantly, she opened her eyes to find that she was indeed in the air. Her heart skipped when she looked down to see the dome, split open like a peeled banana. She soon lost sight of it as the nnunu woman sped through the ice-speckled air, zooming towards the crater of land hovering above them. The Main Land, where the Amaghị were said to reside.

Sinai's stomach dipped, but not from the flight. She agreed with Naala's rationale; or at least she thought she did. It was a good rationale. They *should* gain more information before doing something that could impact the entire kingdom. Isn't that what the Mami Wata, herself, had said: *you must learn for yourself.* Perhaps what they had to learn lay somewhere in the mysterious Amaghị. A sour taste entered her mouth.

Perhaps it didn't.

The Mami Wata's foreboding words were frustratingly indecipherable and time hadn't helped. They remained jagged and opaque, so unlike the force that had drawn Sinai to those crystals. Nothing about the crystals was mystifying. They held none of her usual doubts. Had she made a mistake by resisting that pull?

Sinai felt heavy as they settled down onto the new land. Unlike the scarce and bare land below, this land was bountiful. Viridescent vegetation smothered the ground and sparkling crystals peppered across the horizon, growing alongside shrubs and small wiry trees. Like the lower island, translucent lights showered the land, coating it with streams of dazzling blues and pale whites. It didn't have the same wet powdery patches that had covered the lower island but it too was far from warm.

Sinai could feel the pinch of the cold on the tips of her nose and ears as she hugged the feather robe that the nnunu women had made, grateful that Naala had asked for it before they had ventured out.

'Is this the Amaghị?' Sinai murmured. There was not a single soul about.

'No,' Nwamara muttered, raising her wing and pointing behind her. 'That is,' she noted before inspecting an unsteady Naala.

Sinai squinted at the mammoth structure in the far distant. It was the crystal structure she had seen when they had first flown into Urukpuru. She could now see that it was positioned on a curved rock. *Strange.* She frowned; the rock looked almost like a man, a man bowing under the weight of the crystal settlement. A shiver escaped her.

'If it's all the way there … then did we *have* to stop here?'

'We didn't,' Naala protested, her body jolting slightly as she held her stomach and puffed her cheeks.

'Oh,' Sinai grimaced; she had almost forgotten how badly flight seemed to affect Naala.

'Yes, we did,' Nwamara replied, watching Naala carefully. 'Esinaala was going to be sick and I do not wish to become anyone's kpofuo dump.'

'I was fine,' Naala protested, taking a deep breath and straightening up. 'I *am* fine,' her voice growing steadier. 'Let's go,' she sniffed.

'We walk,' Nwamara said, 'it's better, it's safer.' She turned to the other nnunu. 'Nene, you should go back home. No need for any more people to be around this *place*,' she chirped. Nene nodded her head and took off into the sky without a seconds delay.

'Wait!' Naala cried before snapping to Nwamara. 'I told you I was fine! We don't have time for these *dramatics*.'

'You tell many lies,' Nwamara said with a smile. 'Follow me,' she added, as she drifted towards the Amaghị settlement.

*

'So, are you related to the nnunus in the city?' Sinai finally asked. After an hour of Nwamara's recounting of the encounter they had all *just* shared, Sinai was desperate to change the subject.

Nwamara levitated slightly into the air for a few brief seconds before settling back down; Sinai noticed that the bird-woman seemed to do this every time that she got excited.

'Yes and no,' she sang, lifting the corners of her beak into a smile.

Sinai waited for further explanation, but when it was clear that Nwamara wasn't going to continue without prodding, she added, 'How so?'

'I was a nnunu in the palace, yes, but I am not the same any more, no,' Nwamara said.

'*You* were in the palace?' Sinai marvelled. 'How?' she exclaimed. She couldn't imagine *Nwamara* begging alongside the demure, songful bird-women of the Palace of Nri.

'Yes,' Nwamara chirped, 'I was, but then you and your sickly sister—'

'I am not sickly,' Naala snapped, 'or anyone's sister,' she added quickly.

'More senseless lies,' Nwamara tutted, and Sinai snorted a laugh, clasping her hand over her mouth.

'Sorry,' she murmured but Naala didn't respond. She was too busy storming ahead. The closer they had got to the Amaghị settlement, the more agitated she had grown. Sinai had thought she would be elated but then she guessed she didn't really know the girl at all.

'You were saying that we …' Sinai said, hoping to get the conversation back on track.

'Until you, Sinaikuku and Esinaala, activated the Chi part of the Mother's Crystal.'

'That *changed* you?'

'It changed everything,' Nwamara said. 'I felt something in my body, a pulse that did not belong to my heart, and I knew that the time had come. Soon after my language came back to my tongue, then the air came back to my wings.'

'But you're different – to the others,' Sinai said thoughtfully; Nwamara was far more focused, more communicative than the other nnunus.

'Yes, we are all exceptionally different, and all practically the same, like sand,' Nwamara chimed.

'Eh, yes, but I meant, well, I was referring to the other bird-women. You speak … *more*?' Sinai said, not too sure how to put her thoughts into words.

'I speak more?'

'She's trying to say that you seem more intelligent,' Naala called from ahead.

'Intelligent?' Nwamara repeated as she shook her head. 'No, I am not. I assure you I am quite unintelligent. Though I do see how your kind might be confused, brains as small as you have. Poor things. No, no, what you mean is I have a stronger grasp on language … well, your language anyway, since I was never transformed into a hamerkop.'

'You mean,' Sinai said, wetting her lips, 'that the other nnunus were hamerkops?' The transformation from nnunu to hamerkop had always puzzled her, but the reverse seemed … well, *astounding*. 'So, the hamerkops brought the Amaghị here too?'

The nnunu didn't reply at first. The skin around her beak was pulled downward into what Sinai could only assume was a frown.

'Strange magic,' Nwamara said after a while, smacking her beak as though she had something vile stuck in her mouth.

'Why do you keep saying that?' Naala said exasperated as she turned around.

Rather than answer, Nwamara planted her feet on the ground as she fell into a fighting stance. Her large eyes narrowed into slits as a bizarre hissing sound came out of the corners of her beak.

'Nwamara?' Sinai exclaimed as a chill ran through her. It hadn't been caused by the cold or even the conversation they had just had. She turned to look at the empty land, her throat tightening with dread. She felt as she had when they were in the forest before the beast escaped. Something was following them.

'Can the Aido-Hwedo get up here?' Sinai asked hastily, trying desperately to still her quickening heart and concentrate. Nwamara didn't answer; instead she continued to hiss.

Naala's eyes darted to and fro, looking for the threat she couldn't see.

Sinai snapped her head back. Slapping her hand against her neck, she could have sworn someone was breathing against it. She shivered as fright coursed through her veins.

'There's someone here,' Sinai whispered hoarsely as they looked around the open land. The shrubs were low, the gleaming lights hid no shadows, the crystals looked clear, save from their dull blue glow. 'Something is *wrong*.' The sensation washed over her and before she could say another word, she felt the ground give way below her and they all fell into blackness.

CHAPTER 13
FOUND

Urukpuru

'Hello?' someone croaked as Sinai coughed ferociously. Dust scratched the back of her throat and stung her eyes. After what seemed like an eternity, her throat cleared and she could breathe again. The black, thick air was littered with coughs and spluttering. The sounds of feet crunching on rocks bounced through the darkness.

'Naala, Nwamara,' Sinai wheezed out in the darkness.

'Is everyone okay? What happened?' a voice that sounded like Naala replied.

'The ground fell,' Nwamara chirped.

'I can't see you,' Sinai replied as she felt around for anything she could grip. Her palms suddenly slapped against a cold rocky wall and she cautiously followed it.

'Sinai, is that you?' she heard Naala ask.

'Sinai?' a familiar voice replied. 'Sinai!?'

'Ina,' Sinai said softly, not believing what she was hearing.

'Who said that?' Naala exclaimed.

'Sinai?'

'Ina! Is that you?'

'Sinai,' Ina breathed out in relief.

Sinai blinked as shadowed figures formed out of the pitch black. *Was it brighter?* Sinai turned to the wall closest to her, a dim orange light grew beneath its surface.

She dropped her hand before turning to Naala, Nwamara *and Ina.*

'It's you, it's really you,' Ina gasped, dropping the rock cradled tightly in her hand and embracing Sinai.

Sinai beamed back at the friend she had left in the palace. The cloth that Ina wore was peppered with small tears and patches of dust-stains. Her long, dreaded hair, tied loosely at the nape of her neck, was now coated with soft fluffs of hair – a far cry from its usual flaxseed-gelled smoothness. Sinai had never seen Ina look so erratic, and yet the girl still somehow exuded a sense of regality. She let a small smile play on her lips, her dusk-black eyes gleaming in the dull light.

'Who is this?'

'A friend from the palace.' Sinai laughed – to imagine Ina was *here.*

Ina's smile faltered as her gaze flicked from Naala to Sinai. It crawled over their faces and left Ina deep in thought. If she was shocked, it could only be detected by a slightest purse of her thick lips. 'Is this … part of your *thing?*' she asked Sinai as she gestured to the both of them, 'Did you create an alter ego or something?'

'Alternate ego? Odd conclusion. Can you not see them? They are clearly twins,' Nwamara noted as Ina's eyes narrowed into a cutting glare.

'*You,*' Ina spat, edging closer to Nwamara with her finger pointed and violence spewing out of her dark eyes, 'you trapped me here!'

'I did not,' Nwamara said, cocking her head to the side as Sinai stepped in between them.

'Wait now,' Sinai pleaded with both hands raised.

'No. That nnunu and her little bird friends tried to kill me!' Ina proclaimed, leaving Sinai wordless. She turned back to Nwamara who seemed unruffled by Ina's accusation.

'That is false.'

'The nerve you have! They flew me here on their backs. I nearly died, my heart gave out at least twice and then, instead of going to Oyo, as *I told them,* they took me *here.* A floating city in the *sky.* Then they trap me in this … this – whatever this is and left me here for days!'

Sinai's initial shock settled and she began to remember who she was discoursing with.

'For days?' Sinai repeated as she glanced over Ina; she looked a little worse for wear, but not like a woman kept in a cave for *days*.

'Yes,' she said firmly before throwing her hands up. 'Well, curse me, Sinai, I don't exactly have a sundial lying around to keep track, but, yes, I'm sure it's been days – it's been a long time, look at me … I'm wilting away like some *commoner*.'

'Ahh bad nnunus,' Nwamara muttered. 'You know, I *did* tell them to report when they bring people to Urukpuru, but alas they can be forgetful those birds.'

'They *forgot?*' Ina gritted as she nudged Sinai out of the way. 'I am the first daughter of *Oyo*. No one forgets *me*.'

'Oh, yes, but they did. They forgot you here, it seems,' Nwamara replied, blind to Ina's growing rage. The light in the pit brightened slightly, and for the first time since she arrived in Urukpuru, Sinai felt warm.

'You left her here?' Naala asked as she looked around the pit.

'I did not say that.'

'Oh, you *lying* …' Ina fumed taking yet another step towards an unsuspecting Nwamara. 'It was definitely you,' she said, squinting at her, 'I remember you.'

'I don't remember you and I have an excellent memory. I see. Yes, yes, I see it. You have mistaken me for one of my sisters? Yes? Common mistake amongst your kind. You, humans, have such *dreadful* eyes.'

Ina eyed the nnunu woman before taking a deep breath. 'I have excellent eyes,' she bit finally before taking a step back, 'and a *fantastic* memory. What you nnunus have done to me is wrong, and trust there will be consequences,' she murmured before turning to Sinai. 'Did they snatch you too? Because I'll add that to my list,' she said, pointing at Nwamara whose eyes gleamed at the word list.

'Eh, no, well, yes, but not in a bad way,' Sinai rambled. 'Anyway, we can save those details for another time. Right now we need to—'

'Leave,' Naala mumbled, as she studied the cave.

'Yes… Nwamara, what is this place?'

Nwamara looked around unperturbed. 'Unclear, but it appears we have found ourselves in a set trap.'

'We need to get out of here,' Naala said before closing her eyes, her brow furrowed in thought and her jaw set. When she opened her eyes, they shone brilliant gold.

'What on earth,' Ina gasped, pulling away.

Naala ignored the cry as she darted her gold gaze around the cave. She was clenching her jaws so hard that she had begun to bare her teeth. The sound of rustling emitted through the pit but nothing moved. After a few tense minutes, she released the breath she held. Her gasps were ragged and short, her eyes blinking as they returned back to their dark-brown colouring.

'I can't shift this earth,' she said eventually, her voice smaller than Sinai had ever heard it, before she let out a frustrated sigh. When she looked up, her eyes were black with rage. 'Nwamara, is there a way you can fly us out? I don't see a ceiling.'

A small cloud of dust erupted into the air as Nwamara flew to the top of the pit.

'It is closed at the top,' the nnunu woman called down. Sinai could hear her scratching against the surface. 'Strange magic.'

'Oh, I can't breathe,' Ina announced, using her hand to fan herself. 'I am not supposed to be *here*.'

Before Sinai could reply, a deafening sound exploded through the pit. Dust and rubble sprinkled from the ceiling. Sinai's heart thudded in her ears. She didn't have the wits to scream.

'Oh my,' Nwamara whispered, flying back down to the girls as they watched a crack forming in the ceiling.

'Naala? Is that ...' Sinai started but her throat closed when she noted the girl's widened dark eyes.

'It's not me,' she whispered.

The crack widened and the bright dazzling light flooded the crevice. Sinai squeezed her eyes shut to the blinding pain, before squinting through her eyelashes. A thick rope had descended into the pit. Sinai's heart pounded as a figure clambered down. Nwamara hissed, spreading her large wings over them, as though it were a shield. The winds threw dust around the pit as Sinai felt power rippling through her.

The air shifted.

Naala gasped before breaking away from Nwamara's cover.

'Naala!' Sinai called. She reached out at her but missed her by a hair's breadth. She faltered at the look smoothed over Naala's face. It was not fearful nor was it angry; it was *elation*.

Naala stepped towards the figure; a boy with as many years as her, perhaps a little older. He stood tall with sharp features and eyes that cut into Naala. His lips parted though nothing escaped but the air he had been holding. A smile tugged on Naala's lips. A smile that gave her the most captivating glow. His eyes danced over her face but it never left it; he didn't even seem to blink. It was as though the act of looking away might cause her to disappear. By heavens, it was clear that he didn't want her to disappear. Finally, words began to form on his slackened mouth.

'What are you doing here?'

CHAPTER 14
THE HEAD OF THE SNAKE

Urukpuru

Earth, vanilla pods and pine. That was what hit her first. The scent that had stalked her beneath the mist of the Furuefu forest, dragging with it memories of the past. A hand holding her steady, a finger grazing her ear, a distant laugh deep enough to cause a flutter in her own stomach.

Eni stood before her. A ghost turned real. He gripped the erhọ rope, his face obscured with shadows, as he scanned the room until his gaze found hers.

Even under the cloak of darkness, Eni looked at her as though he *knew*. As though he could see everything. Every misdeed, every delight, every dark thought, every stumble. He had seen it all and nothing, it seemed, would make him turn away.

Naala's chest tightened as an image of the Eze returning to dust entered her mind. Would he still look at her the same when he discovered that she had since turned into a killer of men; a killer of kings, no less?

Warm breath kissed her forehead. When had she got so close to him? Her palms itched. All she wanted was to move closer still. She held herself steady.

'What are you doing here?' he said. Beneath the rich tones of his voice, Naala detected something rough, almost desperate.

It took her back to the night that Eni had found her eavesdropping on the group of survivors. He had growled that same statement at her, his hand clasping her scream. It had been the first time she had felt his skin against her lips, his body pressed into hers.

Naala's breath caught in her throat as Eni's long fingers guided her face upwards. 'It's really you,' he murmured, and her eyes pricked painfully.

'Who is this man?' asked the haughty girl that Sinai had called Ina; she seemed rattled.

Naala jumped back; her head felt so light she feared she might fall. Heat scorched her cheeks as she took in the eyes peeled on her. She crossed her hands over her stomach.

'Eni,' Naala said quickly, her heart pounded manically. 'A friend from the forest.' Why was she so out of breath?

'A friend from the forest?' Ina repeated dubiously, as she tossed her dreads back.

Naala gave her a stony look before turning her attention to the light streaming through the pit.

'The ceiling is *open*,' she muttered under her breath. 'Can we get out of here?'

As soon as she said it, she realised how much she needed to escape. The air was too stuffy here. She glanced over at Eni. It was near impossible to breathe.

Before anyone could reply, a gust of wind flung dust mercilessly around the pit. Naala spluttered as something lifted from the ground, only to land back again with a powerful thud. When the dust settled, Nwamara stood beside her with a smile across her beak.

'We *can* get out. I just did,' the nnunu chirped as she spread out her wings. 'Quick, get on my back.'

'What are *you* doing?' Ina said, smacking Sinai's hand away before she could approach. 'Didn't you hear a word of what I said? You jump on that nnunu's back and you will end up in another pit in some underground dungeon.'

'Oh? Which one?' Nwamara asked, brightly bouncing on her clawed feet.

'See!' Ina hissed as Sinai shifted uncomfortably.

'So do you plan on staying down here indefinitely?' Naala asked. Ina's mouth pressed tightly and her eyes narrowed. Naala couldn't help but feel a little satisfied that she had got under the girl's skin.

'Of course not,' Ina snapped back.

'Exactly, so surely you can see that it's best to go with Nwamara. I mean, what is the other option?' Sinai offered as Ina folded her arms.

'Am I the only one that sees this perfectly fine rope just dangling here?' Ina replied drily. 'Isn't that how *he* entered this cesspit?'

'Yes, I had planned on getting you out,' Eni said, 'though to …' He gestured to the nnunu woman.

'Nwamara,' Naala offered.

'… Nwamara's credit, flying is probably much faster.'

Naala tensed at the prospect of flying out of the pit. Given the choice between the two, she would have actually chosen to climb her way out. She certainly couldn't say that now, not with the early signs of a smirk playing on Ina's lips.

Ina inspected the rope carefully, taking hold of it with one hand. 'Well, I'd prefer to climb.'

Naala grinned as she pictured Ina clambering up the rope. She glanced at Ina's palms; just as she'd suspected, they looked as soft as butterfly wings, softer even than Sinai's.

'*You* are not climbing,' Naala snorted but before Ina could protest, Nwamara bolted into the air, and hovered.

'Oh,' she said, circling the rope, 'I see. Yes, yes, I see.'

'See what?' Naala asked nervously; something about the bird-woman's tone whispered of trouble.

'Hold on!' she called down below and seconds later Naala felt a strong arm wrap tightly around her waist before she was hoisted up through the pit. A scream cut through her throat as she was hauled up high into the air and her stomach dipped as she came crashing down. The air tore in and out of her chest as she lay on the grassy grounds with Ina and Eni at her side.

Naala's mind spun as she crawled back to the pit opening.

'Sinai?' she managed to croak. Nwamara had pulled them out of the pit using Eni's rope and the poor girl had been left behind.

'Kai!' Nwamara exclaimed, before dashing back into the pit, emerging soon after with Sinai planted on her back.

'Thanks,' Sinai murmured to Nwamara before throwing a glance at Naala.

'Don't say a word,' she warned but it did nothing to stop the grin spreading over her lips.

'It would be you,' she chuckled, shaking her head as Sinai's lips tightened.

The fun did not last. Her smile melted away as Eni approached them. His eyes widened as they flicked between the two girls. *Of course*, Naala thought bitterly. Their bizarre likeness must be gleaming in the unforgiving sun.

'Sinai, Sinai, Sinai,' she heard Ina muttering under her breath, 'wasn't it enough to be an efuola? Now *this* …'

Sinai flashed a burning look back at the girl and Ina's hands sprang up in protest. 'Sorry, it's just so … it's just so …' Ina trailed before deciding to keep her thoughts to herself.

Naala didn't care to hear more of Ina's opinion. Eni's was the only one that mattered. What was he thinking? Did she even want to know? Naala hadn't considered this when she had dreamt of their reunion. Why hadn't she considered *this*? She had imagined his face, what he might say, even his voice, but not what he might think about the *situation*.

Naala held her breath as Eni shifted towards her.

'Naala,' he said carefully, before flicking back to Sinai, 'wha—'

'Sinai,' Naala said briskly. 'I met her in the palace,' she added definitively. *Not now*, she pleaded. They had just met again. Now was not the time to address the questions that she herself had buried within her mind. Not when Eni was Eni … she knew he would burrow into her most shielded thoughts. She had no doubt that he would tear through them one by one. Naala wasn't ready for that. Not now.

Eni regarded her carefully before closing his mouth. She noted the crease that had formed on his brow. She knew he would let the discussion go for now, but not for long.

'This is crazy,' Ina said, looking around the land. Naala wasn't sure what she was referring to, but she had to agree: all of it seemed crazy to her. 'How do we leave?'

'We don't,' Naala said as Sinai bit down on her lip. Naala turned to Eni. 'At least not yet.'

'Oh, we certainly do,' Ina insisted, jutting out her chin. 'I refuse to stay in this sky contraption a second longer.' She stormed off for a couple of strides before turning back to Sinai, her eyes widened expectantly.

'Ina, it's more complicated than you can imagine. There is something happening with the Kingdom.'

'I don't need to imagine anything. I've *seen* it. Why do you think I needed to escape for Oyo? Sinai, we are floating in the *sky* with no food, no shelter, deranged nnunus who can grab us at any second – and now this cursed *girl* is talking about *staying*?'

'I'm not talking about staying for a festival,' Naala scoffed before turning to Eni. 'We seek counsel from the Amaghị. Sinai and I, we've discovered something in this sky city, something that could destroy or help the Kingdom. We need to speak to someone, Bayo maybe?' Bayo, the insufferable man who had first told her about the Black and Gold realm. He had called himself a Dibias, a man who could see and feel magic. He was a pain, there was no doubt about that, but he knew much about the world of magic; he could help, she was sure of it.

'There's also a beast in the forest, a terrible beast,' Sinai added, and Naala's heart squeezed at the thought of Siwunmi. *They're safe*, she told herself as she held fast to Nwamara's comment. The beast would be dormant for days to come. *Hopefully.*

Ina's eyes bulged at Sinai's words. She tucked her hands under her armpits and shuddered. A stark contrast to Eni who seemed unmoved, as though Sinai had been merely recounting the sun's movements.

For the first time since they'd met, Naala really appraised him. He stood before her in deep red gear. His neck was coated with ruby red fur; his chest was covered with a wide strip of crimson leather sewn onto his fur necktie. His forearms were bound with red leather bands, as were his calves and waist; the leather material on his chest also covered below his waist up until his knees. Was he wearing a uniform?

'You already know this?' Naala asked quietly, watching as Eni nodded his head slowly.

'Some of it, yes. That's why I'm here, to bring you to the Isi.'

'The who?' Sinai blurted.

'The Isi Agwọ Ahụ, the Head of the Snake; it's what the Amaghị call their leader,' Eni explained.

Their leader? Something shifted within Naala. *He was tasked to bring us to the*

Amaghị's leader. The thought swirled in her head and weighed her down. He was tasked to do this *alone?*

'Madi and Kora?' Naala said; her voice came out lower and more sullen than she had intended.

Eni frowned at that, his eyes lingering on her lips.

'They are in the Amaghị's Idu; they're waiting for your arrival,' Eni said distantly, and Naala's lips tightened.

'Naala …' Eni tested lightly.

'What?' she snapped and immediately regretted it. She could feel the group shifting uncomfortably. Nwamara was the only one that seemed not to pay her any mind. The bird-woman had her back turned to them all as she looked ahead, stoically, at the crystal structure at the heart of the land.

'You've got that look on your face,' Eni said; his dark eyes were lit with mirth. Heat jolted up and down her body as her eyes narrowed in on his smirk. 'I see it right there. All the assumptions that your brilliant mind has formed, the assumptions that you are acting on before they've even become a reality … what is it this time?'

'You've joined them, the Amaghị,' she said, and Eni let out a laugh that made her question everything.

'Don't let the garments fool you; you'll be in these in no time.' He chuckled as she bit her inner lip.

'Fine,' she mumbled wearily, 'but …'

'But?' Eni said, sweeping close to her. Too close. The hairs on her arms lifted under the threat of his touch.

'You knew we were here,' Naala said. She had wanted to sound angry and biting. She had wanted to shield her hurt, but it came out all the same. Eni's expression softened.

Naala felt like a stone, moving from hollow to hollow in a game of Mancala. She had once imagined Eni there alongside her, but he now seemed to be more of a spectator than a pawn.

Moon-cycles. She had spent moon-cycles fretting and failing to find them, and all the while he had known. He had *waited?*

Her words hung between them before Eni pressed forward. His large hands clutching her arms, his head lowered so that their foreheads almost touched.

'I didn't want to leave,' Eni said, his voice low and rough. His black eyes burned.

'I know,' she replied. She didn't.

'I fought,' he continued. 'I fought *hard*. I didn't stop fighting, even when they took us here. I would have never stopped looking for you … but they said, they said that our best chance would be for you to come *here*. I didn't believe them at first, but then I saw …' His voice trailed. 'I didn't want to leave.' His face was so close to hers, his breath entangled with her own.

'Strange magic,' Nwamara suddenly chirped and Naala remembered where she was. She drew back from Eni and swallowed down her thundering heart.

Nwamara remained fixed on the distant crystal settlement. Her feathers were lifted and ruffled. 'This is where I must leave you.'

'Leave us? Nwamara, we still have quite a while to go until we reach the Amaghị. What about the crystals? The kingdom?' Sinai protested.

'Here,' Nwamara replied, pointing to an invisible line on the ground. 'Strange magic lies beyond this point and so this is where I must leave—' she cocked her head towards Naala '—unless you no longer wish to see the Amaghị? Unless you are ready to evoke the crystals?'

Naala shook her head curtly.

'Very well,' the bird-woman sighed. 'The boy can show you the way from here. Try to stay alive. Your weak bodies can only take so much,' she said, lifting into the air. 'You know how to find me.'

'Wait!' Sinai called after the nnunu woman who had already soared too high to hear her. 'We have no idea how to reach you,' she muttered, shaking her head.

'Do you really know the way back to the Amaghị?' Naala asked Eni who nodded back his response.

'Yes. We're here,' Eni responded.

'We are?' Naala said, looking ahead. The settlement still looked at least another hour or two away from them.

A firm hand circled her waist and pulled her to the side. Naala's heart sped as she looked up at Eni who offered a quick smile before reaching down at a crystal cluster behind her. At first glance it was unassuming, but as she peered closer she noticed a red glint to it. Thin, ruby vines crawled up the surface of the cluster.

Eni tore off a large flat leaf from a nearby plant and pressed it against the crystal, muttering something inaudible under his breath. Naala's forehead furrowed as the leaf crumbled into ash before her eyes. Something flickered in the light rays that coated the land. Naala blinked and the scene before her melted into a large crystal door.

'What?' Naala bellowed as she took a step backwards. Her head snapped from left to right. They were no longer on the pastured lands. Rather, they were now positioned on top of a large rock structure, facing the entrance of the Amaghi's settlement. The crystal door before them was smooth, almost glass-like. Similar to the crystal cluster that Eni had tampered with, its surface was lined with red, dull vines. It made the frost-coated doors look as though they were dusted pink.

'What is this witchcraft?' Ina cried out loud.

'It's the Amaghi's Idu—' he shrugged before grinning at their expressions '—you really thought it stopped at hamerkops and a city in the sky?' He looked ahead at the large door, and added, almost darkly, 'It's not the most secret society in the world for nothing.'

'Strange magic,' Naala murmured as she recalled Nwamara's apprehension.

The door cracked open, revealing a hallway paved with rose gold. The walls were not smooth like the doors, but crusted, with bits of rose metal poking out sporadically. The hallway sparkled before them, reflecting thin streams of gleaming white light. No one said a word.

'Are you sure about this?' Ina murmured to Sinai. Naala could feel Sinai's eyes bore into the back of her head. *Are you?* The thought sprang into her head; it felt foreign and out of place. A chill ran up her back. Eni stepped into the hall before turning back to her, beckoning her to join him.

'Yes,' she said, entering into the hallway, with Sinai and Ina following shortly after.

As she entered, Naala glimpsed up at the high ceilings. She had never seen anything like it. It wasn't anything like the thatched roofs in her village or the flat sand ceilings in the palace. These ceilings were made of thick shards of crystals, contorted over one another like piles of logs. She could still see bright-blue sky through the occasional gap in the structure. The Amaghị's Idu was grand and decadent in a way that differed from the elegant palace; its beauty was unrefined, almost forceful. It made her feel small.

As though he could read her thoughts, Eni took her hand and squeezed it. It did not alleviate her fears, but it certainly improved them.

'I know it seems daunting,' he said gently. 'They have set up quite a life for themselves here in Urukpuru. It is not perfect, but at its heart it is a good community with a shared goal, to set people free.'

'Uh-uh,' Ina muttered behind her. Naala couldn't help but concur.

'Let me take you to the Isi,' Eni said, taking a sharp breath.

'Now?' Naala halted. Eni appraised her with a smile tugging at the corner of his lips.

She wasn't ready to meet another king. She wanted to speak to someone familiar, someone closer to her level; dare she say it, but she wanted to speak to Bayo.

'Aren't all visitors to a village greeted by the chief?' he laughed.

'Surely there is someone else that can welcome us; Bayo, perhaps?'

Eni chuckled. 'I never thought I'd see the day when you would actually *ask* to be greeted by Bayo.'

'This is important,' she insisted, and he sobered for a moment.

'I know,' he said. 'I've learnt things from the Amaghị, about the crystals and the beast you speak of. I don't know much, but I know enough to not take anything you say on the matter lightly. Not during these times. That is the reason why you must see the Isi. Though skilled, Bayo is not the most learned person in the art of magic and strategy; *she* is.'

'She?' Sinai sputtered. 'The leader is a woman?'

Naala was dumbstruck as Eni nodded back with a smile.

The Amaghị had always felt like a silent force, mysterious, quick and stronger than one initially imagined. The idea that this society, the most secret one in the Kingdom, the society that had defied the Eze's tyranny over the villages, was run by a *woman* was unimaginable. Naala's blood pumped with fresh adrenaline.

Eni gestured towards a door on his right before stopping in front of it.

'We're here,' he warned before knocking. After a few seconds, the door creaked open. Naala's palms became warm as she stepped cautiously into the large room.

The blushed, crusted walls were lined with bright-green plant vines. A series of big akwete cushions lay on the rose gold floor. There was a large window on the left-hand side of the room, coated with thin, clear glass.

At the far end of the room, there was a grand chair made from dark mahogany wood and cushioned with a plump, soft mound coated with white leopard fur. Naala raised her eyes and glanced at the woman who sat on the magnificent seat, the only thing in the room, perhaps in the whole settlement, that seemed to be made from earth materials. Naala didn't know how much she missed the feeling of *real* wood but she didn't dwell on that too long; it was the woman who had really caught her attention.

She sat clothed in layers of white, thin cloth. Her face was so striking that Naala felt a sharp thud in her chest as she witnessed her. The woman's eyes were bright violet coated with bleached white eyelashes, her nose was flat and curved, her cheeks raised in the air defiantly. Her full, wide lips, rich with a peach colouring, were pressed in the slightest of smiles. Her thick afro hair was a small white halo resting on her head, with golden thorns spiralling around it. Her skin was devoid of any colour; it stood as pale as the cold powder that formed on the lower island of Urukpuru. Naala recalled a boy from her village that had come out of his mother like this: his hair, his eyes, his skin devoid of the rich carob skin that his older brothers and sisters had.

'He is an albino,' her grandmother had explained to an inquisitive Naala. She recalled how the village would have to hide the boy whenever the army came through on their patrol. Though being an albino was not officially against the law, it wasn't unheard of for people to try to steal the colourless children to sell to Amoosus who would use them in forbidden rituals.

It was hard to place the woman's age; her face didn't seem to have more than 40 years, but the way she carried herself, and the bright white of her hair, spoke to many decades living on the planet. Her eyes scanned the room and Naala could sense Ina and Sinai gasping at the sight of her before they bowed to the ground.

Naala looked to Eni who nodded at the woman before bowing himself. Naala found herself bowing her head slightly too.

The woman rose from her seat and walked towards them in a tranquil manner. She stopped in front of Naala and Sinai, inspecting them with a gleam in her violet eyes.

'So the time has come for the Amaghị to welcome the daughters of Nri into our midst,' the woman said, her voice cool and chilling. 'Get up my children, Ndewo.' She brought her crossed, gloved arms to her chest and extended her palms towards them one by one.

'Ndewo,' Naala murmured as she returned the gesture.

'Ndewo,' Sinai breathed.

'Ndewo,' Ina murmured. She added in a whisper, '… Lolo Obioma.'

Naala flashed back to the regal woman. *Lolo Obioma?* she thought, startled as her heart quickened … *the Eze's lost wife?*

CHAPTER 15
DUSK

Urukpuru

Sinai felt stuck between reality and the realm of her visions. Lolo Obioma swept forward, bringing with her the sharp cooling scents of grapefruit, sandalwood and crusted sugar cane.

Sinai recalled the gentle woman who had offered the efuola one of her first smiles in the palace. She also recalled a shadowed-eyed woman from her visions who had so swiftly declared a man for dead; which version was *true*?

Perhaps they all were. Different versions of the same woman walking down a path that led her here; a leader, the Isi of the Amaghị. A queen in the sky. Sinai thought back to the Eze and the sick feeling that had engulfed her when he had described the fate of the fallen Lolo. He had said she had been mauled by his mammoth lion, Asilia. Sinai gazed at the Lolo's unmarked skin and her bright, sharp eyes. She couldn't speak to whether the Lolo had truly been mauled, but there was a stillness about her, as though she had been forged from marble, frozen in the crisp cold air of Urukpuru.

'Ina, Daughter of Oyo,' she said, her voice as cool and crisp as the room they resided in. Ina lifted her head. 'I'd recognise those locs anywhere, our own resident dada,' she hummed, her speech slow and deliberate. 'Do you remember when I used to help you oil them? You used to prattle off the wildest of things. Tell me child, are you still love-struck over that Ife boy?' The Isi gave a honeyed laugh.

'No.' Ina scowled before she recognised the Lolo's jest. 'I've grown out of that,' she managed as the Isi's violet eyes twinkled.

'I'd imagined that would be the case,' she said. 'You always had a fire within you, whereas the boy always seemed rather—' she paused, holding her gloved hand to her pale-orange lips '—weak.'

She turned her head and looked Sinai squarely in the eyes. Her expression brightened into the one Sinai remembered from her childhood. She had always looked at her as though Sinai were *special*.

'Sinai, what a child you were. I couldn't imagine that anyone could get more beautiful, and yet, look, here you are.' Lolo Obioma's gaze found Naala. 'How remarkable to see you two here like this.'

'We thought you had died,' Ina whispered.

'Yes,' she murmured, 'a lot of people do think that, and why not? I was *meant* to have died. And all the Kingdom's twins were meant to be killed at birth,' she said, as her eyes swept over the girls. 'I thank the lost gods that my late husband's intentions were not carried out, otherwise none of us would be here right now.' Her voice brimmed with emotions and yet somehow seemed controlled. Her face remained ruthlessly expressionless – only the delicate turn of her lip corners and the flash across her violet eyes gave anything away. Sinai thought back to the chief village in her vision; had this woman really ordered the death of that innocent man?

'Late?' Ina noted and Sinai's heart halted; she shot a sideways glance at Naala. 'You know about the Eze's *passing*?' Ina said the last word in a cautious whisper, as though simply mentioning the Eze's death could taint her somehow. What would she say if she knew she was rubbing shoulders with his killers?

Sinai shifted uncomfortably. When she looked up, she found that she was under Lolo Obioma's gaze. Before the woman could say a word, a man emerged from the shadows behind her.

His dark face was framed by contrasting white tufts of sprouting hair. Sinai's throat closed at the sight of him. Something about the man's mannerisms, his gait, even his presence, reminded her of the faceless man. Whilst he did indeed have a face, there was something unassuming about him, something shadowed.

'Chukwudi, how nice for you to join us,' she said, before turning to the group. 'This man is my most trusted advisor, a genius if I ever knew one.'

'You're far too kind, Isi,' he replied; the crimson crystal around his neck blinked as he scanned the room. His white brow was furrowed, fixing his face into a sharp and studying look. 'I did hear word that we had received guests,' he said tightly to Eni. 'I thought I made it clear how we operate things here. No one must enter these gates without the Aturu's approval.'

'And what of my approval?' The Isi laughed as Chukwudi gazed back at her with bulged eyes.

'Your approval?'

'Yes, I saw the detection and I sent our guest out to fetch our latest visitors. I trust that is okay with you?'

'Of course,' he sputtered, 'I only meant – I did not mean—' he paused and took a sharp breath '—I only feared for you, Isi; you above all must be *protected*.'

'As kind as the sentiment is, Chukwudi, I must ask you to put aside your fears and, if possible, to stop throwing daggers at young Eni. As I've been told, he has a history with our guests, and they were in need of help,' the Isi said, fluttering a gloved hand in the air, 'so we helped.'

'How did you know?' Naala asked, echoing the question forming in Sinai's mind. The Isi regarded her, her violet eyes glittering.

'I looked,' the Isi said, her body as still as granite. 'Very little is truly hidden in this world. We all leave little clues here and there; if you observe long enough something is bound to reveal itself.'

Naala frowned at the obscure answer.

Sinai was once again reminded that Naala wasn't used to the ways of the palace. Obscure speeches came as easily as breathing in that place.

'So, you spied on us?' Naala replied.

Nope, not used to it at all, Sinai sighed inwardly, thinking of how badly they needed the help.

The Isi gave her a gentle smile. 'Call it what you may but we are always looking to help.'

'We do need your help,' Sinai jumped in before Naala could give another brazen response.

'… Yes, we do,' Naala said. 'We have something important to share.'

'In that case, Chukwudi, gather the settlement to the Rie quarters. Ensure a meal is prepared.'

'A meal?' Naala frowned. 'There's no ti—'

'Thank you, Isi, but perhaps the dinner could wait? Our news is really quite urgent and a meal now is … well, *unnecessary*.'

'Little one, nothing in this life is ever necessary but our lives are immeasurably enriched by our commitment to what we *must* do.'

'Yes, and what we have to discuss, our news, is very important and *urgent*,' Sinai stressed.

'That much is written all over your face, and then, of course, there's the signs. The indicators that point to the danger coming for the Kingdom.' The Isi smiled curtly at their widened eyes. 'I know all too well about the urgency and importance of what you have to say.'

'Then you understand why we can't wait to discuss next steps. As we speak, the Aido—' Naala started but the Isi held her hand up. With great restraint Naala quietened down.

'As grave as it is, we must discuss it with the entire settlement.'

'But—'

'We may have been dubbed a "secret society", but we hold no secrets amongst our own. What you *must* discuss in front of me, you must discuss in front of us all.'

'I don't think …'

'You don't need to think,' Chukwudi interjected sharply. 'You must simply know that this is our way. A way that will not change based on your thoughts.'

There was little else left to do. Sinai glanced out at the darkening sky. Another day was coming to an end. Her chest tightened. Another step closer to the Aido-Hwedo's reawakening.

CHAPTER 16
WHISPERING WALLS

Urukpuru

'Did you hear that?' Sinai said, turning to the crystal-clustered walls, but no one paid her any mind. They were all too preoccupied with the Rie hall itself, a long, narrow room that curved like a fat snake. In its centre lay a rose-coloured thick rug, with Nsibidi symbols sewn into it with glistening gold thread. At either side of the rug sat rows of large plump cushions.

Sinai turned back to the walls; her heart raced as she drew a finger towards the rose gold clumps. It seemed to be almost *breathing*. Ice slipped down the nape of her neck. There! Again, she was sure she had heard a whisper. Had she not? Sinai sucked in a breath before pressing her finger against the rough surface, half expecting it to move under her touch. Instead the red vines beneath it grew. She dropped her hand and stepped back.

'The Isi always sits here,' Eni said, pulling Sinai out of her thoughts, as he gestured to the large cushion that sat at the head of the table. He paused, and grimaced at a thought. 'She ... indicated she wanted both of you to sit by her.'

Sinai's stomach dropped. Seeking her counsel was one thing, but the thought of sitting by *the Isi* for an entire meal made her throat tight.

'Oh,' Naala said, inspecting Eni, her eyes narrowing at something hidden in his expression, 'what else?'

He grinned ruthlessly. 'Those seats *unofficially* belong to Chukwudi and Bayo; neither of them will be too glad about the rearrangement.' He bared his teeth apologetically as Naala's face sagged.

'Oh. That's ... great. Two major egos to straddle.'

'They're not so bad,' Eni said as Naala arched her brows. 'Okay, they are but they're not the worst.'

Naala snorted. 'Who is then?' she said before her eyes widened. 'Don't say me.'

'You, definitely you.' He chuckled before relaxing into a grin. '... No, I suppose as bad as you are, you don't hold the main spot either. I can think of someone else, someone far bigger with a tiny, tiny brain. You must know who.'

'Azu,' they said together before falling into an easy laugh.

Sinai didn't understand the joke but she did understand the sentiment behind the look Eni poured over Naala, his face softened and warm. *He loves her,* she thought. Why else would he look at her so?

The door flew open and a squeal tore into the air followed by the sound of pounding feet as someone dashed towards them. It was a girl, small in stature, with hair cut close to her scalp and powdered red. On her forehead, there were a series of raised circle tribal marks; her soft face was stretched in a wide smile.

'Naala! You're back! You're *really* back!' the girl screamed as she jumped on Naala.

Naala was taken aback at first but she soon returned the embrace, grinning up at Eni as she did so. The girl had been followed by a large boy. He stood tall, his muscles almost bursting out of the same attire that Eni wore, his hair hung around his ears in small braids curled at the ends in white cowrie shells. He watched Naala for a moment, his honeyed eyes melting at the sight of her. Once the girl had stepped away from Naala, he, too, took her into a deep embrace, his eyes closed as he pressed his face into her hair.

'Don't do that again,' he murmured richly.

Naala pulled away from him, her face brighter than Sinai had ever seen it.

Sinai shifted on her feet. She should say something, shouldn't she? It would be strange not to; she had been standing there for so long, staring at a reunion she had no part in. But what could she possibly *say*?

At least she wasn't alone, she thought, turning to Ina. Though Ina didn't seem the least bit put out by the display; at most, she seemed bored.

'What … who … what is this?' a voice boomed in the room. At first, she thought someone had noticed the whispering walls but the large boy's wide eyes were fixed on her. Suddenly, being ignored wasn't so bad. She watched his gaze darting from Naala to Sinai and his mouth had fallen open so wide it was almost comical. He seemed genuinely terrified … of *her*? What a thought!

'Another Naala,' the short girl gasped, darting away from the large boy's attempts to pull her back.

'She's …' Naala began before trailing off.

Sinai made to complete her sentence but all the options felt wrong. My sister? Twin? Fellow destroyer (or saviour, depending on who you asked) of our doomed kingdom?

'Sinai,' Eni offered with a smile. The room collectively exhaled. Sinai had a feeling she had Eni to thank for that. His calm, casual manner had clearly translated to the others. 'Naala met her in the castle. They are twins,' he said, before he noticed something flash across Naala's face, '… we think.'

'Twins?' the large boy repeated, flinching back from the word. '*Twins?*' He continued to hold Naala back from the threat of Sinai. 'Twins are—' he looked back at Naala, pained '—*cursed.*'

'See, I'm not the only one who thought of it,' Ina muttered.

'According to who?' the small girl scoffed. 'The Eze?' she rolled her eyes before walking towards Sinai. 'Just *look* at that. It is amazing – beautiful, *amazingly beautiful!*'

'Uh-huh,' Naala muttered.

The girl sighed. 'Still opposed to compliments, I see?'

'Don't start,' Naala groaned, shaking her head as the girl beamed.

'I think I will,' she hummed as she bounded over to Sinai; her eyes brightened playfully as they studied her. 'Ndewo,' she said eventually. 'I'm Kora and this big lug is Madi; it is so good to meet you,' she said, as she performed the greeting to Sinai and Ina. As they exchanged their welcomes, Kora began to circle Ina. 'Your hair is magnificent,' she gasped.

'Thank you,' she said, swallowing down a smile. 'Well, yes, I am in fact a dada.'

'A what?' Madi asked blankly.

'A dada,' Ina repeated. 'I'm a daughter of Oyo,' she continued but they simply stared back at her. 'My people have *special* children, dadas, whose hair is naturally loced. I'm a – oh, never mind.' She waved away the air as Madi offered her a wide, forced smile. The frown returned to her plump lips, as though it had never left.

'Sit down, sit down,' a tall man said as he entered the room, with a short smiling woman by his side. Madi's expression darkened and Kora rolled her eyes.

'Sorry,' she whispered to Naala.

'For what?'

'For doubting you when you said Bayo was a huge pain in the …' Kora winked before taking her place on the cushions just as the thin man approached.

'Oh look, the girl with no ears,' he called out.

'What?' Naala said, tilting her head as her lips pulled downwards.

'The instructions were simple. The operation was fool-proof, and yet you still managed to mess it up. So I must assume that you have lost the functionality of your ears.'

'Right,' Naala replied stiffly.

'Ndewo, Bayo,' Eni said tightly. 'You're quite mistaken. She didn't mess anything up; she—' Eni said.

'Failed,' Bayo interrupted, before throwing a glance at Sinai; something glittered behind his beady eyes. 'Still,' he drawled, 'it did lead to an interesting turn of events.' He nodded at them before taking a seat next to Madi, who did little to hide his disappointment. 'I said sit. She'll be entering soon.'

Sinai settled down on the seat close to the cushion at the head table, opposite Naala and beside Ina. More people had started pouring into the room. Their eyes peeled on her as they whispered eagerly to one another.

Sinai looked away from their glares, sneaking glances whenever her curiosity got the best of her. They all wore the same outfits. The men wore Eni's and Madi's red garments, whilst the women were draped in layers of cloth similar to Lolo Obioma, only in crimson as opposed to white.

A hollow sound rang through the room and the room settled into a hush. It came from two small nnunu women seated, cross-legged, by the doors. They seemed to her more akin to the nnunus in the palace than the ones she had encountered in Urukpuru. Their heads were bowed and their expression faded. Her eyes grew hot at the sight of them. Sinai blinked fast and looked down at her hands.

The nnunu continued to pound on a bulbous udu. Rounded, deep sounds with high and low frequencies echoed through the room, entwining with the flat ogene in the other nnunus arms.

Baom.

Baom.

Baom.

Sinai glanced to her side as the Amaghị began to pound their fists against their legs, adding a slapping sound to the music. The nnunus increased the frequency of their pounding and the high-spirited song began to emerge as it reached its fever pitch.

Everything stilled.

The door swung open to reveal the Isi. She walked into the room slowly, with Chukwudi following behind.

'Ndewo, my dear people,' the Isi said gently, as she took her seat, 'today, we share our home and meal with guests.' A low whisper erupted through the room and the Isi drew a kola nut out of the fold of her garment. She held it high before breaking it. 'Welcome them as I have welcomed you,' she said, placing the broken kola on the rug in front of her. 'When the kola nut reaches home, it will tell where it came from. Whatever good they are looking for, they will see it.'

The Isi looked ahead with a slight smile but she didn't say anything after that. A slow murmur washed over the room. The welcome had ended, it seemed. Sinai looked at the broken, lone kola, discarded on the luxurious rug. Her stomach hardened at the sight of it.

The hall was alive with conversations sprouting to and fro, though their section remained uncomfortably quiet.

'Isi?' Naala piped up when the food had been served. 'If your customs permit, we need to discuss the matter of the Kingdom. I don't know how much you know but the Aido-Hwedo is—'

'The Aido-Hwedo? Is that what you wish to discuss?' the Isi asked.

Naala shot a quick glance around the room. Her forehead rumpled before she let out a sigh.

'It *is* urgent.'

The Isi broke into the faintest of smiles. 'Please, speak your mind.'

'We were attacked by the beast in the forest. Sinai and I were lucky to get out, even with our ...' she searched for the word '... *abilities*. There are villages in the forest, families, children. I fear it could spread out of the forest even; I fear it could destroy the Kingdom. We need to stop it at once, and there is a way to the beast's demise. It involves us *evoking* the Earth Mother's Crystals.'

'Evoking?' Madi frowned. 'Evoking what crystals?'

'Have you not been reading the parchments that I've been giving you?' Bayo hissed as Madi released a sigh. 'Do you enjoy being blissfully unaware about *everything*?'

Madi's fist balled up and the bird-woman clearing the table jolted backwards. Her eyes darting around him as one would do as they approached a snake. Strange. The boy was large, yes, but as far as she could tell, he was gentle. Sinai couldn't imagine him harming a plant, let alone a person.

'I took the parchments,' Kora announced before Madi could reply.

'No, she did not,' Madi protested. 'Bayo, why must you insist on playing this game? You know that I'm not the most skilled reader, you know Kora has been helping me, and you know that means there's only so far I can go. I need—'

'Kai, come and see this agbaya,' Bayo tutted. 'As big as you are, you still crave to be hand-held through life, a whole Descendant?'

Madi's eyes widened at the statement before lowering them down to his efere.

'A Descendant?' Naala repeated slowly.

The Isi held her hand up and they all went silent. 'Naala, you mentioned the Mother's Crystals ... do you know their whereabouts?'

Naala pulled her gaze from Madi before regarding the Isi carefully. 'We do; we know of two: the Àlà and Ikuku.' Whispers tore through the room.

'Two,' the Isi repeated, as Chukwudi grew unsettled.

'Àlà, Ikuku, but what of Chi?' he blurted.

Sinai's eyes bulged at the comment. Did they all know of the nine stones? It

113

would seem so. All but Madi seemed unmoved.

'I lost the crystal,' Naala admitted and Sinai snapped her head up at her.

A lie.

As soon as Sinai saw Olu's forest-green eyes, she had *known*. It came to her in a vision. The crystal, buried in the ruckus they had left in the Eze's quarters, lodged deep in a broken shard of the Eze's stone table, cast beside his akwa nest. Sinai had stood, arms stretched between Naala's vengeance and Olu, pleading for his life.

Naala had spared him and Sinai had repaid the girl by whispering the whereabouts of the crystal to the man who had butchered Naala's grandmother.

Sinai's cheeks burned hot. Olu was the only person she could have entrusted it to before they fled. There was no time to wait, no chance of re-entering the Eze's guarded quarters, no moment to *think*. What else could she have done? She glanced over at Naala and a wave of nausea settled in her stomach. More, she could have done more.

'We ...' Sinai murmured weakly, 'we lost it.'

'Lost it?' Chukwudi rasped, his mouth opening and closing. 'The Chi ... It was your *sole* task.' Spittle flung to his white beard as he shook with growing rage.

'They surpassed the task, did they not?' the Isi said calmly. 'They vanquished the Eze, a feat that thousands, including myself, had tried and failed to do. A task we were hoping to do with that crystal.'

'You did *what?*' Ina exclaimed, her impenetrable expression falling into shock.

Sinai might've smiled at the girl's outburst had the room not fallen silent. An army of eyes crawled up her face. She wanted nothing more than to disappear.

'You did it? You really did it?' Kora whispered, her eyes filling with tears. 'You're, you're ...'

'Amazing,' Eni said, his eyes fixed on Naala. 'You, both, are amazing,' he added, flicking his gaze between the two of them.

'I suspected,' Ina blinked brightly, 'but, well, I suspect a lot of things – most true, granted, but this, this I ...'

Sinai shifted in her seat as whispers gathered. All around her, she was met with looks of admirations, looks of fear and looks of contempt. She didn't know which was worse. A slow clap exploded through the room. Chukwudi wore a foul look, clapping long after the room fell silent.

'Beware the fool that hails a winner before the game has been won,' he said stoically.

'The game has been won. The Eze is dead,' Eni replied, his low voice low and cutting.

'And who will rise in his place, *boy*?' Chukwudi replied. 'We've already heard reports of this *General Ikenna*. Look at what he did to the nnunus.' Sinai blinked over at the nnunus, noticing for the first time the gold clasps squaring off the tips of their wings. Her heart thudded in horror. *They'd been clipped.*

'He doesn't have the crystal,' Sinai said quietly, mostly to herself, as she recalled General Ikenna standing beside Olu. It was the General that had organised their escape from the city upon Olu's request. General Ikenna who had warned them that if they ever returned to the palace they would burn before they could mutter a greeting. Olu wouldn't … he couldn't …

'Yet,' Chukwudi said sharply, 'he doesn't have the crystal *yet*.'

Sinai's heart plunged.

'Shall we avoid talking in hypotheticals?' the Isi said, her thin frosty voice piercing through Sinai's thoughts. 'Young Naala and Sinai know the location of the Àlà and Ikuku crystal. Two crystals that can protect the realm, should Chi fall into undesirable hands. Two crystals that they can evoke.'

'We can't – no one can,' Naala protested, and Bayo shook his head violently at her outburst.

'Why in heavens not? Do you wish to see the Aido-Hwedo grow stronger with each new day?' Chukwudi cried.

'I don't,' Naala said, turning to the Isi; 'and that is why we must approach with caution. We were told – Sinai was told – that a great evil will be unleashed into the world if the crystals are evoked.'

'Impossible.' Chukwudi snorted.

'Yes, she said a pit, right? A pit, a pit of …' Naala insisted.

'The pit of Eriri Uhie,' Kora said with a strange look on her face. 'I saw it – well, read about it.' She blinked before throwing a sideways glance at Bayo, whose eyebrows were raised.

'Read it where?' Bayo said slowly as Kora winced.

'Yes. So – strictly speaking it wasn't in my *set* reading,' she hurried, 'but I thought it would be okay because I completed my reading early, and I ... *found* this red parchment and I thought I might as well ... read ... it?' she flinched at Bayo's growing fury.

'It was you that broke into the Oba Akwu̩kwo̩,' Bayo said accusingly.

'No!' Kora exclaimed, a little too vehemently to be convincing, 'but perhaps the person that did, left it for me to find—'

'It was you,' Bayo repeated with narrowed eyes.

'Let's focus on what's important here,' Kora insisted, avoiding Bayo's glare. 'I thought the parchment was nonsense, it was pretty, but nonsense, but now I think ... I don't know, I think it is connected. It mentioned the Nine Ikusas – the nine breaks in time – and one of them would result in this pit. A pit that could kill us all. What else comes in nine? The crystals, boom – a pit of evil.'

'The Kingdom,' Naala whispered. 'We can't risk the Kingdom.'

'No, we cannot,' the Isi said quietly; her violet eyes had darkened as the conversation deepened. She closed her eyes. 'Perhaps, there is another way?' she opened them at Chukwudi.

'There is,' he responded tightly. 'The Aturu can devise a plan to subdue the beast,' he assured, 'though it will be *difficult*. Near impossible. Lives could be lost.'

'No, we can—' Naala started before Bayo raised his hand to silence her.

'What if you had help? The girls?' Bayo offered. Chukwudi glared at him but the Isi brushed a gloved finger over her lips, brightening at the suggestion. 'You could teach them the ways of the Aturu. I'd wager it would be a more efficient solution ... in the absence of the crystal.'

'Teach?' Chukwudi said with a quick snort. 'Is that your solution for *everything*?'

'Yes and why not? Should not information be shared? Is that not the crust of who we are?'

'Knowledge is power and power in the wrong hands is catastrophic,' Chukwudi said glaring at Naala. When he switched his gaze to Sinai, she couldn't help but look down.

'What are you talking about?' Naala asked.

'Oh, don't bother yourself; they do this all the time,' Kora said, reaching out for more steamed beans. 'Best to leave them to it; they'll explain eventually.'

The Isi didn't take her eyes off of Naala and Sinai, her forehead creased. 'What of Madi?'

'What of Madi?' Naala said, jerking back before throwing a glance at the large boy. He avoided her gaze for the first time since they had been reunited.

'The boy is not ready for that ...' Bayo started.

'Must we do this now?' Madi said, his voice tinged with stress.

'Do *what* now?' Naala demanded, attracting glances but no answers.

'Don't,' Madi warned as Bayo opened his mouth. The thin man regarded Madi carefully before sighing as he turned back to Naala.

'What do you know of the Descendants?'

'Bayo,' Madi cautioned, his fists tightening.

'That is the last time you will use my name so callously, boy. This has as much to do with her as it has to do with you; maybe even more so,' Bayo snapped.

'The Descendants?' Naala muttered under her breath. Had Nwamara mentioned it? Perhaps the Mami Wata?

'The Descendants of the First,' Kora interjected excitedly. 'It's what you are,' she said to Naala, before glancing over at Sinai, and, stranger still, Madi. 'What you all are.' The large boy returned her excitement with a dark stare.

'A Descendant?' Naala frowned. 'You said I was a mmo?' she said to Bayo. 'Now I'm a *Descendant?*'

'Yes.' Bayo paused carefully. 'Yes, I did. I thought – I didn't know,' he added, his voice quietening. 'I didn't know that you were *possible*. That the Descendants *could* return. Even when the theory began to curl in my mind, I rejected it for folly. I needed to be convinced—' he glanced at Madi '—and by heavens I got it.

'When I first encountered you, Naala, I could sense your power as clear as day. I could feel your connection to the Black and Gold realm, but your abilities didn't map to any of the gods, so I assumed mmo. A mmo can shift the earth, they can even touch the crystal, but you, child, *wielded* it with the realm itself. No mmo could do such a thing.' Bayo's far-off gaze focused on Sinai. 'But now that there are two of you. Well, that is something else entirely. You control the earth and she the air;

on its own not very assuming, but you two together … well, it's like a puzzle that looks remarkably like … the Earth Mother, Ala.'

'Bayo,' Chukwudi warned.

Bayo blinked rapidly at the outburst before giving a tense nod to the white-haired man.

'I'm getting ahead of myself.' He shook away a frown. 'There's no need to delve into the gritty details just yet, but you see,' he continued, 'something has happened; something is happening.'

'Yes, but with no control,' Chukwudi snapped, 'it is unacceptable. The Mother's Crystal was evoked, *carelessly*. Left unchecked, these *Descendants* will destroy everything that we've worked for. We're already seeing it; how much damage will the Aido-Hwedo inflict? Yes, we may be able to *contain* the situation, as we did for Madi when he went on his rampage, but what of the others—'

'Madi?' Naala interjected; his frame stiffened at the mention of his name. He waved his hand in quiet protest.

'Let's not—' he began.

'It wasn't a *rampage* – it was an accident,' Kora insisted protectively. 'It wasn't even *that* bad.'

'Another time, we can discuss it another time,' he said weakly. His eyes appeared pained as they darted around the room, avoiding anyone's gaze.

'Bayo?' the Isi said crisply. 'Tell me, are you proposing a plan that *combines* the art of the Aturu and the Descendants?'

'Yes,' he said curtly as the woman turned to Chukwudi.

'Will it work?'

He considered her words before nodding stiffly. 'If they can be controlled … perhaps.'

With his words came a sudden flurry from the whispering walls. A chill crept up Sinai's spine as they formed into coherent words:

A terror …

Comes … child born of both.

A fate worse than death.

The horror is … near. The horror is here.

Sinai snapped her head back to the gathering. Sweat trickled down her temple as her heart raced.

A horror, she thought, hands shaking as she dared to reach Chukwudi's cold glare.

CHAPTER 17
SOURCE

Urukpuru

'You *have* to let me do your hair,' Kora insisted as they strode through the grasslands behind the crystal settlement.

Naala was at a loss for words. A beast was on the loose, the Kingdom was at risk, but Kora's pressing concern was *her* hair?

'Just think about it; once I'm done, no one will dare call you a vagrant.'

Naala snorted. 'Kora, you're the only one calling me a vagrant.'

'And if you want me to stop—' Kora pushed.

'I want to know how the research is going,' Naala interrupted. Kora glared at her before releasing a long, low sigh, and Naala knew that she had won their tug of war, this time.

Since the welcome feast Kora had yet to find anything else on Njem, the Descendants or – what was most bothering her – The Children Born of Both. Even the parchment that Kora had found on the Nine Ikusas had vanished.

'No,' she frowned, clutching at her forehead.

Naala wasn't surprised but a heaviness came over her all the same.

'I still can't believe I lost that parchment.'

Naala pressed her lips into a smile that she couldn't quite commit to before turning her head back at the gleaming crystals that housed the Amaghi. As Madi and Sinai joined them, the fleeting look Chukwudi had on his face when Kora had mentioned the parchment at the feast sprang into Naala's mind, cold and daring. 'Don't be so sure you did.'

'You—' Bayo clapped across the field as he approached the group, his eyes fixed on Kora '—leave.' He drew his thin, bark cane out of the holster on his hip.

'Leave? But I can help,' Kora protested, the corners of her eyes tightening as her eyebrows pressed together.

'Are you a Descendant?'

'No but—'

'Then you have no place here,' Bayo interrupted, flicking his wrist at her.

'I won't be a bother, I—'

'You need to do your reading.'

'Ah-ha! I've already done it,' Kora said with a smirk that faltered as Bayo gave her a hard smile.

'In that case, I have an assignment for you on—'

'Glass beads? Done. I've also completed the parchment on numbing agents,' Kora sang as Bayo's eyebrow arched.

'What of the mission equipment?' he asked, and Kora's bottom lip dropped.

'The mission equipment? You didn't say I was to hel—'

'Leave,' he snapped.

Kora lingered for a moment before releasing a sigh. 'Fine,' she mumbled, walking solemnly back to the settlement.

'What is *power*?' Bayo asked as he swivelled around to the group; his gaze hunted across their faces but no one spoke. Naala could tell by the twitch in the corner of his mouth that his debate with Kora had left him with little patience to spare, and he didn't have much to begin with.

Madi cleared his throat. 'Strength?' he said.

Bayo snapped towards him before wrapping the bark cane against Madi's head. The large boy yelped as he rubbed at his ear.

'Strength is strength. What is power?' he repeated to the silent group.

'Well, we hardly have an incentive to try,' Naala muttered before quieting at

Bayo's glare.

'The ability to *do* things?' Sinai suggested, flinching as Bayo got closer.

'Access.' He nodded as Madi's eyes widened.

'Is that not what I sai...' he trailed, stepping back from Bayo's stride.

'Power,' Bayo continued, 'is simply *access*. The ability to *do* that which others cannot do. As Descendants of the First, your blood grants you access to one of the greatest energy sources in the universe.'

'The Black and Gold realm,' Naala said, edging forward, despite herself.

'Yes, the Mother ordained the blood of the first man and the blood of the first woman with a key that gives their Descendants access to the Black and Gold Realm. This is the blood that runs through your veins. This is your power.' He ran his gaze across the group. 'Your access is dependent on you, your chi – your *soul*.' Bayo pivoted to Madi. 'You have access to strength, a deep strength that goes beyond what you can ever imagine. This one—' he gestured to Naala '—has access to the earth, the soil and bark, and you,' he said, turning to Sinai, 'you, my dear, have access to the air. Your power is dictated by your access. The more you practise, the more you learn your triggers and points, the more access that you have to the realm and the less limitations that you have.'

He looked upon their faces as he watched them carefully. 'After years of practice,' he continued, 'years of manipulating and drawing energy from the Black and Gold realm, your body will be able to use that energy as life fuel. A fuel that will sustain you for hundreds and hundreds of years. You will not bleed as we do, you will not die as we do; you will be *great – if* you can practise discipline.'

Bayo had alluded to this a few times and it had never sat well with Naala. The thought of living for hundreds of years felt impossible, unnatural and lonely.

'Is that what the Eze used to keep himself young?' Madi asked, before receiving another wrap on the ear.

Naala noted the flare of bright pink tinting his brown skin. Poor Madi, he always had the roughest time in these sessions. Sinai was Bayo's favourite, and Bayo knew if he pushed Naala too far, she'd retaliate, whilst Madi, as strong as he was, never would.

'Was the Eze a Descendant?' Bayo snarled with his hands behind his back.

'No,' Madi replied gruffly.

'No, but the Eze had the Chi Crystal – but even then, could he use it?' Bayo asked Madi as the large boy bit his lip in grimace.

'No,' Naala interjected, and Madi mouthed thanks.

'I wasn't asking you,' Bayo sneered before nodding reluctantly, 'but, yes, that is correct. He couldn't. Not without a *key*.' He cut a glare at the group. 'What do you know of Ọbara magic?'

'It is evil,' Madi said firmly.

Naala groaned internally as Bayo twisted at his cane.

'Ọbara magic is simply magic. Same as the magic that runs through you. The only difference is its *source*. Your magic stems from the Black and Gold realm; Ọbara magic stems from blood. Blood packed with life energy – Ọbara magic extracts this energy, and, much like the Black and Gold realm, it requires mastering to make it *efficient*. A poor practitioner will need to kill hundreds to simply raise a peanut into the sky. A good practitioner, a *trained* practitioner, could extract that energy from a small mouse. Every Aturu practitioner is *trained* and none have spilt human blood. But others have.

'The issue with blood magic is it has easy access, anyone can do it – not a handful of Descendants, but *anyone* who learns of the practice. That allows for the poor practitioners who have given a bad name to blood magic, but it in itself is not bad.'

Madi shifted uncomfortably.

'Do you have something to add?' Bayo asked raising his eyebrows.

Madi hesitated. 'It's … it's still wrong.'

'Was it *wrong* to save you and your friends? *Wrong* to clothe and feed you? Was it *wrong* to protect the Kingdom?'

'I don't unders—'

'What magic do you think we have been practising here? What do you think powers the settlement? What powers the hamerkops, the illusions, the efe-efe baskets?' Naala's throat burned at his words. Blood magic? The Amaghi used *blood magic*?

'Strange magic,' Sinai muttered, repeating Nwamara's words.

Naala shivered.

'Ọbara magic, blood magic is the backbone of this settlement and it's the principle of Aturu. If you are serious about defeating the Aido-Hwedo, you must make peace with that.'

Naala exchanged glances with Madi. His expression was almost as tight as hers. When she turned to Sinai, Naala found her attention had been taken by something else. Naala followed her gaze to a window at the east side of the Idu where a shadow stood; its dark eyes fixed on her.

CHAPTER 18
CHASING FLOWERS

City of Nri

Crisp ruby petals drifted in the hidden Nzuzo garden. Olu watched them fall as he held tightly to the memory of *her.*

Hollow bones had pressed against his arms when he had carried her to these gardens. She had been so frail. Grief had claimed her like nothing he had seen before. Olu had feared she would follow Meekulu Kaurandua to her place of rest. Yet moments after entering these very gardens, Sinai had arisen. She had danced with the flame tree's velvet petals and come back to life. Now, long after she had left the city, they still danced for her. Olu swallowed the lump in his throat.

The sun had sunk low in the sky, and the world was cast in deep indigo. He came here often, too often, searching for … something. For her.

Yet all that was left for him were ghosts. Whispered memories of nights and people long gone. Meekulu Kaurandua. His heart twinged. He had failed the old woman. He let her fall victim to the Eze's regime.

A deep ache consumed him. It should have been him who had burned that day. Olu's vision blurred as the flower petals whirled at his feet. He blinked as they began to gain height. Crimson petals dancing weightlessly in the air, picking up speed until they began to spiral. Olu nearly doubled over when they began to bunch together and form a shape that looked eerily like the old woman herself.

Olu let out a strangled breath as the flowered figure walked towards him, its gait identical to the ancient cook.

'And wouldn't that have been a waste,' the apparition said, its voice a shimmering echo of the dead woman.

Olu recoiled as his guts twisted. The flower figure offered him a crooked smile and Olu drew out his abara. His heart pounded as he slashed uselessly at the figure. *Run!* he screamed at himself, but his body was frozen in place.

'And wouldn't that have been a waste,' the apparition repeated. He let out a retching breath.

'What?' he managed, his mouth dry and his head spinning. It was not real. It could not be real. He glanced at the abara in his hand; save for a folded petal at its rim, no one would have been able to tell that he had used it.

'A waste of life. If you had gone instead of me.'

Olu's racing heart paused. He shook his head as a bitter laugh clawed out of his mouth. He had conjured it. He was finally broken. A strange calm came over him as he pondered it all. It quickly descended into rage. 'My life alone has cost countless others,' he spat. 'You have no idea the things that I've done, y-you—' The words caught on his throat.

If he had found life difficult under Eze Ochichiri, it was near impossible under Ikenna. Not even an Eze yet, and Ikenna had already racked up his fair share of bodies, with Olu, his swordsman, by his side. It wasn't just the killings; it was the *cruelty* that got to Olu.

When Ikenna had noticed a dwindling in the number of nnunus in the city, he had decreed a mass clipping of the bird-women's wings. A senseless act that Olu had been tasked to lead. The memory of their screams still chilled his blood, sounding through his ears as he drifted off to sleep. Worse was the silence that had engulfed the city. After what they had done, the nnunus no longer sang – a fact that had thrown Ikenna into a blind rage.

'Everything must move towards a better reign, *my* reign,' Ikenna had spat, 'so *how* could my reign *lack* what the Eze had in abundance?'

Ikenna could huff and puff all he wanted but he simply couldn't force them to sing. Any attempts nearly always resulted in their death. So instead he had forced them into a back-breaking servitude instead. Olu had never felt shame as he did when a nnunu waited on him.

'And what of the lives that you have saved, little green-eyed Chi? What of the help you gave to Sinai?' the apparition argued.

He could taste heat rising on his tongue. His fingers itched to grab the apparition's head and squeeze as hard as he could.

'I haven't saved anyone,' he said, head pounding. Olu may have organised her safe travel outside of the city, but heavens knew where she was now. 'I deserve to die for my crimes.' It wasn't the first time he had thought it, but it was the first time he had said it out loud. The figure drew closer to him and smiled the same smile he had seen spread across Meekulu's wrinkled mouth thousands of times,

'Remember what I told you, the first time we met. You harboured similar notions back then.'

He paused. He remembered nearly everything the old woman had said, clinging on to her words like a vine wrapped around a tree. 'Your life matters because you want to do better.'

'Is that still the case?'

'I took the blood oath,' Olu said defeatedly.

'Yes, you did,' the apparition said, swiping its hand across his forehead; the flowers fluttered in the gust of air. 'Silly boy. What a senseless path to choose, after being *warned*, no less. Nonsense.'

Olu gazed at the petals queerly. 'You sound just like her.' Olu couldn't make sense of the trick his mind was playing on him. Was this it? Was he to live the rest of his life gaunt, spewing out obscenities like the soldiers who had sustained invisible injuries in their mind? He looked back at the apparition; its brows were raised and arched.

'But then again, green-eyed Chi, whilst your path may not be set, your destination is, and everything you do, good or bad, will take you to it. That is, after all, what is written.'

Something about what she said grated at him. 'Why do you call me that?' he finally asked. It wasn't a name that Meekulu had given him whilst she was alive.

'Because that is who you are,' it said, and Olu marvelled at the creases he could see spread around the apparition's flowered eyes. How different things might have been if she were still alive. *She would have been the first person I would have gone to when Sinai had been taken.*

'Don't dwell on things in the past. What has happened has happened; the only thing to consider now is what you *will* do—' the apparition turned around '—and you didn't answer my question – is that still the case?'

'What?'

'Do you want to do better?'

Olu looked back at the apparition, his answer hovering reluctantly in his throat.

'Well, then,' the apparition said, before collapsing into a flower heap on the ground.

'Ma!' Olu called instinctively, catching himself when it dawned on him that he was only chasing flowers.

CHAPTER 19
THE DOOR THAT BLED

Urukpuru

Naala's breath created smoky clouds in the crisp night's air. Though it pinched at her cheeks, she was far from cold. The drapes of fine crimson cloth that the Amaghị had provided her with trapped warmth far better than she had imagined. One of the many tricks of the Aturu, she supposed.

Walking would do her good, she had decided. Her quarters were far too large. Nearly the size of her family's entire ụlọ in Igbakwu. An obscenity that made her head hurt. Then, of course, there was her hair. Naala fingered the fresh braids that tugged mercilessly at her scalp. She had given into Kora's demands. They were heavy, intertwined with dyed, pulled sheep's wool, so long that it fell well past her waist.

If she was honest, it was not the braids that kept her up, nor her excessive quarters, nor even the too-soft akwa nest. No, it was this *place* and the many secrets buried in its walls. Naala slowed. The plump moon glittered behind the hallway's thin windows, which were lined with sprawling frost. Walking, it seemed, wasn't helping at all.

'Of course,' a voice suddenly said from behind her and her heart jumped out of her body.

'Eni,' she breathed, clutching her chest as he approached. Her heartbeat drummed loudly in her ears.

'Why is it that I can always find you lurking around in the middle of the night?' he said, shaking his head as a smirk flirted on his lips.

'If you weren't *lurking* yourself, you wouldn't have that issue.' She smiled as he closed the gap between them. The wind, whistling through the crystal pipes above them, was their only company in the deserted hall.

Heat rose to Naala's cheeks. It was the first time they had been alone since Furuefu. Her lips tingled with the memory of Eni's pressed against hers. The feel of his firm grip on her body. She dropped her gaze to the ground.

'I couldn't really sleep,' he said, bringing his finger to her chin and raising her head high. His gaze fixed on hers as he traced her face with his finger, trailing a stray braid behind her ear. 'Your hair looks nice.'

'Thank you,' she murmured; she could feel the pulse of her heart vibrating off her parted lips. He dropped his hand and tilted his head with a grin.

'So, where were you creeping off to? The Oba Akwụkwọ, I presume?' Eni said, glancing behind her.

'No, I …' the words left her as she followed his gaze to the decadent door behind her. She hadn't noticed it before but now that she did, it seemed most peculiar indeed. It didn't have any handles or other opening devices; it just stood before her, a block of thick crystal.

In the pale moonlight, she could see that the thin red vines sprawled within it. The scrawling didn't seem random and haphazard as the others within the Idu. No, they seemed to be *deliberate*.

Naala turned and drew closer. *Nsibidi*, she thought. The written script. She squinted at the symbols but the words were nonsensical, randomly meshed together with no meaning. 'This is the Oba Akwụkwọ?' she asked. She had never been in one before; Igbakwu had been too small to have its own, and her uncle had insisted that the nearest Oba Akwụkwọ was too far for a young girl to travel. A statement that had left Naala in a bitter rage for moon-cycles after.

The Oba Akwụkwọ were described as a well of knowledge. An ụlọ brimming with parchments, etchings and statues. Rows and rows of information in all the physical forms they could possibly be put in.

'It is,' Eni said, coming up behind her. 'Before you get any ideas, you should know that it's protected by the Aturu. Meaning it's impossible to get in.'

Naala tensed at his words. It felt like her uncle's refusal all over again.

'I thought there were no secrets in the Amaghi,' Naala said tightly.

Eni's mouth curved into a smile. 'Rules don't always hold up when you live in the shadows.' He shrugged but Naala caught something darkening in his eye.

'You don't trust them?'

His eyebrows gathered at the question. 'I don't trust anyone,' he said finally.

It stung more than she would have liked to admit. Did he include her in that statement?

'At some point, everyone lets you down. Whether they mean to or not.' His words were meant for someone. That much she could tell. She was desperate to know who, but she couldn't bring herself to ask.

'You don't trust me?' she asked instead. She had hoped to deliver her words in a teasing tone; she had to stop herself from cringing at the pricks of pain she had detected instead. Though Eni hadn't seemed to have noticed; a grin spread over his face.

'Trust you?' he chuckled. 'You are the wildest of them all, determined to kill yourself at every corner!' Something sparked within him and his grin widened. 'Why do you think I'm stationed at your door? I'm on the watch in case you decide to flee again.'

A laugh started deep in her belly and sprang unfiltered from her mouth.

'Shh,' Eni sniggered. His head leaned into hers, but she couldn't settle; the startled look on his face tickled her even more. Finally he gently pressed his hand over her mouth; his other hand gripped her waist in place.

Naala's body soared hot against his touch and she stilled. Far too quickly he released his grip. His chest heaved up and down as his black eyes roamed over her.

'You said that you couldn't sleep,' she managed.

'See where *trusting* lands you.' He smiled, stepping towards her before taking her head into his hands. A charge ran through her as his thumb grazed across her bottom lip. She stopped breathing.

'You should stop that,' he added, his voice low and vibrating.

'Breathing?'

He creased at her response. 'Trusting,' he corrected as he pressed into her.

Naala stumbled backwards towards the door. She slammed her hand against it for support before something sharp stabbed at the tips of her fingers.

'Ow,' she yelped, pulling away from the door.

'Sorry—' Eni pulled away, his widened eyes scanning her face '—did I hurt you?'

'No, I felt…' Naala frowned, turning around to find a bright red colour bleeding through the Nsibidi symbols on the door. 'Is that an alert call?' Her heart was racing. She had no desire to meet with Bayo's wrath this evening, or, worse still, Chukwudi.

'I don't think so,' Eni replied distantly as three symbols began to glow.

'Born from secrets and bound by blood?' Naala read aloud before a scratching noise erupted into the hall.

She jumped back. She should have run but something held her firmly in place. *Click.*

Naala backed into Eni. They watched, unmoving, as the door creaked open to reveal a brightly lit room.

'We shouldn't,' Eni said quickly.

Naala snorted and her eyebrows rose so high it lifted the corners of her mouth.

Eni let out a sigh. 'I forgot who I was dealing with.'

'Come on,' she insisted, slipping her hand into his and tugging him forward.

CHAPTER 20
WORDS OF THE NIGHT

Urukpuru

It was not as she had expected. The Oba Akwụkwọ's rose gold floor spanned out a sea's length without a single object placed on it. Yet its back wall brimmed with rows of plaques and crevices filled with parchments. Narrow, crooked stairs led to a landing with even more plaques and an archway in the centre. Naala released a breath as Eni came up behind her.

'That's the symbol of the Aturu,' he said, staring up at the symbol over the archway.

'Blood,' Naala read before shifting over to the plaques on the ground floor. Positioned at their tops, they each had a small symbol. She went over to the one with the scorpion, reading the header below: *Words on Fear.* Naala glanced ahead at the other plates: *Words on Health. Words on Romance.*

'Sections,' she muttered to herself, as she began to read the script in the *Words on Health.*

The balance of the universe is reflected in the intricate balance between the body, the mind and the spirit. Balance in all three will result in strong health. To understand what an individual needs to reach this, they must look to their ancestors.

Naala grabbed one of the parchments tucked in the crevice at its side.

One iku of nuts or one efere of shellfish will impact those born from the house of Ogemedi severely.

Naala pulled out another parchment and read.

The Biloko that stem within the Kingdom of Kongo may be as small as a child, but their years and wisdom is that of the elders; beware crossing their paths as they have been known to swallow people whole.

She placed the parchment back. Her breath caught in her throat as she read the next section. *Words on the Descendants.* Her head lightened as she took a step towards the plate.

'It's a section on the Descendants,' she said to Eni, who had never learnt to read the written script.

'Read it out,' he said.

Naala's stomach dipped but she did not hesitate.

'In the beginning, there was nothing but Chukwu. The All-Knowing one filled the corners of the universe with a singularity. Until Chukwu introduced chaos into the realm. Chaos began with what we now call the Black and Gold realm.' A tingle ran up Naala's back. She drew closer. 'The realm had nine sections, each one with its own keeper. No two keepers or realms were alike in personality or abilities, a fact that caused—' Naala frowned at the word, re-reading the section for more context before finally resuming '—thunderous? Thunderous clashes at times, but overall, they coexisted in harmony.

'Time passed and the nurturing keeper, Ala, asked for the All-Knowing's permission to create a realm that excited outside of the Black and Gold. The All-Knowing agreed, knowing that she would create Earth.

'And so she birthed the Earth and became the Earth Mother. Soon after, she created a new type of chaos. A chaos that reflected herself. She called this humanity. It began with eight. Four women and four men made from ofo sticks and coated in umber leaves.

'Within six of the humans, she placed fire, water, wood, soil, salt and stone. But within the First Man and the First Woman, Ala placed something special. She placed a part … a piece of herself.' Naala traced over the words with her finger.

'This piece was special, too special,' she continued. 'If two with the piece were to mate, their offspring were fated to be …' Naala frowned '… astounding?

No. Catastrophic …?' Naala paused. Neither word felt right; it seemed to be a combination of the two. She found her throat tightening but she continued. She had to continue. 'So Ala created a law. Like the law of the sun rising in the East and setting in the West. Like the law of death to all who lived. Like the law of night and day. A law of the First that decreed no Descendant of the First Man and no Descendant of the First Woman must ever mate. No Children Born of Both can enter the world, for with them comes the start of Njem and – with that – the end.'

Naala knees weakened. *Children Born of Both.* Was that not what Nwamara had called Sinai and her? A slight tremor ran through her hand but she continued to read. 'The First Man and First Woman were free to mate with the other children of Ala. The piece Ala had hidden within them would flourish within their children on a rare occasion.

'These children that bore the piece, the Descendants of the First, had access to the Black and Gold Realm through the piece within them. Access that allowed the keepers of the realm to explore Ala's world. Over time the keepers and the Descendants became one and they became known as the gods of Earth.' Naala stopped and looked up at Eni, her heart pounding mercilessly.

'Gods,' she whispered, clenching her fists to stop her tremors. '*That's* what the Descendants are?' The old gods *returned?*'

Eni blinked back at her. 'What else could you be?' he grinned, though the play didn't reach his hardened eyes.

'Impossible.' She needed to sit down.

'Maybe not,' he mused. 'You forget that I *saw* you in the palace. I've never seen anything like it, the things that you can do, and Madi …'

Madi. She had seen it when they had been reunited. Yes, he was warm and jovial – he was Madi, after all – but there was something else. Something haunted resting in the corners of eyes. Something that hadn't been there before she had left.

An ache panged at the back of her throat. Naala couldn't help feeling as though Madi's change was her fault. As though she had polluted him.

'There was an incident,' Eni said gently. 'Madi smashed through a few walls, and … a few people got hurt … some quite badly … it really broke him.'

Of course it broke him, she thought bitterly. Madi was a member of the Mpako tribe who placed honour above all. She knew it would burn him, the very thought of hurting others because he had lost control.

'He smashed through the walls,' Naala repeated as Eni's words settled on her. She recalled the boarded-up section of the Amaghi's settlement that she had seen on their way to the Rie quarters. *Surely Madi couldn't have done that?* She glanced over at the thick crystal walls, standing with unyielding sturdiness. Naala simply couldn't imagine a human body tearing through the rock-hard material, even one as large as Madi.

'He's strong,' Eni said, watching her mind churn. 'Very, very strong.'

'Ikenga,' Naala whispered as she recalled stories of the old god of strength. The god said to be able to crumble mountains with his bare hands. Her gaze flicked back to the plaque; could it be *true?*

You control the earth and she the air; on its own not very assuming, but you two together ... well, it's like a puzzle that looks remarkably like ... Ala. Bayo's words stung at her temples.

'Naala,' she heard Eni say softly behind her but she couldn't stop. Not now.

'I have to ...' she trailed off, scanning the parchments.

The Ogeri family claimed to have a Descendant bloodline, with claims of Idemili being a distant cousin of their ancestors.

Naala's eyebrows furrowed, flicking to another parchment.

The oracle said that it would be the Nine Guides that will reveal the path to the broken crystal.

Naala halted. 'Broken crystal?' she muttered, before she continued to read. 'The green-eyed Chi, the black-eyed Àlà, the clear-eyed Ikuku, the rose-eyed Ihunaya, the grey-eyed Ọnwu, the purple-eyed Ndụ, the brown-eyed Okike, the silver-eyed Udo and the golden-eyed Ala. Can you make any sense of this?'

'No,' he said beside her; his hands filled with the parchments that she had discarded.

Naala blinked at him. She had gone through the entire section and *nothing.*

Eni's forehead crinkled and his lips pulled down.

'Perhaps it's time we leave; we've been here for too long now and though I jested, the Aturu are very serious about their ways. This is not something that they will take lightly,' he warned.

'Uh-huh,' she said, looking up at the archway, 'Kora said that the parchment she found was red, right?'

'What?'

'She said it was red,' she mumbled, as she stretched her neck to catch glimpses of red on the landing. Perhaps that was where they hid the *real* information.

Eni groaned as she headed towards the stairs.

'There was a time where I believed that you were fearless,' he mused as he followed after her, 'or mad.'

Naala spun to face him when she had reached the landing. He was closer than she had thought and she staggered back. Before she could lose her footing, his arm clutched around her waist. He pulled up, holding her tightly in his arms. Eni's warm, sweet breath brushed against her nose. Her stomach tightened. 'And now?' Naala said breathlessly.

'Now, I feel as though Azu was right – you are simply a troublemaker.' His lips parted slightly as his gaze found its way to her lips.

'A troublemaker?' she said exasperated, pulling herself out of his hold as she recalled the annoying man who had 'led' the survivors of the Eze's attack, not knowing that it was Eni, Madi and Kora orchestrating their every step, assisted by the Amaghi.

Azu hadn't been the first person to call her a troublemaker; it had been near enough her nickname in Igbakwu. A pang throbbed in her chest as she wondered what they would have called Sinai.

'She really looks like me,' Naala said.

Eni's smile faltered as he searched her face. He settled into a frown. 'You know,' he said, 'I've met them before … twins – in my village. They're not like what they say. They're not evil.'

She stared back at him. Is that what he thought her problem was? Did he think that she had believed the Eze's heretic claims? She pictured him in his last moments, unhinged and baseless. That wasn't it at all.

'They never did,' she continued.

Eni's frown deepened until something clicked in his dark eyes. He understood. Naala's throat tightened.

Her grandmother, her uncle, her family … none of them had looked anything like her. As much as she loved them, she had never felt like she belonged. Perhaps she never had. The most painful part was how different it felt with Sinai. She couldn't deny their connection, though it felt like a betrayal against the people who had spent years nurturing and caring for her. The people she had let down.

'They are still your family,' Eni said, cutting through the rabble in her mind. 'No matter what they looked like, no matter what your blood says. They are still your family.'

'Perhaps,' she murmured, before turning back to the archway. It opened into a dark room filled with blood-red parchment that glimmered with gold writing. She would find out the truth. She needed to. She edged closer to the archway when Eni began to fuss.

'Naala, wait, no really—Naala! Wai—'

She rolled her eyes at Eni's protest before she felt something pull at her forcefully.

'What are you doing?' she grunted.

He growled back at her, his eyes wild with rage.

Ice gripped at her throat. 'What is wrong with you?' her voice came out thinner than she would have liked. She had never seen him so angry.

'Me? What is wrong with *you*?' he breathed through gritted teeth as he scanned her face.

'Eni, I—'

'*Look* – look at those ridges in the corner,' he explained.

Naala pulled her gaze away from him and followed his finger to the raised lines on the archway wood.

'They are creating a field, similar to the illusion at the Idu's entrance, but far more dangerous,' he panted as he looked around for something before grabbing a discarded parchment on the ground. He flung it through the archway. It didn't drop to the ground; instead it sizzled into a heap of dust.

Naala stared wordlessly at the mound on the floor.

'You see why *sometimes* it is important to listen to someone other than that blasted voice in your head?' Eni lectured as though she were still a child.

Her cheeks burned but for once she had nothing to say.

Eni released a sigh before inspecting the archway with a frown. 'What are they doing using something like that in the Oba Akwụkwọ?'

The question stirred something within Naala. Something that left a bitter taste on her tongue. 'It is a place of knowledge,' she said, 'and so a place of power.' An image of Chukwudi floated into her mind but then—

Eni threw a glance at her, his frown deepening at her expression.

'What is it?' he asked, but Naala shook her head, straining her ears for something in the distance.

'What is that?' he said, disconcerted.

'Screaming ... someone's screaming!'

CHAPTER 21
BLACK SMOKE

Urukpuru

Kora blasted the door open before bounding into the room.

'Why can't you just announce yourself like a normal person?' Madi sighed as she leapt onto his akwa nest.

'Because then I wouldn't see your shocked face,' Kora grinned. 'It is by far your best face, second only to that irritated one you are wearing now.' Madi grumbled back at her before turning back to the ọgụgụ nook. A deep cubby placed in every room in the Idu, fleshed with thick vines that lined the crevice and sprawled across its edge. Layers of hartebeest fur formed a seat, and a thin slab of protruding crystal created a flat surface for those wanting to write.

Kora loved to see Madi stuffed into his ọgụgụ. He sat so *awkwardly*. His large frame folded queerly in the tight confinement. She warmed at the crease that had formed on his forehead. It always popped up when he was trying to read.

Reading didn't come easy to Madi, but he was determined to learn. He told her repeatedly that he didn't want to rely on her reading for him forever. Though she would have been glad to.

Kora sank into his akwa furs, her heart lifting at the scent of him. A rich enveloping musk. If she closed her eyes, it almost felt like his arms were wrapped tightly over hers. She didn't dare do it, though, lest he catch her. Instead she looked out at the sky; it was pitch-black, dusted with sparkling stars and the looming, heavy moon.

'You should be asleep,' she said to him.

'*You* should be asleep,' he retorted, offering a bemused smile, 'and at least *I'm* in my own room.'

Kora's heart raced, as it often did when Madi played with her. Although their rooms were similar, Kora had always preferred Madi's; like him, it felt safe.

'I'm not the one with *omnipotent* god training tomorrow,' Kora declared.

'Learning the Aturu ways is not god training,' Madi said, laughing, and the cowrie beads at the ends of his braids rattled as he shook his head. 'And don't pretend like you won't still be there to bother me.'

She *had* been planning to try her luck again. Why shouldn't she attend their training? Bayo was *her* mentor. It was preposterous that he was shutting her out of this. It burned her to think of how much she was *missing*. How much she could learn.

It was not as though it would interfere with her studies. Her innate curiosity always kept her ahead of her schedule, no matter how hard Bayo tried to set her back with more tasks and those lessons had piqued her interest like nothing before.

After moon-cycles on Urukpuru, the Aturu were a mystery to her. A group of eight people who seemed to wield the world's information at the tips of their fingers.

A hard slam brought Kora back to reality. She watched new tiny cracks forming and spreading across the crystal slab. More of those and he'll be needing a replacement.

Kora stood up and peered into Madi's ọgụgụ nook. 'Sounds like it's going well,'

'Excellent,' Madi huffed. 'How can you tell?'

'You need to be easier on yourself.'

'I don't. Bayo is right; I can't be hand-held through this.'

Madi shrugged as Kora's fists tightened. *Blast Bayo and his loose tongue.*

He climbed out of the nook, and towered over her. 'I just want to make sure that I have the tools that I will need,' he said, 'now that I'm ... you know.' He sat down on his akwa nest.

'A god reincarnated?' Kora suggested as she went to join him. His large frame created a slight slope in the nest that pulled her towards him. She could feel the warmth from his body and her heart quickened.

Madi's lips were pinched together before he released a heavy sigh. It was the best and worst thing about him. This drive he had to do the right thing.

She watched him return back to the conversation, his face scrunched.

'I'm not a god. I just … might have something in me that allows me to do *godlike* things,' he concluded before throwing her a smile. 'If I really *were* a god, you would fear me a whole lot more than you do now!' he added as Kora giggled. He laughed along with her before his expression shifted.

'I can't believe she's here,' he said, punctuating each word with brightening eyes. Cold water slapped against her back as she watched him.

'Eni did say,' Kora added lightly. It was a terrible habit she had formed. Whenever Madi got that *look* in his eye. Whenever he felt compelled to bring her up, she would follow up with a comment on Eni. She wondered if he had noticed it.

His face darkened. 'Yeah, he was right; we just needed to wait.'

Kora could see the memories flood over his mind, tormenting him as they tugged on his guilt and jealousy. She shifted closer to him.

'It wasn't a great time,' she said sympathetically, 'for any of us.'

It really wasn't. They had not left the palace of Nri willingly. One minute they were in the palace, the next they were *here* on Urukpuru and Naala was nowhere in sight.

Any feeling she had on the matter had been quickly overshadowed by Madi and Eni, particularly Eni. In the early days, it got so bad that he had to be kept under constant sedation.

Everything shifted once they received word on the Eze's death. Eni had even calmed down long enough to spearhead a plan to find the lost girl. It might have even worked had Eni not backed out of it at the last minute.

No explanation. No reason. Just no. That was when Madi, in a fit of rage, had desecrated a section of the Amaghị's Idu. In hot pursuit of Eni.

'She's here now … she's a *twin*,' he said, shaking his head incredulously. 'I'm still trying to wrap my head around that one.'

'So is she, I think,' she added. She could tell that Naala hated the term. 'Hopefully,

Eni can talk to her.' Madi tensed and Kora realised she had just entered dangerous territory.

'Right—' he bit the word '—or I could.'

Kora felt a scorching heat burn across her chest. How could anyone be so oblivious? 'It's probably best coming from one person, and Eni is likely to be the most *effective*,' Kora pressed. She shouldn't have. She could see he was seething and yet, 'Oh, come on, Madi, you can't be oblivious to it.'

'Oblivious to *what?*' he said, eyes narrowing.

'Why are you getting annoyed at *me?*' A lump had formed in her throat. She *hated* when he looked at her like that. Like she was nothing.

'I'm not,' Madi said, softening; 'I just want to help my friend, but apparently, I'm *ineffective.*'

He looked young with his eyes drooped and mouth pouted. Kora could see him now, a little boy with folded arms, hurt at how unfair life seemed to be.

'I am her *friend* too,' Kora said softly, 'but notice that I'm not annoyed by the fact that Eni might be the best person to talk to her.'

'It's not a fact. You don't know that for sure.'

'I think it's clear that they have a ... connection,' Kora insisted. At times they looked at each other like they were prepared to kill, or die. She couldn't tell which one but both made her uncomfortable. She glanced up at Madi's hardened face. 'Madi, come on – you've seen it too; for all the time you spend looking at her, you must have seen the way she looks at him.'

'I don't look at her,' Madi said quietly and Kora's heart squeezed out a weak beat.

'You're lying.' she murmured as she cut past her pain. 'I know you're lying because I spend a lot of time looking at you.'

He threw a pained glance at her. 'Kora,' he said, wavering.

'Oh, don't do that,' Kora huffed, waving her hands as she stepped up from the akwa nest. 'Don't pity me. I'm not the least bit troubled by this situation. It will resolve itself. You will understand that they have a connection and that we ...' she stopped and turned to hide her expression from him. 'That we ... we ... we'll see,' she managed, throwing her hands up in the air and looking back at Madi with an impudent smile. 'Then you'll stop being annoyed at Eni.'

'I'm not annoyed with him,' Madi protested as Kora scoffed. 'I'm just ... he's not what he seems to be; he's not perfect.'

'No one is, Madi.'

He paused. 'I just don't understand how he could be so *determined* to find her and then change his mind like that,' he said as he snapped his fingers. 'Yes, he was right – she did find us – but what if she didn't? He was so steadfast about it, all because the Isi said so. I hadn't taken him to be such a *puppet.*'

Kora sighed as the ghosts of past arguments flourished within Madi's eyes. He still resented the Amaghị for trying to use his brother to get to the Eze's weapons.

'I just don't understand why no one else can see it ... they are liars, Kora. Full of secrets—and not to mention the weird things that they do, holding those nnunus captive, spying with those blasted hamerkops.'

'It's complicated.' It was all Kora could manage. It wasn't that she couldn't understand Madi's reservations. She had always been able to understand them. It was Madi who couldn't seem to understand the other perspective. He never seemed to remember that it was the Amaghị who had saved all of their lives twice over; first from the village attacks and then in the palace.

Kora opened her mouth to say more but a strange tickle caught her throat and filled her nostrils, causing her to cough. It was tangy and sharp like ... smoke?

'Is something burning?' Kora said, glancing at the ọkụ flame, but it looked perfectly normal.

'I don't—' Madi started as the sounds of screams engulfed his words. Kora's eyes widened as they both bolted out of Madi's quarters.

When they entered the hallway, clouds of thick, dark smoke drifted over them. Kora could see crowds of people rushing up and down the hallway. Her eyes stung and her throat closed up so tight that she began to choke.

'You need to get out of here,' Madi shouted at her as she coughed violently.

She looked around, gasping; she couldn't see which way was in or out. All she could see was herds of people scattering this way and that as they tried to escape a danger that they couldn't see.

Someone slammed into her and she fell back into Madi. He held her up as she let out a whooping cough. A sudden gust swept across her face and she found some relief as clean air filled her raw lungs. Her throat still tickled but she found that she could now breathe. She let out another wrenching cough and tears ran down her eyes.

Kora blinked them away to see the hallway filled with huddles of people, recovering as she was. They were surrounded by black soot. The walls were spotted with frayed holes. Kora couldn't imagine what substance could have burnt the crystal like so. With the smoke cleared, the people began to empty out of the hallway in a hurried rush.

At the end of the hall, she saw someone she thought to be Naala with her arms outstretched in a dark robe and her thick hair flowing in the air. She frowned; she had never seen Naala's hair out like that before.

'What is going on, Kora?' Eni said from behind her.

Kora glanced at him and jumped when she saw that Naala was in fact standing beside him, the hair still in the same plaits that Kora had helped her to do just hours ago. She glanced at Naala and then back to the other girl, her heart thundering as she realised the girl must be Naala's twin, Sinai.

'I don't know,' Kora croaked.

Naala frowned; she squinted at something in the distance.

Kora followed her gaze and her heart thudded at what she realised was a door engulfed in amber flames. Curls of dark smoke escaped from its corners.

'It's that room,' Kora whispered. 'It's still on fire.'

'We have to stop the spread,' Eni wheezed as he approached it.

'We'll need to get in and put it out,' Madi agreed.

'Do you think that there's someone in there?' Kora said distantly.

'If there was, I don't think that they're still alive,' Eni said tensely as flames beat against the door.

'That's Ina's room!' Sinai said rushing towards them, her eyes sparkling gold. The flames beat relentlessly against the door despite the high winds.

'We *need* to stop the fire,' Eni said.

'I could barge the door open,' Madi suggested.

'You'll burn,' Kora protested. Madi was strong, yes, but he still bled, he still hurt.

She looked at the crystal walls, gaping with large holes, as though they were nothing more than burnt parchment. This was no ordinary flame.

Madi frowned. 'You need to leave,' he insisted.

'Sinai, do you think you can use the wind as a barrier, between Madi and the flames?' Naala asked before Sinai gave a sharp nod, her eyes coated with tears.

'I can try,' she whispered, glancing back at the room.

'I don't think that's a good idea,' Kora murmured as her eyes ran over Madi's soft skin. *He thinks he can take this; he can't. I know he can't.*

'We need to do something, otherwise the fire will spread,' Eni said before glancing over at her. 'He'll be fine, Kora.'

For a moment she believed it wholeheartedly. Her worry subsided enough for her to take a step back.

'Cover me,' Madi said to Sinai, who nodded as the winds started to pick up. The air moved so fast that it formed a white mist. 'You!' Madi suddenly shouted to Kora, raising his voice to match the whipping winds. 'Step away!'

'Madi,' Kora whimpered as she let Eni pull her further back.

When Kora and Eni were far down the hall, Madi turned to Sinai. 'Ready?' She gave a brisk nod before he burst through the door, shattering the thick crystal as though it was nothing but glass. A burst of hungry flames flew into the hall.

Even from where Kora and Eni stood, the heat was unbearable. It pressed itself against her skin with a force that knocked her to the ground. Her relief came in thick swirls of air coating her, and allowing her to breathe, though it wasn't enough. The heat against her skin was scorching and the air barrier was getting thinner and thinner.

A cutting scream ran through the air. *Sinai.* The flames were too strong. *She can't keep the air barrier up.*

Okay. A strange calm washed over her. *Okay.* Kora tried to turn to Madi … she wanted to see his face … she wanted to feel safe before the flames took over.

But she couldn't; she couldn't find him; she couldn't turn; she couldn't do anything but face the flames as they started to lick her skin.

Then it all stopped.

The flames sizzled into nothing and Kora staggered to her feet, edging closer to Madi. He was still standing; for the most part, he was intact. The smoke had smudged him with soot, and she could see fresh welts sprouting on his arms. Madi stood deathly still, his gaze fixated on the room before him. One by one, they all staggered to meet him by the opened door. Kora was the last.

Her heart gave out when she saw it.

Ina lay in the destroyed room, sleeping soundly, her akwa nest untouched by the flames.

CHAPTER 22
STRANGE MAGIC

Urukpuru

Naala had never encountered a more infuriating girl. Ina stood, unabashed, as she glowered back at Madi, Naala, Sinai and Kora.

'But why should I put that foreign substance in *my* body?' she drawled.

'I felt the same way too when it was suggested for me but the ọgwụ isn't that *bad* – fine, it is a bit tangy, but it's not *bad*,' Madi tried as the girl stared blankly back at him.

Naala wanted to shake her, and for once, she wasn't the only one.

'Who cares what it tastes like! Think about what it *does*,' Kora stressed, her eyebrows curved and eyes wide. 'You are a *Descendant* and you nearly *burnt* down the settlement. The ọgwụ will help you control those powers. Madi hasn't had a single incident since he began taking it; what is there not to like?'

'Rubbish,' Ina spat, shaking her head. Despite the motion, her smooth long dreads stayed firmly placed, held tight by her extravagant *gele*. Though she wore the Amaghị's mandated robes, she had completely refashioned them. She had split the crimson skirt at the side so her dark long legs were visible and the gold cuff at her ankles shone through. At her top, she wore two long strips of cloth anchored by gold chains at her shoulders and rippling down her back alongside her foot-length dreads. It wasn't even close to protocol, yet it seemed as though the girl could get away with anything. 'I am *not* a Descendant; I am a daughter of Oyo.'

'Why does she keep saying that?' Madi muttered exasperated.

A crack cut through Ina's stoned expression, but it vanished just as quickly as it had arrived.

'Because it is true,' she replied sharply. 'I am aware that *something* bizarre happened that night. But I'm also aware that it had nothing to do with me. It is impossible. Impossible. I am a daughter of—'

'Oyo, we know,' Kora said, rolling her eyes to the heavens.

Ina stared at her silently with something cold and biting swirling through her dark eyes.

'Not only am I a daughter of Oyo, but I am a daughter of a king. The high Oba Ọsínlọ́wọ̀' she said, taking a step forward so that she towered over the other girl. 'I wouldn't expect *village folk* to understand the meaning of such a statement, but let me assure you, it puts me in a completely different remit to the likes of you.' Naala moved to Kora's side as Ina spoke; heat crawled up her skin as she fought the urge to pummel her.

'Ina, don't—' Sinai started.

'No,' Ina cut sharply before turning back to Kora. 'Let's be frank,' she said, 'let's not mince words here. I am *different*. I was born different, so I do not play by your rules. I will not take your *potions*, not when there's no *real* proof; not one single soul saw me do anything with that fire.'

'But—'

'But nothing. I'm not taking some unknown substance on a whim that relies on a logic that I know to be false. If it makes you all uncomfortable, then find solace in the fact that I am leaving for Oyo soon. Until then, do not come to me asking for rubbish,' she said curtly before turning to leave.

Madi sighed. 'I don't get it; why is it impossible for her to be both? Do they not have gods in Oyo?'

'They do, just not one that displayed the power that she did,' Kora said, staring after Ina with a frown etched on her lips. 'The Orishas had Oya, of course, but her power *really* came in the form of lightning and storms, not fire, not to the extent that Ina displayed. There was Ogun, he was a fire god … but he presented as male, and Ina … well, her powers look more like Anyanwu.'

'But *still*, lightning and fire, they're pretty much the same thing. She might still be …' Madi suggested as Kora shook her head.

'She is *not* a daughter of Oyo and she knows it,' Naala said. 'That's why she's fighting so hard.' Her words hung over the group's pressing silence.

'She's going to end up killing someone if she carries on like that,' Kora eventually muttered before turning on her heel. 'Come on, we need to head to training.'

'We?' Naala smirked at her friend. The group walked through a large set of crystal doors and out onto the patch of flat grassland sprawling down the back of the mammoth rock that the Amaghị settlement sat on.

'Yes, *us* – this time I know he'll let me stay. I've finished all my assignments, even the ones he has yet to set.'

'You read his mind?' Naala teased.

'I saw his planner,' Kora said triumphantly, but the confidence drained as she turned to face Bayo. He stormed past them with a wooden box in hand. Someone had already annoyed him, which meant Kora had no chance. 'Bayo, I...' she began pausing as his eyes darkened and nose flared, '...I know, I know,' she murmured defeated before she had started, her hands outstretched towards him in surrender as she mouthed her goodbyes.

'You're late,' he barked at them.

'We were here bef—' Madi started before he caught Bayo's expression; he flinched instinctively for his ear. '… Late, we're late.'

'Today, we move from theory to practice,' Bayo announced, placing a box by his feet.

Naala's stomach churned. Discussing Ọbara magic was one thing, but practising it? Well, that was another.

'It is not as gruesome as you may think,' Bayo muttered, his tone softening at their apprehension.

He went over to his box and opened it, bringing out an agitated mouse and a dried lily before handing it to Madi without a word. He went back to the box twice more to give a pair of mice and dried lilies to the girls also. Naala's grey mouse was calm and still, twitching curiously in her palm. Nausea gnawed at her.

'You don't want us to harm the little furry thing, do you?' Madi said, as his mouse sprang around, eagerly twisting around his fingers as he tried to control it.

'Asks the boy who wolfed down a whole goat the other day,' Bayo snapped as Madi shifted his gaze away with a deepening frown pulling at his lips.

'Do we *really* need to hold it?' Sinai said nervously, holding her mouse at arm's length, her face scrunched and her mouth downturned.

'You will do more than *hold* it. You will transfer energy from the mouse to bring fresh life into the flower.'

'Errr,' Sinai said uncertainly, jumping slightly as her mouse twitched, 'I don't know how to do that.'

'You will, and once you've mastered this, you will have a fighting chance against that beast. Right now, your powers alone cannot defeat it. You're babies. Still so inexperienced, and the Aido-Hwedo is stronger than you can imagine. Its bones are infused with centuries of power seeped from the realm. You have no chance against such a thing, unless you know how to drain its energy force.'

'But surely—' Madi paused, turning the words around his mouth '—you said that well-trained people were most efficient, right? That they didn't have to hurt … that they didn't need to drain as much energy? Well, shouldn't the practitioners who have been doing it for years handle this side of things?' Madi said.

Bayo's mouth twisted. 'Lazy boy,' he said, rapping Madi across the head. The uneasy mouse sprang out of Madi's hands, and he scrambled to get it back. 'As Descendants, what you pay will always be less than even the most skilled practitioners. Enough with the baneful questions. *Concentrate* and find your mouse's lifeform. It will feel like a heartbeat, a hum almost – find it.'

Find it? Naala thought, glancing down at the little mouse. She opened her mouth to protest but Bayo tightened his grip on his cane. A dare came to life behind his eyes.

Naala sighed, staring down at the mouse. 'You didn't really teach—'

'Concentrate,' Bayo barked. 'You have all accessed the Black and Gold realm; you do not need to be hand-held through this. Concentrate on what you are doing, and locate the *hum*.'

Naala felt for the Black and Gold realm as the warm mouse nestled between her fingers; perhaps that would help her locate the hum. That plan very quickly fell short. The power surged through her but that was the beginning and end of it. No hum. *Nothing*, she thought exasperated. Her lips were pursed so hard that they tingled.

'What is it?' Bayo drawled.

'It's not working,' she said, through clenched teeth. Of course it was not working; the Black and Gold realm had long deserted her. Her heart hammered at the thought. No, it hadn't. It couldn't have. Not when they *needed* her.

'Try hard—'

'Something has happened to my *access*,' Naala blurted. She hadn't meant to say it. She hadn't discussed it with anyone yet. She felt Sinai and Madi's gaze fall on her as heat scorched at her cheeks.

'What do you mean?'

'I can't access *things* in the same way again,' she said under her breath and Bayo arched his eyebrows with the early signs of a grin flashing across his lips.

'Of course you cannot,' Bayo said. 'You control earth materials, no?'

'I do,' Naala said carefully.

'Well, what do you expect? There are no earth materials in this land – or rather, very little. Hence why you can't feel it, but you can still feel the Black and Gold Realm, can you not?'

'Yes,' Naala said as her body relaxed. Perhaps she should have come to him with this a little sooner.

'Then, con-cen-trate,' he sounded out to her as if she were a child.

Instead of striking him, Naala shifted her position and let out a breath. Her gaze fell to the mouse and she watched it intently. Paying close attention to every movement, even that of its little hairs. She watched the beat of its heart pulsing through its body. She began to visualise the creature's warmth, its energy. Wider than its shape, light and airy. Moving to the sound of a slight thud—

'You found it?' Bayo asked, taking a step towards her.

'Maybe,' she muttered. Had she imagined it?

Bayo ignored her hesitance and nodded back to her approvingly before frowning at Sinai, who still held her mouse at a distance, bouncing at its every sudden move.

'Relax,' Bayo said, 'you'll never hear it over your own fearful heart otherwise.' He clasped his palm over hers, holding the mouse still. 'Calm yourself and feel for it.' They stood like that for a moment before he lifted his eyelids. 'You feel it?'

Sinai bit her lip as she nodded back, drawing the mouse back towards her gently.

'I need help,' Madi said nervously as he tried to catch his leaping mouse. 'Mine is broken.' His eyes widened before he grimaced. 'I think it bit me!'

'Calm down, boy,' Bayo said as he walked over to Madi. 'Be still.' He wrapped the bark cane on his shoulder. Madi grunted angrily as he tried to settle down, holding the mouse still and trying to breathe. After a moment or two of relative stillness, he sighed.

'I don't feel anything.'

Bayo looked at him curiously before taking out a small long dagger.

'Hey! Hey!' Madi cautioned. 'I can take the bark but if you cut me, I'm leaving – let the world be damned,' he warned as Bayo smirked at his outburst, shaking his head as he brought the dagger to Madi's palm and pricked the mouse. The group gasped as the mouse stirred disturbingly before settling down. Naala could see blood lining Madi's fingers.

'Try again,' Bayo said as he wiped the dagger down.

A sad look came over Madi as he looked down at the quietened mouse in his hands.

'I—' Madi started.

'Try or the mouse gets another cut ... a fatal one.'

Madi's face hardened before he concentrated. 'A hum?'

'A hum,' Bayo repeated as Madi closed his eyes, his face scrunched up until suddenly it began to relax.

'A hum,' Madi repeated nodding his head.

'You see – the blood aspect isn't always necessary. If the creature is simple enough, or the practitioner is skilled enough, you can access the energy source without opening up the being. Your access to the Black and Gold realm gives you *sensitivity* to the energy that most don't have. Madi, your access has been dulled somewhat by the ogwu – but blood ... well, blood makes it all that much clearer. The beast that you will fight is not a mouse; it's not even a boar nor an elephant or like any other earthly being. The Aido-Hwedo is a *mystical* beast and therefore in order to access its life force you will *need* to make it bleed.'

The field settled into silence. A heaviness pressed on Naala as she watched the blood now trickle down Madi's fingers.

'You are all feeling your mouse's energy-source, its *Ike-Obi*. Tap into that frequency, become accustomed to its hum, breathe with it – and when you have control over it, or at least some of it, try and pour it into the flower at your feet, as you would pour water from one bucket to the next— Ay! Madi, I would hurry it up if I were you; your mouse might not have very long.'

Naala closed her eyes and tried once again to feel for the energy force, but her mind was filled with the image of the bleeding mouse in Madi's palm, Eni, the Isi, Siwunmi, the Eze. Her eyes sprang open and Bayo's beady eyes came into sharp focus.

'Concentrate,' he snapped. Naala sighed but she closed her eyes all the same. 'Count with it. *Understand* the frequency.'

Naala followed the hum as it resonated in even beats through her palm. She reached out for it, letting out a gasp when she grasped something *solid*. The hum. She held on to it, and tipped it down at the flower at her feet.

An ache rang through her as her knees buckled. Her eyelids were as heavy as lead. She blinked and she was on the ground, the mouse escaping from her slackened palms.

'Whaa,' she tried to speak but the words were like boulders in her mouth. She was so tired. Beyond tired. It took all her energy to open her eyes, and when she did she saw Madi on the floor. Bayo was bent down to his knees, grinning at the two spent students.

'Good,' he chuckled as he gestured at the flowers by their feet. Her heart squeezed limply. The petals were no longer dry. They were now fleshed with new life. Their crumpled pale beige tone was now brilliant white.

Naala felt a wave of nausea run over her body as Bayo lectured: 'As is expected, you transferred some of your own life forces. As bad as it feels, it is good. No one is able to do it on their first try, but it's important that you understand how not to do it. Taking from your own energy is very inefficient and dangerous – but also part of the process. Most practitioners end up in a week-long sleep on the first attempt, or dead. Be glad you have access to another energy force other than your body.' Bayo stood up, grinning, before throwing a glance over at Sinai. Something cold gripped at Naala's neck.

Sinai was still standing. Her eyes were closed and her mouth moved slightly as the mouse shifted in her grasp. A flush of flowers began to grow at her feet – not just the dead lily, but bright coloured-flowers, thick and rich with life.

Stop, Naala thought as she saw the flower mound grow. If one measly flower had done *this* to her, how much more would it be for the girl who had created a mound? Naala tried to pull up to her feet. Every fibre of her body screamed in agony.

'Stoooaa,' she tried. She wanted to scream. She wanted to shake the girl, but all she could do was stumble backwards. Instead of the floor, Naala found herself in someone's arms. *Eni?*

'Rest on me,' he said gently, his eyebrows pulled together as he scanned her face.

No, she wanted to say as she tried to look back at Sinai. Her lips were parted and her wide eyes glazed with tears. Sinai opened her hands and let out a strangled sound as the wind carried dust particles into the air. All that was left of her mouse.

'Interesting,' Bayo breathed, his brightening eyes fixed firmly on Sinai. Her breaths turned quick and shallow as she looked down at her empty hands. When she looked back up, streams of tears had coated her cheeks. She shook her head before bolting off.

Naala tried to lift herself and go after the girl but her body shook from the effort.

'Just give her a moment,' Eni said into her ears. 'Give yourself a moment.' His arms clung around her and her slumped head rested against his chest.

'Eni, did you disrupt my lesson to get a hug?' Bayo said, as he crouched to inspect Sinai's flower mound.

'No – I've come with a message from the Isi. She needs you; the council is meeting.'

'What meeting? There's no meeting today,' Bayo said, looking at Eni for the first time.

'It is … last minute,' Eni said carefully. 'Things have got worse.'

'Worse how?' he said, getting up to his feet. 'I'm not going anywhere without an explanation.'

'The beast.'

Bayo froze. His eyes gleamed with fresh understanding, but he asked all the same. 'What about the beast?'

Eni took a deep breath. 'It's started killing.'

CHAPTER 23

A POOL OF SILVER

Urukpuru

The crystal pipes above him whistled with the high winds. A storm was coming.

Good, Eni thought. A storm would mean no reports. The gusts would filter through the hollow pipes that formed the Idu's ceilings, flushing out the little birds hidden within them.

It wasn't *quite* right to call the folded crystal pipes a ceiling. On its surface, the pipes were innocuous. They sat so high that onlookers would have to bend their necks to see them. During the day, the crystals would shoot off bright reflected sunbeams; at night they seemed to blend seamlessly with shadowed night. Making it near impossible to spot the yellow-spotted hamerkops perched within the pipes, ears preened to listen and record the unsuspecting speakers below.

Naala shifted and Eni's attention fell on the girl nestled in his arms. Her mouth, now slightly ajar, released a steady stream of soft snores. Warmth spread across his chest. How long until she too discovered the Amaghi's tricks?

He could see it already: her sharp mind peeling through the layers of the settlement; her bright eyes bursting with questions at every corner. The Amaghi had no idea what they had got themselves into when they had brought Esinaala to their Idu. His smile deepened.

On more than one occasion, Eni had even contemplated telling her. Countless times he had been but a hair's breadth from telling her all he knew of the Amaghị – their secrets, lies and plots. Only, he knew she would ask the one question he wasn't prepared to answer: how did he know?

'Fo, fold-ed went tickle boar,' she mumbled and a laugh escaped from his chest. Though still deep in sleep, she moved at the sound. He brought his hand to her temple to soothe her. Tight soft curls of black hair rested on the edges of her scalp, and he brushed them to and fro until her breathing was slow and steady.

She had been asleep for nearly two full days since her session with Bayo. No one could deny that the timing couldn't be worse. His throat tightened, as it always did, when he thought about the beast's rampage through Furuefu. His only relief was that the Aturu had contained the Aido-Hwedo, but for how long? Soon their energy would wane, and then what? What else could they do but wait?

They had tried to force Madi to wake to no avail and Eni refused to let them experiment with Naala. He had kept at her side to ensure that they didn't try anything underhand. He was well-versed in how far the Amaghị would go to get what they wanted.

Eni traced her face gently with his finger; as he turned his wrist, he couldn't help but take note of the garish scar he now bore. A relic from his time in the palace, when an abara had pierced his skin. With Naala in his arms, the memory of that day, moon-cycles ago, played vividly in his mind.

*

Naala's eyes were wide and pleading as she stepped away from him in the palace of Nri, with the emerald crystal in her hand. At first he hadn't understood what she had meant; the words had rushed out of her mouth but they hadn't seemed to reach him.

She turned and, finally, he understood. She was leaving him. *No! Why?* They were so close. They *had* the crystal. They had won.

His heart hollowed as Naala sprinted down the palace halls. *Go after her,* his body sang, but before he could move, their guide, Okeke, pulled a daga out of his garments.

'She's leaving! The girl is leaving! She's taken the crystal!' he bellowed, forfeiting his disguise as he called out to the shadows.

'No,' Eni grunted, blocking Okeke as he sprang towards Naala with bloodthirst in his eyes. In that second, Naala had gone from friend to enemy. Out of the shadows more assailants thundered over him – each one hungry for blood they would never taste. His fists pounded on flesh as he dodged most, but not all, of their blows. Still, he felt no pain. How could he? If he let his guard down for a second, if he allowed himself to feel *anything*, he would stumble. They would get to her.

Naala. He turned his head to the end of the hall. She was nowhere in sight. Nothing was in sight. The darkness had come for him.

Eni woke up thrashing in the back of a dark cart. The weight of sleep almost suffocated him. He heaved against it. *Where is she?* His head was too heavy to lift, the right side squashing against his arm. Kora lay in front of him, her eyes closed, blood trickling down the side of her face. Tension released from his shoulders when he noted the rise and falls of her chest. Eni darted his eyes around the room. Madi's large legs sprawled beside him. There were others here but ... not *her.*

The cart bounced. They were moving. They were leaving the city. Eni tried to speak but it felt as though cotton filled his mouth.

'Silence, boy!' a voice hissed from behind him.

Eni used all of his strength to turn his body and his heart stopped. She really wasn't here. They were leaving and she wasn't here. He let out a cry, but it came out as a series of grunts stuck in his throat. He felt the strength return to his limbs and he began to fling them to and fro. He felt a heavy weight hold his arms steady.

'Settle,' a voice warned in his ear.

Eni kicked back and came crashing down. He delivered punches as hard as his numbed body could offer. Yet none of it mattered when he felt a sting at his neck and, again, the darkness came.

He woke up, slow and heavy. His mouth was still full of cotton. When he turned, he jolted at the pale woman standing over him. The Isi watched silently as he thrashed.

'What is wrong with him?' she asked Chukwudi, who stood by the door.

'We don't know, but he's been like this since they took him.'

'Could it be a reaction to the darts?'

'There are side effects, yes, but not like this.'

'Then what is it?' she asked, drawing closer as Eni fought to form words.

'Where. Is. She?' he managed, tugging at the ropes clutching his arms.

The Isi's head snapped back to Chukwudi.

'The girl?' she asked, aghast.

'We believe so.'

'Emenike,' the Isi hushed softly, her eyebrows pulled tightly and her violet eyes glittering with emotion, 'this will do you no good.'

'Where. Is. She?' he was pleading now, his voice wet and desperate.

'Isi,' Chukwudi warned as the woman moved closer to the manic boy.

'The girl will return. We know of this for certain now,' she said, before gesturing to the tearing ropes, 'but *this*, this will do you no good. We can't keep you in the deep sleep indefinitely. It's not good for the body. Whatever this is, you must wipe it away. Give way to your common sense. Or there will be consequences. Consequences that you may not have bargained for,' she noted, her voice turning cool with each word.

The rope holding his right arm snapped. He attempted to clamber out of the akwa nest but a familiar sense of heaviness overtook him.

'No,' he garbled, as he looked down at his chest to find a dart embedded deep in his skin.

The darkness came.

He woke up slower this time, his mind waking before his body. It gave him time to think. This time, he wouldn't thrash. It wasn't effective. How would he find Naala if he was constantly sedated? No, this time he would exercise patience. He would listen and then he would act.

He quietened down. He ate his meals and he settled into being a good guest.

'I'm getting good at flying those things,' he said quietly to Madi and Kora one day. They were in Madi's quarters, scheming in the dead of the night, as they had once done in Furuefu. 'And I think they're beginning to really trust me.' He had been watching the riders fly the efe-efe baskets in and out of Urukpuru, and he had even begun to build up a rapport with some of them. 'If I offer to start working with them, they'll agree, and when they do, I'll have access to the stable key. We'll wait till nightfall, take one of the baskets and start our search. First at the palace, and then we scour the lands for her.'

'You don't think we should *at least* talk to them about it?' Kora said hesitantly. 'They might let us go, so then we wouldn't have to sneak around or steal anything. What? Don't look at me like that. Let's consider *who* we're dealing with; they have eyes *everywhere*. The chances of us getting caught are—'

'Low,' Madi insisted, 'but if we tell them, they will refuse. You know they will, Kora. How many times have they tried to convince us that she'll come here? But I've asked around and they are doing *nothing* to find her. Nothing at all.'

'She might come here, she might find us,' Kora suggested, her eyes dimming as she spoke. Eni knew she didn't believe that. Kora had given up but Eni couldn't.

'We can't tell them,' Eni said. He didn't enjoy enforcing his opinion on any person or situation. His way was to listen, weigh up all sides and express his take on it. He had no time for that now. He couldn't rely on a miracle and he certainly had no capacity to weigh up the balanced view. He didn't care if he would have to leap off from the floating island himself, he *would* find her.

Nights later, Eni entered the stables. The looming moon hung low in the sky, painting the dark night with pale strokes of white dust. The only other source of light was from Madi's window, where he and Kora waited for his signal.

Eni took a deep breath. He could do this, couldn't he? His last attempt at riding the efe-efe basket had resulted in a crash, but he didn't have time for any more practice. The longer he stayed here, the further Naala pulled from him. There was no time for doubts. He took a deep breath and drew open the stable doors. He exhaled as though he had been punched in the gut. He felt like he had.

There, in the stables, stood the Isi. Eni's stomach pulled at the sight of her.

'Fools are predictable,' she said to him, her lips pressed tightly together before she released a sigh, her fingers rubbing at her temples. A chill ran up his spine as her violet eyes settled on him, her white afro glistening under Urukpuru's pale light beams. She brought a gloved hand to his cheek. 'But endearing at times.' Her face was as still as marble but he felt the sea of rage crashing within her. Eni gently focused on ripples of her emotion, smoothing them where he could.

'I was just—'

'Do not lie to me,' the Isi said sharply and his heart seized. She scoffed lightly. 'You really think I don't know what you're doing? Your little trick? Your childish attempts to pacify me?'

Eni's heart thundered against his chest. She knew. He had always been sensitive to people's moods. He had always known when people were angry, happy or excited. They wore it on their skin, a light mist that only he seemed to be able to see. As he grew, he had realised that he could *adjust* those moods. He could calm a frantic person down simply by concentrating on the ripples within the invisible layer that housed their emotions. He used it sparingly, and only when it would help people. He felt it wrong otherwise, like he was cheating at a game with players who didn't even understand the rules. He had never discussed it with anyone.

'You think you're good at lying, Emenike, but you are not. You're just willing to do that which others wouldn't do,' she said, looking back at him blandly. 'You are not skilled; you are brash and that is only ever effective when people *want* to believe you, but I do not. I want to keep you safe.'

He didn't reply. Two members of the Aturu emerged from the shadows. *She's going to kill me.* The thought came and went. He hadn't known the Amaghi to kill but what did he really know of them? For all he knew, they had already killed Naala; perhaps that was why they discouraged them from trying to find her. *Naala.* He couldn't die without seeing her again.

'I just want to see her.' His voice wavered as he spoke. When had he become so *tired?*

'And so you shall.' The Isi gestured to one of the men. 'If that is what it takes,' she murmured.

The man bent down to the ground, drawing a daga from his waistband. Eni tensed but the daga didn't touch him; instead the man drew it across his own wrist.

'What are you doing?' Eni gasped, snatching at the daga. He was the only one who had reacted. Was this man *mad?* Were they all mad?

They stood there, still, as the blood trickled down to the ground, pooling in a silver liquid.

Eni paused. 'What...?' he gasped, backing away as both men began to chant. Their voices drifted in the moonlit night like fireflies. Eni threw a glance at the Isi; her stone face was impassive as she motioned to the bleeding man.

When Eni glanced down at the silver pool, a figure formed. Her hair was rougher than he had last seen it, thin spirally tufts broke out of her braids; it coated her with a softness that made his stomach lighten. A thin layer of sweat sat on her deep, earthy skin. She gleamed fantastically in the sun. Her dark eyes were sadder than he had ever seen them, punctuated by the slight curl in her full lips.

'Naala,' he whispered; his heart crunched under the weight of her. He shook his head. 'It's a trick.' Yet he couldn't seem to look away. 'It's ...' Her eyebrows knitted in thought, she brought her finger to her lip and brushed it back and forth. 'Her,' he said, 'it's her.'

'Naala,' he called out, falling beside the pool that contained her. She didn't respond. Rather, the image scattered into a chase. Naala was running through the forest, a voracious beast lumbering behind her with bloodthirst in its eyes.

'What is this?' he yelled. 'Is this happening now? Naala!' he called, but in a flash, the image transformed once again. She was clinging on to the back of a nnunu woman, her eyes firmly shut. The image shifted and she was *here* in Urukpuru. She stood in one of the ẹkas, her hand pressed against the rocky walls. The pool flickered back to silver.

'What was that?' he said, his voice scrapping across his throat.

The Isi regarded him coolly before speaking. 'What you saw was the chain of events that would happen, if you stay here and wait. You see, Emenike, you've made this situation far more drastic than it ever needed to be. It has always been that simple. You will see her again *if* you do as I say and wait. If you let this foolishness consume you. If you attempt to leave, steal an efe-efe basket or whatever else, you will throw everything off balance, and I promise you, you will never see her again.' She guided him up from the ground by the chin. 'Unlike you, Ọbara magic does not lie. Unlike me, it is not forgiving.'

She shifted her gaze down to the ground where a feeble groan sounded. A frown tugged on Eni's mouth. The man who had opened his arm was slumped and still, in a pool of blood. A cold sweat ran down Eni's back.

'No,' he roared, crashing down to the man. His hand gripping his cold wrist in an attempt to stop the bleeding. There was no pulse. 'He's dead. *He is dead.*'

'Choices are important, Emenike,' the Isi said above him, 'even when you think you aren't making them. This was an unnecessary sacrifice; I hope the next choice that you make will come at a lower cost.'

*

Naala shifted again in his arms, pulling him out of the memory. Eni blinked as he found that she had been watching him; for how long, he couldn't say.

'You have that crease on your forehead,' she said, her voice still thick with sleep. 'What were you thinking?'

'Nothing,' he replied. 'Nothing at all.'

CHAPTER 24
CALL IN THE SKY

Urukpuru

Whispers followed her every step as Sinai walked through the halls of the Idu. They no longer bothered her as they once did. Something else had taken that role. Something she couldn't seem to settle. In a matter of days, hours even, they would be called to fight. Her fingers trembled at the thought.

'You have an unprecedented aptitude for Ọbara magic,' Bayo had said. Sinai had never really had an aptitude for anything in her life. Now that she did, it felt more like an insult than a compliment.

Sinai paused, glancing down at her palms. She could still feel the weight of the mouse drop to almost nothing. She could still see its ashes swept away in the wind. When Naala and her had used the crystal, she had felt driven, as though it was the crystal itself acting, not her. It had been different with the mouse; she had felt no better than a thief.

A flutter turned her attention to the ceiling. The storm had settled and the birds had returned to the crystal tunnels. Sinai glanced up at the honeycomb structure; through the gaps she could see the sapphire-blue sky clear as though she were outside. A crease formed on her brow as she spotted a lone cloud. Odd. From that angle, it almost resembled Nsibidi.

'Fly?' she wondered out loud, as she pieced together the three lines that met at the middle with two curved lines either side of it. She had seen images in the clouds before – a rabbit or a giraffe, sometimes even a face – but nothing like this. Nothing that was so *precise*.

Her forehead knitted. What was that? A black spot had formed in the centre of the cloud. Pricks of fear ran up her neck. It was *growing*. No, not growing; it was falling, fast enough to crush her.

Sinai leapt backwards just before the dark figure landed in the spot in which she had previously stood.

'Nwamara?' Sinai asked, clutching at her chest. The gold-tipped nnunu woman ruffled her feathers.

'Ndewo, twin girl,' the bird-woman said, before hovering towards her. Her head tilted to the side as she blinked her large eyes. 'You are scared?'

'I'm not,' Sinai breathed as Nwamara frowned. 'Well, okay, I'm *shocked*. You just sprang up out of nowhere.'

Nwamara watched intently before breaking into a smile. 'Is this a human pastime?' she beamed as Sinai creased her forehead. 'You called for me and now you are shocked; is it a requirement for me to be shocked as well?' She spread her dark wings, her feet lifting off the ground, as she bobbed up and down in the air.

'No, it's not,' Sinai replied, caught on Nwamara's words.

'Call you? I didn't call you.'

'Curious,' Nwamara said, before lifting her chest and placing her claws on her hips. 'Yes, I too am shocked as I didn't know that I had been called.' Nwamara's voice was now unnaturally low and raspy. She blinked at Sinai. 'Am I doing the pastime correctly?'

'It's not a pastime, Nwamara,' Sinai said, 'and were you *mimicking* me? Is that what you think I sound like?'

'That is how all humans sound.' The bird-woman nodded before fluttering up and gesturing toward the broken cloud. 'Given that we can both see the call, I'm confused as to what the goal of this pastime actually is.'

'Nwamara …' Sinai started, her eyes still fixed on the clouds. It had been a call?

The bird-woman's eyes widened; an impressive feat given how large they had been to start with. 'Oh. Oh, I see. Yes, yes, yes – I see! The point is, there *is* no point?

Oh, you humans are good,' she said excitedly. 'At pastimes,' she added quickly, 'but on a whole you can be quite disastrous at almost everything else.'

'Nwamara ...'

'Very curious beings,' the bird-woman mused.

'Nwamara, I didn't send any message,' Sinai said. *So who did?* She glanced at Nwamara's wings, free and majestic, unlike the nnunus she had seen roaming the Amaghị's halls.

'It is what they wish,' Chukwudi had declared stonily when Naala had inquired. 'Their way of repaying us, I suppose.'

Sinai had felt uneasy about his response; she couldn't quite understand why, upon *saving* the nnunus, the Amaghị had kept them in servitude in their Idu. On more than one occasion she had tried to ask the nnunus directly but they didn't respond to her. They would back away from her, trembling at her words and filling her with guilt.

'Is it safe for you to be here?' she asked, ushering the nnunu to a corner.

Nwamara suddenly let out a hawking sound.

'Nwamara,' Sinai hissed, glancing around, her ears strained for any sudden movements.

'Strange magic,' Nwamara said as she turned to watch the crystal walls.

'Strange m—?' Sinai murmured as she followed the bird-woman's gaze. 'You hear the whispers too?'

'I hear longing, fear, pain, love and hope,' Nwamara said as Sinai watched the red vines beneath the wall glow.

Sinai shuddered. 'What is it?'

'Strange magic.'

'Ọbara magic, you mean?' she said as Nwamara shook her head in disgust.

'Twin girl,' Nwamara said.

'Yes? Oh, my name is Sinai, in case you forg—'

'Why did you call me to this place? Are you ready to escape?'

'Escape?' Sinai laughed at the serious expression plastered on the bird-woman's face. 'Nwamara, we're not prisoners!'

'I think you might be,' Nwamara added, 'like my poor sisters.'

That wiped Sinai's smile off her face. Her chest tightened as she looked back at the nnunu woman.

'They say … they say they wish to stay …'

'They don't know what they wish,' Nwamara hawked as she beat her wings. 'Strange magic.'

'It's not all bad,' Sinai said quietly. 'Ọbara magic, I mean – strange magic … it's a tool. If it's used by bad people then it's bad, but good people can use it too,' she said, repeating Bayo's words. Though saying them out loud, it felt as hollow and senseless as the crystal tunnel ceilings.

'No, twin girl.'

'Honestly, Sinai is perfectly fine. In fact it's preferable.'

'Good people use magic from the Black and Gold Realm or no magic at all; they don't use strange magic because strange magic always takes and never gives.'

A shiver ran through Sinai's spine as the feeling returned. A sudden weight leaving her palm. Dust grating between her fingers. Was that what she had done? Taken that which did not belong to her? She'd be lying if she said that wasn't how she felt.

'Well, you should probably know that I've used it. If you truly think it's bad, well, you should know.' Sinai's cheeks burned as she struggled to meet Nwamara's eyes.

Nwamara shook her head. 'You *have* to stop, twin girl.'

'Sinai,' Sinai muttered.

'Strange magic seeps into your soul and breaks it apart so that eventually you will need it to fill the cracks that it left,' Nwamara said, gesturing to the cavitied ceiling.

Sinai's mouth dried. The heaviness that seemed to be permanently at her chest pressed down further. *Unprecedented aptitude.* If the art was indeed evil, what did it say about her that she could grasp it like so?

'Nwamara, the Aido-Hwedo has started to *kill*; what else can we do?'

'Is that why you asked me here?' Nwamara said, as she ruffled into her feathers. 'We heard about the killings too.' She pulled out a small object wrapped in brown cloth.

Touch.

Sinai knew it long before Nwamara pulled the cloth open. The double crystals.

She could feel their energy pulsating as Nwamara brought them into the light.

'I can't use that,' she whispered as she edged towards Nwamara's claw. Something seized her stomach. *The kingdom will burn.* 'No!' She pulled away and turned her back on the nnunu. 'You don't understand. If we evoke those crystals, things get worse; we exchange one big problem for a colossal one.'

'Yes. Such is the path to balance.'

Sinai turned back at her incredulously. 'No, Nwamara, you're not human so you don't understand: we can't throw away lives like that.'

'Humans understand nothing of life, of Ndu. You must evoke it,' the nnunu woman protested, flying in front of Sinai. 'Only this will restore order.'

'There is another way,' Sinai insisted, stepping away. 'We have devised a plan and we can defeat the beast another way.'

'Oh,' Nwamara tutted, her expression softening, 'your outlook is very narrow. Your approach dictated by what you think is correct and not what you *know* to be right. You must open your eyes, or we will not survive this.'

There was something hard in her gaze. Sinai had seen that look before in Meekulu Kaurandua's eyes before the guards took her away.

'I don't want to mess this up,' Sinai said, her voice thick. She couldn't be this person forever, always moving to the wrong beat, always with one foot out of step. Look at what it had cost her. The old woman should have been alive had Sinai been more *focused.*

Nwamara looked at her carefully before attempting to place the crystals in the girl's hand.

Sinai jumped back, letting them clang on the rose gold floor.

'Then don't. Strange magic is not an option. Take the crystals and deal with what happens head-on. Yes, yes?'

'Nwamara, that's simply not a good idea.'

'Why?'

'Because I might use it.'

'If you use it – it is because you *should* use it; it is because given all the options that you have at that moment, you've chosen that – no?'

'Well, in theory, yes—'

'You are Amuru ha abuo; you should keep it, and if you don't want to use it and prefer to break your soul down with blood magic, you can – else, you can decide to use the stone, but in both situations, you should have it.'

Sinai looked down at the crystal. 'Nwamara, I just don't—' Sinai started before the bird-woman suddenly took flight.

'Open your eyes!' Nwamara called as she flew up into the air.

Sinai watched her go, speechless, until something gripped at her throat. She looked down at the brown cloth pouch at her feet.

'Oh, she didn't,' Sinai muttered, her stomach dropping as she looked around at the empty halls. 'She didn't!' she exclaimed.

CHAPTER 25
THE PRICE

City of Nri

'Back again, are we?' Ikenna emerged from behind him. Olu wanted nothing more than to rip the grin plastered on the man's face but he willed himself as still as granite. What was he doing *here* of all places?

'Olu,' Ikenna chortled, 'don't tell me that *you're* surprised? Don't tell me that you are just *now* discovering that I have you followed. I expected more vigilance from you.' He peered around the Nzuzo garden. 'I know all about your visits to this place. Fear not, I won't tell anyone that you talk to yourself.' A gleam formed in his eyes. 'I won't tell anyone about your *other* nighttime visits either.'

Olu's face warmed. Chiaza. Her face burned in his mind. Her thick rolls of black, moss-like hair that reminded him so much of Sinai's. Her skin, softer than fresh hibiscus petals. Her akwa nest, empty since her husband had been sent off to the Kingdom of Nekor on Olu's command. So Ikenna knew about Chiaza. He felt naked before the man he had once considered his friend.

'That's not—' he started, his heartbeat thrumming in his ears before forcing himself to pause. No. He refused to enter that discussion.

Ikenna watched him with an arched brow before he shook his head. 'Olu, when will you see that no one cares? You want so much to be holier than thou, whilst doing the same things that we *all* do. You want to paint a picture of yourself as this benevolent saviour? The tortured hero? Why? For who?'

His questions seemed almost genuine but Olu kept his mouth tightly shut all the same.

Ikenna released a sigh. 'You *wanted* her and so you took her; why is that so hard for you to bear?'

'You don't know what you're talking about,' Olu said tightly. What did Ikenna know of the situation? He had no inkling of how cruel Chiaza's husband had been. He hadn't seen the dark bruises scattered over her supple skin. It had been a choice between killing the man and sending him away. Olu had entered her nest, on her request, long after his departure. It was shameful, yes, but not his design.

'But I do,' Ikenna said. 'I know you. Why do you think I requested the Obara oath? You think after years of watching you, killing alongside you, that *I* didn't know that you would keep a promise? Of course, you would have – but it would have broken you. You, my friend, needed something to blame. Something concrete to hold on to as we do what is necessary to move this kingdom forward.'

Ikenna tilted his head as he examined Olu. 'I see how you have begun to look at me. Brother, it is okay. If you need to pin it on me, that's fine. I can take it. I can be the demon in the fantasy that you lean on—' he shrugged '—but know this—' he stalked towards him '—under your excuses, under your pretty language and manufactured woes, you are far worse than I, and *I* accept that. I accept *you*, brother!' he slapped his hand on Olu's face. The two men regarded each other sternly before Ikenna sneered and pulled away.

'Any word on the search for that crystal?'

'It has yet to be found by those searching,' Olu said, his heart quickening. He hated discussing the crystal. It felt worse than an abara sword burning against his back.

When Sinai had whispered the whereabouts of the crystal all that while ago, Olu had known that he was dead. He was bound between a promise to Sinai and an oath to Ikenna. There was no question that he would fulfil the girl's wishes, which meant that his blood would be forfeited.

Olu's blood was tied in an oath he had made to Ikenna. An oath to help Ikenna become the next Eze. What greater help could there be other than the Earth

Mother's Crystal? What greater betrayal was there than Olu keeping it from the man?

When he had entered the Eze's quarters, Olu had expected to feel the excruciating sensation that would overtake him every time he attempted to act against the blood oath; a warning of sorts. The pain would seize his heart first, leaving him gasping for air, before it rippled across his whole body. He would feel as though he was being torn apart from the inside out. The pain would cease once he had aligned himself once again on a path that would ensure Ikenna's place on the throne.

He hadn't felt it. Even when he had followed Sinai's instruction and discovered the crystal embedded in a shattered stone. Olu had even brought a hamerkop with him, praying that he would have enough time to hand it to the bird, who had been instructed to take it to Ina.

But he had felt nothing. He had pocketed the crystal in a thick cloth without issue, carrying it around with him, unsure as to what to do next.

His next fright came when Ikenna had first asked about it. Olu had stiffened, feeling the small weight wrapped within the folds of his garment. He had cursed himself for not discarding it earlier. He would lie, yes, but what of when they discovered the crystal on his dead body? Yet he had survived without so much as a twinge.

Over time Olu had realised that his blood oath did not stop him from keeping the crystal from Ikenna. It didn't stop him from lying to him or even going against his wishes. It prevented him from acting in a way that would hinder the man's ascension to the throne. That was it. It seemed as valuable as Ikenna thought the Earth Mother's Crystal was, it would do nothing to get him on the throne. At least, for now.

'Damn them,' Ikenna said under his breath. 'I need that stone. Especially now with that blasted plague spreading across the city. Those filthy squalors are ruining everything.'

The egbu, the blood illness, had come suddenly and cruelly, capturing the Kingdom within a matter of weeks, taking hold of its victims and ravishing their bodies from the inside out. It started with blistering sores and ended with a horrific death. The Timbuktu students theorised that the illness had stemmed from a contaminated well in the squalor and that, if it wasn't isolated, it would spread catastrophically throughout the Kingdom. The city was on standstill as the palace healers worked tirelessly for a cure.

Ikenna had barricaded the palace to keep the illness far away from the nobles. Every person within the palace walls now needed to undergo an inspection every morning. If they exhibited any signs of the deadly disease, they were banished immediately – a fate that had only impacted the servants.

Ikenna's approach to the illness had been the only thing that the Obis had collectively agreed on since the Eze's disappearance.

'We were gaining control,' Ikenna said, swallowing hard. 'I *had* them. I had nearly all of them on my side; Akunna was the last one and then this illness comes and ruins everything. Now with his son dead, Akunna is *untouchable* and he's rallying them, Olu – I've even heard word that Arinze and Wale have deserted to his side.'

'We're still ahead.'

'Ahead? We're rods behind where we need to be. I *had* them. They would all rather this city be a body without a head than have me lead it.' He chewed on that thought. 'If I claim the throne right now, Akunna will dry up our funds. Arinze would halt trade, and with production so low with this blasted illness, we wouldn't last a month.'

'If Akunna claimed the throne, Iben would halt the health efforts and reports, Jideofo would disrupt the water supply, and you hold the army.'

'They wouldn't last a week.'

'Exactly – you are still in this game. You still have the upper hand.'

'In the game,' Ikenna scoffed. 'But can I claim a victory?' His thin lips tightened into a deep scowl. 'Every day we endure hours of back and forth at the Obi meetings. Projects are being dropped and little is getting done. All because we do not have a *leader* – we have a group of squabbling birds, and there's nothing that I can do to change that. Obi Akunna would never side with me after what happened with his son … but if I had that crystal, do you think any of them would dare to side with him? Do you think I couldn't get to Akunna, force him to reveal the secrets to the financial crypts that he holds so dear?'

Olu took a deep breath. 'It is here somewhere.'

'Ọbara magic.'

'What?'

'That's my theory; I have to use Ọbara magic to solve my issues.'

'Surely it has gone too far,' Olu said, his stomach churning at the prospect of more rituals.

'Look how successful it has been; look at what we've achieved with it,' he said eagerly. 'You said it yourself – look at the claim we now hold over the Kingdom. If it wasn't for Obi Jideofo's foolish daughter, do you think we would have any control over the water supply?' Ikenna snorted. 'Now that one was really something else. I mean, what kind of *person* ties their life to an alliance because they think they are taking *a love potion*?'

'A girl of twelve years,' Olu muttered as he pushed away from the memory of Obi Jideofo's reaction when Ikenna had callously told him; Olu had never seen a man cry so ardently in his life.

'I just need more,' Ikenna said hungrily. 'The amoosu women are worn out and spent, their sacrifices are not yielding the same effect. They need an amplifier and I know it's that crystal.'

Olu regarded his old friend. What had power done to him? 'Remember our conversations in the drinking ụlọ? Remember the future we imagined without fear, with innovation, a true collaboration between the Obis? A new system built on merit and not blood?'

'What do you think I am doing here?' Ikenna snapped, his eyes narrowing. 'Everything, everything in this life has a cost. I learnt that young, and I have always made it my business to know the price when I agree to *anything*. Do you think I did not love my uncle? My grandfather? I loved them but they had no place in this new regime. When I killed them I made a choice. Not on a whim or a notion, but because that was what I had to do. That was the price that I was willing to pay. I am trying to attain a *future* for this kingdom. *That* future, that dream, was always dependent on a blood price, and I have always been prepared to pay it.'

His words tore deep into Olu. Ina had been right – Olu was truly a fool. How had he not been able to see the lengths that Ikenna could and would go to?

As if the man could hear his thoughts, Ikenna turned to him, his eyes gleaming with malice. 'And brother, you will do well to remember that the streets of Nri will flow with your blood if you do not help me pay it.'

CHAPTER 26
DRIED LAKES

Furuefu forest

1. Wait for the beast, 2. Drain its energy, 3. Draw blood (don't sleep, please don't enter the deep sleep), 4. Kill the beast.

'1, 2, 3, 4,' Sinai muttered under her breath. The plan was simple enough. She had gone over it hundreds of times. Sinai clenched her fists but it did little to hide her tremors. She let out a long, jagged breath. Her encounter with Nwamara still gnawed at the back of her head but there was no time to brood on such things.

Every second you hesitate, every second you delay, the beast grows stronger. Strong enough to best you. Strong enough to kill you all. Sinai shivered as Bayo's words shook through her. She looked across the scattered forest. Furuefu was almost unrecognisable. The beast's destruction hung to the air like moisture, thick and suffocating. Nothing could go wrong. She couldn't fail them. She glanced over at Madi and Naala. If either of them shared her fears, they certainly weren't making it known.

'1, 2, 3, 4 … 1, 2, 3, 4 … 1, 2—'

'We should go,' Naala suddenly announced.

Sinai couldn't make sense of her words. Go? Go where? This was the *only* place they were meant to be.

Days ago, the Aturu had contained the beast within a section of the forest. They had conjured a shield, of sorts, by dispelling their energy outwards. Every time the beast approached it, it would become disorientated and change its direction. It was no easy feat. Nearly all the Aturu members were on a rotating shift to keep the shield up, leaving the Idu powerless.

The land at the North side of the confinement was decimated, peppered with exposed tree roots, shrubs, and flat dry land layered with rubble and stone. According to the Aturu's observations, it was also the best place to be. Close enough to the shield to disorientate the beast but not too far to deter it. The Aido-Hwedo was said to come here every day at midday, when the sun was at its highest and the beast at its weakest.

'The sun has passed its midpoint,' Naala noted, 'by an hour at least, and the beast is nowhere in sight. The longer we wait, the weaker the Aturu become and the stronger the beast. We need to finish this today or we might not get the chance.'

'We were told to wait,' Sinai replied; her voice came out small and distant. It wasn't as though Naala's words didn't make sense. They did. It was no secret that the Aturu's strength had begun to wane. Soon the shield would give and the killings would restart.

Naala was right; they couldn't afford to waste any time … but to simply leave? To throw away the plan just when she was so close to being *comfortable* with the whole thing? Sinai clutched her arms to her chest.

'The situation has changed, Sinai; what we were told no longer applies.' Naala squinted across the horizon. 'Look,' she said, gesturing to the ground. 'The top layer is dry but beneath is still moist. There's no vegetation, and see those trees over there?'

'What does this have to—?'

'A lake. This *must* have been a lake. Perhaps that was why the beast ventured over here when the sun was at its highest – to drink. Perhaps that is why it is no longer here; those trees have created an artificial dam, which means no water, which means it has no reason to be here. It won't come by this way. We have to find it, which eats even more into our time. So, we don't have time to wait.'

Sinai frowned, looking around at the dead uprooted trees and plants scattered across the once thriving forest. The usual sounds that punctuated the forest had been replaced with a heavy silence, with most of the birds and land animals long gone.

'I think she's right,' Madi said, his voice lower than usual. *Of course, she's right,* Sinai thought, *but that doesn't make it easier to face.*

Sinai threw a glance over at Madi. He stood stiff, with his lips pressed tightly; a stark contrast to his usual demeanour. Sinai didn't have to ask what was wrong with him. Madi had stopped taking the ọgwụ. Though the remedy helped him better control his powers, it also weakened him and they needed all the help they could get. Meaning Madi would have to focus, and focus hard, on not losing control.

As Bayo had described it, their bodies were still not accustomed to the power they were able to access. It showed up in different ways for each of the Descendants. With Sinai and Naala, the issue became apparent when their emotions overwhelmed them. During those moments, they would use up more energy than they had to spare. It had happened to her when she had watched Meekulu Kaurandua burn to death. She would have died that day too had she not been able to recoup her energy in the Black and Gold realm.

It was different for Ina. They had theorised that her powers were most temperamental when her defences were down. When she was relaxed, calm and vulnerable. Whilst Madi believed that for him it was shock. Something unexpected that threw him into a violent rage where destruction was the only thing that seemed plausible.

It was not the best of traits to bring to a fight, but what choice did they have? The beast had started to *kill.* It had ravaged an entire settlement in the North. Sinai was ashamed to admit that she had felt a moment of relief when she had heard. Siwunmi was in the South, so Siwunmi was safe. Her chest had ached soon after. She might not have known those who had died, she might not have seen their faces, but they deserved more than her relief. Like Siwunmi, she had no doubt, the perished settlement would have once been filled with families, with children and love. They deserved more.

Sinai followed Naala's gaze to the sky at the efe-efe basket hovering above them: the Amaghị's flying device. A large blackwood-framed basket with flat iron rims that scattered the sun rays. If she looked hard enough, Sinai was sure that she would see the faint glow from the crystal at its heart powering the whole contraption.

Somewhere within the basket Eni sat alongside another rider, a tall woman with knotted hair who did not speak a word to them. Naala had been violently opposed to Eni joining on the expedition, but, with most of the efe-efe riders stationed to swap out the Aturu, they had no choice. Plus, as he had pointed out repeatedly, Eni was handy with a bow and arrow. With Kora's specially crafted archery set, he joked he might even be of use in the fight itself.

'Fine,' Sinai muttered as she looked down from the sky.

'Let's go then,' Naala said, signalling to the efe-efe basket above before treading through the broken forest.

'What about a Cross River?' Madi asked as they walked on; his honeyed eyes were squinted from his discomfort but somehow found room to be bright with jest. 'Come on, you've had to have seen one of those.' They had been walking for goodness knows how long, with Naala marching ahead as usual. Madi had decided to keep her pace even though he could have easily kept Naala's, something Sinai suspected was more for her benefit than his.

'No, well, I don't think so – there was one time when a goril—'

Feed.

The word burst into her head followed by an insatiable desire. She stopped and gasped sharply.

'Sinai,' Madi called, concerned, as Naala whipped around, watching cautiously as she approached.

'Sinai, are you okay? Is it—' Before Naala could finish, a screech erupted in the air, maniacal and inhuman. It pierced through Sinai's chest and left her vibrating. The lessons that Bayo had drummed into her vanished in that second. Her mind was not centred. Her breathing was not calm. She was wild, erratic and no longer the master of her body. Fear and anguish boiled within her. Black mist clouded her vision.

'No!' Naala called at her. 'Focus.'

Her shrill voice laced with desperation cut through Sinai's distorted mind. The haze cleared and she found herself nodding, though she was not certain what to.

One, two, three, four.

If she acted too rash, if she consumed herself with her power, if she lost control, she could become lost in the Black and Gold realm. She could enter the deep sleep. She wouldn't be a help to anyone. She would be a liability. A dead weight that Madi and Naala would have to drag as they faced the beast alone. No, she *needed* to concentrate. She needed to drain the beast of its energy and leave it primed to kill. Another screech rippled through her and, despite herself, Sinai forced air in and out of her mouth. Her eyes closed as she sharpened her mind.

Listen, Bayo's voice echoed in her head, *concentrate and you will find it, the heartbeat, the hum.*

Sinai's eyes sprang open.

It wasn't so much a heartbeat as it was a stream. A loud crashing noise that fell over her. The beast's Ike-Obi. Her heart plummeted to her stomach as it rushed over her. Just listening to it was overwhelming; how on earth was she to *drain* it? Naala's expression looked like how she felt; her mouth had parted and the whites of her eyes, almost fully exposed. She had felt it too. She knew they were doomed.

'You can do it,' Naala said gently. *You have to.*

'I have to,' Sinai breathed, her palms opening and closing until she balled them into fists. She began.

The mice and goats she had practised on in Urukpuru had been a joke compared to this creature. She had pulled their Ike-Obi as easily as a string. They had been weightless and easy beyond words. This creature, however, was drowning her. Her attempts to drain it were completely futile. Its Ike-Obi was erratic and manic, slipping from her grasp as easily as rain in the highstorms.

Concentrate! But try as she might, she couldn't contain it. The mere efforts were draining *her*. She felt herself weaken under the weight of the beast's mighty Ike-Obi. *Concentrate,* she pleaded as the earth vibrated under the weight of the beast. It was approaching. It was coming fast, and she couldn't seem to—

'Concentrate!' she screamed. Another screech ripped through the air and a flurry of flowers burst out of the vast forest floor. Sinai collapsed to her knees as a wave of exhaustion hit her. She had done it. She had pulled some of the creature's Ike-Obi. A sick feeling ran through her as she felt the stream pour over her. She *had* done it. Sinai knew she had, and yet, if it wasn't for the plants at her feet, the exhaustion tearing through her limbs, she would have never known. As she reinspected it, she realised with deathly dread that the beast's Ike-Obi appeared unchanged.

Sinai looked back at Naala and Madi's expectant faces. There was no winning this fight. They were dead.

CHAPTER 27
THE SCENT OF BLOOD

Furuefu forest

'RUUUN!' she yelled, as the beast clawed through the trees. It was no use. Seconds before they could move, it was *there*.

The Aido-Hwedo stood before them, even larger than she had remembered. Its lumbering body extended far higher than the tree tops. It gave another screech as it crashed to the ground; dust and debris flew into the air and the energy of its movement knocked Sinai over. Her ears rang and the cold metallic taste of blood entered her mouth.

'Get out of the way!' Madi roared at her, but she couldn't. All she could do was look up at the cracked branch falling towards her. Before she could scream, it flew to the side, crashing against a nearby trunk.

'Get down!' Naala screamed, her arms raised as she swivelled the hefty branch towards the beast. It landed against the beast's stomach but it didn't so much as flinch.

Madi bounded for the beast, his arms outstretched and his face widened in a scream. The beast swatted him away in one sweep, throwing the boy across the field. He landed with a large crash, the weight of his body crushing the mammoth tree he fell on.

Sinai reached for the power from the Black and Gold realm, gritting her teeth at the attempt. She breathed out as the large streams of air flowing in and out of the beast started to form. She held the air steady. She would suffocate it. Only the beast jolted and turned, faster than she could react. It threw another screech into the air and Sinai was forced to release her grip. *We're going to die.* The thought was swift and final. No. Not without a fight, not withou—

A whistle cut through the air followed by a sudden cascade of arrows. They ran so fast that Sinai saw them as blurs.

Eni leapt out of the efe-efe basket, and landed on a treetop with the gracefulness of a panther. He propelled himself off each branch, all the while shooting a series of arrows into the air. Each one of them lodged deep in the Aido-Hwedo's skin before exploding on impact.

Eni landed softly on the ground, his aim unyielding, and his pace swift. Sinai had never seen anything like it. She stood dumbstruck as he fired with perfect execution, dancing around the legions of incoming materials flung to and fro by the temperamental beast before yelling—

'Drain it!'

That's when it hit her. The pungent smell of iron that filled the air. The violent gashes on the creature's skin gleaming red. *Blood,* Bayo's words echoed. *Blood makes it all that much clearer.*

Sinai took a deep breath; as she did, the beast's large and formidable Ike-Obi sounded in her head. It was still huge, still overwhelming, but it had slowed somehow. Its erratic movement had stilled to a steady flow, a flow that she could cup and expel. Sinai grabbed at heaps of the Ike-Obi, pouring it any place that she could find. Around her, the cracked trees straightened, their wounds fleshed out and their dried leaves flushed with new life. Step by step, she felt the beast weaken.

'Attack!' she screamed, though she had little reason to. They had all picked up their pace.

Eni continued to fire arrows and the earth shook violently as Naala pulled out dead trees from the ground, sending them crashing towards the beast. The creature staggered backwards and let out a sound. Not a screech this time, but a whimper.

Please. Stop, a weak voice sounded in the back of her mind.

Sinai hesitated for a moment as Madi reared up and thundered into the beast. The hit sent ripples through its translucent skin as garish pink splotches formed. The beast backed away, as though it were – as though it were *scared*? A myriad of thoughts suddenly burst into her mind. Confusion, pain, hunger, loneliness, a *child*?

Please.

Something wasn't *right*. Madi geared for another hit and before Sinai could think, she had raised her arm towards him, sending a stream of air to hold him back.

'Sinai!' Naala screamed, her mouth slack and her eyes wide. 'What are you doing?!'

'It's weakened,' Sinai said through gritted teeth. Madi was fighting hard against her hold.

'Exactly!' Naala roared. 'Now is the time to kill!'

'We can't, it's a child, it's – it's confused. It's innocent,' Sinai claimed, and Naala's bottom lip quivered as she fought to find the words.

'Innocent?' Naala spat. 'This beast has killed hundreds of people. We can't leave it here to kill mo—'

Madi roared in frustration. He had given up his fight against the invisible air and had now, it seemed, entered into a fight with himself. He pulled out clumps of his hair and tore at the ground around him, his fists and legs kicking out viciously in the air.

'Madi,' Eni said. His voice was steady, almost calm, and yet it seemed to ripple through all of them. Madi whipped his head towards Eni. The glare he gave him was murderous. 'Madi,' Eni repeated cautiously, 'remember who you are.'

Madi bolted at him. A scream echoed in the air; Sinai wasn't too sure if it was hers or Naala's.

Madi rushed towards the boy with all the strength of a thousand men. He would have crushed Eni to death, had Eni not been faster. He jumped out of the way, letting Madi crash into a tree. The tree didn't simply crack; it vaporised into dust before her eyes.

Sinai stepped back as though she had been punched. Nausea crept up from her stomach and settled in her throat as black spots scattered across her vision. *What have I done?*

Madi's fear of losing his control was no longer the quibble of an overly anxious boy. It was real and deadlier than she could have imagined. Sinai tried to use the air to slow him down, but every time she did, her hold over the beast loosened. She couldn't risk setting the beast loose, not until she understood what it would do.

The earth shifted around her as Naala tried to block Madi's path with the trees, but he smashed them one by one. With each crash, the violence brimming from his eyes intensified.

Sinai couldn't breathe. *What have I done?* A cry cut through her chest and she swung her head to witness the horror.

Somewhere in the pursuit, Eni had caught his leg on a rock; he came crashing down, but not before whipping an arrow into his bow. Beads of sweat ran down his face as he pulled the string towards his cheek – aimed and ready for Madi.

Breath caught on Sinai's throat. He hadn't let the arrow go. If he did, it would stop Madi in his pursuit. It would save his life. It would kill his friend. Eni wrung the bow tight but he didn't release.

'Madi, please,' he said as he scrambled backwards; even from Sinai's standpoint, she could see the unnatural twist in Eni's leg. He wouldn't be able to stand, let alone run. Something wavered in Madi's honeyed eyes and for a strangled moment Sinai had thought … she had *hoped*.

Madi bolted towards Eni with murder gleaming in his eyes. Eni's expression tightened before sagging into despair. He lowered his bow.

'Get up!' Naala cried as she leapt in front of him, pushing herself under his arm as she attempted to lift him up.

'Get out, Naala,' he roared as he grimaced up to his feet. Madi slowed, his face contorting as he flicked from Naala to Eni. Again, Madi seemed to have returned. His lips trembled as his eyes glazed over.

'Kill me!' His voice cracked under the strain. 'Eni, please kil—'

He was gone. His softness, his kindness, his sense drained away and in its place was a monster, foaming at the mouth.

Naala tore away from Eni but she didn't run. Instead she stood in between the both of them.

'Get out of the way,' Eni said, his voice so deep it shook through Sinai. He raised his bow to Madi as he stalked towards the both of them.

'Madi, it's me, it's us,' Naala pleaded, fresh tears running down her face as thick vines snaked from the ground and tugged at his arms and feet. He tore them away as though they were nothing more than dried leaves. He paused for no longer than a breath. Then he began to charge.

Eni released the arrow.

Sinai's heart stopped, unblinking; she threw both hands towards him. Knocking him to the ground with a gust of air so powerful his skin rippled and flapped.

Sinai didn't see the beast escape. She didn't hear its heavy feet or its screeching roar. One moment it was behind her and the next it was crashing through them all.

Sinai fell back from the force of its movement, the left side of her body scorched with blinding pain. When she looked up, the beast was nowhere in sight. Madi was still on the ground. His chest gashed open from the claw marks the beast had left before it bolted deep into the forest.

'No, no, no,' Naala said as she crawled over to him, her voice nothing more of a whisper. 'No, no, no, no.'

Sinai scrambled towards them, shaking as she neared. She didn't know what to do. Blood, there was so much blood.

'I'm s-o sorry,' Madi said. His eyes were soft again, filled with tears. Sinai couldn't breathe.

'Shhh,' Naala said, cradling his head; her hands were bright and red. She looked up at Sinai, her lips quivering. 'T-transfer my energy to him.'

'Naala, I—'

'NOW! He doesn't have time, help him heal, like, like the flowers. I can take it.'

Sinai swallowed, her mouth so dry that the motion hurt. The sensation of the mouse in her palm turning to dust filled her. She couldn't do that. She couldn't take that risk.

'Sinai, please,' Naala cried as Madi's eyelids lowered.

Sinai felt tears pricking her eyes.

'It won't work,' Eni said as he limped towards them.

'It will,' Naala shrieked.

'It won't, Naala; you are a Descendant. You can't be drained. Sinai, try, you'll see.'

Sinai forced her mind to settle and she tried to find Naala's Ike-Obi. There was nothing there. 'I can't,' she said. She didn't know what pained her more, the look that spread across Naala's face or the fact that on some level, she was glad. *Madi.*

Naala gasped as though she had been punched. She looked down at Madi before scanning the forest. Sinai could see her brain at work behind her restless eyes.

She looked up at the efe-efe, no doubt thinking if they could make it back to the Idu in time …if they could get the Aturu, the healers, anybody …

It was not possible. A pool of blood surrounded Madi, more blood than Sinai had ever seen. He had minutes left, if that. That thought hit her squarely in the chest. *Madi.*

'The crystal,' Naala said, her voice hoarse, her fingers outstretched.

'What?'

'I know you have it, I can feel it,' Naala snapped, clicking her fingers. 'We can use it, we can heal him, I *know* it.'

'We can't evoke—'

'THE CRYSTAL!' Naala demanded, and Sinai looked down at Madi. In the brief time she had known him, he had become the kindest person she had ever met. He would die because she had acted to save a ferocious beast. What had she been thinking?

Sinai felt out for the pouch folded in her garments. She pulled it out, her fingers shaking as she unravelled the cloth to reveal the two crystals welded together.

They both reached out for it at the same time. A loud crack broke into the air when their fingers touched its smooth surface. In a sudden flurry, the crystals were flung into the air. Sinai reached up and, as she did, the murky white crystal landing in her hand, she staggered backwards as the power from the crystal tore through her lungs.

Distantly, she could hear Naala.

'Heal him, heal him! Heal him!' she cried. The girl had the onyx crystal pressed in her hands. Nothing was happening. Naala sprang her head up at Sinai. 'You touch it with me. That's what we did before and—'

Sinai shook her head. No, that wasn't *right*. Her heart was racing. Naala's words scattered towards her but she pushed them aside, she had to.

The crystal, Ikuku, was in her hand, and she needed to listen. The fear that she had worn slipped off like a cloak, and in its place, clarity sheathed her. She looked down at Madi. She could see it now, as clear as day. Whether he lived or he died, it was all the *same*. A memory brushed against her, crimson leaves, a grand tree, a whisper of Meekulu Kaurandua. Sinai surrendered to that feeling and a dazzling gold light exploded through the air, followed by pitch black mist, speckled with gold. The mist engulfed the two girls. A scream tore out of her. Life itself seemed to have torn out of her. Sinai could feel everything, every breath, every heartbeat. It scorched through her until it suddenly stopped.

Boom!

She was flung into the air before she came crashing down. Sinai's head rang but she managed to lift herself up.

'Madi? Madi!' she heard Naala cry as she crawled over to him.

Before Sinai could follow, she felt something prick at her leg. She looked down to see the beast's huge head backing away from her, its misty white eyes drawing up as it watched her intensely.

'No,' she gasped as she caught a gleam of fresh blood at the tip of one of its long, thin tooth, and the world melted into darkness.

CHAPTER 28
A MESSAGE TO THE UNDERWORLD

Urukpuru

It was a grating sound that had woken Naala. A low scratch that occurred without fail in even intervals. It spiked its way through her head. Her *head*? Why did her head feel so heavy, so raw, so bruised? She felt as she did, moon-cycles ago, when she had woken up chained in the tall towers at Nri.

She lifted her eyelids slowly and her heart leapt to her throat. Four nnunu women peered down at her curiously, their claws clutching at the edge of her akwa nest. Their eyes widened as she woke.

A garish noise rippled through the room and the bird-women scurried away with sudden haste. Naala pulled her head up in time to see them flutter through the crystal doors. The effort made her head spin and she crashed down once again. *Golden clamps*, she thought, recalling their wings. *I'm back in the Amaghi's Idu?*

'You're awake,' Kora exhaled as Naala cracked one eye open.

When did Kora arrive? She thought it had been the nnunus in her room no more than a second ago.

Kora wavered slightly as she lowered herself to the ground, balancing a broad basket on her head. She ran to Naala's side, before pressing the back of her hand against Naala's head and turning back to her basket. She rummaged until she brought out a crystal bottle and a thick cloth.

'Kora?' Naala croaked.

'You're doing well,' Kora said with a smile, as she poured a bright blue liquid onto the cloth.

Her hands shook and Naala could see dark rings under her bloodshot eyes. Naala frowned as Kora brought the salve to her head. It felt cool against her skin and gave her a short bout of relief.

'You probably need some more itucha to help heal the wound on your head, but you're definitely improving,' Kora said, as Naala watched her blot the material against her forehead. 'Oh, don't look at me like that; I've been studying.'

Naala didn't care about her head. Memories of their expedition came back to her one by one, each memory worse than the last.

'Madi, is he …?' Naala asked hoarsely. She noticed a slight tremor at the corner of Kora's eyes and her heart plummeted. *No!* Naala forced her heavy limbs to move but as soon as she lifted her head, the dizziness engulfed her. Not Madi, not Madi.

'Settle, settle,' Kora hushed. 'He's okay, they say…'

Naala's eyes widened as she watched her. Her heart thundered against her chest. He's okay? He's alive but—

'But what?'

'They won't let me see them,' Kora said and Naala felt her body collapse into the furs. Her throat was so dry, it felt as though it would tear.

'As far as I know, they're alive, but they won't let me see them and I know, I am a novice, but I'm *skilled*. I know things and I just wish they wouldn't shut me out, and when they do, then I have to ask *why?*' she rambled before she caught herself. 'But the important thing is, you are fine, and you are awake,' she said before her eyes darkened.

'What is it?'

'Now that you're awake,' Kora said gently, 'they'll want to see you.'

Naala walked down the hall slowly. Her head was still pounding but the salve that Kora had given her had helped. She paused at the crystal door. It was the same door that Eni had escorted them to when they had first arrived. Yet, it was *different*. She gazed at the door and she *felt* it. The tiny earth particles scattered across the Idu. Particles that she had not been able to feel before. Particles she could now grasp on to.

Naala looked down at her palms before staggering backwards. A cold sweat formed on the nape of her neck as she took note of a black mark on her wrist, the same deep black colour of the symbol at the side of her palm. The symbol was made of two straight lines, a horizontal line positioned at the bottom with a vertical line sitting in the middle of it.

'Ikuku,' Naala muttered, as her heart thundered. The second crystal had been evoked. A knot formed in her belly as the door creaked open.

Chukwudi stood at the other side, an unforgiving frown plastered on his face.

'One should always announce themselves at a closed door,' he said stiffly, 'else one might think you are sneaking around.'

That's rich coming from you! she thought; all Chukwudi knew was sneaking around. He seemed to thrive in hidden shadows. For once, though, she kept her mouth shut. It seemed that the remedies they had given her had blocked the lightning connection between her mouth and her mind. It gave her a moment to reflect before she spoke, and if she could help it, she would have liked to avoid a quarrel with the white-haired man. Instead she nodded at him.

'Ndewo, I'm here to see the—' she began.

'The Isi?' he said, before moving out of the way to reveal the woman seated behind him. 'You should have greeted her first,' he muttered, shaking his head as he allowed Naala into the room.

'It is good to see you well,' the Isi said, her voice almost as cooling as the salve. She sat composed on her grand mahogany chair, regal as always.

'Thank you,' Naala said, her gaze turning to the necklace that the Isi wore. It had nine crevices, one of which was occupied by a dark onyx crystal. The Àlà crystal. Naala's heart gave a violent thud. She pressed her mouth together to stop the gasp from escaping; instead it came out as a short cough. How had the Isi got a hold of it, and why was she *wearing* it? 'And the others? Are they well too? Kora couldn't get access to them.'

The Isi's violet eyes brightened as she spoke. 'We will get to that matter shortly. First, please sit.' She rose from her seat, extending an arm to the array of cushions on the floor.

Naala blinked as the Isi lowered herself onto one of the plump cushions, gesturing for the girl to join her. From the grumble that escaped Chukwudi's lips, Naala could only guess that he disapproved. She looked at the Isi hesitantly before taking a seat.

They sat in silence for a long time. Naala stole occasional glances at the older woman, who she sat unmoved and serene.

Naala tried to stop fidgeting. She wasn't too sure if she would be permitted to speak but the restlessness within her was spiralling. She wanted to know about the others. Where were they? Why couldn't Kora go to see them? Why was the Isi wearing the onyx crystal? These questions ran through her mind and something told her that it was in her best interest to remain patient. Naala bit against her lip, a sensation that provided some respite from her pounding head and her anxious heart.

'You have love for your friends,' the Isi said.

Naala had to fight the scowl from claiming her expression. She was trying, she really was, but her patience was wearing thin. She didn't want to talk about her *love*; she wanted to talk about their health.

Still, she found herself nodding.

'I do,' she said, sharper than she had intended. The Isi placed her gloved palm over Naala's marked wrist. The gesture was gentle, perhaps intended to be soothing, but Naala couldn't help but draw away.

'I had feelings for a man once,' the Isi continued as though she hadn't noticed Naala's flinch. 'I discovered later that I did not love the man, but I certainly loved those *feelings*. I enjoyed being *his* woman and yet I couldn't live with being under his rule.'

'I'm sorry, but I don't understand what this has to do with anything. We have so much to discuss — the beast, Madi, the crystals,' she listed, her gaze falling on the necklace around her neck. 'Are you sure it is wise for you to be wearing that?'

'You are so very young,' the Isi replied, her eyes softening as she regarded Naala. 'Sadly, you cannot stay that way; not any more. You must transcend your youth and there are only two ways to do that: pain or wisdom. The latter is what I offer you now.'

Naala shifted uncomfortably in her seat.

'You will have *all* your answers but first you must listen. Is this something you can do?'

Naala looked back at the Isi and a cold chill ran down her spine. She glanced over at Chukwudi. Did she really have a choice?

'Do you know what occurred between Ochichiri and I?' the Isi said suddenly.

Naala faltered. *What?*

'No,' she replied quietly. It was something that she had wondered about, even before she had met the Isi; when the woman had been known as Lolo Obioma. The visitors to her village used to come with stories about the Eze's Lolo. Singing praises about her humility, her strength and her beauty. *Strange*, Naala thought to herself. *None of them ever brought up her albinism.*

The Isi smiled demurely. 'I was his puppet,' she said almost *proudly*. 'His little fool and oh, how I loved that role. That was, after all, what my father had raised me to be: a dutiful queen to a powerful king.' She allowed a slight smile to play on her peach lips. 'And what did I do?' her nose flared at the thought. 'I created *a god*. Or so I thought. It was I who taught Ochichiri how to use the crystal.' Naala's head snapped towards her, and the Isi smiled.

'You see, like Bayo, I have always been gifted with the sight of magic. I can see things within people, within artefacts. I used that sight and I formed him. I *created* him, and I knew,' she said, her eyes dropping, 'I *knew* that below the surface there lay something … *repugnant*. But you see, we made a promise to each other, he and I; I promised to make him the best he could be and he promised to never let me see the worst of it.' She let out a bitter laugh before stopping abruptly.

'Anwuki,' she added softly, and Naala saw Chukwudi stiffen for the first time in the conversation. Naala was about to enquire further into what this name meant but she needn't have bothered.

'He gave her to me,' the Isi said. 'A gift.' Her frozen face was more animated than Naala had ever seen. Her violet eyes sparked with the memory. 'She was a wild woman, exciting, uncontainable. She opened my eyes to a new love, a *pure* love that I hadn't known existed.' She glanced purposely at Naala. 'I fought it at first but Ochichiri encouraged me. "Why shouldn't my wife have a wife of her own?" he would say.'

The Isi's small smile fell from her face and she sat still for a long moment. Naala shifted.

'Then one day, after I had lost yet another child, Ochichiri invited all the kings across the Kingdoms to the palace. He asked me to attend, as he often did. I used to find it pleasing at first, how accepting he was of my *condition*. Soon I saw it for what it was. A parade. He would strip me of my garments and parade me around for all to gawk at.' Her full lips stiffened at the memory. 'I was always prepared for the worst, *always* – but I wasn't prepared to see *her*, my Anwuki, sitting in the middle of the room with an executioner at her side.' The Isi's eyes creased at the thought; water had begun to pool within them. 'An *executioner*, as though she were a *commoner*,' she spat before taking a pause. Her chest heaved as she deepened her breaths. 'As was the custom, Ochichiri had a message for me to send with her to the underworld. Do you know what it was? The message he made me whisper in her ear before she was sliced to pieces by abara?' She paused before leaning into Naala's ear; her words, as soft as feathers, grazed against her ear. 'I will feed you more.'

Naala jolted back. The faces of her family and friends slaughtered on the Eze's command flooded over her. She clutched at the cushion to steady herself.

'Everyone thinks it was the time that he dragged me through the streets, or when he kept me in that abara cage while Asilia tried to snap at me. But it wasn't, all of that was … easier. All of that I was prepared to handle. But Anwuki – that was something else. That was when I refused to come down. I refused to parade at his whim. I refused to be *his* woman, and *that* was when he put a mark of death on my name.' A ruthless look cut across her face. 'But look who lived and *who* returned to dust. Look who ended up joining her in the underworld.'

The Isi entered yet another bout of silence and Naala felt as though she should say something, but all she could manage was, 'You wear the crystal.'

'I do,' the Isi said, grazing its surface with her gloved hand. 'You did not tell us that it was in your possession. Why?'

'It came when the fight occurred,' she said quickly as the Isi regarded her. Naala had noticed it as soon as she had seen Sinai that morning. It had called to her just as it had done in the nnunu's cave. She had been furious, ready to call her out, and demand that she return those crystals to wherever she had got them from.

Then she had seen the girl's face. Wracked with worry. Any fool could see that Sinai was on edge. They hadn't had time for *anyone's* breakdown, least of all the girl who was shouldering the bulk of their impossible task. Sinai had looked as though she would break if someone mentioned she had a hair out of place, and so Naala had bit down on her tongue. She would wait. She would give the girl the benefit of the doubt, and if at any point Sinai should try to use those crystals, *that* was when she would intervene. Naala had a feeling that the lost gods were still rolling with laughter.

'That's not what our reports say,' the Isi murmured. Naala returned her gaze unflinchingly. 'Naala, do you know why I told you that story?'

'No,' Naala said.

For a second, the Isi gave her a murderous look. Unlike the looks that Chukwudi routinely offered her, this felt *real*. As though the Isi could very well wrap her fingers around Naala's neck and squeeze until no breath would ever escape. Naala glanced at the crystal on the woman's neck as a shiver ran down her spine.

'I made a mistake with the crystal before, and I empowered the wrong person, and now I have blood on my hands. Countless deaths that now sit on *my* head. I will not make that mistake again; I will rectify those wrongs.'

'The crystals aren't yours to take.'

'Says who?'

'You're not a Descendant,' Naala said frustratingly. 'You can't even *touch* them.'

'And yet I have been able to use it in better ways than those that can,' the Isi said. 'Where you have neglected, overused and discarded these crystals, I have protected them,' she said, running a gloved hand over the onyx crystal. 'Not every child belongs with the woman that bore it, Naala, and these crystals belong to the people that treat them best.'

Naala frowned as something dawned on her. 'You hit me with the darts.'

'*I* did no such thing.'

'I was fine,' Naala insisted, 'I was fine until something drew me to the deep sleep, and now the crystal is in your hands and you refuse to tell me the whereabouts of the others.'

'Madi and Eni are being taken care of,' the Isi said, '*because* I was able to use this crystal to assist with their healing. If I had left it in your reckless hands, they would be dead right now. Listen to *reason*, Naala; I've tried my best to heal them but we need *both* of the crystals before they can fully recover. We need both crystals to survive the reckoning that you and your *twin* have unleashed.'

'Madi and Eni are being taken care of?' Naala repeated as she looked at the onyx crystal; an image of Sinai with the milky white crystal in her hand flashed before her. 'But what of Sinai?'

The Isi glanced over to Chukwudi before her gaze settled back on Naala. 'That is why you are here,' she said. Her words sliced coolly through Naala's chest. *No.* 'We were hoping you would tell us.'

CHAPTER 29
THE GUIDE

Urukpuru

All she could see was cobalt blue. It flooded over her as she drifted through the air, her limbs dangling uselessly at her sides. Sinai was floating. Her nose wrinkled as the air brushed against it. No, that wasn't right. *Flying.* She was flying? She was flying!

Questions and doubts welled within her, each one heavier than the last, until her stomach knotted into iron pulling her down into sickening dread. She didn't have time to scream. Her hair slapped against her cheeks as the air was snatched from her lungs. Adrenaline tore through her body as she plummeted through the torturous blue sky.

A loud thwack ran through the air when she landed. She pressed her quivering hands against her body, searching for the broken bones and torn skin. She found neither. Sinai glanced around but she couldn't *see* anything. Her heart was pounding too hard and she couldn't seem to suck enough crisp air to satisfy her aching lungs.

You keep lifting up to the sky only to tumble down again. Could you perhaps stop? It makes me quite nervous.

It was only then that she realised she was sitting on something. Something warm and solid, soft like beaten snakeskin. Something *alive*.

Sinai jumped up so hard that she began to tumble off the creature. Her fingers dug into whatever she could find as she struggled to stay onboard.

Oh. Well, that is far worse.

'Ndewo?' she called out shakily as she regained her position.

Ndewo, little one.

The voice echoed through her mind. Sinai was clutching onto something translucent; below its surface lay a web of rainbow veins. Her heart stopped.

'The beast,' Sinai gasped, springing to her feet. The sudden motion knocked her down almost instantly. There was little else she could do but to grasp on to the murderous Aido-Hwedo.

You must be careful. The baritone voice sounded in her head, steady and rich. There was something else buried beneath its tone. A thickness that reminded her of tears. Was it *upset?*

Yes, the voice sounded. *It is cruel to call one a beast when one is simply being. My name, after all, is Dogbari. Dogbari of Abomey.*

'Dogbari,' Sinai muttered as a lightness thrummed against her chest. She didn't understand. This beast – this creature had *killed*. If she closed her eyes she could still see an image of Madi, laying still, his chest torn and gleaming red. So why did she feel guilt? A sharp sting pulled her out of her thoughts, and she looked down to find a long thin cut crusting over on her calve.

'You took me,' Sinai whispered.

You were the only one that listened.

'Where are they?' she asked, her voice smaller than she had anticipated as she looked out at the empty blue sky. Was she even alive?

The ones you seek are with the ones that take. Dogbari folded his long neck to face her. Milk-white eyes peered at her, distant and yet somehow focused. Up close like this, he didn't seem frightening. He seemed almost vulnerable. During the fight she that vulnerability had felt child-like but now, she knew that wasn't quite right. Dogbari felt older than time itself. Like the frail, greyed old men who hobbled on sticks and gave toothless grins.

Don't be stupid, look at him! Dogbari's head was almost as large as she was. *Vulnerable*, she scoffed internally, her eyebrows narrowing as she beg— the images hit her almost all at once. She was alone. Everyone was *gone*. She did not know *how* she knew, but God help her, she *knew*. She was all alone. Hunger and thirst ripped through her senses. There was no rest. She couldn't remember what rest even tasted like. A cold grip squeezed at her throat. They were here. The ones that take. She recognised one of them, his white hair reflecting the pale moonlight, his face shadowed: Chukwudi? A blinding pain exploded within her. She was burning. Hot flames licked down her veins.

'Feeeeed,' she shrieked manically as a violent thirst overtook her. A thirst for blood and carnage.

Sinai lay back, panting, as the memories faded away, until all she could see was the cobalt blue. She felt Dogbari rouse her with the edge of his cheek. Sinai pulled herself up again to meet his murky eyes.

'Please don't do that again,' she managed. Try as she might, she couldn't stop herself from trembling.

As you wish, little one. Dogbari lowered his misted eyes but not before she could see them gleaming with crystal water.

'Who did this to you?'

The ones that take, he said. An image of Chukwudi formed in her mind and her throat tightened. The Aturu had tried to contain the Aido-Hwedo when they had first encountered it. Did they know that it was their efforts that had driven Dogbari to rampage? She looked curiously at the creature. She could no longer sense its bloodthirst but what had settled it?

Ikuku, of course.

Sinai froze. Her heart pounded manically as looked down at her empty hands. A dull ache hit her chest. She had *evoked* it. She had *lost* it. The sour taste of bile entered her mouth.

Dogbari tilted his head pensively before opening his mouth.

Touch.

Laying on his tongue sat the Ikuku crystal. Sinai's legs weakened as her hands flew to her mouth. *It was here*, she thought, as she kept her gaze fixed on the misted white stone.

'You have the crystal,' she whispered dumbstruck. 'You can *touch* the crystal?'

Touch the crystal? Dogbari exclaimed, and a deep hearty rumble shook through him, so hard that Sinai began to vibrate. *Little one, I am of the crystal. Ikuku cannot hurt me, nor can I hurt it. We exist together as one. Its touch can never change me to dust. Its voice can never be quiet in my mind. I cannot be complete until it is restored.*

'You are of the crystal?' Sinai repeated. Goose pimples ran up the back of her neck.

Your kind has given me many names. Aido-Hwedo, The Clear-Eyed Ikuku, Guide, Protector. I call myself Dogbari.

Her gaze shifted back to his mouth; Dogbari's razor-sharp teeth were the size of her entire arm. The thought of him wielding the power of the crystal made her shiver.

'Will you continue to kill?'

Kill? I haven't killed since the Mother walked the earth. Sinai regarded the creature carefully. Was he lying? Sinai peered deep into his eyes. No, he wasn't. She could feel it as easily as she could feel the wind against her skin. Sinai found herself, yet again, perplexed. If Dogbari hadn't attacked those people, then who had?

Before she could reply, something brushed against her leg. Sinai quickly lost her balance when she looked down to see that she was no longer seated on Dogbari. She was *flying*; hovering over him, following the creature's trajectory with nothing but … herself?

Sinai instinctively felt the Black and Gold realm, the usual source of such occurrences. It rushed over her as easy as breathing, and she sprang into the air with ease. Tears pricked at her eyes as power rushed over her.

It seems, little one, I am not the only one that the crystal has changed.

CHAPTER 30
CRYSTAL TUNNELS

Urukpuru

Sinai lowered herself onto the contorted crystal pipes that housed the Amaghi's Idu. Adrenaline crashed through her chest as she inspected the large pipes. *How had Nwamara done it?*

The crystal structure had no opening, just rudimentary punctures every now and again on the pipe skins, no bigger than a hand. Sinai was filled with a sense of emptiness as her plan soured before her eyes.

Sinai had asked Dogbari to drop her off at Urukpuru. She needed to speak to Naala. Speaking to Dogbari had left her with endless questions and very little answers. She needed help. She needed to find out whether Madi and Eni were …

No. She pushed that thought aside, fighting against the tightness in her chest. She needed to focus. She needed to speak to Naala. Together they could figure this out.

Sinai hovered over what looked like an opening but turned out to be a shadow. 'I could always go through the doors.' She sighed. She could; she had no doubt it would be easier. She also had no doubt that it would lead her face to face with Chukwudi. The echoes of Dogbari's memories pounded against her head. She needed to speak to Naala first.

A shard of light caught her attention and Sinai shifted over to a jagged piece jutting out of one of the crystal pipes. As she approached, the tension in her body gave way and her feet rested on the crystal surface. *An opening!* she thought, clamping her hand over her mouth to stop the squeal from escaping her throat.

Sinai looked around before slithering into the large gash. The jagged edge of the rim pulled unforgivingly at her skin but after a couple of twists and turns, she was in.

Sinai hadn't expected it to be so beautiful in the pipes. Pockets of light came alive in the tunnel, scattering shimmering blues and whites as they danced through the crystal channel. Sinai had expected to have to crawl through the pipes, but she could stand straight without a problem. She could see now that the structure itself wasn't haphazard at all; it was a network … a criss-cross of paths that sat above the Amaghi's settlement.

Sinai walked along, almost aimlessly. She didn't know what direction she was heading in, yet she followed on, turning left here and right there. Something was pulling her and, after a while, Sinai knew with certainty what it was. It was *her.* Naala. At least, that's what she hoped.

'Oh, don't do that!' a voice said from behind her.

Sinai stopped instantly. She swallowed her scream.

'Why? I thought you preferred your parchments by your akwa nest?' another voice, a woman, said.

Sinai turned to face the voice but the crystal tunnel was empty. A cold sweat pricked on her forehead as her heart hammered in her chest.

'Only during the rainy season when the wet travels down the walls; does it look like the rainy season?'

'I don't see a crystal around your neck.'

'What?'

'Throwing demands at me like you're some sort of Aturu,' the other voice grumbled and Sinai's forehead furrowed. The ghostly voices didn't seem to be aware of her presence at all. She looked down at her feet. The crystal coating of the pipe was thick, but she could still see the blurred heads of two people. They weren't talking to her; they were talking to each other.

She held her breath as the man threw his head up to the ceiling. He had seen her. He had to have seen her. Sinai stayed frozen in place, waiting for a shout, a mention of the dark figure in the ceiling, *anything*.

'You say you want to help, I tell you how to help. You complain, bah!' the man exclaimed, looking back down at the woman. He hadn't seen her at all.

No one saw her as she walked through the pipes. Yet, she could hear everything below, as clearly as if she were sitting right by them. Private conversations throughout the Idu filtered upwards and found their way to her. She looked out at the crystal pipes as a frown pulled on her lips. Who else knew about the secrets hidden within them?

Crack!

Sinai's stomach dropped as a creak sounded through the air. Soon after, her body followed. The crystal ground opened up from beneath her and she tumbled down with it. She would have crashed down to the floor had she not grasped at her control of the winds. She lay there suspended in the air for seconds before she heard the cry.

'You!' Naala exclaimed and Sinai collapsed. Her forearms flared with sharp stings as the shards of scattered crystals dug into her skin. Sinai gritted at her teeth as she peeled herself of the ground.

'What are you …? Where have you …? You can *fly*?' For the first time since they met, Naala seemed truly lost for words.

Sinai smiled half-heartedly back at her as she brushed away the shards, unsure of what else to do or say. She hadn't expected this reaction; she had expected rage. Naala's face darkened. *Here it is.*

'Footsteps,' Naala mouthed as Sinai's brow gathered. She followed Naala's gaze to the broken ceiling. 'Can you take us up again?'

'Yes, but—'

'Now!' she hissed. Sinai acted before she could think, pulling them up into the air with an ease that hadn't failed to surprise her. As they entered the pipe, the shards of crystals that had been scattered on the ground followed them up, landing in a heap by Sinai's feet. Naala's eyes were glistening gold as they gave her a sharp look, her finger pressed against her mouth. Below them, the door sprang open and two people entered the room.

'Blast it!' a woman said, stomping around the room. 'I told you I heard something.'

'I – well, she couldn't have gone far. Call for her hamerkop?'

'What hamerkop? They've all been directed to the palace! That's why *we* were supposed to be watching her.'

The man shook his head as he watched her fruitless search. 'Kai! This is not good. What are you going to do?'

'Me? You were the one that told me ...' Her voice faded as they both left the room.

'They're keeping you prisoner?' Sinai whispered once she was sure they had gone.

'Unofficially,' Naala muttered, inspecting the crystal pipes. 'Things have been ... strange.'

'Very,' Sinai replied. Her chest ached as she anticipated what would come after she asked the question burning at her throat. 'Madi?'

That drew Naala's attention quickly. She gave Sinai a wary look, and her stomach plunged. *No, heavens no.*

'He's fine,' she said, 'we think. I don't know. They won't let us see him ... or Eni.' Her voice was strained as though each word was more difficult than the last. Heat pricked at Sinai's cheeks.

'I'm so sorry, I just didn't ...'

'Don't,' Naala said, her expression softening, 'It was impossible, I ... we all acted *questionably*. I shouldn't have ... I'm sorry.' Her eyes lowered.

What did she have to be guilty about? Before Sinai could ask, Naala's head sprang up.

'From what I've gathered, Eni and Madi are in the North East wing of the Idu.' She ran a finger over her lips. 'We should be able to navigate to it from here. This way.'

As they ventured through the ceilings of the Amaghi's Idu, Sinai retold of her encounter with Dogbari in a hushed tone. Naala kept her gaze forward, but Sinai knew that the girl was listening because every now and again she would throw in a question.

'But who killed them then?' Naala suddenly interjected.

'The villagers? I don't know.' She had been hoping that Naala would be able to fill out that puzzle. The girl was good at putting two and two together.

'You left the crystal with him?' Naala asked.

Sinai hadn't got round to that yet. She shifted uncomfortably. She was certain that she had made the right decision. The crystal didn't belong with the Amaghị and she was certain that Dogbari was trustworthy. Yet, she wasn't keen on explaining why she had left something so valuable with a creature that had almost killed Madi. It echoed too closely with what she had done with the Chi Crystal.

'I did ... I trust him,' she said, fighting to keep the weakness out of her voice.

Naala regarded her carefully. 'It may be for the best,' she said, as a dark look passed across her face. 'The Isi has the Àlà Crystal.'

'For *what?*'

'I don't know. She believes that she's more capable of handling it. Don't look at me like that; I didn't *give* it to her. I wouldn't ... I think they shot me with the darts.'

'Why?' Sinai had asked, her mind reeling at the very premise.

'I don't know,' Naala said exasperated. 'But if we could avoid handing them over another crystal before we figure it out, that would be great.' She stopped.

Sinai poked her head around Naala to find that the tunnel itself had come to an abrupt stop. A flat crystal wall stood before them, impenetrable, as far as Sinai could see. Sinai edged to go back around but Naala stopped her gently.

'Look,' she whispered, pointing at the crystal wall. Sinai drew nearer, squinting her eyes until she began to make out something dark below. It sat at the far end of the room below their feet, a white blur sat in the middle of it whilst a red blur hovered before it. The Isi's quarters?

'She's there,' Naala said quietly. The hairs on Sinai's arms lifted as Naala pressed her ear against the wall and tsked.

'That's convenient. Every room in this place is open except for hers.' *It is not just convenient*, Sinai thought, *it's deliberate. Like everything in the settlement.* 'I can't hear anything.'

'What now?' Sinai asked. She half wanted to turn around, find another way to Madi and Eni, but Naala gazed intently at the crystal wall with a hard look on her face.

'I break the ceiling,' Naala muttered as her eyes shimmered in gold.

'Surely they won't continue their conversation if the ceiling collapses?' Sinai exclaimed as Naala shook her head.

'It won't collapse; I'll just make a little hole,' Naala insisted, as she placed her hands on the crystal and closed her eyes. A low scratching sound erupted and thin lines curved within the glass. When they had formed three circles, they gave off a sharp *ping!*

The sound rang through the air as Naala caught the shards in her hands, her eyes wide and lips pressed tightly together.

'What was that?' a deep voice said, his words were slightly muffled, but comprehensible. A cold trickle ran down Sinai's back.

Chukwudi, Naala mouthed, and Sinai nodded back slowly.

'The hamerkops at the wall, I believe,' the Isi replied. 'Go on.'

'Ehh … yes, as I was saying, they can't find the girl.'

'Surely her hamerkop will know her whereabouts?'

'… occupied,' Chukwudi said, his voice low and muffled.

Naala turned to Sinai, her face scrunched in confusion. Sinai shrugged back at her.

'Occupied? What could be more important?'

'There have been many *developments*. Isi, the time has come to put away the crystal to somewhere saf—'

'Chukwudi,' the Isi said; her voice cut through the air like an iced daga.

'Yes, Lolo?' he said, bowing his head as she approached.

'Do you know the best place to hide something precious?'

'Ehh, in, well—'

'In plain sight,' she interjected calmly.

'I …'

'It took me years to teach that lesson to Ochichiri; it's disappointing that you don't know it by now.' Her gloved hand stroked his cheek and he seemed to shiver from her touch.

'I do *understand* but the crystal is precious and I see what's coming. It's getting more dangerous than we imagined.'

'*We?* I spent years of my life following the genealogy of those Descendants, finding each and every one. Finding scraps and pieces to the puzzle that will lead us to the stones. You tell me that the crystal is *precious*? Chukwudi, this is my life.'

'*Precisely*,' Chukwudi implored, 'and if they got their hands on it, well, it could be a disaster.'

'Yes. So why are you leading them to it?'

'I'm not.'

'Do you imagine that you would calm their curiosity if the stone suddenly disappears? The stone that *calls* to them?'

'Well—'

'Did you imagine that they won't ask any questions, go sniffing around for more clues?'

'Well, I—'

'You are forcing me to play a hand that I don't want to play, Chukwudi.' She turned away, her long neck curved as she looked off to the distance. 'I don't like force. I do not like *overtness*. It is ineffective.' She turned back to him. Even from her distance Sinai could see the gleam dancing within the Isi's violet eyes. 'We must *guide* people to make the right decision. Look at what we have already achieved with this strategy. They evoked the crystal. Just as I wanted, and why? Because I gave them the truth that *they* wanted to hear.'

Sinai snapped her head up as something cold trickled down her spine. *Just as I wanted.* The words bounded sporadically in her mind. She turned to Naala and saw that the girl was rigid with fury, her eyes narrowing with laser focus.

'Do you think if I told them to use it, they would have?'

'I can only suppos—'

'You don't need to *suppose*,' the Isi said sharply, 'you *know* they wouldn't have. You saw how they responded to you when you suggested it. We would have lost them before we had the chance to begin.'

Sinai felt sick. It all seemed so obvious now. She thought back to the day Nwamara gave her back the crystals. The bird-woman had been *called*; like a fool she had dismissed it. Sinai bit at her lip to stop herself from screaming.

'I dreamt of the palace last night,' the Isi suddenly said, so low that Sinai almost missed it.

Tick tick. Sinai turned at the sound and froze when she saw a hamerkop gazing at them.

'No,' Naala whispered as the bird took off in flight. Sinai heart plummeted to her stomach. If that hamerkop got away they would have seconds before the Aturu was alerted.

'Hold still,' Sinai hissed as she held it down with gusts of wind. Eventually the bird stilled. Sinai released a breath.

'… so don't flatter me, Chukwudi, I don't need it,' the Isi said.

'Lolo.'

'So, do you have it?'

'I do,' Chukwudi said, as Sinai shifted back to the wall in time to watch Chukwudi pull something out of his garments. It was a crystal horn filled with something bright and red. It moved like a mist or a shadow.

'The Eriri Uhie,' the Isi murmured.

'We've started mining the pit,' Chukwudi said, wetting his lips. 'The process is not as simple as we originally thought but it's promising.'

'It's more than promising. It is everything. *This* combined with the Ọbara magic and the crystals …' she said. 'We'll have everything ready for his return.'

'Yes, Isi,' Chukwudi said.

'What was that?'

'What? I didn't hear anything.'

'In your voice, a hesitance. What are you keeping from me?'

'It's the crystals …'

'I need those crystals. The Eriri Uhie is the beginning but if I really want to control them – control *him* – I need those crystals. All of them.'

'Yes, it's difficult, Lolo,' Chukwudi said. 'We have no idea about the whereabouts of the Ikuku crystal, and the Chi Crystal …it …'

'Out with it.'

'We still haven't been able to locate it, we've searched the far kingdoms and still no word on it.'

'Impossible,' the Isi eventually said; 'it has to be *somewhere*. It has been evoked for heaven's sake, there must be—'

Tick tick.

Sinai groaned inwardly, glancing back. An iron grip tightened its hold on her heart.

'A shame,' the Isi muttered. 'We have to get them back − both of them. We are so close and I'm tired of fighting with scraps.'

'Naala,' Sinai croaked as beads of sweat formed on her forehead.

'Shhh,' Naala insisted, pressing herself further into the crystal wall.

'… I paid for that palace with blood; it will not be snatched away from me by another version of Ochichiri.'

'She wants to rule?' Naala whispered.

Any voice Sinai had left had quickly dried up; all she could do was tug at Naala's arm.

'What?' Naala huffed before letting out a short gasp as she cast her widened eyes on the flock of yellow-spotted hamerkops blinking back at them.

'Can you hold them back?' Naala asked.

'I'm trying; they're too temperamental,' Sinai puffed. 'Too many of them … keep losing concentration. It's like trying to hold a hundred balls in my hands.'

'They can't know we're here,' Naala said as Sinai's head spun.

'I can't hold them,' she realised.

Naala's eyes scanned her. 'Then we have to leave *now*.'

Sinai felt them slipping, one by one. Finally, she let out a breath. For a brief moment, she almost felt relief but that quickly morphed into a sick despair as she watched the birds soar through the tunnel in sudden and frantic haste.

CHAPTER 31

LAND OF DUST

Urukpuru

Naala didn't have time to think. If she thought too deeply, she might lose the courage to act on what was on all accounts an *insane* idea.

The hamerkops had knocked her flat on her back, their wings slapping against her skin as they fled. Naala knew, with almost absolute certainty, that a swift reckoning from the Aturu would follow the blasted birds' departure.

She threw her arms up and a cascade of cracks tore through the crystal pipes. Naala felt the power surge through her body as she created a new path out of the crystal pipes. She didn't have to say a word to Sinai; the girl sprang them up into the air and soared them out into the sky. The winds swept across Naala's face as she let her gaze fall down to the splintered ceiling.

Violet eyes, cold as death, looked back at her.

In one heartbeat, Naala swept her hand across the broken structure and the crystal shards flew to find their old positions until the ceiling gleamed as though nothing had occurred. Still, a shiver ran through Naala. She could still feel the cold glare of the Isi against her skin.

She didn't have much time to dwell on that. Something large and warm swooped in below her. An animal, a beast—

'Waaargghh!' she screamed as it propelled her into the air. The winds whipped across her face and Naala *knew* that she was going to fall and crash to her death. Her body lurched up and down like a doll. Her screams ran high and long and didn't stop until the world stilled. A cloud of dust engulfed her and she gave out a retching cough as she pulled herself up from the powdery floor. Too fast. Her head spun as she buckled down to her knees, her body vibrating and her mind blank.

'Naala,' Sinai said from beside her. The girl's tone was worried and somehow that made Naala feel worse. Something large nudged at the side of her body. The gentle touch acted as an anchor and slowly she returned to herself. When Naala managed to open her eyes, she was met with huge orbs, white as milk, looking down on her. The orbs blinked and Naala was filled with an overwhelming sense of relief and guilt. Naala shivered. Those feelings didn't belong to her.

'The beast?' she whispered and something sharp stabbed at chest. 'Sorry!' she said quickly. Naala didn't know who she was apologising to, but she had a sense that she had *hurt* someone.

'He doesn't like that,' Sinai said beside her. 'He prefers Dogbari,' she said, as Naala lifted her body up.

'Sorry, Dogbari,' Naala said hesitantly. Her gaze ran across the mammoth creature. Could he really *hear* her? She got her answer quickly when a rush of gratitude hit her. A smile threatened to form on Naala's mouth; it was chased away by the reality of their present situation. She turned to Sinai.

'They *knew*,' she spat and Sinai's expression darkened. 'They *wanted* us to evoke that crystal. They knew! Blast it!' Naala could feel heat ripping through all of her senses. Her fingers dug painfully into her palms. She had been deceived, played as though she were a simpleton. Sinai didn't chime in, her expression remained sullen. 'They have Madi, Eni and Kora.' The words felt like dust on her mouth; as they scattered out she was hit with another wave of nausea. *They have Madi, Eni and Kora.* She had to get them out of there. She inspected the land that Dogbari had brought them to for the first time.

The land was completely bare, save a handful of structures and walls. The ground, the structures, even Sinai and Dogbari, were coated in a sea of fine grey dust. There was something hanging in the air. It tasted of death.

'What is this place?' Naala asked.

'I'm not too ...' Sinai wavered before turning to Dogbari. Naala watched for what felt like eternity until Sinai said, 'The land of the dust?' with a crease forming on her brow. 'I think it's the third land in Urukpuru.'

'Fine, but we have to—' Naala's heart thudded painfully before she could say another word.

'What is it?' Sinai asked as Naala stepped closer to a wall carved with an etching she had seen before.

'It is the blood symbol,' Naala said as she came up to it. The same one she had seen in the Oba Awkado that night with Eni. 'It is the Aturu's symbol.'

'The whispers,' Sinai replied distantly, 'like the walls of the Idu.'

Naala took a step towards the slab of concrete. There was something behind it. Something that needed her. 'It's not a wall,' she said, grazing her hand against the stone. It pricked against her skin, drawing blood. Symbols began to appear, glowing a deep red. 'The soul that pumps blood through the snake,' she read.

Snap!

A breaking sound exploded into the air and the stone door creaked open. An old smell sprang into the air, stale and stagnant. It was all-consuming, filling every space with an entitled ease. She felt strangely drawn to this place. She walked ahead into the darkness despite Sinai's silent protests, stopping only when she felt something brittle crunching under her foot.

'What is this?' Sinai said, flinching at the shadows in the air.

Naala looked down, her stomach churning as she stared at a material she had seen before until her vision blurred with tears.

'Strange magic,' she whispered, tears choking each word. She picked the navy garment from the ground, embroidered with tiny elephants. The smile of the boy she had met in Siwunmi, visiting from the North village, scorched across her mind.

'No,' Sinai said hoarsely, her voice thick and low, 'they said they were using *animal* sacrifices; Bayo said they had only sacrificed a *goat at most.*'

'They sent us on a death mission to trick us into evoking the crystal. Madi almost died,' Naala said flatly as she shifted through the scattered bones. Her stomach tightened and she could feel bile building up at the back of her throat, but she kept her body still. 'How many animals do we see roaming about Urukpuru? How could we have thought that a couple of stray jackals were enough to keep the entire Amaghị settlement powered? To keep Dogbari contained? To fly the efe-efe baskets? We saw how much energy it took to grow a plant; how much more so to power an entire settlement?' Why hadn't she seen it before? She hadn't wanted to.

'Nwamara said that Ọbara magic seeps into your soul and breaks it apart,' Sinai whispered as a haunted look ran across her face.

'Well, it doesn't get much soulless than this,' Naala muttered, blinking away her tears as a thunderous heat raged within her.

'We should get out of—' Naala started before a muffled remote sound echoed through the dark caves. 'Someone's here.'

'I think it's the hum,' Sinai murmured as Naala shook her head.

'No, *I* can hear something,' she said, as she crept forward into the cave.

'Naala,' Sinai hissed, 'we don't know if it is safe.'

'Of course it isn't,' Naala muttered as she walked further in; from the scuffled noise behind her, Sinai must have decided to follow along.

The air darkened and Naala couldn't see a thing. Only the faint murmur, sporadically cutting through the thick air, kept Naala on course. She blinked as the pitch-black began to soften. She saw the curves of the caves and artefacts that lined the walls. She halted. There was something glowing in the depth of the cave. A deep red glow. She approached it carefully, her breath quickening, though she couldn't say why. The red glow sprouted from the centre of the room, and fanned out through vines embedded in the surrounding grounds.

It was an ofo stick with a serpent's head. The jewelled eyes shone brilliant red.

'This must be what they use to power everything,' Naala whispered. She could feel it pulsing in the air. It wasn't lost on Naala that the red glow was similar to the glowing vines that lay beneath the Amaghị's crusted crystal walls.

Sinai let out a slight, strangled noise.

'S-Sinai?' Naala cried, freezing at the sight of Sinai toppling over, her fingers digging deep into her head so hard that Naala could see pricks of red mixing in with her tears. Sinai's breath was jagged through her clenched jaws. 'Stop it! Sinai?!'

The girl let out a sobbed cry. 'So many voices, s-s-o many souls.'

Ice ran down Naala's back as she turned back to the ofo sticks. She hadn't noticed it before but now she *knew*. They were not *alone*.

'Souls,' Sinai whimpered as a tear ran down Naala's cheek.

'They're trapped,' Naala said hoarsely, glancing around at the skeletons around her. *The soul that pumps blood through the snake.* Naala's throat closed up so tight she choked as she doubled over. It wasn't enough that they killed them, that they drained their blood … they drained their *souls* too.

Sinai let out another cry and Naala's body seemed to move without her direction. She picked up the ofo stick. The heat bit fiercely into her hand. Invisible flames crawled up her arms, scorching at her flesh though they left no mark. Naala roared as she smashed the cursed artefact on the ground.

The world stilled.

Then it broke.

A force flung her against the stone walls before pulling the world into darkness.

CHAPTER 32
THE SURVIVOR

Urukpuru

'Chief, the council meeting has begun,' a distant voice said.

'Yes, they tend to do that at this time,' a man said, smiling down at her, his dark almond eyes crinkled as she tried to reach for him. 'I'll be there in a moment,' he added, turning to the distant voice before her whimpers drew him back.

He bent down to plant a kiss on her forehead. Her hands were balled up into little fists and she sprang them into the air.

'Esinaala!' the man exclaimed with a laugh that warmed her belly. 'Is it me that you want to beat?' he chuckled and she began to laugh with him. A laugh that made her head lighter than the air.

She stopped when she noticed it, the wet sadness creeping into his eyes. 'Ahh, you're just like Zy,' he said in a low voice. He shifted her slightly before placing a gentle hand on a bundle sleeping soundly at her side, 'and you, Sinaikuku – always sleeping, eh?'

'Chief.'

'Eh-he.' The man sighed before shaking his head. 'Na me who be chief, yes?'

'Ahh, yes, Ozo.'

'Okay, good. I'm glad you remember.' He chuckled lightly. 'Don't stress, I'll be right there. Can you not see that I'm finishing up another important meeting with my daughters?' he laughed before shaking his head and getting up.

*

Tears ran down Naala's cheek when she opened her eyes. She sat up and the dust air tore at the back of her throat. She let out a violent cough. Dust clung heavily in the air, broken up by tiny beams of light. Indigos and violets slowly flooded the cave. She looked up to see that the cave's ceiling had completely blown away. Beside her, Sinai stirred.

'Eyya,' a voice groaned incoherently.

Naala frowned; it hadn't come from Sinai. She staggered to her feet and followed the voice to a set of cages in the corner of the cave. They were full of skeletal figures, slumped over and wasted.

'Hello,' she said; her voice was so raspy it was almost inaudible. She let out another cough. 'Hello?'

'Naala,' the skeleton whispered. Naala took a step back, her heart thumping violently. Was the skeleton *alive*?

'How-how do you know my name?'

'Survivors must train,' the figure whispered.

Her heart stopped. She had heard that before, surrounded by the green forest and sweltering heat. 'Survivors must train,' the skeletal man repeated, and Naala could see the ghost of a huge ox of a man, Azu. He would repeat that phrase as he led the training sessions that had served as a mask for Madi, Kora and Eni to scheme with the Amaghi. Naala peered at the stick figure before her.

'It can't be,' she muttered.

'Survivors must train,' he said again and she sprang back, her mind reeling with shock.

'*Azu?*' she asked and the skeletal figure turned to her, his sunken eyes boring into her soul.

'You,' he said, shaking his head at her.

'Azu,' Naala choked, 'be still — I'm going to get you out of here, but you need to save your energy.' She tugged at the cage bars. They had been weakened by the blast and creaked under her pressure.

'En,' he whimpered at her and Naala felt her heart shatter. She thought back to all the times when she had ridiculed him behind his back, mocked him to his face.

She had openly despised him. Now seeing him like this made her wish that she had been kinder. 'I'm getting you.'

'Ena,' he whimpered.

'Just hold on,' she said as she used her powers to fling off the cage door.

'Eni,' he whimpered and Naala stopped dead in her tracks.

'What did you just say?' she murmured but Azu didn't reply. There was a stillness in his body that irked her.

'Azu, what did you just say?' Naala asked again, reaching out at the man but he didn't respond. Sinai came up behind her.

'Did you hear what he said?' Naala asked but Sinai just shook her head.

'I think …' Sinai whispered, 'I think he's dead.'

'No,' Naala said, grasping onto his arm, and waiting for a slight thud of a pulse that never came. She dropped the cold arm and a dark silence washed over them.

'Naala,' Sinai called. Only then did she realise that she was walking. Her feet moved with a deadly purpose. 'Naala, where are you going?' Sinai scrambled behind her.

'I'm going to find them,' she said through clenched teeth, her heart beating frantically. She felt as though she could feel and see *everything*, and yet it all seemed surreal. *Eni.*

Had he really said Eni? Had she imagined it? If not, what did it *mean*? Naala stormed out of the cave. She needed answers.

'Find who?'

'The people who did this. We are going to get answers, Sinai, and then we're going to burn them all down.'

CHAPTER 33

JADED BONES

City of Nri

A pale-green hamerkop landed with a soft plop on Olu's workbench. A smile pulled on his lips as the old bird tottered towards him. He ruffled its unkempt feathers before taking out the scroll tied to its neck. He couldn't say why he had adopted Sinai's old hamerkop as his own, but he was glad for it. There was humour in its greying eyes that lightened his spirit whenever he chanced to notice it.

Olu's smile faded as he read the parchment.

General quarters. Now. —Eze Ikenna

Olu gritted his teeth at the title. 'Fool,' he muttered under his breath as he stormed out of his quarters. Everyone knew that the hamerkops were easily infiltrated, so what was Ikenna playing at? If the Obis caught Ikenna referring to himself as Eze, then the fraught alliance Olu had fought to form over recent moon-cycles would crumble. Nri would be at war.

Olu tugged at his gloves. His heart juddered when he caught sight of the horror that lay beneath the beaten leather. The horror that had answered his prayers and sealed his fate forever.

'Olu,' a voice said from behind him and he turned to find himself faced with Obi Ife. Olu sighed inwardly as the slender man strutted over to him with purpose. He tried to force a smile for the Obi but the most he could muster was a glare.

'Ndewo, Obi Ife,' Olu said as Obi Ife approached him; he crossed his palms at his chest and brought them down towards the agitated Obi.

'Eh, yes, Ndewo Olu,' Obi Ife replied, performing the standard introduction lacklustrely. 'I need to speak to him.'

'You know he has refused to speak to any of the Obis outside the council meetings.'

'I am not *any* Obi!' Obi Ife spat, jerking towards Olu with every word. He paused, drawing up his chin so that his pitch-black locs fell behind his ears. On another man, it might have been interpreted as threatening, but for Obi Ife it was awkward, and somewhat embarrassing. Once the Eze's favourite, Obi Ife was now at the mercy of the other Obis. In the absence of their old leader, their ripened resentment was now open and vengeful.

Olu thought briefly to nudge the man back, but Obi Ife's ego was as fragile as an indigobird's egg. He had no desire to clean up that mess.

'I am practically the Eze Ochichiri's *heir*,' Obi Ife hissed. 'The natural next in command. If Ikenna really expects me to convert the Obis to his cause – so that we can rule *together* – then I must be able to speak to him freely. I have *urgent* news.'

Olu gave the man a hard look. Obi Ife faltered before taking a weary step back, clasping his hands together as he let off a nervous chuckle. 'After all, we are on the same side.' He shrugged.

'Indeed. This is why you must learn to understand Ikenna's *nature*, it can be … temperamental. Not always suitable for a *refined* Obi like yourself – at times a filter is simply necessary. Why should you bear the brunt of such aberrant moods?'

'*Surely* this is something I must learn to handle if I am to be the Eze,' Obi Ife said, whispering the last word as though it were a secret he couldn't help but share.

Olu tensed. The statement was reckless. He couldn't afford any recklessness; not when things were so delicate. Olu had only just managed to convince Ikenna to slow down on the Ọbara oaths; imploring that the Obi system only worked when the Obis were *truly* on his side. They needed something else. They needed someone on the inside, someone hungry, ambitious and conceited enough for him to be easily controlled. They needed Obi Ife. The senior lord could bring the reluctant Obis to their cause, simply by speaking in their language.

Olu didn't tell Ikenna that he had bought Obi Ife's compliance with the promise of a joint partnership. Olu had no doubt that Ikenna would see it as no less than treason. He looked at the glee forming across Obi Ife's face. *Fools*, he thought as he released a heavy sigh. *They're all fools.*

'How are the negotiations with Obi Arinze?' Olu threw in. The Obi of trade was pivotal in all of this; if Obi Arinze shifted his alliance from Obi Akunna, then Olu was certain that the others would follow. They would have won.

'That is what I am trying to tell Ikenna: something is wrong.'

'What could be wrong? Wasn't it you who said that the majority of Obi Akunna's followers could be easily converted to our cause?' Olu asked.

'Exactly!' Obi Ife said. 'You said it yourself, I command respect; but something is happening within the Obis. They are becoming more arrogant and less willing to *engage.*'

'What do you mean?' Olu frowned.

'They are no longer listening to reason,' Obi Ife huffed. 'Once it had been almost a fact that most, if not all, of the Obis, with some persuasion, *would* choose Ikenna over Obi Akunna – but it would seem that the situation has since *changed.*'

'Changed how?' Olu snapped, ever more tired of the Obi's flowery language.

Obi Ife looked around guardedly. 'I believe that there is something new in the mix.'

Olu frowned as a knowing expression spread across Obi Ife's face. 'Well, what is it?'

'I'm not certain yet but something has them afraid. Something to do with Akunna,' he said, pulling up the corner of his mouth in a sneer. 'I believe he's dabbling in Ọbara magic.'

Ọbara magic? Ikenna's affiliation for the practice was uncommon for the noble class. He certainly couldn't imagine someone like *Obi Akunna* dabbling in it. Olu regarded Obi Ife carefully. 'Are you certain?'

'I know the signs,' Obi Ife noted, his eyes crawling up Olu's dulled skin disapprovingly. 'I know he is planning something big.' He drew a little closer before looking around cautiously. 'Something to do with that ghastly commoner's illness,' he added quietly. 'Hey!' he called as Olu darted off. 'Make sure you let him know that we *need* to talk!'

*

Olu steadied his breath as he entered the Army's Nkebi. The General's quarters were at the west side of the palace, and unlike most quarters, it didn't have walls. It sat like a large fat caterpillar, the sides of its belly were curved white pillars that allowed the warm air from the neighbouring fields to waft through.

The ceilings were layered with blocks of wood and raffia, varying from dark camel to sand. The ọkụ lights hung by the pillars, dancing faintly to the sounds of the cicadas as they welcomed the mauve evening sky.

Olu let out a staggered exhale when he saw Ikenna. He did not look well. The dark circles under his eyes had deepened since he last saw him. The only thing that seemed to have remained the same was the piercing hunger beneath his slit eyes. *No, not the same*, Olu thought. *It has worsened.*

Olu's chest tightened when he saw who was seated on Ikenna's lap but he didn't change his stride. Chiaza, the woman that Olu had defended in the city squalor. The woman he had gone to nearly every night since. Chiaza would cling to him under the blanket of the deep night. She did not complain when he would disappear before daybreak and she did not flinch when he would call her by someone else's name.

She shifted in embarrassment when he approached. Olu noted Ikenna's grip tightening at her hesitation.

'Ndewo, Olu,' Ikenna said.

'Ndewo, Ikenna,' Olu replied, letting his palms fall towards the both of them. 'Ndewo, Chiaza,' he added.

Her eyes fell to the ground as she began to mumble a reply before Ikenna shook her into silence.

'I see you've gone ahead with the extensions,' Olu said as he saw the rubble in the far distance where the oxen stables had once been. He did nothing to hide the disapproval in his face or tone. Olu had warned Ikenna that Obi Arinze, the *one* Obi they truly needed on their side, would surely take offence for that overstep, that he would be unforgiving. *Stupid, stupid, stupid move.*

Ikenna watched him with cold eyes. 'Tell him,' he said, jostling his knee.

Chiaza blinked back at him with widened eyes.

Olu's jaw clenched as what felt like a daga pierced through his belly. The sight of Chiaza had rattled him far more than he would have thought. He could taste her discomfort; it was bitter and cruel.

'Eze Ikenna does as he pleases,' she said softly, still unable to meet his eyes.

'Indeed,' Olu said.

'Oh, yes, of course, you two are *acquainted*,' Ikenna said with a glint in his eyes. He threw Chiaza off his lap.

Olu cursed himself as he lurched forward. The best thing he could do for her was feign apathy. At least then, there might have been a chance that Ikenna would have grown bored. He had lost that now. Olu stood rigidly as Chiaza struggled to her feet, her eyes wild as she adjusted her loosened garment.

'It's quite a lesson, isn't it, Olu?' Ikenna got up to his feet and stalked towards the other man. 'Watching someone else take what is yours. My father taught me it young. A few times actually,' Ikenna said distantly. 'I didn't realise at the time but it was an important lesson. Sometimes with family and friends, over-familiarity can skew the true hierarchy that must be in place, but *this*,' he said, gesturing to Chiaza, 'draws a line under everything, doesn't it? This makes it clear who the real Onyeisi is.' His slit eyes burned into Olu before he broke into a cruel laugh. 'Of course, I did go on to kill him, so there's that ... but *you* won't be doing that, will you, Olu? Not after our little ceremony.'

'This is unnecessary,' Olu said tightly.

'I didn't even have to try,' Ikenna said, his eyes wild and bright. 'I just told her my name and she leapt into my nest.' Ikenna grabbed a fistful of her hair and Chiaza let out a shrill cry.

Olu's abara was in his hand before he could think. At the corner of his eyes he saw two large bodies approach.

The Nkịta Ọhịa: Ikenna's private platoon. Olu hadn't known the meaning of ruthless until he had met them. Why wouldn't they be, after what they had to go through to even call themselves a member. They would spend years training and bonding with the wild ọnwa wolves from the North – a strange breed of wolf, twice as large as a common gray wolf, with golden coats and silver eyes. Before the Earth

Mother disappeared, they were said to be able to shift into the spirit realm during full moons. Ikenna would make his men bond with the animals before forcing them into a brutal hand-combat. Those who survived joined the famed platoon, wearing the dead wolf's fur as a badge of honour. At times Olu could swear he could detect shards of silver in their deep-brown eyes: ghosts of the wolves they had slaughtered.

'No,' Ikenna called out, his eyes fixed on Olu, 'I will deal with him alone.'

'Let the girl go home,' Olu tried. Chiaza flinched as Ikenna spat at her. Olu felt his blood boil so hot he truly thought he would die if he didn't strangle the small man.

'I-I do not know what I have done to displease you, E-Eze … I don't want to displease you. I just want to be with you,' she said gently, as Ikenna laughed bitterly.

'She wants to be with *me*?' Ikenna said, curving his eyebrows mockingly. 'Olu, what nonsense have you spewed to this street urchin?'

Chiaza shrank away from the glow of Ikenna's drawn abara sword.

'Don't you ever insult me like that again, do you hear?'

Olu's heart plunged. Any hopes he had of rectifying the situation dissipated into the warm air like steamed water.

'Yes,' she said, shivering at his tone.

'Yes, what?'

'Yes, Eze Ikenna.'

'Ah ha!' Ikenna announced.

'Ikenna,' Olu said sternly. The small man glanced at him briefly before turning back to Chiaza mockingly.

'Sure, he seems so innocent now, but trust me, urchin, this man is a *snake*. Rather like you,' he muttered, before lowering his abara and turning back to Olu. 'You think I don't know what you have been up to? Prancing around with the Obis?'

'Of course you know, we *agreed*,' Olu exclaimed. 'Is this what this show is about, Ikenna? Your poor memory?'

'Nothing about me is poor or weak or less than,' Ikenna said, his voice so low that Olu could feel its vibration throughout the Nkebi. 'Nothing!'

Ikenna grabbed Chiaza by the hair, pulling her head so far back it exposed the full extent of her neck.

Olu bolted towards them but stumbled as a familiar sensation brought him to his knees – crippling pain that tore at his skin and squeezed at his innards.

'You, on the other hand, *do* have a weakness,' Ikenna added with a wicked grin.

Olu coughed violently as the poison from the Ọbara oath coursed through his veins, claiming his blood as penance for his attempt to cut down the other man.

Chiaza's feverish eyes were glossed with tears. Her mouth moved silently but Olu knew what she was begging for: her life. If he was quick, he could do it. He could plunge the abara into Ikenna's chest. If he did that he would die. Then what? The Nkịta Ọhịa would kill her. He knew that. The kingdom would be doomed. Sinai would be left alone to deal with what he knew was coming. He *had* to stay alive. He had to be there for her.

'Olu,' Chiaza choked before she let out a piercing scream.

Olu felt sick as the abara metal burst through her stomach. His head pounded as the world slowed. Chiaza jerked at the pain, her mouth filling with red foam and her eyes bulged. Olu watched as the curse of the abara metal filled her with the worst of its pains. It was torturous to have it in a body. It was so cruel.

'Pull it out!' Olu growled.

'But then she'll die,' Ikenna whined. '*Too quickly*,' he added with a cackle. 'I am about to teach you a truly valuable lesson, brother. A lesson in pain and loyalty.'

Olu felt a cold chill run through him. He looked at the other man dead in the eye, dropping his abara sword as he rose to his feet. Olu pulled off the glove and a gasp echoed through the open space.

Olu rarely looked at it. His hand. Not since the incident. Now, he brought it to his face for inspection. He couldn't really call it a hand any more. It was simply frayed scraps of muscle over jade-green bone.

'Kedu?!' Ikenna shouted but Olu paid him no mind. He placed his hand into his garment until he found it. The crystal that had transformed him. When Olu finger grazed its cool surface. He could see the thin thread that tied Chiaza to life. He squeezed at the crystal and Chiaza's whimpers settled down to nothing. Chiaza was no longer in pain. She was no longer there; instead a pile of dust scattered over Ikenna.

'How?' Ikenna jumped up, frantically slapping the dust off of his garments before looking up at Olu. 'The crystal?' he gasped, revealing the whites of his eyes. 'Give it to me now!' Ikenna roared. 'I demand that you give it to me now!'

'I tried to die,' Olu said to him, ignoring Ikenna's petulant cries. He could hear the lightness of feet moving behind him. Two men were at the edge of the Nkebi's neighbouring fields, another two behind the door. Two on the roof and two more located near the rubble at the end of the Nkebi. All eight of the Nkịta Ọhịa had arrived. They were all deadly quiet. He shouldn't have been able to hear them, but Olu had always had an uncanny knack for the art of war.

'I held it, hoping to die. Hoping to be rid of you and your sick demands. After endless moon-cycles, holding on for a promise that I made to *her*, I was willing to throw it all away because of you.' The hatred he had locked away spewed out of his pores, as sweet and sticky as honey, coating him from head to toe. 'I didn't die, but I *saw*. I saw that which will come. What the amoosu saw the day we enacted that blood curse. It is coming for this kingdom. It is coming for *her*. We have to be prepared. We have to be unified, and this—' he gestured to the dust at his feet '— must stop. Otherwise, brother, I will kill you. And if you make me do that, if you make me fail her *again*, our souls will never rest. That I promise you.'

'You're insane,' Ikenna said, his eyes darting out into the encroaching darkness.

'Do you really want all of your men reduced to dust? With all the people out to kill you, do you think that's wise? I'm only one man, Ikenna. I can only do so much.'

Ikenna's eyes widened at the threat. 'You can't do this, any of it. You are bound to me by blood.'

'Did you think I could forget?' Olu said quietly to him. 'I am bound by blood to put you on the throne, Ikenna. But there is a lot behind that, isn't there? If I give you the crystal and it kills you, *ncoh*? I would have failed, yes,' Olu said, nodding, as he stepped towards Ikenna, 'but if I use the crystal to help you get to the throne, to help you keep it, to help rid you of your *tendencies* that would otherwise get in your way – then I have succeeded, yes?'

Ikenna let his mouth hang. 'Olu, this isn't *you*.'

'You pride yourself on *knowing* me, Ikenna, but you weren't the only one listening in the drinking ụlọ. I know that you want to rule, and you will. They will sing your praises and shout your name, I will ensure it. You will be able to do whatever you want to do as long as it is within my boundaries.' Olu stalked closer. 'You see, a man like *you* will always thrive under boundaries, but take them away and you become manic. Ikenna, I have faith that soon you will come to understand and appreciate these boundaries.'

'You filthy—'

'Ikenna – come on, *brother*, this is not the time for harsh words; this is a celebration after all. Don't you see? You will be the Eze. You have so many things to be happy about. Your uncle and father may be dead, but your mother and dear sisters and efuola daughter are still alive and well in the Kingdom of Aksum,' Olu said as Ikenna's eyes widened. 'It is just as you said, Ikenna. Everyone can be got,' Olu added quietly, 'and together we are going to transform Nri to a new glory.'

CHAPTER 34
THE SHADOWED MAN

Urukpuru

'So, you agree that this is the best thing to do?' Sinai asked, glancing over at Naala nervously. She hadn't said a word in a long while. Her expression was hard as stone. Sinai had spent the last hour trying to convince Naala not to be too rash. They needed to get Ina, Madi, Eni and Kora out of the grasp of the Amaghi before they proceeded to 'burn them all down'. After all, they both knew what the Amaghi were capable of.

The land of dust had left a cold chill buried deep within Sinai's bones. She didn't want to think about it, yet she couldn't stop her thoughts from wandering back to that cruel abyss. The feel of the dust between her fingers, the brittle bones that punctuated her treads, the sorrowful voices. Sinai sank into all of it. At times, her hand would fling to her chest, clutching at the space as though to tear it out.

Ina, Madi, Kora and Eni were all locked in the crystal Idu with the people who had committed those evil acts. It was too much to bear. *We'll get them out*, she thought to herself for the umpteenth time. *We have to.* The chant soothed her a little but Naala wasn't helping.

She was hiding something behind her shrewd gaze. Something that could lead her to do something wild and unexpected. Something that could jeopardise it all.

'Naala, did you hear me? I said, do you still agree that this is the—' Sinai tried again, halting at Naala's curt nod. Sinai could see that if she pushed any harder it could inspire the worst of it. Instead she followed Naala's hard glare towards the Idu below.

Sinai was holding them steadily in the air right above the crystal pipes where Dogbari had left them. In truth, Sinai would have liked Dogbari to have been with them. She would have felt safer with the large creature by her side, but Dogbari fetched too much attention. Even when he coated himself with the clouds he was a sight to be seen. Rather than take the chance, Dogbari had brought them to the Idu, far past the reach of human eyes. Soon after he had left, Sinai had guided her and Naala down closer to the crystal pipes that coated the Amaghi's Idu.

Now they stood watching. Waiting. The shimmering lights danced and dazzled below. Strange, she had not expected it to be this *alive*. She had expected gloom, sorrow, something that reflected their horrific deeds. Instead, she was met with jubilance. How were they still able to power the Idu without the souls that Naala had released? A shiver ran down her spine. *It must not be their only source of power*, she thought darkly. There must be more lands of dust. More trapped souls coursing through the walls of the cursed settlement.

'Let's go,' Naala said thickly.

'What about the—' Sinai started before a loud crash drowned her out. Naala must have started the diversion. A series of pits starting off in the Rie quarters, large sunken holes in the ground, certain to take all the attention as they entered the Idu once again through the pipes.

'Let's go,' Naala repeated sharply. Sinai sucked in a breath before allowing the power to surge through her flesh as she tugged at the winds, sweeping the clouds low enough to feed through the pipes. Sinai hoped that they would serve as a cover to hide them. With that, they began to descend down to the spot that Naala had theorised would be housing Madi and Eni.

As they reached the crystal pipes, Sinai let the high winds roar. The sounds masked the loud cracks that formed as Naala tore into the pipes. When the gaps were large enough, Sinai lowered them both in. Her chest hammered with fright as she half expected to find the Aturu hidden in the shadows. They weren't. The crystal pipes were as empty as they had been when she had first entered. Yet, Sinai couldn't let her muscles unclench.

Naala and Sinai had passed through three sets of pipes already, layered over one another like logs. They now stood within the last pipe, and at her feet Sinai could see a hazed image of the room below.

It was filled with akwa nests, four of which were occupied. She recognised the people in the bed. They were too blurred to know for sure, but something about their shapes, their hair and colouring reminded her of Madi, Ina, Kora and Eni. Could it really be them?

Naala stiffened beside her.

'They're sleeping, not … they're breathing,' Sinai said quickly; that was one thing at least. Naala's shoulders dropped at Sinai's words, but her lips remained pursed.

'This isn't right,' Naala murmured. They had expected Madi and Eni to still be recovering in the Healers' Wing, but what were Kora and Ina doing with them? 'Why have they put them all here? Sedated?'

Sinai's stomach churned. It was a honey trap. 'What do we do?'

Naala peered through the crystal pipe floor unmoved. 'We go. We go through with our plan and deal with what we have to deal with when we get there.' She looked up at Sinai squarely. 'We just have to keep our eyes open.' Dread pumped through Sinai. Keep their eyes open to what? The unknown? There was only so much they could see or preempt when they were going into a situation completely blind.

Are you sure? The words were stuck in her throat, but before she could get them out, she heard a crack resonating below.

Sinai's weight plummeted to the ground. She grasped at the air before holding both Naala and her suspended. Shattered shards of crystals scraped over them, nicking her skin as they crashed to the ground. Sinai clenched her jaw at the proceeding stings.

'Could you please warn me next time?' she said quietly, her cheeks blazing hot as she lowered them both to their feet. She shook the crystal shards that clung to her. At the very least, Naala could have exercised greater control over the crystals.

Naala looked back at her with eyes as wide as eferes. 'It wasn't me,' Naala muttered as her eyes narrowed around the room. Sinai's mouth dried as she glanced up at the gaping hole in the ceiling. Had they been too heavy? Sinai ran her eyes over the room. Lingering at the akwa nests, her heart thumping at the sight of Madi, Ina, Eni and Kora. She followed the rhythm of their breath carefully, until—

Sinai let out a strangled noise.

'What is it?' Naala demanded as Sinai turned to the far right corner of the room. The space was completely empty, and yet, she *knew* that there was someone there. The air shifted around something and flowed in and out of a figure. Someone was breathing.

'Naala,' Sinai said gently, her eyes fixed on the invisible person. Naala turned and looked at the spot.

'I don't …' Her words faded into silence as a figure emerged before their eyes. Chukwudi.

'Impressive,' he said, the white wisps of his beard twitching with glee. 'What was it? My breathing?' He didn't wait for a reply. 'Very impressive. It narrowly makes up for your earlier blunder,' he said, taking a measured step forward, a smile spreading across his face. 'The sheer hubris you must wield to dare to enter the crystal pipes again. Stupid. Incredibly stupid. Even with your silly little pit tricks. I'm curious, did you actually want to be caught?'

Naala wasted no time. She flicked her wrist and the shards of crystals scattered on the ground lifted and zoomed hastily towards Chukwudi. Their target was clear and their path unyielding, yet not one of them hit him. Before they could so much as graze against his skin, they shimmered into dust. Chukwudi snickered cruelly; the blood crystal at his neck shone crimson.

'Behold, the Descendants of the First. The would-be gods,' he said bitterly as he reached into his garments and pulled out two darts. 'In the end we are all the same. You will yield just like the others. Your souls will feed the Amaghi with more power than you can even dream of. We really should be thanking you.' In a near undetectable motion, Chukwudi flung the darts at them but as soon as they left his grip, Sinai shifted the air and changed their course. They shot up to the sky, lodging deep into the pipes above and shattering on impact.

He grinned. 'Another mistake on your part. I offered those darts to you as a mercy. What follows will be rods worse.' At that Sinai felt a force squeeze against her stomach. She gasped as she was flung into the air.

No! she wanted to scream but there was no air left in her lungs. Her back slammed against the crystal ceiling before she felt her weight drop. They pulled to the ground faster than a heartbeat. Sinai mustered all of her strength to swivel the air below them in what she hoped would be a cushion against the impact.

Blinding agony ripped through her all the same when they crashed. Before she could draw another breath he did it again. Then again. Again. Agai— She couldn't see any more. Everything was a sickening blur. She could scarcely think and yet with each blow she managed to pour the air below them.

Only, the air was getting thinner with each crash. Her body was too heavy. Her mind too clouded. Sinai couldn't keep going.

The crystal ground raced towards them. Her heart ached. This time she would fail. She knew it. Her bones would shatter. Her mind would go dark.

Sinai released her hold. When she opened her eyes, she realised she wasn't spinning. She was on the ground watching as the crystal ceiling tore into a thousand shards and crashed down on her.

CHAPTER 35
RAINS OF CRYSTAL SHARDS

Urukpuru

Sinai didn't flinch as the glittering dagas of crystals poured down on her. She welcomed them. They would stop the pounding in her head. They would end the roaring ache scraping under her bruised skin. They would send her to sleep. She closed her eyes.

Get up! something screamed within her. *Help her!* Help who?

Sinai's eyes sprang open and she turned to see Naala, her teeth gritted and stained with blood, her body bruised but her eyes sharper than she'd ever seen them, fixed on the endless cascade of crystal shards raining down on Chukwudi.

His hands were raised high and his neck bulged as he struggled to turn wave after wave of the crystal shower into dust. The crystal at his neck was no longer ruby red but a dulled pink. He was weakening.

Sinai drew all the energy she had left and sent the full force of the winds rushing towards him. Caught off guard, Chukwudi fell flat on his back, his hands still raised as he fought off the oncoming slaughter of the endless shards. He was starting to miss. They sliced through his skin and blotches of dark red started to form on his robes. Sinai chortled hysterically as the smell of blood darkened her mind. *Drain him. Turn him to dust.*

Sinai could feel his Ike-Obi. It wouldn't be hard. In seconds she could have him writhing, begging for his life. In minutes he would be dust. She shook her head. The skeletal figures from the land of dust nudged into her mind. Never. She would never use that form of magic again.

Instead she drew on the air that circled him. He resisted her with great strength, but still he had begun to struggle for air. He twisted and turned and Sinai's eyes widened as she saw the floor swallow him. It wrapped over his body, pulling him in place, sinking him deeper into its hold until only his head could be seen.

'You were saying?' Naala said, out of breath, as he wriggled and writhed, roaring in defiance, but the crystal around his neck was clear. He had no way of getting out.

Sinai quickly tore off a strip of cloth from her garments. They may have been able to subdue Chukwudi, but she had no intention of dealing with the rest of the Aturu. She walked over to the screaming man and hesitantly wrapped the material over his mouth. He bit at the air, snarling as she did, but soon his yelps were muffled and low.

When she looked up, Naala was by Eni's nest, a quivering hand on his chest.

'Sinai.' Her voice was so thin; she looked up at her with glazed wide eyes. 'Something is wrong with them. They're all *frozen*.' She waved her hand over Eni's face. 'Eni, can you hear me?'

'He can,' a cold voice said from behind them.

Sinai turned to see the Isi standing before them, her white robes gleaming in the moonlight. Her heart-shaped face was raised high, and her violet eyes gleamed behind her crystal white lashes. A smile perched on her peach lips.

'I must say, it's a pleasure to have you girls back.'

CHAPTER 36
BY HER HAND

Urukpuru

'I would stay where you are, girls,' the Isi murmured at the door. The room fell into a stiff silence, broken by the muffled cries of Chukwudi. The Isi. Lolo Obioma. The woman who headed the Amaghị. The woman who had defied all odds. The woman who would kill them all.

Naala's rib cage tightened as her gaze fell to the Isi's necklace; the Àlà crystal gleamed at her chest. It seemed to mock her, a symbol of her failure and loss. Naala's heart pounded hot blood through her body as she raised her head high. They had defeated Chukwudi. Wasn't he the head of the Aturu? The champion in Ọbara magic? If they could defeat him, then they could defeat her too. They had to. Something in her gut told her she had more to lose than her life.

A cold chill ran down Naala's spine as she felt Eni's unblinking eyes peeled on her. Would they be able to fix him? Did they even want to? She didn't know what to think of him. Why had Azu said Eni's name? Was it the creeping madness of a dying mind, or was it more?

He was so close to the Amaghị, closer than all of them. Why? Could he be involved in their atrocities? Her gaze found his and her heart ached. No. He couldn't. She *knew* him. There was no way he could be involved. Could he? Naala sucked in a breath. She needed to hear from him. For that to happen, she needed him alive.

'Let them go,' Naala demanded and the Isi frowned.

'No.' There was power behind her voice that Naala hadn't noticed before. It held no doubt, no question. It spoke of cold and certain cruelty.

'Let them go,' Sinai echoed, and a light breeze flew through the room. The Isi's mouth curled slightly. Her nose flared as she stepped back with her hand to her neck. Gold scattered across Sinai's eyes as she snatched the breath from the Isi's lungs.

Before Naala could feel a moment of relief, her stomach dipped. Movement. Small, violent jolts juddered through their friends. At her side, Eni was baring his gritted teeth, his eyes were bulged and unblinking, despite the sweat trickling into them.

'Stop,' Naala screeched.

Sinai blinked back, her mouth open and moving, but no words escaped. She let out a sigh and the Isi took a step backwards.

'I did *warn* you,' the Isi croaked, her speech quick and breathless. Naala's blood hardened.

'A Descendant?' Naala whispered.

The Isi coughed out a short laugh. 'Oh, child, no. My abilities were not handed to me by some higher power. Everything I have, I created.' She stepped towards her. 'I made the power I yield.'

'Ọbara magic,' Sinai said.

'Indeed. How did you suppose that I, an albino woman, became the head of the snake? *This*, all of this, is mine. The Aturu is *mine*. Chukwudi and the rest are all *my* students. I taught each and every one of them the art that I mastered as a child.' Her violet eyes became dim and distant. 'I was as young as five years old when they started to hunt me. I decided one day that *I* would be the hunter. I turned to the thing they sought – blood – and I made magic. I learnt exactly what blood could do. What it can *create*.' The Isi regarded them blankly before her gaze narrowed. 'Where is Ikuku?'

'We don't have it,' Naala said evenly.

The Isi's lips pursed slightly. 'Then, you must find it. Both of them: Ikuku and

Chi.'

The Isi's words pressed like hot coal against Naala's skin. 'Never,' she snarled.

The Isi hiked her eyebrows and, not for the first time, Naala cursed her quick tongue. She looked at her frozen friends, turning in time to see the Isi pull out a plump June plum from her robes.

'Food is fascinating, isn't it,' she offered, almost casually.

Naala watched her carefully.

'It nourishes us and eventually it *becomes* part of us. Ingrained in our very otomys. What do you think happens when you blend that power with a *special* agent? An agent only made available when you girls opened up its pit.'

No.

Naala's stomach lurched as she looked to Eni, Ina, Kora and Madi.

'Yes,' the Isi said coldly. 'Your friends have consumed a portion of Eriri Uhie enchanted by me and so every cell in their body is at *my* whim,' she said, pursing her lips. 'You two are *different* – Amụrụ ha abụọ, Children Born of Both. Two Descendants, so alas, no human blood to corrupt. A fact that kept me up for many nights, until I realised it. Your mistake, a mistake I made a while back too.' Her eyes brightened. 'You have both created deep weaknesses that live outside of your invincible bodies,' the Isi said, as she stroked Ina's arm. A scratch forming on the girl's arm, bright red blood lining it. Naala had to bite her tongue to stop herself from screaming.

'Stop it, please,' Sinai gasped.

'We have a prisoner too,' Naala said quickly as she looked down on Chukwudi. 'Let them go, and we will spare him.'

The Isi stared hard at Naala. Ice clutched at her throat as the Isi moved over to the man.

'You won't be able to free him,' Naala insisted, tightening the crystals that held him. The Isi ignored her as she bent over to remove the cloth from his mouth.

He let out a gasp as she cupped his cheek with her palm.

'Lolo,' he murmured, pressing against her touch as though it were life itself.

The Isi planted a kiss on his cheek and he let out a bone-chilling scream. It tore through Naala, filling her eyes with tears.

'Stop,' she said, rushing to pull the woman away but her feet turned to lead. Chukwudi's face tore apart before her eyes, shredding into tiny pieces until he was nothing but red dust on the ground. Bile rose to Naala's throat as she keeled and wretched. She couldn't shake that image from her mind. Open or closed, she saw it over and over again … Chukwudi tearing to nothing before her.

The Isi stood up again, a tear shining in her eye. 'No one,' she hissed rigidly, 'no one can be used against me again—' her gaze flicked towards Eni '—but can the same be said about you?'

'I will tear this castle down if you even dare,' Naala seethed, staggering in front of Eni as the Isi released a small smile.

'I know,' she said, 'and when I'm dead, Eni, Ina, Madi and Kora will reach Chukwudi's fate.'

'You lie.'

The Isi looked at her, confused. 'For what?' she paused and the corners of her mouth lifted. 'Test it. Kill me, or hurt me as you tried to before. See how long they last.'

The girls didn't say a word. Naala glanced over at her suspended friends and her throat tightened.

'You will get the crystals.'

'We don't know where they are,' Sinai sobbed.

The Isi looked over at her curiously. 'I did not ask for excuses. I demanded a result. You are the Amụrụ ha abụọ, the rarest beings to ever walk the planet, and you want me to believe you can't find a few stones?' she said coolly. 'You can find anything if you want to,' she added quietly.

The Isi's hand sprang to her necklace, her darkening eyes narrowed on Sinai. 'Do that again, and she dies,' she said, as she grazed her hand over Ina's hair. 'Wouldn't that be a waste? Do you know how long it took me to find her? To find all of you. I cherish you all, more than you'll ever know. Especially *her*, my Anyanwu.

'I wanted her the most, outside of you two, of course, I wanted *her*. The power she yields is unbelievable; it is intoxicating. Would you believe, I practically *created* her? I poured over thousands of records before I found him: Chibuhe, a Descendant of the First that held the flame igodo. He was just a commoner, a philandering commoner at that. A beautiful man with a charm that could trap anyone with a pulse. Of course, he had children – many children – but none of them had the igodo. It would take a particular mix to get that flame out. Imagine my delight when the Oba of Oyo brought his precious Ayaba to Nri. That woman was a fool. A little fool with *something* about her, a *fire*. I orchestrated a happenstance meet up and before I could blink, Tiwa, the Ayaba of Oyo, was with child by Chibuhue, the ogene player.' She laughed lightly.

'Ayaba Tiwa had him killed, of course, him and all his other efuolas, in case anyone showed up looking like the child in her stomach. Then she offered the girl in the treaty. Tiwa always knew how to guard her neck. She couldn't have the girl growing up to look like the commoner who had played her husband music on their visit to Nri. He never forgave her for that. The Oba, he loved that child, and she sent her away before he could say. By the time he had realised it was too late. Taking the girl back would risk war. Pity, she hardly should have bothered. The girl takes more after her mother in looks. Ironic, isn't it? The measures we take to protect ourselves so often become our own cage.' The Isi glanced at them coldly. 'Get the stone to me or your friends die. It's as simple as that.'

Naala's mind raced. She couldn't test her. Chukwudi's remains were still dusted on the floor. If the Isi had no qualms about killing him, a man that had stood by her side for decades, she certainly wouldn't spare their friends. She took a deep breath, letting her head fall back to the heavens. The indigo sky glimmered through the mighty gash she had created in the ceiling. A lone cloud passed through and her heart jolted. *Dogbari.*

Naala snapped her head back to the Isi. Dogbari? Could he help? He could kill her. No, she can't die. If she dies, they die. He could distract her while they got away. No, she would use her hold over their friends, torture them until they came back. Naala's heartbeat slowed. He could *bite* her. Just as he had done to Sinai. He could send her into a deep sleep. Would that work? She didn't know. Her heart faltered. She could see no other way.

Sinai's bottom lip was trembling when she looked at her. Naala flicked her gaze to the Isi, then to the sky, then to Sinai, widening her eyes for emphasis.

'What are you doing?' the Isi said.

'Nothing, Dogbari.'

'Dog *what?*'

Sinai's eyes widened in recognition.

'What if we can't find them?' Sinai said quickly.

The Isi regarded her carefully. 'Then your friends will die,' she replied sharply.

Sinai let her head fall into her hands and let out a cry. 'You can't do this to us,' she blubbered. Between her fingers, Naala thought she could see specks of gold. *Good girl,* she thought as the winds picked up.

'I cannot abide with dramatics,' the Isi said uncomfortably. 'It won't serve anyone, just find th—' A loud crack tore through the Idu.

'What are you doing?' the Isi roared at Naala.

'Nothing,' the girl cried as the wall behind her collapsed.

Naala had to fight to maintain her footing. She flung her hands in front of her and the akwa nests housing their friends flew to the back of the room, safe from the crumbling ground. A screech ripped through the air as Dogbari slithered across the room. His long neck bent forward and his huge head faced the Isi.

Her violet eyes blazed against her pale skin as she squared at the beast. She snapped off her pendant and began to chant, her words inaudible against Dogbari's high screech.

'Yes! Take it!' Sinai screamed and before she could blink Dogbari brought his snarling mouth towards the Isi. She held her hand up just as the creature sunk its razor-sharp teeth into her wrist, leaving nothing but a stump gushing red.

The Isi's eyes widened but she didn't break her chant. The crystal dust on the ground sprang up into the air and latched onto her wound, until a white crust coated over the raw stub. The Isi stumbled, her eyelids drooping, but she continued her chant. A large crystal cocoon grew from the ground and enveloped her. Only once it had been sealed did she collapse onto the ground.

'Is she dead?' Sinai asked worriedly.

'No,' Naala said, watching her chest rise and fall, 'she's asleep. Dogbari's venom.' She looked about the room, deathly afraid she would find lumps of dust instead of her friends. The tension released in her body when she caught sight of Eni, Kora, Ina and Madi. Not only were they still alive, but they were stirring.

'The venom,' Sinai repeated as she watched them. She drew closer to the cocoon, bringing her finger towards it before pulling away as one would do to a scorching pot. 'It stings!' she yelped, sucking her finger thoughtfully. 'She knew the venom would knock her unconscious; that's why she created that structure.' Sinai turned to their rousing friends. 'Look at them, they're no longer frozen. She must need to be conscious to keep the hold. Did you know?'

'I'd hoped.'

Sinai didn't smile. Her face fell as she turned to Dogbari. 'The Aturu are coming. They've already started attacking.'

A whisper ran past her ear and Naala turned to see a dart lodged in the wall behind her, having missed her by a hair's width. She turned around to see where it came from but the area was clear. Dread sliced through her chest.

'Now!' Sinai cried. 'We have to leave now!' she yelled as a forceful wind swept Naala off her feet roughly. She found herself on Dogbari's back with Kora looking back at her, her eyes widened with terror.

'It's going to be okay,' Naala said as she felt the creature move below her. 'It's going to be okaaayyyahhh.'

CHAPTER 37
THE MAN IN ODICHEKU

City of Nri

Meekulu's cave sang to Sinai. A sad and soulful melody that churned through memories she had long forgotten. Nsibidi ọkụ lights hung around the rock stalactites, dancing to that sorrowful tune. *Please*, she whispered, *help me save them.* No one answered back. Madi, Kora, Ina, Eni and Naala stood beside her in the cave, their expressions hard as stone.

None of them had objected when she had led them to the old woman's cave. Sinai hadn't even realised that this was where Dogbari had taken them, not until she saw the hills, a patchwork of varying shades of green.

'Come with me,' she had commanded, standing amidst her friends who had laid dazed on the grassland. To her surprise they had listened, following her through a shallow lake, past the waterfall and into the cave without a word. Now she was here, she had no idea what to do next.

'So, there's something here that can help?' Naala asked, running her fingers over the items on Meekulu's brimming shelves, stopping at what looked like a cube of molten lava moving within the confines of its shape.

Sinai didn't know. The only reason she had thought to come here was because it was the only place she knew to go. Pressure steadily built in her chest and she realised that she had forgotten to breathe.

'I hope so,' she said shakily. 'I really do.'

'Help?' Ina blurted, shattering out of her stone demeanour. 'Did you not see what *she* did? *What she's capable of?*' her voice was rough and Sinai could see veins beating under her dark skin. 'There's no help left for us now. Only death.' Ina held Sinai's gaze as she said those final words. Death. It hung around her, following her everywhere she went. Sinai didn't want to face it again, not yet. Not after Meekulu.

'Death is not an option,' Naala said, and Ina released a laugh that morphed into a sob; she clutched at her chest before turning her back on the group.

Naala looked at Sinai. 'You brought us here for a reason, right? So what do we do?' her gaze burned into Sinai, her jaw hardened by will.

Sinai gaped back at her.

'What do we—' Naala repeated.

'I don't know,' Sinai said under her breath. The corners of Naala's eyes creased and Sinai dropped her gaze. Silence swept through the cave until Kora broke it.

'We should discuss what happens if we can't find a cure,' she said hollowly.

Madi stepped in. 'What is there to discuss? If there is no cure then Ina is correct. Death is what lies ahead of us.'

'Death is not an option!' Naala declared, her lips tight and the large whites of her eyes wet with the threat of tears.

'Naala,' Eni whispered, her name carved out of his mouth like a prayer.

She shook her head at him and squeezed her eyes shut. 'It's not an option,' she repeated through clenched teeth.

'It is and it's not the worst one we have,' Madi said gently. 'If the Isi wakes – *when* the Isi wakes – she'll have full control over all of us. She could kill us one by one, or, worse, make us kill others at her whim. I-I can't take that risk. What is death in the face of that?'

'Death is so final,' Kora murmured distantly.

'No, it is not,' Madi retorted.

'Either way,' Eni said, his gaze fixed on Naala, 'we will *try* to overcome this. We will try.'

'What if we can't?' Kora whispered.

'If? Of course we can't overcome this,' Ina insisted, her hair frosted with a pale light from the monument Meekulu had called the ọnụ ụzọ. It ran down from the ceiling, a stream of silver curved into a ring, before looping back up.

'Stop saying that,' Naala snapped.

'There is another option, you know, other than death,' Kora said, and they all turned to her expectantly. 'We give her the crystals,' she said, gesturing to the necklace that Sinai wore.

Dogbari had given it to her, still clasped in the torn and bloodied hand of the Isi.

'What lies ahead will require Àlà, Ikuku and Chi,' he had said when she had objected. She had asked him to explain, but he had said that was all he knew. The cold metal bit hard against her skin.

'Are you *insane?*' Madi sputtered as Kora's eyes tightened.

'No, I – we don't have to *die*. We could give them to her,' Kora continued, 'and bargain for … for …'

'A life in servitude?' Ina muttered drily. 'What do you think happens when she gets what she wants? Do you think that she leaves us alone? Do you think she won't want to use the additional power we hand over to her?' Ina's voice was laced with so much venom it almost made Sinai flinch.

'Kora might have a point,' Eni said softly as Madi threw his hands in the air.

'You can't be serious,' he huffed.

Eni paused, clenching and unclenching his jaw before he answered. 'The Amaghi work by playing games. If we play along to win, if we hand it back to her with *intent*, then we may be able to take back control.'

'This is not a game,' Ina spat, pointing at the scar that the Isi had left on her arm. 'What she did to Chukwudi was not a *game*.'

'We're not giving the crystal to anyone,' Naala said, her gaze fixed on Eni, cold and hard.

'Naala, we have to consi—'

'Where is Azu?' Naala said. Her words held no emotions, and her eyes were blank and yet they cut through the air like an arrow landing squarely on Eni's chest. He grimaced, his eyebrows pressed together, darkening his gaze.

'Azu?' he repeated, his mouth slack.

'Where is he?' Naala repeated, stressing out each word, her frame deathly still, save from the slight quiver over her lip.

Sinai stepped forward, her stomach clenched as she watched the conversation unfold.

Eni blinked back at her. 'Odicheku. Where we sent them after we left Furuefu. Naala, I don't—'

'You are a liar.'

The cave stilled. Naala's expression was as tight as Sinai had ever seen it. 'Azu is in Urukpuru. Dead. Along with the villagers who *you* told us Dogbari had killed, and goodness knows who else.'

A sound escaped Eni's mouth as though he had been punched in the gut. 'Impossible,' he breathed.

'W-what is she talking about, Eni?' Kora asked, stepping between them.

'Impossible. He can't be,' Eni said, his eyes fixed on Naala. He stepped past Kora as he edged towards Naala but Madi stood in his way.

'It's time to tell the truth,' Madi said stiffly.

'The truth?'

'Yes. The truth. Or have you forgotten it completely?'

Eni looked back at him aghast, shifting to meet Naala, who had begun to pace up and down. 'Azu is not dead. He's in Odicheku. I—'

'Sent him to his grave!' Naala yelled.

'No, I—' Eni fell silent from the glare Naala threw at him.

'I saw him die with my own eyes,' Naala spat as Eni shook his head furiously. 'I saw him, I heard him call out for you. You, you liar, you are a liar.'

Eni took a step back, crestfallen. 'I ...' he started, before stilling. He clamped his mouth shut before straightening his back and moving past Madi to Naala. 'I lied,' he said, broken.

'Eni,' Kora gasped, clasping at her mouth.

Naala choked. The rage fell from her face like water. She looked as though she would crumble.

'I lied,' Eni repeated, hoarsely, 'but I *did not* send *anyone* to their grave. I didn't ... I wouldn't. I lied. I didn't grow up in a village; I-I grew up in the city squalors. Sold to the palace at five years, she – Lolo Obioma recruited me to spy. I can ...

I'm good at—' He stopped himself and took a breath. 'I lied, when you met me. I am a part of the Amaghi. I've always been; they raised me. They sent me to help. The survivors of the village attacks, I was helping them. They said I was helping them.' He stepped towards Naala, his eyes feverish and bright. 'Azu is not dead. He is in Odicheku. He is safe. I saved him,' he said roughly as he blinked back tears. 'He is. He's in Odicheku.' Naala lowered her eyes and Eni's chest caved in as he surrendered his hold and fell into anguish.

Naala opened her mouth to speak but someone else got there first.

'My, my … isn't this tense.' A deep voice sounded distantly, commanding all of their attention.

Ina screamed as she got up to her feet, stepping away from the two shadowy figures that had appeared beside her. One a tall bald man, the other a small girl that Sinai recognised with bright eyes.

Chisi?

CHAPTER 38

JIKỌỌ

City of Nri

'Who are you?' Madi growled, seizing the both of them with one arm.

Chisi cowered under his grip and Sinai moved to her instinctively. Chisi was so different now, gaunt where she was once plump. Far older than her years would suggest. What had happened to the kitchen girl?

'Chisi,' she called, and the girl looked down at her with large wet eyes. Sinai placed her hand on Madi's and he cautiously let them down.

'Lolo,' she breathed, her widened eyes darting around the room.

'You know them?' Madi asked hesitantly.

'I know *her*,' Sinai said, shifting away from the man beside her. His eyes were dark and his face shadowed, not in the inconspicuous way that Chukwudi had seemed to her. No, this was different, more menacing, like shadows of something lurking in the dead of night.

'Lolo, you're still making the air swirl,' Chisi said, drawing Sinai out of her thoughts as she gestured to the swirls of dust at the corner of the room. The smile on her lips was not as curious as Sinai had remembered, though it still held some of its charm. Something had hardened the girl. *Meekulu*, she thought. Sinai had known the old woman for just a few moon-cycles; what was that compared to the sun-cycles Chisi had spent by the woman's side? Sinai's throat tightened.

'Chisi, who is this?' Ina demanded. 'Has he hurt you?'

'Hurt me?' Chisi said, her face scrunched. 'No, no, Healer Agymah saved me. I ... I was one of the first to get the egbu illness, and he helped me, and now we help others.'

'The what?' Ina said, recoiling back.

Chisi shivered. 'It is a bad disease ... a terrible blood illness. Very deadly. Everyone who has had it has died, except the people that Healer Agymah has treated,' she said, rubbing at the back of her hands, her gaze bouncing around the room.

Sinai frowned as she regarded the man. He didn't look like a healer, not in his tattered grey garments. He snapped his head back at her before pulling his lips into a smirk. Something cold slinked down her spine.

'Chisi is too kind,' he said, his voice low and sticky, 'I'm no miracle worker. Egbu is a disease of the blood, and that is my speciality.' He studied the room and his grin widened.

'Lolo,' Chisi said quietly, looking Sinai in the eye for the first time, 'why are you back *here*? The city isn't safe for...' She quieted herself but her tight eyes voiced the source of her concern as they darted from Sinai and Naala.

The healer released a slow chuckle. 'Safe? No place is truly *safe* for anybody. Including here.'

'What does that mean?' Naala asked, studying the shadowed man with her lips pressed flat and eyes narrowed. Flickers of gold shone in her eyes and Chisi's hands flew up to her head.

'Don't hurt us, w-we just needed some supplies for t-the remedies,' Chisi piped, jumping slightly at each word.

Sinai's stomach hardened.

'Chisi,' Sinai started gently before the healer stepped in.

'Settle down, pet. Your friends do not have time for such *episodes*.'

'What do you mean by that?' Naala asked and he snorted in response.

'Do you—' the healer stalked towards Naala before Eni stepped in his way; he sneered at the boy before releasing another smile '—have time?' he sniffed the air around Eni before running his tongue over his cracked lips. 'A jikọọ as sweet as they come.'

'Jikọọ,' Kora gasped, her eyes widened as she studied the floor. 'I … I read …'

'Pah!' he slapped his hand through the air. Sinai jumped at the sound, her thumping heart lodged in her throat. 'One does not *read* the jikọọ. You need to feel it in your hands, squeeze it, kill it, to truly know of the jikọọ. It is a contamination of the greatest order. A taint. A stain. A cancer poisoning you all.' Each word served as a daga, twisting away at her gut.

'Speak plainly,' Madi insisted. 'What is this jikọọ?'

'It's a curse,' Kora whispered, 'a form of the Eriri Uhie, the substance that drives us … to live, to survive. It can be manipulated in ways that can enact a curse. The contaminated Eriri Uhie then latches on to the host's Eriri Uhie, tying their life to it.'

'An Ọbara oath?' Eni asked, his coal-black eyes cutting into the smaller girl.

'Mba! Far worse, my boy,' the healer said, 'an Ọbara oath forces you to *choose* between life and abiding by its rules. With the jikọọ, there is no choice: you do or you do.'

'Chínēkè,' Madi muttered under his breath, taking a step back.

'Make no mistake, God has nothing to do with this one. *This* belongs to something else,' the healer said almost *gleefully*. 'This is the work of chaos.'

'Do you know how to fix it?' Naala said sharply with an unbreaking focus. He returned her gaze silently.

'Yes,' he said carefully, before turning to point at Sinai's neck, 'with the help of that.'

Sinai placed her palm over the crystals, as one would do a child. Heat surged through her and the shelves rattled with the rising winds.

'Kai,' the healer laughed, looking around the room. 'Now, isn't that *something*.'

'The last person that took those crystals for the sake of *healing* cursed us. So forgive us if we're not receptive to the idea,' Naala said curtly.

'Oh, hush. It's just a little chant, a dash of blood and just like that all your troubles will be away,' he said, waving his hands in the air.

'Lolo Sinai, if you need to be healed, you must heed the healer's advice,' Chisi said, holding Sinai's gaze steadily. 'He can save you.'

'Hold your tongue, Chisi,' Ina said, her gaze pinned on the shadowy man. 'Men like him often lie.'

'Well, there is your cure,' the healer boomed, 'right *there*.' He threw his hands towards Ina. 'Anyanwu herself ... tell me, have you tested out those *cleansing* flames?'

Ina flinched at the mention of the lost goddess' name.

Sinai's mouth dried. How did he *know*?

The healer shook his head. 'No?' he said before drawing a deep breath, his eyes closed as he did so. Something softened his face. 'No,' he said in nothing more than a whisper. He flinched at a thought. 'Should she try, she'll burn the Kingdom down.' He opened his eyes and scanned the room. 'Pity.' A smile spread over his face. 'Of course, there is always my *way*, but—' he sniffed at the air '—fear and mistrust are standing in your way.'

No one said a word. Sinai felt something gnaw at the pit of her stomach. She didn't like this man. She didn't trust him, and, yet, what else were they to do?

'No,' Eni said, his sharp jaw hardened.

'Now, Eni, shouldn't we, at least—' Kora started.

'No,' he said, 'what he speaks of is Ọbara magic, blood magic, the cost of which is always higher than it seems. I never really grasped the meaning of that saying until now.'

The healer watched him before letting a smile spread across his lips. 'Very well,' he said, tilting his head to the side as he delivered one final sneer before turning to go.

Chisi looked back at Sinai expectantly before following him out of the cave. Sinai wanted to go after him, but her feet seemed to be locked into the rocky ground.

'Are you sure that was wise?' Ina asked, watching after them. 'I know what I said ... but I don't *want* to die. Not if there's a *real* chance.'

'Kora, you've heard of this jikọọ; is there any other way?' Naala asked.

'I ... there, no, not that I ...'

Ice cold ran down Sinai's body as she watched the line of thick blood that trickled down Kora's nose. She stumbled forward as Kora's scream tore mercilessly through the air.

CHAPTER 39
RED MIST

City of Nri

'No,' Sinai gulped as she rushed over to the girl, jumping back when Kora's head jerked up and a voice as thundering as the darkest storms broke out of her mouth.

'They will writhe in the worst of pains. They will rot from the inside out. They will claw themselves to shreds before your eyes until you return those crystals to me. Then, and only then, will they die. Try and give them peace, try to end their suffering, *I* will keep their hearts beating, *I* will ensure that their minds are alert. I offered you mercy and you spat in my face. Now all that is left for you is vengeance.' Kora snarled fiendishly, the corners of her mouth wet with spittle and blood. She collapsed, convulsing on the ground, as Sinai fell to her side.

Thump!

Thump!

Thump!

Dust fell over her eyes as Madi pounded against the cave walls, his teeth gritted, his vacant eyes brimming with tears. Sinai couldn't see Ina over the dark smoke that had engulfed her but she could hear her shrieks.

Eni lay on the ground, unmoved, but sweat formed on his brow and anguish painted his face. He couldn't scream. Something was happening to him, something terrible, and he couldn't scream.

'It seems you've run out of time,' a voice said over her as nausea crept up her throat.

Sinai looked up, and through the blur of tears, the healer formed before her eyes. She sobbed weakly at the sight of him.

No. That was all she wanted to scream, but instead her hands quivered as they found their way to the crystals at her neck. He looked at her hungrily before turning his back on her.

'No,' Sinai blubbered as she scrambled to her feet. 'Come back,' she shouted above the shrieks of her dying friends. *They were dying.* The healer stopped in front of Chisi before taking her small palm in his, as he drew a crimson daga out of his garments.

'What are you doing?' Sinai started hoarsely.

'Just a cut. A simple cut,' Chisi recited, with a faraway look as though she was lost within herself.

'Not her, cut me,' Naala said, thrusting her hand at the shadowed man but he didn't so much as look up; instead he ran his finger along a line on Chisi's palm.

'Your blood has no use here.'

'Fear not, I've done it before,' Chisi said, her voice small and flat.

Sinai didn't say a word as the healer pressed the daga into Chisi's palm until blood sprouted. It was just a cut; a thin cut against her pink palm. He guided her hand towards Sinai, and beckoned for the necklace. Her clammy palms fumbled at the necklace before she edged it closer to the shadowed man.

Drip.

One blood drop fell on the Àlà.

Drip.

The other on the Ikuku.

A sound expelled through the room with each drop of blood. It sank into Sinai, filling her with a nauseating fear. She had to bite her lips to stop herself from spewing. Beside her, the healer chanted. At least, she thought it was chanting. He didn't use any words. He spoke as though he were the wings of the hummingbird.

Soon she couldn't hear anything over the screaming. She looked back nervously. She found Madi, Ina and Kora, all convulsing on the ground. Their bodies rocked violently, their eyes bulged and their jaws sprung open. Red mist began to slowly gather over their mouths.

Clouds of red hung over them before clumping to one another. Sinai squinted at the sight before scrambling backwards; it was coming for her. Sinai sprang to her side just as the mist poured into the shadowed man. When he opened his eyes they were blood red and a heavy force slammed into her chest.

*

The world spun when Sinai awoke, sprawled on the ground. Her elbows were raw and scraped, and a bell sounded from her head. She blinked away the dust and debris lodged into her eyes. Slowly she began to see bodies scattered around her. She crawled over to the nearest, Kora. She was still alive. Sinai's heart burst with joy. She was not in pain; her face was as calm as if she were simply sleeping. Sinai glanced over to Naala. There was a look on her face, a pained look, a look of horror. Sinai followed her gaze to the healer. He stood in the centre of the cave, his eyes fixed on the ọnụ ụzọ.

Sinai's blood hardened as an image formed within the ring of silver. Sinai's throat closed when she saw it: a dark pit at a corner, rimming with red mist. Not the small particles that had been drawn out of her friends, but an infinite amount, swirling in the broad daylight.

'Isn't it beautiful?' he said, his voice breaking. 'And now I know where it is.'

'Where's the girl?' Naala growled.

Sinai's heart stopped. *Chisi*. A sob escaped her mouth as she took in the pile of red dust that sat where the girl should have stood. *No, please.*

'The boy said, *Blood magic always takes more than it claims.*' The healer turned around to face them with his blood-red eyes. 'False. It only ever takes what it is due. Nothing less, nothing more. It is *you* who take. You who always want *more*. Three lives. That's what you asked for and what were you willing to pay? Two drops of blood? Impossible.'

Hot blood rushed to Sinai's ears as winds flung the demon man to and fro.

Naala sprang at him, her teeth clenched as cracks in the earth raced towards him. His eyes bulged as he hopped up and down. Something heavy slammed into her gut when she realised he wasn't afraid. He was *laughing*. Red mist sprouted from his body and by the time Naala had reached him, he was gone.

'Thank you, truly, for your help,' a voice boomed in the distance. 'In exchange, I will offer you some advice. Leave this place. There is nothing left for you here but death. You can no longer stop what is coming for this kingdom. Accept that now, and we may get the chance to duel another day … ' As the voice crackled into the distance, Sinai could see the ọnụ ụzọ transforming into another scene.

Iron gripped mercilessly at her throat as she fell to her knees. Yet she couldn't look away at the image before her. Thousands of demons, their faces ashen, their eyes blood red, marching through the city of Nri, tearing down everything in sight.

Chapter 40
The Favourite

City of Nri

Anger clutched at his neck. Pain ripped at his skin. Envy twisted his gut. Rage, fear, anguish. They piled, one by one, over Eni. Tearing at what they could.

He had fought at first. He had tried to scream, to beat them away, to *survive* but now … now, he was still. His racing heart had slowed to sluggish thuds. He could no longer breathe. All Eni could do was drown in the sea of people imposing their will on him.

That's what he had deduced them to be. The fragmented pieces of people that filtered into him. He had originally thought them to be emotions but no, they were more. More demanding, more relentless and more raw. *Will,* he thought. *It's their will—*

NO.

The thought burst into his mind seconds before she did. Naala came into sharp focus and agony followed. Scorching thunder exploded within him as a blinding pain began its reign over his body. He couldn't even scream for respite. Not unless he could force her behind the iron wall in his mind.

He couldn't.

Something brushed against his cheek, as soft as warm rain. Her words caressed against his ear: '*Please, please wake up*'. Eni sucked in a raspy breath and for the briefest moment he had his wits about him. He flung up his wall before settling back into himself.

'I think he's waking,' Naala whispered above him.

'I am,' he tried to reply but all that came out was strangulated gabble.

'He is,' a voice that sounded like Kora exclaimed. Her relief trickled over him like sand.

Eni's head rang as he forced himself up, sinking his elbows into the grasslands.

'Wo-wai-wai-wait,' Naala said hurriedly, her hands firmly holding on to his head.

Eni lifted his eyelids and a dull thud escaped his chest when his eyes met hers. They were wet and bright like the new morning behind her. She released a gush of warm air.

'He's awake,' she whispered, her cheeks round with a smile.

Eni didn't want to look away but something else caught his eye. A dull glow emitting from the Aido-Hwedo who sat curled on a distant hill; its clear eyes pierced through him. So, they were no longer in the cave?

'What happened?' Eni said, grimacing as he warded off their internal replies. Rage. Despair. Fear.

'He tricked us,' Sinai said. Her eyes were dry but even in the dim light they still gleamed red and her voice was thick with tears. 'He—' she gulped '—*he killed her.*'

He killed her. Eni's gut twisted at her words, though he was not certain about what she meant.

'We let him trick us. We let him – *I* let him kill her,' Naala said stiffly, her hands tightly clasped on her lap.

He killed her. Ice ran down his back as he looked around. Kora, Madi and Sinai stood huddled around him, Ina a little further back and Naala close by his side. Two people were missing: the healer and the girl. The memories crashed into him all at once. The girl.

No. The conclusion planted itself unabashedly in the centre of his mind. *A child,* he thought, *she was nothing more than a child.* Had the so-called healer killed her to rid them of the Isi's curse? His stomach knotted.

'Where is he?' he growled. He would avenge her. The thought felt more like a fact than desire. Another name to add to the ever-growing list of people who had died because of *him*. His throat tightened but Naala caught his eye before he could sink any further into his thoughts. Carelessly, he reached for her hand. She didn't pull away.

Something about that irked him. Why didn't she pull away? He watched her heartbeat vibrate beneath her chest, matching his own. He could feel it there at the edge of the iron wall; the pull she still felt towards him. His pulse sped at the thought but he let his dark desire twist into rage. Why was it still there? After everything he had revealed, after everything she knew.

He didn't know why he was surprised. After all, it was her only true flaw. Naala was infuriating, yes, stubborn, oh yes – and so, so very annoying, but it was this – this *recklessness* – that topped it all. He despised it almost as much as he wanted her. A liar, she had called him, but he was far worse. He belonged to the shadows. He knew that. She knew that. So why did she look at him like he didn't?

'He fled,' Naala said quietly. The world stilled. Of course he did. Eni had smelt the stench permeating off of him. The same stench he had overlooked for years amidst the Aturu. *The takers, the users, the shadows crawling in the night.* A deep scowl settled onto his face before he caught Madi's gaze.

They must have worn the same look. He knew then that Madi would join him on his conquest to kill the demon healer. He could taste Madi's need to stop the man from acting out in such a way ever again. He seemed to see the man as a wild boar that must be put down before he could hurt again. Madi felt obligated.

Eni did not. He shifted as once again he faced the difference between the two of them. Eni didn't feel obligated; he felt compelled. He would certainly prefer that the man should never kill again but that wasn't what drove him. It was vengeance. Justice for the girl.

He had felt that girl's will, her hope. It was damp like a cotton cloth soaked in sweet zobo; darkened around the edges but *good* all the same. He had felt all of their wills. All the people he had moved wherever the Amaghị had bid him to, he had used his sensitivity to make them feel safe and secure. Blast his foolishness! He had thought them to be *safe*. The Isi. Bayo. Now this healer, Agymah. All those who had played him for a fool. All those who would pay for it with blood.

'We'll find him,' Eni said as Madi nodded curtly. Something sharp caught at his throat and the warmth of Naala's hand felt *uncomfortable*. He didn't move. After all, it wasn't his will; it was Madi's.

Madi's feelings for the girl had flourished on their return from the hills of Udi. Almost a sun-cycle ago, when Naala and Madi had stowed away in an attempt to save Madi's brother. Eni's mouth tightened at the memory. Reckless. She was so *reckless*.

Eni's shoulders sagged as his gaze fell on Madi. He couldn't find it within him to despise the boy. His will was like quartz: so clear and focused. Duty and honour was all he ever strived for and that made him safe. It made Madi good. Yet even now he could feel Naala's gaze settled back on *him*. Moments like this made Eni want to scream at Madi, *Blast your honour, pursue her. Take her.* He could never find the words. He knew he never would.

'No, we can't,' Naala said, getting up for the first time; the ghost of her touch left him cold. 'We have a bigger *thing*. We have. I have. It's all gone wrong.' Eni could feel the tears building up within her, but as always, she plunged them back down violently.

'There's something coming for the Kingdom, Eni,' Kora said quietly when Naala couldn't get the words out. 'Thousands will die because of us. He ... Agymah has – or will – use the jikǫǫ he took from us to create something monstrous, an army of the dead—' she shivered at the thought '—the bụrụ-ọnụ ... a curse.' Kora turned to Ina. 'You were right: we should have died.'

Ina didn't say anything; she sat still, a cool rage burning within her.

'Bụrụ-ọnụ?' Eni repeated.

'Yes, we all saw it through the ọnụ ụzọ. You were—'

'Sleeping,' Madi jested, though it didn't reach his eyes. Whatever they had seen had sunk deep into them, terrifying them at the core.

'You were hit harder than us,' Kora corrected, 'you ... she nearly killed you.'

'She nearly killed all of us,' Eni replied bitterly.

'You were clearly her favourite,' Ina said drily. The word stung him more than he wished to say.

'So, this Agymah has created an army of the dead with the jikǫǫ?' Eni said, changing the subject. 'To do what?'

'To destroy everything,' Sinai said. She had been quiet. Sinai was always quiet, to him at least. Where Naala's will was thundering, Sinai's was no more louder than a hush.

'They will ravage the city,' Ina said, her emotions erratic.

Eni couldn't quite tell if she was upset by the prospect or *pleased*.

'They could do much more,' Naala said. 'If he gets his hands on the Chi Crystal then—'

'He won't,' Sinai said. Her response was sharp though her gaze remained fixed on her intertwined fingers. There was something behind that answer and, of course, Naala knew it. Eni grimaced as her will flared. She wanted answers.

'You don't know that,' Naala said. Her voice was low and flat. Sinai regarded her carefully.

'I do because I gave it to someone else. I-I gave it to him,' Sinai said.

Gave it to who— Eni's hand flew to his forehead as the air flew out of him. He had to force himself not to double over from the pain. Naala was beating against the wall. She was furious, that was clear, but it was worse than that; she was hurt. Everything in his body told him to pull away and yet he found himself moving towards her. She was hurt.

'Why?' The pain in her voice twisted a daga into his gut.

'Because not everything is as it seems,' Sinai said, brimming with tears. '*Nothing is as it seems*, not the Isi, not Dogbari, not … Olu.'

'Olu?' Ina interjected, her creased brow smoothing as her face settled into stone.

'You *knew*,' Naala spat, jabbing her finger at Sinai, 'you knew what he did and you still gave it to *him*.'

'I *had* to, Naala. I—'

Naala flinched as though she had been slapped. 'You *had* to?' she said; her hard words were no louder than a whisper but still carried over the waking day.

Sinai threw her hands at her sides before she ran her tongue over her lip, edging cautiously towards Naala. 'We had to leave the city—t-there was no way around that. I saw the crystal in a— I knew where it was and I couldn't just *leave* it unattended. What if Agymah had got to it? Or someone worse? The palace is full of terrible people, and Ol— He, he was the only person there that I could trust. I had to trust that. Just like I had to trust that I couldn't use the Ọbara magic against Dogbari or that I couldn't trust Chisi with that man.' The tears streamed down Sinai's face.

Naala shut her eyes to them; her lips trembled as she balled up her fists.

'Naala.'

'It's too much,' she croaked. 'It's all too much, it's—'

Eni's head split as he stood in front of her, grasping her shoulders with his hands. 'It's too much.' He nodded and her eyes found his.

'He killed her,' Naala whimpered, she tried to keep her voice steady but it broke with every word.

Her emotions were so violent that he could almost *see* them. Images of an elderly woman merged and mixed with the young Chisi. Eni had no idea who Naala was referring to. He didn't believe that she did either.

'And those demons will kill the whole city, spread out through the Kingdom, because I ... I should've *known*,' she said, turning to Sinai. 'I should have known.'

Eni smirked at her. The pain began to ease as her eyes narrowed.

'Are you *laughing* at me?' she said, stepping out of his grip, trying and failing to hide the smile forming in the corner of her mouth.

'No – not laughing ... it's just ... you really think you know *everything*,' he said, shaking his head as her nose flared. 'Well, you don't, and that's okay. You're not alone.' He sobered with his last statement. He didn't know how many ways he could tell her that so that she might finally understand.

'You're not,' Sinai insisted. 'I can go to the city and get the crystal from Ol – from him. Then we'd have three crystals. We can use them to stop the bụrụ-ọnụ. Or I can use the wind or you can shift the earth.' Sinai edged closer to Naala.

'I can knock a few of them out,' Madi threw in.

'I can blow a few of them up,' Kora piped. '*With some supplies*,' she added, rolling her eyes at Madi's scoff.

'I can shoot a few of them down,' Eni found himself saying. The laugh felt strange on his tongue, but he was grateful for it all the same. The mood was no longer overpowering. He could finally regain some control. Ease the burden pressed so tightly against their necks.

'I could burn them,' Ina muttered. The air shifted as she released a sigh before clicking her finger; a flame roared between her thumb and index fingers.

'You control it?' Madi exclaimed.

'Yes. Since you came back from the forest.' Ina tilted her chin but she couldn't seem to meet his eye. Instead she let her gaze fall on the Aido-Hwedo.

'So … does this mean we have Anyanwu on our side now?' Kora asked as she bounced on her knees.

'Kora—' Madi warned.

'It's fine,' she snapped back at them. 'I – well, we all heard what she said about my … my mother, and her … It *never* made sense. I *knew* it never made *sense*. I was their first-born. I had juniors that could have – he should have gone to war to keep me. I-I thought it was me. I thought he believed me to be broken.' She threw her hands in the air, turning her back on them all. 'I wanted to prove him wrong. Show him that … he should have fought.' Her emotions draped over her, a dark blanket sucking at her like a leech.

Eni was tempted to pacify her, but he knew better. He had to let her feel it, feel all of it; otherwise she would never be able to move past it.

'You are not broken,' Madi insisted. 'You are blessed with two strong homes: Nri and Oyo. I envy you.'

Ina looked back at Madi before letting her gaze fall to the ground; a smile formed on her lips.

'Well,' she said, flinging her long hair back, 'if any of you should speak one word of this to anyone, I will know and I will burn you to a crisp.' Laughter spread across the group like wildfire. Ina, eventually, joined in.

'We can do this,' Madi said once they had settled.

'We have to,' Naala added.

'We just need a way into the palace …' Sinai said pensively.

'Well, that should be easy enough.' Eni shrugged.

'Easy? The army has been instructed to kill me and Sinai on sight,' Naala protested.

Eni regarded her curiously as the corners of his mouth lifted into a smile.

'What?'

'There are about ten different ways to sneak in and out of that palace, and I know them all,' he scoffed. The words had tumbled out of his mouth before he could think. That was stupid. Sloppy. He was never sloppy. He glanced down at Naala, his pulse pounding against his temples. It came to a stop when he saw her face. She wasn't disgusted, he concluded, as he took in the gleam forming in her eyes. She was *tickled*.

'Lead the way, Onye Nyocha.'

CHAPTER 41
THE LEOPARD AT THE WALL

City of Nri

Eni's jaw stiffened as dust filtered down from the ceiling of the tight burrow. He shifted upward, peering out at the land above, where the armed guard stomped before the city walls.

'To the left,' he said in a low hush.

He was guiding them to a hidden latch; the best of the ten ways that Eni knew to get into the city. Naala pressed her lips together as the sinking feeling at the pit of her stomach resurfaced. If someone had told her that Eni was a full-fledged member of the Amaghi, she would have laughed in their face. If they had said he'd grown up in the city, that he had been trained as a *spy*, she would have declared that they were only fit for Mgbapu with all the other people that had lost their minds.

Looking at him now, it all somehow made sense. Eni was constantly shrouded in secrets. He had *always* been shrouded in secrets. Yet, she *knew* him. Didn't she? In some ways she felt she knew him more than he knew himself. But what of the other part? The part that neither of them had ever seen? Naala studied Eni's settled expression. *Who are you?* She shivered as a pair of green eyes shifted into her mind's focus.

Eni squinting down at her, scattering more moist rich soil into the burrow. 'Naala?'

'Yes?'

'To the left,' Eni repeated.

Her forehead furrowed as she gaped back at him. He didn't say another word; instead he placed his hands on her waist, lifting her up to the top of the burrow. She could feel his breath on the back of her neck and her stomach tightened.

'See, to the left … can you see the leopard statue? That's where you need to direct us,' he said, his voice competing with her pounding heart.

Naala took in a deep breath.

A big mistake. Fine dust scratched at the back of her throat and her eyes watered as she suppressed a violent cough. She nodded her head as he put her down. She clasped her hand over her mouth to muffle the sound as she cleared her throat.

'Was that really necessary?' Madi muttered. 'Look at her.'

Heat rose to Naala's cheeks. 'I'm fine,' she insisted, ignoring the lightness spreading across her head. Eni watched over her with a frown that broke into a grin. He brought his palms to her face and wiped away at the dust from her cheeks with his thumbs. Her skin tingled under his touch.

'Yes, you are,' he murmured as heat raced through her chest.

'Left,' she said hoarsely.

'Yes,' he affirmed as she began to shift through the land. 'Perfect, it's just straight on from here.'

Sweat trickled down her back and she was glad that she wasn't the only one. Each one of them were covered with a sheen of sweat; their breathing sounded as quick and strained as hers. Even the air that Sinai shifted through the tight space did nothing to help. The hot air moved around them, offering no sense of relief. *Ina*, Naala thought, as she watched the girl fling her long locs behind her ear as though nothing was amiss.

'Why is it so hot? I can't take it a second longer,' Kora huffed, fanning her face uselessly.

'Ina can answer that,' Naala said, returning Ina's glare with a knowing arch in her eyebrow. Admittedly, she didn't despise Ina as she once had, but there were times she wanted nothing more than to wring her neck. This was definitely one of those times.

'Do you want to see or not?' Ina said through gritted teeth, pointing at the flames burning in her hand.

'It's not just that flame and you know it,' Naala muttered. She had seen them, tiny sparks emitting from Ina. She could still feel the faint sting from the one that had latched onto her arm. Ina had yet to utter an apology.

'It's not my fault that there's no air in here,' Ina hissed.

'I am trying,' Sinai insisted.

'*You* are,' Naala replied, 'but Ina seems determined to block all your efforts.'

'Yes. Yes – that is *exactly* what I want, and do you know a great way to make it stop? Rattle me up more!' Ina exclaimed and Sinai lunged at the girl, clamping her hand over Ina's mouth as movement sounded from above.

Eni ducked down as soil crumbs rained over them. Loud thuds rang through the air as the soldiers stormed.

Blast it.

CHAPTER 42
HIDDEN KPO

City of Nri

'Did you hear that?' a muffled voice said from above. Naala bit down on her lips so hard she could taste blood. Not now, not when they were so close.

'Why aren't you at your station?!' another voice demanded.

'I heard someth—'

'Get back to your station, now.'

'But I heard—' His voice was carried away in the intensifying winds.

'You heard the blasted winds!' the other man roared.

'But—'

'Are you disobeying me?'

'No,' the other man said measuredly.

'Are you looking for a long and painful death?'

'N-no, Ozo.'

Another wave of soil crumbs scattered across the burrow as the men above marched away. Soon after Ina prodded Sinai.

'Don't do that again,' Ina warned as she wiped her mouth.

'You don't do that again,' Sinai hissed. 'Come on, Ina, I know you're nervous but—'

'Nervous?' Ina scowled venomously. 'I am not nervous.'

'Well, I certainly am,' Kora muttered, lifting up her trembling hands. 'Shame, I thought we had finally found something we had in common.'

Ina didn't reply; instead she let her dreads fall to the side of her face as she turned to the wall.

'How long?' she asked briskly and Naala's fists tightened. She was ready to tell Ina exactly what she thought of her when – she felt something.

Naala's heartbeat slowed. There was something ahead. It wasn't soil. It was too hard, too solid. The tunnel wall? She glanced up at Eni, who nodded back at her.

'Why have we stopped?' Madi asked as Ina took a step forward, the flame in her hand throwing warm light against the clay brick wall scrawling with red lines.

'The tunnel?' Ina gasped.

Eni walked up to the wall and gave it a light tap, a dull echo resonating through the burrow.

'Yes, the tunnel,' he affirmed.

The breath ran out of Naala. Green eyes. Ashen demons with the promise of death on the tips of their tongues. The girl – Chisi – turning to dust. Naala jumped as something touched her shoulder. Sinai.

'Are you okay?' Sinai whispered.

No! Naala wanted to scream at her. Sinai had given the Earth Mother's Crystal, one of the most powerful artefacts in the world, to a demon. She wasn't okay. She hated her. At least, she should. She couldn't. How could she? After all, what had she done to protect the crystal?

'Shall I smash it?' Madi suggested.

'Alert the guards, you mean? If we were going to do that, we might as well have asked them politely to let us in,' Ina scoffed, as Kora ran her fingers across the red particles on the wall.

'I didn't mean – I meant now is the time to call on our friend so I can smash it,' Madi grumbled. Madi had taken to calling Dogbari, *friend*; a term that Sinai insisted pleased the great creature immensely. Both of them bore scars from their battle together, but Madi's guilt was by far the largest one.

'Sure you did,' Ina smirked.

'Sinai, call him please,' Madi said through clenched teeth.

'Wait,' Kora suddenly blurted.

'Wait? You've been complaining nonstop and now you want to wait?' Ina's face crumpled as she spoke.

'Look,' Kora said, pointing at the wall.

Naala took a step forward and the red scrawling came into focus. Only they weren't just scrawling. They were symbols or rather one symbol repeated over and over again: three lines sitting on a two-legged stand with a curve spread over it.

'What is it?' Madi asked.

'Kpọ explosives,' Kora muttered. 'If they are disturbed, they will start a tiny reaction that will set off the others. If one of them is compromised, then I suspect that the whole tunnel goes down.'

'What is the point in such a thing?' Madi asked, rubbing a hand over his face.

'So that if someone tries to break in, it's destroyed before they know where it leads to.' Eni frowned. 'I've always come in through the latch; I had no idea.'

'Ina needs to cut out an opening,' Kora announced.

'Why on earth do you keep volunteering me to do things?'

'Because I enjoy it when you're distressed,' Kora replied, offering Ina a wide smile. 'Oh, come on; you are simply the best person for the job. You can localise your flames and draw out an opening without compromising the kpọ explosives.'

'I don't like the sound of this,' Madi said.

Naala shared that concern. If Sinai was right about Ina's nerves, then she was hardly in the position to handle something so … intricate.

'Well, I do,' Ina insisted, shoving at Madi. 'Oh, stop looking at me like that and move out of my way.'

'If you get yourself blown up trying to act brave …' he mumbled as he moved, though not far. His eyes darted from Ina to the wall as his frown deepened.

'Acting is beneath me,' Ina muttered as she wrapped her hand in a ball and threw the flame up into the air so that it hovered a finger away from her forehead. She positioned herself on the dusky wall and took a deep breath as a bright red line began to cut through the thick material, erupting a loud sound into the air.

'What is that?' a voice boomed from above.

'Ozo, I tried to tell you!' another voice sounded.

'Oh,' Sinai murmured, biting on her lip. Seconds later a crashing screech ripped through the air. Naala had known it was coming but she couldn't help but jump at the sound. Showers of dust ran through the burrow as the guards fled above them.

'It's in the sky!'

'Stay alert!' they yelled.

To her credit, Ina paid them no mind. She moved slow and meticulously, blinking away the sweat that had formed on her forehead, her lips pressed tightly together as she wound the thin line around the wall.

'No,' Sinai blurted under her breath, and they all stilled. She blinked back at them before offering a strained smile as her hand rubbed at the back of her neck. 'Sorry,' she gushed, 'it's Dogbari … he's trying to eat them. Something about the iron being irresistible.' She laughed nervously.

Naala snorted. 'Let him.' An image of the soldiers storming through her village came to mind and then a pair of emerald eyes. She shuddered.

'Do you want to talk?' Sinai whispered, and Naala bit at her cheeks to stop herself from rolling her eyes. Talk about what?

'No—' she shrugged '—thank you.'

'There,' Ina announced, and Naala let out a gush of air she hadn't known she had been holding. The line that Ina had drawn was far wider and taller than she was.

Ina looked proud. She glanced over at Madi quizzingly. 'You should be able to get in, shouldn't you?'

Madi smiled at her, ruffling the top of her head. To Naala's surprise, Ina offered him a small smile, and not an onslaught of insults, before fixing her hair back in place.

'Shall we?' Madi said as he took a step forward, pushing the heavy concrete back. It scraped against its edges before it twisted open, releasing a sudden rush of cooling air.

*

How long is this tunnel? Naala groaned inwardly as they came to yet another turn. Her legs were heavy and pricked with dull aches. She felt almost as empty as her stomach, which had started gnawing on itself.

No one had said a word for a while now. Naala presumed that, like her, they were all trying to conserve their energy.

'How long is this going to take?' Ina proclaimed.

'We're essentially walking through the entire city of Nri,' Sinai said.

Ina's eyes narrowed at that. 'How long is it going to take?' she repeated.

'A while,' Sinai bit back.

'Look, I'm tired,' Ina snapped, 'we need to rest. We are not mules.' She glared at them expectantly before shrugging. 'Well, I am not a mule.'

'Ina, we are not going to carry you if that's where you're going with …' Kora trailed off, distracted by the look that had come across Sinai's face.

Naala frowned. She knew that look. The look Sinai gave her whenever she had an idea, a good idea, that she knew Naala would despise. Naala ran her hand through her face as it dawned on her. She wants us to fly, Naala groaned inwardly.

'No,' Naala said, shaking her head.

'It'll be so much quicker,' Sinai protested.

'No.'

Sinai bit her lip. 'We'd be there in no time.'

'We can walk.'

'Ina can't – she just said.'

'Ina can,' Naala snorted back.

'Don't drag my name into whatever this is,' Ina said, folding her arms.

Naala sighed. The thought of flying through the cramped tunnel twisted at her gut. She could feel green eyes boring into her back. Or was it the destination that troubled her?

'She wants us to fly,' Naala grunted.

'Fly? In this tunnel?' Madi said.

'That will not happen. Not after what I suffered on Dogbari's back. You must be joking,' Ina muttered.

'Exactly!' Naala exclaimed, for once grateful for Ina's strenuous nature.

'Weren't you the one that said that you needed to be carried?' Kora protested. 'And you're right, this is taking too long, way too long. What would be the point if we miss our opportunity?'

'It would be faster,' Eni mused, and one by one the faces turned to Naala; even Ina awaited her answer.

Naala's chest hollowed. 'Fine,' she surrendered.

'Sorry,' Sinai grimaced but, before Naala could reply, she was swept unceremoniously off her feet.

Naala had to clamp her hand over her mouth to stop herself from screaming. They swooshed through the tunnel and with every new turn came another round of subdued cries. Soon enough they began to slow down, and Naala noticed a light shining through the otherwise dull tunnel. Shortly afterwards, Sinai lowered them onto the ground and Naala was immediately hit by a wave of dizziness. She pressed the tips of her fingers against her forehead as she willed herself not to expel her empty guts.

'Hey, Naala, are you okay?' Eni said, placing a hand on her back.

She shrugged it off, shaking her head as she slowly felt her body return to her.

'I'm sorry, Naala, but I thought it was better to get it over with,' Sinai chimed beside her.

'I'm fine,' Naala said, swatting them away.

'You're shaking.' Madi frowned before pulling her into a hug. She considered pulling away. It wouldn't have been hard, as big as he was; Madi always handled her so gently. The nausea seeped away with the embrace and Naala found herself melting into his large arms, shifting only when she caught a dark look brewing across Eni's face. Heat flushed up her back.

'I'm fine,' she said as Madi released her.

'So am I,' Ina said, rolling her eyes, 'in case anyone was wondering.'

'You want a hug too? I suppose I could—' Madi started before jolting back when Ina sparked up a ball of fire in her hands.

'You dare,' she warned as she fought away a smile.

Madi backed away, clutching his chest mockingly until he hit a wall. His eyes widened before he turned around.

'I think we're here,' he said, turning to Eni. 'Where did you say this led to?'

'It should lead into the ox stables but something feels wrong.' Eni frowned.

'Wrong how?'

'I can't place it – it's a … feeling.'

'A feeling?' Ina repeated sceptically.

'Yes, a feeling,' Eni said sharply.

Naala was taken aback by the edge in his voice. If she didn't know better, she might have thought him panicked.

'This was your plan, Eni,' Naala said quietly.

He looked to her, his black eyes roaming over her face as he shook his head. 'I know but it's no longer good.'

'Eni, are you sure this feeling isn't nerves?' Kora tried.

'It certainly seems illogical to me,' Ina said under her breath.

'Eni, the bụrụ-ọnụ is going to come at any point and we still haven't even got into the palace. We need to warn people. We need to get the crystal to help them prepare for this attack. If you really think your feelings are more important than that, then fine. Let's turn around now, but it's pretty high stakes for something you can't put your finger on,' Madi said, as he looked over the other boy.

Eni's jaw tightened before he took a sharp breath. 'Fine,' he said, 'but stay alert. I don't understand it – this feeling – but we must all stay alert. There's something behind that door that shouldn't be here. That much I know.'

Before Naala could question him, Eni pressed his hand against four corners of the wall. Naala's breath caught at her throat as bubbles began to form on its surface. Soon, the liquified wall began to form a door. When it solidified, Eni began to turn a lever at the left side of the door, back and forth. The door creaked open to reveal a small empty room with wooden walls.

'This doesn't look like stables,' Kora whispered as they crept forward.

'It's not,' Eni said, his jaw clenching. 'We need to go.'

'Madi, don't shut the—' Naala began but a dull click told her all she needed to know '—door,' she finished, throwing Madi a filthy look.

'Sorry,' he replied before tugging at the lever. It didn't give. He shook it again before turning back to them. 'It's locked,' he said, frowning.

'Well, knock it down,' Ina said as she walked over to him.

'What about the noise?' Madi protested.

'I don't care. I don't like this. I don't like it one bit.'

'Knock it down,' Kora whispered, 'before she burns us all down.'

Naala had noticed them too, the brightening sparks scattered across Ina; some of her locs were even caught in a slow-burning flame.

Naala turned to Eni; he had pulled away from the group and was inspecting the wooden walls carefully.

'Fine,' Madi muttered before drawing his knee to his chest.

'Wait!' Eni roared as he swivelled around with his arm outstretched towards Madi.

He was too late.

CHAPTER 43
THE TASTE OF ABARA

City of Nri

A blur of fluorescent green poured down from the ceiling followed by a mighty crash. The sound vibrated through Kora's chest but it was the sight of Madi's fall that stole her breath. He withered on the ground; bright red seeped through his gritted teeth. Her heart stopped and she couldn't seem to move. Beside her, Naala and Ina rushed over, dropping to his side.

Madi. Her Madi. A rushing sound crashed against her head and she felt the walls close in around her. Madi shook violently. His clenched fists pounded into the marble floor and cracks spread with each new thud.

Kora squeezed her eyes shut as the screams of her village tore through her mind. The stench of the waste hole her father had flung her in to save her life. Thud. Thud. Thud. The sound of muscle against soft flesh. The sound they had made as they took his life and reduced him to a bloody pulp.

'M-Madi,' Kora whimpered as she forced her eyes open. Thud! Thud! Thud! Arms engulfed her before she could scream. She looked up to find Eni staring down at her; his deep black eyes held her steady and the ache that had crept up her neck eased a little. For a moment, she could breathe.

'Madi!' Naala shrieked, driving Kora back to the present. Her stomach plunged as Madi's honeyed eyes bulged wide. His rigid body shook violently.

'Naala, move away from him,' Eni barked as Naala ducked out of the way of Madi's strong arm.

'He's in pain,' Naala called back. Kora blinked back at her comment. *But you will die.* If Naala didn't get out of the way, if she got caught in Madi's swings, she would die. Kora grew hot at the thought.

'Move out of the way!' she called out, stepping out of Eni's grasp and tugging Naala back.

She should hardly have bothered. Kora was still clutching on to Naala's garments when Madi stilled. Thud. Her heart gave way as Naala let out a strangled cry.

Ina looked up at them, the expression on her face tight and unreadable. 'He has fainted,' she finally said, her voice hollow and distant, 'from the pain. It can … happen like that sometimes.'

Kora blinked back at Madi and saw that Ina had spoken true. Though his face was as still as the death, his mighty chest still heaved up and down. She peered at him carefully. His blood-tinged garments were spotted with burn holes and his bare arms were blotted with raw welts. *What could have—*

'Ouch,' he croaked and Kora snapped her head up. Her eyes stung with fresh tears as she watched the smile grow on his face. It seemed the most natural thing for Madi to do.

Ina and Naala backed away as he began to sit up but Kora simply couldn't keep away. He winced as she wrapped herself around his neck. She pulled back, cursing herself for her ever-present thoughtlessness, but he held her steady, patting his large hand against the back of her head as she sobbed into his neck.

'I'm fine,' he repeated until she almost believed it.

The lightness within her chest turned to lead as Madi pulled her away. Only then could she see the bright green poles that now surrounded them. Spread across every wall within the tiny room. They were trapped.

Eni flinched as he pressed a finger against it.

'Abara,' he murmured.

Kora felt her gut twist within her.

A squeaking noise erupted into the room. The wooden walls began to pull up into the skies.

Kora squinted at the bright light. When her vision cleared she saw a man standing beyond the bars – his emerald eyes fixed on Sinai.

CHAPTER 44
THE BROKEN

City of Nri

Sinai ached at the sight of him, an eroding pain that anchored her in place as it tore her down. It hurt. She had tried to prepare herself for the worst. *You may have to face him as an enemy, what then?* she had asked herself. Sinai realised now that she had never given herself an answer. He stalked towards her. She had no defence.

Olu's scarred face was hardened, more gaunt than she remembered, his jaw locked in place and fury burned in his eyes. He scanned the group until he met her. His brows knitted and his frown deepened. Sinai nearly doubled over. What exactly had she expected? A warm smile? Olu rushing to her, crystal in hand, ready to help them fight against the bụrụ-ọnụ coming for the Kingdom? *Yes,* she thought weakly, *that and more.*

'What are you doing here?' his voice was rough, almost pained.

Sinai's heart flung against her chest. She was a *fool.* A true fool. Scorching heat slammed into her chest as she lunged forward, stopping short at the luminous bars. The cage. Olu had put her in a *cage.*

The room the cage sat in was not a room at all. It was a long strip of marble topped by wood and raffia. Large marble pillars held up the roof. The structure opened up to vast fields at either side of the strip, littered with shooting ranges, daga stands, benches and other equipment she couldn't recognise. *The army's Nkebi.*

The one section of the palace that she had never managed to sneak into. This was where he had trapped her.

'Olu, get us out of this contraption,' she heard Ina say beside her. Her voice was so low it seemed to scratch against Sinai's skin.

'I can't,' Olu said. His words cut through her and the ever-present dip in her stomach deepened as his forest-green eyes found hers. 'You shouldn't be here, not now. I'm not ready. I—'

'*Murderer!*' The word was brutal. It clawed out of Naala's mouth like a scorpion.

Olu tensed before glancing behind himself. 'She needs to be quiet. *Tell her to be quiet.*'

'No. You need to let us out, Olu,' Sinai snapped. She refused to silence Naala. She refused to dampen her pain. Not again. Naala's rage pricked at the edges of her consciousness, pure and unyielding. This time, Sinai didn't hold it back. She let it sink into her. She let it mix with her crippling disappointment until Olu's name felt like dust in her mouth. Until all she wanted was to crush his stone heart with her bare hands.

'Tell her,' he pleaded, 'please, I can't protect you fr—'

'Protect?!' Naala spat, her eyes black and fierce. 'How dare you?!' she raged, plummeting towards the bars. Eni grabbed her tight before she could make contact. Her legs and arms flayed as she continued to scream, 'You monster! You murderer! You demon!'

Naala's voice had broken under the strain. The sound tore deep into Sinai. The pain Naala had bolted deep within herself had cracked open for all to see. Tears pricked at Sinai's eyes as the floor shook. Her knees buckled under the motion.

'Naala,' she whispered but it was too late. A loud crack, rods deeper than anything Madi had created, tore through the marbled floor before fanning out far and wide. Sinai stopped breathing when she saw the cracks tearing up the pillars. Dust and debris rained down from the ceiling. If the ceiling gave way, the cage would crash down on them. They would be buried beneath the abara metal. A ringing noise sounded in Sinai's ear. *Screaming*, she realised. Someone was screaming.

Before she could think, it all came to a stop.

Sinai only had time to suck in a breath before the cracks that Naala had formed began to *reverse*. They left the marble and earth unmarked as they crept back towards their cage.

Sinai couldn't recall when it hit. The force from the reversing cracks. One moment she was staring out in horror as the cracks raced towards her; the next she was flung into the air. She slammed against the floor, against bone coated with thick muscle, until finally she felt a soaring pain run up her back. Her teeth shattered and she couldn't see anything except a hot white glare. She was burning. She was shredding. Her body shook violently and then it was still.

Sinai, Sinai, Sinaikuku. Sinai!!

Her eyes slit open. A dull ache echoed through her spine. She was overcome with the desire to rest – to fall into a sleep that would last and last and last until it never came to an end. Something weighed heavy on her chest. She tried to tug away at it but as her hand grazed a hard surface, strength trickled back into her. The crystals. She pulled herself up, coughing out painfully as she made the effort.

She opened her eyes to find them all scattered on the ground, bruised and weakened by the encounter.

'It doesn't know how to react to your powers,' Kora said weakly, her brown skin peppered with dark angry bruises. Madi held her in place. 'It's reversing it back on us.'

'In other words—' Ina coughed '—don't do that again.'

Naala didn't say a word. Her arms lay limp at her sides. Her eyes, though dull, remained fixed on Olu.

'You killed her,' Naala said, her lips trembling as she spoke. Sinai buckled under the pain in Naala's voice. An image scorched through her head. Olu standing in a village Sinai had never been to, pulling a blood-soaked abara sword out of an old woman she had never seen: Naala's grandmother. 'You started *all* of this.'

The words seemed to slice at Olu like shards of glass. He stood rigid, his jaw clenching and unclenching before he finally spoke. 'She was calm with sharp eyes,' he said roughly, his forehead crumpled. 'She wore her white hair in a fanned braid. She smelled of some sort of flower.'

'Frangipani,' Naala choked. 'I used to pick them in the forest and she'd blend it into her mango butter.'

'I remember her,' Olu said quietly, stepping back as he jabbed a finger at his head. 'I remember them all. They all live with me in here.' He looked back at them. 'I-I selected them. The most vulnerable. At first, I darted them, smearing them with blood from an insignificant wound in a hope to keep them alive long enough to survive the attacks. But that—' he looked away distantly before tightening his brow '—that turned out to be worse. They were too vulnerable to be so *alone*.' A quiver ran across his lips and he ran his tongue over them before clearing his throat. 'So then I started to follow up the dart with a clean wound to the heart. I thought ... if they had to die, I wanted it to be *painless*. I wanted to help.' Olu laughed bitterly, his eyes brimming with tears. He settled into stone.

'I've taken a lot of lives. Innocent lives,' he continued, raising his eyes to meet Naala's. 'That, I have accepted, is my lot. My curse. I have worn it as best as I could.' He smiled weakly. 'I supposed I could have killed him, the Eze,' he said, shaking his head slowly. 'You know, in battle they call me fearless but it's far from true. Every battle I faced, every person I've duelled, I've known that I could best them as sure as I've known the sun would rise in the morning. But the Eze ...' He pointed to the scar that lined his face. 'Death and I have met many times and we've each left scars on the other. Still, I've never been ready for our final meeting. I've always feared it.' He turned to Sinai. 'But *you* ... I knew when I found you, still breathing after a fall that should have left you no more than a splat on the dirt, I knew that *you* could do it. I knew that you *must* survive.' Olu shifted closer to the radiant bars. The heat pressed against his dark skin but he didn't so much as blink.

'The Kingdom must survive,' Sinai said, her throat so tight that it distorted her voice. 'Olu, let us out.' She saw him now, not as the saviour who had held her in the Nzuzo gardens, not as the monster who had trapped her in a cage, but as something else ... someone broken.

'No, you must survive,' Olu said, drawing his hand out of his garments.

Sinai gasped at the sight of his gnarled green hand clutching on the Chi Crystal.

'How ... how is he able to hold the crystal?' Kora asked.

Sinai didn't know. All she knew was that he needed to give it back.

'Olu,' she pleaded.

'I've *seen* it. I've seen what is coming to Nri. An army of the dead. They will destroy everything and then they will *burn* us all down.' He paused. 'You with them,' he added in a low desperate tone.

Sinai felt a chill against her skin. He had a strange look in his eye, as though he could already see her dead.

'You don't know that,' Sinai whispered.

Olu opened his mouth to speak before something dark flashed over his face. He plunged the crystal back in his garments.

'Question,' a voice slurred behind him. 'Does anyone else see that large glowing box in the Nkebi, or is it just me?'

CHAPTER 45
THE FALLEN OBI

City of Nri

Ina stiffened as the man staggered into the room. His eyes widened at the sight of her before he settled into a mocking smile. Marachi, Obi Iben's wayward son. Why was he sneering at her like that, as though she was some sort of … the word burned deep in her mind. *Efuola*. Did he know? Did *everyone* somehow know of the illegitimacy of her birth? Ina's palms moistened. No. Impossible. She shook away the thought, catching sight of her dull garments, her roughened hair. No wonder he had given her that gloating look. All heavens, she was in a *cage*.

All Ina could do was raise her head high. *Remember, you are the first daughter of a king,* she told herself. As she had done thousands of times over. This time, however, it left her feeling cold. Goose pimples ran up her skin. As far as he knew, she *was* still the daughter of a king. That would be enough. It had to be enough.

Ina clenched her fists as she eyed him up and down. What was he to her? A son of the least impactful Obi? By the looks of the drink in his hand and slur on this tongue, he had become an ọmuti? *Pathetic.* Ina narrowed her eyes as she inspected him. She paused. Something had flashed across his face. A look that didn't suit his usual carefree demeanor. He was … changed? Her anger slipped as she began to regard him properly. She could see now that a heaviness hung over him. A darkness she had seen one time too many in her own looking glass.

Before Ina could dwell on that, *they* entered the room. The Obis. All of them. Ina took a step back, shielding herself behind Madi. Marachi was one thing, but *all* of the Obis. It was too much.

Ina's heart thundered as they sauntered into the room alongside General Ikenna. The General stood between two towering members of his horrible golden wolves. Ina threw a glance at Olu. He was so rigid, so tense. Her mouth dried.

'What is all this commotion?' Obi Arinze commanded before he squinted at them. The whites of his eyes grew as they shifted within the cage. Had he seen her? He threw a stabbing glare at General Ikenna, whose gaze remained fixed on Olu.

'So you can see it too? Yes, yes, this – that's so very goo-good news,' Marachi hiccuped, jostling the clay pot in his hand, no doubt full, or by the looks of him, drained, with the drink of his choice. He pursed his lips, his eyes sparking when they found Sinai's. 'Kai! Aren't those the-the twins that hacked the Eze into dust?'

Of course, Ina thought, for once grateful for the attention that Sinai drew. Marachi hiccuped before he took a long swig from the pot. 'It would seem they have come to f-finish us too … aha!' he laughed darkly.

Ina could see it now. It was his hair. It had been recently twisted into the customary Obi locs. She scanned the group of Obis again, Obi Akunna and Obi Iben was missing. *Iben must be dead.* Meaning young Marachi was the new leader of education and health, a position that ill-suited him. A grim look spread across his face before he brought the pot to his mouth and gulped down its content.

'*The abumoonu! Here?*' Obi Arinze boomed. 'What is the meaning of this?'

'What do we do?' Sinai hissed, throwing a sideways glance at the group. Ina didn't know how to reply. It seemed no one else did. Sinai's eyes tightened as she waited for a response.

'We wait,' Eni said quietly.

The notion felt violent to her. *Wait? Wait, for what?*

'Olu,' General Ikenna said cuttingly.

'Kai! They are *something*, aren't they?' Marachi sauntered closer, halting when he caught Olu's glare. He stumbled slightly before letting a grin spread over his face. 'You're quiet, Ife; don't you want to welcome your would-be-bride?'

Ina's head sprang up. Obi Ife? She almost hadn't even noticed him. He seemed to have blended into the door, shifting uncomfortably as he avoided looking anywhere remotely near the cage.

'Blast it, Marachi, haven't you had enough?' Obi Ife muttered under his breath.

The inebriated man rolled his eyes at the statement. 'Every time you ask me that the answer is always the same, so why bother?' Marachi hiccupped. 'Why bother with what another man is putting in his mouth when your Lolo is here.' He turned back to the cage, gesturing to Sinai with the clay pot. Ina felt for the girl. Her body was so rigid. Her fingers dug into her arms. 'Wasn't it you that entertained thoughts of marrying one of the abumoonu?' he laughed as Obi Ife blinked quickly.

'Heavens knows why I agreed to meeting with you today. This is exactly the kind of abomination I was afraid of,' Obi Arinze growled at General Ikenna's ear. 'Ife, I thought you said he was past these little shows? I thought you said the boy-king was ready to be serious.'

General Ikenna kept deathly still during the outburst. He glanced to his side and gave a brief nod. The guards at Ikenna's sides moved swifter than lightning, slamming Obi Arinze against the door in a heartbeat.

Obi Arinze looked unnerved by the sudden action. He looked to the sky and seconds later a round of arrows whistled through the air. The Obis cowered to the ground, though they should have hardly bothered; the targets were clear.

The Nkịta Ọhịa danced around the arrows expertly, jostling Obi Arinze here and there until the arrows came to an end. Arinze looked out in the distance with a gaped mouth. His brow so furrowed that a fold formed at the centre of his forehead. The arrows must have been his defence. A defence that, by the looks of it, had failed.

One last arrow tore through the air but the guard holding Arinze up caught it with his hand seconds before it could lodge into his neck. He grunted as he wiped fresh blood along the strips of golden wolf fur crossed over his bare chest.

General Ikenna didn't say a word to the apprehended Obi. Instead he turned to Olu. 'You know the law and you brought them here anyway. Kill them.'

'I can't do that,' Olu murmured. A hard look passed between the two men.

'You dare defy me? *Here?*' Ikenna hissed. He shook with rage but there was something unconvincing in his tone. It sounded like fear.

'You misunderstand me. I only wish to protect you. It is, as we feared; they have grown too dangerous to simply kill. If we attack them by normal means they will destroy us all. Luckily, you thought of building these entrapments for the spies you believed were infiltrating the palace. I think they can be safely contained.'

'Yes,' General Ikenna said. 'I see.' His voice was flat and thin.

'Well—' Marachi clapped with the clay pot tucked at his elbows '—the Eze's Eze has spoken.' Ikenna threw him a murderous stare. He returned it wide eyed, his palms up in the air, 'Did *I* say something?' he muttered before shrugging and swivelling his drinking pot.

'You keep asking me to test my power,' Ikenna said, his voice low and steady. 'Just say the word and I will do it. Or, better yet, ask your dead father.'

The room stilled. 'You bastard,' Marachi spat, slamming his pot down on an oak table so hard that fat drops of liquid sloshed over its rim.

'Is that a way to speak to your Eze?' Ikenna said, his voice hovering just below a shout as he brought his glowing araba to the back of Marachi's neck.

Olu nudged the sword away as he slipped between the two men.

'Ozos, spirits are high,' he said, ushering back the approaching Nkịta Ọhịa. 'But let me remind you – there is only one true Eze here.'

'Indeed,' a voice said from the fields, 'and it is not any of you.'

A chill raced up Ina's neck. After all she had seen, all she had done, it seemed Obi Akunna could still inspire the same cold fear within her.

CHAPTER 46
THE CHOICE

City of Nri

'Kill him,' Ikenna snarled but, before the Nkịta Ọhịa could move, red mist tore around Obi Akunna. Sinai choked back a cry. *Agymah.*

The Nkịta Ọhịa rushed towards Obi Akunna, unfazed. Only when the mist was upon them could their grunts and shouts be heard.

Then there was silence.

Two bodies dropped to the ground. Their flesh dried and hardened. Bile rose to Sinai's throat as the mist formed into the demon that called himself Agymah.

'Olu, let us out!' Sinai screeched as she pressed closer to the glowing bars. She pushed against the pain scorching at the tips of her finger. If Agymah was here, then the bụrụ-ọnụ were close. Her head spun. Nri was running out of time.

'Akunna, what is this?' Obi Wale said; somehow the old man's voice carried over the chaos spreading across the room. His long grey beard, braided and wound around a wooden circle, shook as he spoke.

'A day of reckoning, old friend,' Obi Akunna replied. The red mist birthed more figures. To Sinai's relief they weren't the living dead. These people were *alive.* Sinai even recognised them. She wasn't the only one.

'Ihedimma,' Obi Arinze gasped at one of the women on the field, his face falling for the first time.

'Akunna, what is this?' Obi Wale repeated before screaming out at the figures, 'Kale, get out of here!' He stormed towards the field but Agymah moved at inhumane speeds. He stood squarely in front of the old man with a lopsided grin pulling on his cracked lips.

'Ah, ah, ah,' he said, wagging his index finger as the Obi backed away, glancing wide-eyed at his brother, who stood wordless amongst the other Obi's family members.

'Olu,' Ikenna warned as Agymah flashed in front of him, baring his razor-sharp teeth.

'The crystal? Is that what you were trying to call on? Rest assured, your pet is trying,' Agymah sneered, his head snapping to Olu. 'You'll find it's not that easy.' He flashed in front of Olu.

A gasp escaped Sinai's lips and suddenly Agymah was facing her. His eyes gleamed humorously. 'Didn't listen to my good advice, did you? Stupid. Predictable. *Stupid.*' He shifted back to Akunna's side, leaving the ghost of a cackle ringing in her head.

'You took something from me, Ikenna,' Obi Akunna said. His voice was as cruel as she'd ever heard it. The Nkebi fell deathly silent. 'The entire kingdom will be torn to shreds until you've paid the price for that.'

General Ikenna stood with his head held high. A frown tugged on his thin mouth. Sinai watched his chest rise and fall. Beneath his hard cutting eyes, a wound seemed to churn.

Obi Akunna swept over the Obis. 'You let that swine take your family—your legacies. You allowed him to lord their lives over you, and now you follow him like puppets. Too weak to do that, which is necessary. Well, these people, your people, stand before you, prepared to make the choice that you could not. A choice between control and death.' Behind him, the gathered people began to raise their fists in the air.

A shiver ran down Sinai's spine. She didn't like where this was heading.

'What are they holding?' Obi Arinze demanded, pushing forward, but before anyone else could respond, Akunna boomed, 'The choice is and will always be.'

'Death!' the group yelled in unison as they drew their hands to their mouths. The stillness that followed crumbled when the first noble dropped to the ground. That was when the wailing began.

Poison? Sinai thought as the skin across her face tightened. She staggered back as Obi Wale let out a sob. The old man fell to his knees.

'My fellow Obis, I grant you the same choice,' Akunna sounded, 'but rest assured if you don't take it someone else will. Ikenna is done for. Where will you stand?'

Ikenna tore away from the group of men, fiercely wiping his face before turning back to the mournful Obis. Olu stalked up behind him.

'Well,' Ikenna said, wide-eyed, 'do I need to spell it out to you?' he side-eyed the men who peered at him with cold eyes. 'Kill them,' he hissed.

'No,' Olu said quietly.

Ikenna looked as though he had been punched. His eyes tightened as he regarded Olu with his shoulders curving downward. The wounded look hidden beneath his hard eyes rose to the surface.

'I wish I could have done this ... better,' he said, his voice wavering as Olu rested a hand on his shoulders.

'As do I, brother,' he said, 'as do I.'

Olu reached into his pocket and drew out the crystal. He paused for a moment and something unsettling passed over his face.

'Survive,' Olu said before throwing the crystal up in the air.

Instinctively, Sinai pulled at the air until the emerald stone flew into her hand. The air slammed around the cage long after she had released her hold of it but she had it. The crystal. The Mother's Crystal gleaming powerfully in her palm.

Sinai glanced up in time to see Olu plunging his abara sword into Ikenna's gut before dropping to his knees.

CHAPTER 47
AN OATH FULFILLED

City of Nri

Sinai thoughtlessly placed her hand on the bar. She felt nothing. No rushing pain. No burn from the cursed abara metal. Instead, the emerald crystal spat out shards of green light as cracks ran up the bars. Sinai felt the energy from the Black and Gold realm resonate within her. She released it without a second thought and the bars crumbled to dust. Sinai let go of a breath, but she felt no relief.

Her chest tightened as she watched Olu's flesh wither before her eyes; his skin looked mottled and stiff against his bones. He looked as though he had been dead for decades and yet even now, he turned towards her, his emerald eyes wide and bright.

Sinai sank by his head. 'Olu,' she whispered, her eyes filling with tears. She didn't want this. She didn't want him to die.

'S-ur-vive,' he repeated as he fought to cling on to one more breath of life.

'Sinai,' Naala said heavily.

'Are we to sit here like shirking Lolos, letting a common soldier take the responsibility ordained to us as lords of this kingdom?' Obi Arinze boomed from afar.

Sinai lifted her head. Her head pounded as she struggled to comprehend what was happening. The Obi stalked towards Ikenna. The smaller man raised his palm up at the approaching Obi, spluttering blood out of his mouth.

Obi Wale followed suit. 'Our Lolos, our *children,* those who we have been bound to protect have acted with more honour than any of us has displayed,' he said, drawing out his abara.

'Blast it,' Marachi said as he too drew forward, plunging an abara into Ikenna's shoulder. 'For my father,' he spat as Ikenna screamed through gritted teeth.

Obi Arinze plunged his abara into Ikenna's ribs. 'For my daughter,' he said and Ikenna dropped on his knees.

Obi Ife looked around nervously before drawing out his abara and digging it into Ikenna's back before stepping away, blinking in horror as Ikenna lay quivering on the ground.

'For Nri,' Obi Wale said as he plunged his abara directly into Ikenna's heart until the would-be king lay still in a pool of his blood.

Olu groaned weakly in her arms.

'Sinai,' Ina whispered beside her, but she had already seen it. Olu's arm. His arm. His *flesh.* His skeletal frame was filling out before her eyes. His breath had returned. Sinai blinked around. She didn't understand. Ikenna was dead, he was dead and— The breath caught in her throat as she watched all the Obis standing over Ikenna except the one, Obi Wale, who had stabbed him in his heart and now lay crumpled on the ground.

'Finally,' Obi Akunna breathed.

Obi Arinze turned to face the man coldly. 'Make no mistake, Akunna, your blood will run dry today too.'

Akunna regarded them all silently, a sneer forming over his lips. 'How like you to find quarrel with *me.* Today, I *made* you strong. Today, I did what was necessary.'

'And today you die,' Marachi said, soberly.

'Agymah,' Akunna barked. The Obis faltered as the red mist spiralled out of the monstrous man. Until he was gone.

A cackle shook the pillars. 'You still think you can call on me, Akunna? Has your order not been enacted? Is your foe not dead? *ɛyɛ sɛ wo yɛ,* you said to me. Well, listen now, here is the wrath I promised you. You will not be spared a second of your death. You will feel it ten times over until time itself comes to a stop. This is my parting gift to you, master.' The voice echoed into nothing as the colour drained from Obi Akunna. He bolted out of the room; the Obis followed silently.

'We need to get out of here,' Naala said, tugging at Sinai's arms until she had risen to her feet. Olu lay on the ground, his eyes still closed but his breathing even.

'What's wrong?' Ina said, looking up from Olu's side. 'It's over; Ikenna is dead.'

Naala shook her head, her eyes wide and wild. Sinai didn't have to ask Naala what was wrong. She could feel them. The tremors beating through her chest. Low and demanding. Her skin crawled with dread as she stumbled onto the field. Sinai pulled at the threads of air that coated her until she was hovering in the sky.

Sinai lost her balance when she saw them. The cold air whipped against her cheeks until she caught herself, just in time to temper her crash to the ground.

'Sinai!' voices cried out to her but she couldn't place who it was, not over the thundering of her booming heart. She squeezed her eyes shut but she couldn't erase the image. It sat there scorched into her eyelids. The sea of the dead marching to stake their claim over the Kingdom.

CHAPTER 48
THE UNDEAD

City of Nri

They had torn down the walls that surrounded the city. The bụrụ-ọnụ … the cursed beings encroaching on the city of Nri. Naala wouldn't have believed it could be possible if she hadn't seen it with her own eyes.

A mass of grey seeped into the city like palm wine climbing through cloth. Naala couldn't even scream, though it was all she wanted to do. All she could do was watch them, her eyes dry and stinging. Her throat was tight and her head spun as she watched the bụrụ-ọnụ head for the palace entrance.

'The squalors,' Eni said thickly. It lay beneath them, ravaged by the cursed ones. Naala's stomach lurched at the sight of scattered scraps of what had once been people's homes, now occupied by the blocks of the approaching bụrụ-ọnụ.

'Some escaped,' Kora added in a quiet voice, looking out to the hundreds fleeing out beyond the wall. Beyond what was left of the wall.

Something pulled at Naala's core. *Thousands,* she thought. *Thousands used to occupy the squalors … what of them?*

Naala's knees buckled on the impact when they finally reached the palace entrance. She flung out her hands for balance but hopes of that left her when she heard the beat of the bụrụ-ọnụ's approach. Hard, even and closer than Naala had imagined. She stumbled over and Eni caught her before she reached the ground.

'Sorry, is everyone o——' Sinai started but her voice was drowned by screaming.

Naala pulled out of Eni's grasp as she whipped around. A breath escaped her as her gut crunched at the scene before her.

Naala didn't understand what she was seeing at first. Rows of people and nnunus stationed at the foot of the palace. *What were they doing? Didn't they know what was coming?* The people cowered at the sight of them, their garments tattered and their eyes wide. Servants.

Naala's eyes narrowed at the soldiers standing behind them. The spears and swords clasped in their hands were fixed at the people in front of them. Above them, more soldiers were stationed at the palace's windows with taut bows pointing down at the people. Naala took note of a handful of bodies crumpled at their feet with arrows poking out of their backs. *The ones who had tried to flee.*

They were using them as a first defence, she realised. A staggered breath escaped from Naala's mouth; it was all she could do to stop herself from screaming. The blood pounded in her ears and her hands tightened into fists.

Tear-soaked faces whimpered as her expression soured. Naala didn't know who they were more afraid of: her, the cursed army of the dead or the soldiers behind them. The ones that should have been protecting them. *Blast them all,* she raged as the earth trembled.

'Kill the abumoonu witch!' someone cried out. The sky darkened with arrows.

Naala's breathing slowed as she felt each and every one of them. The birch wood flexed as they glided through the humid air. She breathed along with their movement, feeling the power from the Black and Gold realm coursing through her veins. She held her breath and they halted in the air. Destruction blossomed on the tip of her tongue. She let the heat within her rise until she was near blind with rage.

Naala clenched her fists and the arrows shattered into splintered shards before scattering to the ground. She let the air pour out of her as her power bubbled to the surface. Thick vines and barks tore out of the palace's bleached walls and began to board up the large windows, closing them up from any other incoming attack.

Shouts erupted through the air as the soldiers pulled out of their formation. More vines crawled out of the stone floors, pulling at their ankles until they crashed to the ground. Naala's skin pricked as another rain of arrows descended. Far less than before, but enough to commandeer her attention.

'Move!' Eni yelled just as she crushed the upcoming assault. She blinked back as he crashed down on two soldiers who had broken through their vine restraints in pursuit of her.

Naala held her breath as Eni dodged the swipe of the bright green sword, delivering hard and targeted punches until both men stilled. Eni didn't even need to see the three others encroaching behind him because Madi did. He smashed into them with his full strength, knocking them down like sticks. They lay on the ground, broken and immobile. The winds picked up. From the corner of her eye, Naala could see a crowd of the soldiers hovering in the air above Sinai before they came crashing down. One lesson from Chukwudi, at least.

Naala's breath quickened as she heard another round of arrows. This one was different. Not synchronised as the others had been. These were random and erratic. They were learning. *Blast them.*

Naala gritted her teeth as her eyes darted to and fro, exploding arrows left, right and centre. Just as she found her stride, something sharp tugged at her abdomen. *Sinai.*

He was choking her. The soldier. He had his elbow wound tight around her neck. She was squawking, her legs sprawled in the air before he slammed her down hard. Naala felt faint when she heard the soft crunch of the girl's head against the hard ground.

Naala's hesitation was costly. She jumped back as an arrow sliced through her arm, soaking her garment with red. Something gripped her stomach and pulled her down to the ground. Eni. He held her down, covering her body with his as the arrows found their targets. *No,* Naala screamed as she halted the arrows before they could pierce through his back. She pulled out of his grasp and her stomach turned when she saw a man, a servant, crawling at the entrance of the palace with an arrow lodged through his neck.

Naala couldn't breathe. Her neck, it seemed, had turned to stone. The only thing she could do was to release the dark energy soaring within her. When she did, the world trembled. The soldiers buckled, the pillars cracked and the man clutching Sinai shifted. His bare hand sweeping over the surface of her necklace.

Poof.

Dust fragments coated Sinai. Her mouth opened wide as shock plastered her face. The sound of the bụrụ-ọnụ pounding in the background made Naala want to claw at her own skin.

'Enough!' Sinai bellowed and the air whipped around relentlessly. Sinai brought her hand over the necklace and all the soldiers fell to the ground, their hands clutching at their necks as they gasped for air that wouldn't come to them. Sinai released them and they collapsed, wheezing and spluttering as they rolled weakly around the floor.

Naala glanced beyond the palace steps; through the groomed gardens and open land she could see the very beginnings of the squalors where grey inhumane figures had started to emerge.

'Get them inside,' Naala shouted to Kora. She didn't have to tell her twice. The girl nodded as she began to beckon the rows of nnunus and servants back into the palace.

Naala looked down at the soldiers. They wore the same uniform as the men who had slashed down her friends and family. A few of them could even have *been* the same men. The thought sat in her mind, cold and distant. It all seemed *redundant* now. Naala had come face to face with the green-eyed demon. Olu. He was not the same man who had stalked her dreams. He was no monster. He was a broken man. Her gaze swept over the struggling men in soldier's uniforms. Many of them looked broken too.

'You have a choice,' Naala said, pushing her voice so that it carried far. 'Stand with us against the true demons who approach. Protect this palace, this kingdom, protect these people, as is your duty, or get out of the way and let us handle your jobs whilst you slaughter children and the elderly and call yourselves *brave.*'

The men glared back at her wordlessly. The sound of the approaching cursed ones punctuated every second. Slowly they rose to their feet, drawing their weapons up with them.

Naala half-expected them to attack but they did not. They looked beyond her to the bụrụ-ọnụ, who outnumbered them more than ten times over. She could feel the fear quaking within them. It quaked within her too.

'Do you trust them?' Sinai whispered under her breath. The soldiers' eyes followed her every move, fixed on the crystals at her neck. Naala couldn't tell if they had respect or fear plastered on their gaze.

'No,' Naala replied, glancing back at distant figures forming along the horizon. They were less than a rod away. 'But we need all the help we can get.'

'Can we slow their approach?' Eni said by her side.

Naala scanned him; he was a little bruised and there was a red stain on his thigh but otherwise he seemed to be intact. She found herself releasing a breath she hadn't realised she had been holding.

'We can try,' Sinai said, her eyes filling with brilliant gold as the high winds spiralled until they formed something of a high wall. It lashed to and fro, so fast it created a thick blur.

'Brilliant,' Madi exclaimed. Naala had to agree. It was a good idea. Naala was certain that it would keep them out, but for how long?

'Heavens,' Ina gasped.

Naala frowned as she peered out into the horizon. Her heart clenched. A handful of the demons were trying to push themselves through Sinai's wall of wind. The effort tore at their skin, snapping their limbs into unnatural positions but still they pressed on.

Eni drew a bow he had snatched from one of the dead soldiers and aimed it at the buru-onu staggering up the palace steps. *It will work*, Naala hoped silently. If Sinai could keep the winds up, then they could divide the sea of the undead into smaller, manageable sections to fight off. Naala waited for Eni to release his arrow, but he never did.

Naala's brow creased when she looked back at him. His mouth gaped open and his narrowed eyes twitched.

'What is wrong with you?' she demanded as he lowered his bow but all he could do was shake his head. Beside him, another soldier followed through with the kill. More soldiers edged closer, slashing through more stray buru-onu.

'What is wrong with you?' she repeated before Sinai let go of a gasp. The air stilled as Sinai let her wall of wind fall. Naala's heart plummeted to her stomach. A sea of the undead stood before them. They had gathered behind the blurred wall;

now they filled the land as far as Naala could see. The soldiers who had ventured down the steps were now retreating.

'What are you doing?!' Naala called to Sinai.

'They are …' The sound of the bụrụ-ọnụ's feet pounding against stone started up again, so loud now it drowned her out completely.

Naala did the only thing she could think to do. She allowed the power from the Black and Gold realm to flesh out within her. She sucked in her breath and let it fill her. Then she let the earth collapse.

CHAPTER 49
CLEANSE

City of Nri

The earth at the base of the palace steps crumbled down deep into a crater that spanned throughout the squalors, beyond the wall even. Most of the bụrụ-ọnụ went down with the earth but some had already reached the palace steps.

Before she could act, Naala was accosted with grey plaid bodies. They clamped down on her flesh, biting and scratching, pulling at her hair. She flung her limbs until they crashed against cold wet skin. She released a scream as she hit back harder and harder.

They were too many.

Naala fell to the ground as a heavy weight pressed against her lungs. She couldn't breathe.

'Naala!' she heard Sinai's scream and the weight lifted. She clutched desperately at the air, letting it fill her lungs. One by one the grey demons were flung into the air.

One of them, however, clung tightly to her. From this close, the demon almost looked like a *girl*. The garments it wore were tattered but familiar. Garments she had seen on many a market girl. Naala's eyes lifted to the bụrụ-ọnụ's eyes and a lump formed in her throat. They looked *human*.

They *were* human.

Desperate, frightened and *human.*

The girl tore away from Naala and hung in the air with the other bụrụ-ọnụ; the other *people.* Sinai gently lowered them down into the crater.

'They're human,' Sinai said as she rushed beside her, helping her up to her feet.

Naala limped to the edge of the palace steps where several rods down the bụrụ-ọnụ squirmed within the crater she had created. They tore at its edges, a few of them even trying to climb out before falling back soon after. They turned on one another, beating, scratching and strangling whoever they could find.

'They're human,' Naala repeated, her stomach churning at the thought.

'Human?' Ina whispered, holding her arms tightly. 'Are you sure? Are you sure they're still ... still even ...'

'Yes,' Eni said, 'they are alive.'

'How do you know? Look at their skin, look at how they tear at each other.'

'I know,' Eni said firmly.

Sinai nodded. 'He didn't create them. They're not the living dead. He *infected* them with the jikọọ. That is what he got from the pit of Eriri Uhie, not them.'

'Like what the Isi did to us?' Madi said, pained.

'Yes, and what Amadioha did to the anwu people,' Sinai murmured.

The anwu people. The thought formed in her head. Perfect and all-encompassing. 'The cleansing flames of Anyanwu,' she said, her voice rising steadily. 'They need to be cleansed.' Why hadn't she seen it before?

'Naala?' Sinai started.

'You said that the Mami Wata told you that we *had* to evoke the second crystal, and should we evoke the third, it could destroy the Kingdom or heal it,' Naala said hurriedly.

'Yes.'

'Àlà,' Naala said, 'I didn't evoke Àlà. Don't you see? The third crystal ... we can still evoke the third crystal. Think about it, Sinai. What else can be destructive or healing?'

Sinai eyes widened. 'Anyanwu's flames. They can either cleanse or—'

'Destroy,' Ina said tightly as she looked down at the crater. A frown formed on her lips. 'Okay.'

'Ina?'

'Sinai, give Naala the crystal,' Ina said quietly.

'Are you sure you can do this?' Naala found herself saying, though she didn't know why. What choice did they really have?

'No,' Ina replied stiffly. Screams tore out of the crater and a tremor ran through Ina.

'You have to be calm; you have to be settled otherwise they could *destroy* you,' Sinai said, biting her lip. 'We should find another way. Perhaps we could wait for—'

'They're killing each other,' Ina interjected. 'They have no choice. Their bodies have been taken from them. I can't let them … not after … just give her the stone.'

'Bu—' Sinai protested before Naala placed a hand on her shoulder. Sinai grimaced at the touch before taking in a deep breath. Gingerly, she took off the necklace and dropped it in Naala's palm.

Touch.

Naala would never get used to the rush of power that flooded her when her finger grazed the surface of the crystals. Swirls of black mist studded with gold wrapped over her. Power surged through every section of her body, drowning her in energy. She didn't lose herself in it this time. She didn't fall into the black. She *saw* it. She breathed it into her and the world began to shake under her feet.

Deep in the core of the world, a tear started. It raced towards Naala, breaking through the stone floor. Naala choked when a stream of fire flew high into the heavens but she didn't hesitate. She raised her hand and without a second thought, she crashed it down on Ina.

CHAPTER 50
A CRATER OF FIRE

City of Nri

Hot air blasted her backwards. Sinai tumbled into the crater, catching herself in the air before she could succumb to the hundreds of feverish hands grasping for her.

She settled back to the ground, stumbling backwards when she saw Ina elevate into the air. She was wrapped in blue flames and curls of black mist. Ina didn't scream; she almost looked *serene*.

She can do this, Sinai willed silently. Ina opened her eyes and they shone pale blue as she hovered over the crater.

She released a roar of crystal blue fire into the crater. Sinai jolted forward as a cold sensation slapped at her back. Her hands stretched out but she soon drew it back to herself. The fear she had felt at the blue flames settled into admiration. She had never seen anything so beautiful. The flames washed over the people and they didn't make a sound. They stood completely still as their grey skin warmed into various shades of brown.

'It's working,' Sinai whispered as her shoulders sank.

'It's worked,' Naala corrected.

She was right. The flames had stopped and when Sinai dared herself to peer down into the crater, she saw them, disoriented, injured but settled. *Alive*.

'Let them out,' she said, her voice barely a whisper. 'Let them out!' she repeated as her pulse quickened to the speed of lightning. Naala didn't respond. When Sinai glanced back at her, the look on her face twisted at Sinai's guts.

Naala's eyes were peeled open, and her lips quivered as she stood transfixed, watching Ina. Sinai followed her gaze and staggered backwards at the sight.

Ina was engulfed in a tangle of blood-red flames. They circled around her like a den of snakes.

Sinai's mouth went as dry as sand. 'Ina!' she screamed so hard that it hurt.

'I-I can't control it,' Ina roared back. Her voice echoed over them as she let out a scream that scorched Sinai's back.

'Yes, you can,' Sinai bellowed back. 'Yes, you can!'

She had to.

The flames wrapped around her, tightening their grip and boring into her skin. Until they were gone. Ina let out a scream and the world itself exploded.

Sinai coughed so hard she felt the muscles in her neck spasm. A haze of red smoke coated the land. Above her a blazing fire roared. A second sun, with Ina at its centre.

Red sparks flew down. One sizzled on the earth by Sinai's feet; another fell onto the forehead of a man within the crater. Seconds later, he was engulfed in flames. It spread like nothing Sinai had ever seen, scorching through lines of screeching people; burning them to a crisp before Sinai could take a breath.

Sinai sent a cool air racing towards the crater until the flame died down. As she did, more sparks showered down.

Sinai looked around desperately as flecks of fire blew onto the palace, immersing a section in flames. At every turn Sinai tried to put them out, but the more she quenched, the more flames scattered down.

'Control it, Ina! Control it!' Sinai roared. For a second it seemed as though she had got through to her. Ina looked down at her through the crimson flames. Her eyes now burned bright red.

'I don't want to.' Ina's face was blank, her voice flat and her arms outstretched as a flood of deadly flames spewed from her palms.

Sinai had no time to think.

Sinai let the air spiral above her. Whipping it around furiously until it formed a dome that enveloped them. Sinai's neck bulged under the strain of the beating flames. How long could she keep this up? She buckled backwards. She had seconds before she would fail them all.

She had to get her away.

Sinai gathered all her strength and pushed with a might she had yet to know. Heat licked against her feet but she pushed anyway. Lifting herself off from the ground as she pressed against the gathering flames.

'Sinai!' she heard Naala call below her. It was only then that she realised that she had reached the sky. Still, Sinai pushed higher. She could feel cold air lick at the tips of her nose and cheeks, but it was no match for Ina's flames. Even though the scorching heat from Ina's flames had eased, the pressure was still there.

Slowly, the flames settled to the point where Sinai could even see Ina. Her heart gave a painful squeeze. Along the way, Ina had collapsed. Her eyes were closed, and her body flopped as though she were being pulled by a string around her waist. The ball of flames that had engulfed her had reduced to a thin blazing coat. Sinai's stomach dropped. She could now see that the flames were scattered with the red mist of the Eriri Uhie.

'Ina,' Sinai cried as she drew them ever higher into the sky. She had to get rid of those flames. If she could do that, Ina would be safe. The Kingdom would be safe.

Sinai felt her body dip down as her strength waned. The higher they got, the thinner the air, and the heavier Ina became.

Sinai slipped.

Ina descended and Sinai watched in horror as her coat of flames intensified. Sinai reached out to Ina thoughtlessly. She grabbed at her hand, and the red mist ripped through her. Strangely it left her unmarked. Sinai no longer had the strength to lift Ina with the air alone so she pulled her up through the air as the flames bit into her arms.

Just a little further, Sinai thought as the flames subsided. She faltered again, letting out a cry through clenched teeth as she clutched at Ina with her other hand. The flames crept up Sinai's arms, sinking deep into her.

She couldn't even scream. She couldn't think. She no longer knew what she was doing. What was she doing? Going up? She had to keep going up. She had to keep going up.

Sinai let go of the buffer of air between her and Ina. She had to keep going up. Scorching flames curled around her. A pain like she had never experienced before tore at her very being. She had to keep going up. The red flames filled every part of her essence until … it all stopped.

She had to keep going up but she couldn't move any more. They stood there suspended in the air. The only glow on Ina's skin now came from the sun as it basked them in a warm blinding light. The ice-cold air slithered over Sinai as her vision turned black. *But I have to keep going up.*

CHAPTER 51
CATCHING VINES

City of Nri

A tear escaped Naala's eye as she fixed her gaze to the heavens. She couldn't blink; if she blinked she might miss something. 'I can't see the flames any more.' Panic clawed at her neck. 'Why hasn't she come down?'

'Give it time,' Eni suggested.

Naala heaved, 'No. No. Something is wrong.' Her heart squeezed out a staggered heartbeat. 'She is too high. She'll lose air. She'll fall,' Naala rambled as the ground broke open for her. Thick entanglements of vines wrapped around her and pulled her up.

'Naala!' Eni cried as she scrambled up the growing vines.

'She's too high.' Naala strained; she could feel her heart pound over the rising wind. She missed her footing, and her weight pulled her down. Before she could fall, a section of vines grabbed her waist, pulling her back up.

Naala couldn't see anything above her, just the blinding sun and whispers of clouds. Sweat formed on her forehead, dampened by yet another gust of wind. It knocked her off harder this time. She tumbled down her vine tower. Vines stretched out to catch her but she broke through each one until she landed with a soft thud in Eni's arms.

'She doesn't have the air,' Naala sobbed into his chest as he held onto her tight.

She pulled away from him and stared up at the wavering vine stalk.

'What's that?' Madi whispered.

'Dogbari?' Eni said.

'Did he catch them?' Naala asked desperately. 'Has he got them?'

'I …' Eni squinted at the sky before looking down at her with a pained look '… I don't know.'

CHAPTER 52
THE ILLUSION

City of Nri

Ina opened her eyes to find Sinai sitting beside her nest. They were in her old quarters. She could tell by the smell alone: a mixture of rose and lavender hardened by earthy myrrh. There was another odour that she couldn't quite place. It was *revolting*. She pulled her eyes open, looking around for its source. Sinai caught her eye.

'So I didn't kill you,' Ina said drily.

'I didn't kill you.' Sinai sighed as she rested backwards on the chair; her thick hair fell over the folds of her tawny garment.

'How many people?' Ina asked. She tried to keep her tone light but she couldn't seem to still her quickening breaths. She needed to *know*.

'Ina …' Sinai started with a frown on her face.

'Oh, don't,' Ina snapped, 'don't do that. Don't drag it out. Say it fast and let's be done with it.'

Sinai looked back at her with what Ina presumed was her version of a hard expression. Ina might have laughed if she wasn't so nervous.

'According to the last count, two hundred and twenty-five thousand eight hundred and sixty-seven.'

Ina choked and Sinai sprang up as she gasped for air.

'I-I killed *how* many people?' Ina managed to squeeze out, her head swimming with the nameless faces that had been engulfed in her flames.

'You *saved* them. That many people are alive because of you; more, in fact! The entire Kingdom has you to thank for today.'

'No,' Ina gulped. 'No, I killed people.' She shook their screams out of her head.

Sinai didn't say anything for a while. 'You weren't the only one,' she said, looking down at her interlocked fingers. 'Some of them died trying to get past the wall that I created.'

'That's it. Turn *everything* into a competition,' Ina snorted.

Sinai looked up with a start, her eyes wide and mouth parted. 'Ina!' she chastised but a smile passed between them all the same.

'I remember the fire,' Ina said after a moment. If she thought deeply enough she could still feel the scorching hot flames burning her from the inside out. 'I remember you taking me up to the heavens and then falling but I'm ... intact,' she said, looking down at her body. She felt exhausted but she didn't feel *broken*. She didn't even feel sore.

'Dogbari,' Sinai said. 'He caught us on the way down to the earth.'

'Remind me to thank the beast ... our friend,' Ina said as she rested back with a smile on her face.

'Mm, let me finish; he caught us in his mouth.' Sinai flicked her fluffy hair against Ina's nose. 'I've done three washes already and the smell has only *just* begun to subside.'

'That smell is coming from me?' Ina shrieked as she yanked one of her locs and sniffed. Her gut twisted. It was grotesque! Worse than grotesque, because the stench was coming from her. How could she ever live this down? 'Urgh, I'll have to soak it in rose oil for days to get the stench out,' she groaned, as Sinai chuckled before settling down into a sad expression.

'I'm sorry,' Sinai said, and Ina shook her head knowingly.

'There you go again, Sinai, apologising for things you have no business apologising for.'

'I nearly killed you.'

'I *did* kill ... several people and not in the fake way you supposedly did,' Ina retorted and they both fell silent. Whispers of her victims' cries drifted back to her. Ina had a feeling that she would be hearing those cries for years to come.

'I know what the illusion is,' Sinai said suddenly.

'The illusion?' Ina replied, shifting away from her darkening thoughts.

'Yes. The Mami Wata said that in order to keep the Kingdom intact, we would have to know the difference between the illusion and the truth and I think ... no – I know – what it is.'

'Go on.'

'Control. The illusion is that we *have* control.' Sinai looked up from her hands. 'You see, I've thought hard about it. At first, I thought it was Dogbari. I thought that he was the illusion. Then the Amaghi and even Olu. It was only when you were in those flames that I knew.'

Ina rested her head on the pillow. 'Control,' she repeated, closing her eyes as she thought back to the flames climbing up her skin. Pouring in and out of her.

'It felt good ... almost.' Ina wasn't too sure what she was trying to say. It didn't feel good. The pain was awful. Killing those people was awful. She would never forget, nor could she forgive it, and yet she couldn't deny the peace she had found in the midst of it all. 'Not the act, but—' she took a deep breath '—losing control. *That* felt good. No, it didn't. Not, exactly,' Ina rambled. Frustration rose with her. What was wrong with her? She pressed her lips together and took a deep breath.

'I carry a lot of pain, Sinai. We all do, I know, but I ... I *really* do. It feels as though with each new year it grows. Something else adds onto the pile. When I was up there, when the flame was *cleansing*, it was as if I was new again; as if I could start again without any of the load, but then ... I remembered. I remembered everything. I remembered my parents. I remembered feeling so out of place. Being alone. I remembered the day *he* cornered me... I remembered it all. I saw the pain as something else, not something to put away, something to fall into. Then I was filled with this dangerous rage. All I wanted to do was destroy everything ... including myself.'

'Chaos,' Sinai muttered.

'Eriri Uhie,' Ina pondered. 'I know Kora said it fuels our survival, but I think it's more than that. I think it fuels destruction. It fuels this need to tear everyone and anyone down so you're the last one standing.'

'Hmmph,' Sinai said, a worried look forming on her face.

'What is it now?' Ina bristled.

'I think something is wrong with me,' Sinai blurted and Ina laughed.

'Something is wrong with all of us,' Ina sighed. Sinai nodded as she attempted and failed to smile back in response. *Oh Sinai.* 'Why do you think that?' she added more seriously.

'The Eriri Uhie fills you with destructive rage. It burns anyone who touches it. It tires out those who try to manipulate it,' Sinai rambled, 'but me … I—' Sinai cast her eyes down '—I didn't die when I touched your flames; blood magic does nothing to me … I might be … what if I'm … evil, like Amadioha.'

'That's a very simple way to look at it,' Ina said, and Sinai looked up at her with a frown. 'What? It is. You know that you are not evil. You also know that the Eriri Uhie is not evil. Destruction doesn't mean evil. Sometimes things need to be destroyed so they can be rebuilt. That's fine.'

Sinai didn't say anything, but her forehead creased in thought.

'The world is broken, Sinai. It doesn't take a genius to see that. You tried to fix it by getting rid of the Eze and how did that pan out? There's no quick fix. No fix that doesn't include destruction. A clean sheet so we can make way for something new, something better. Isn't that what you were saying about control?'

'It is?'

'Yes. The truth is we have no control. Everything we gain, every morsel we grasp onto, can be taken away from us in a snap second,' Ina said, sitting up in her nest. 'That's the illusion, right? That we're safe because we have control, but there *is* no promise, no guarantee. All we have are these moments and we're disconnected from them; we're disconnected from *her*.'

'The Earth Mother?'

'Yes. *She* is the balance. I see it now. I saw it in the flames. You and Naala are going to bring her back with those crystals. I know it. So, see, you destroy, then you build. Simple.' Ina beamed.

Sinai smiled back at her but her smile faltered.

'What now? That was a great speech; if I haven't convinced you now then—'

'No, it's not that, I understand what you mean; it's just ...' Sinai's shoulders slackened, and her face sagged as though something heavy was pressing on her.

'What?'

'The crystals. We lost them.'

CHAPTER 53
THE STRANGER

City of Nri

Eni had woken up before sunrise, the dark sky brightened slightly by a thin beam of light outlining the horizon. He hadn't slept all night. He had lay awake, with Naala nestled beneath him, counting her steady breaths.

He shifted, careful not to wake her, when he rose from her nest. He couldn't help but smile as he looked down on her. She would curse him for leaving. He could see her now, face scrunched, and eyes narrowed. He brushed her temple. How to make her understand? If word got out that they shared an akwa nest, people would assume that he had taken her honour. Eni couldn't allow that.

They had been close on more than one occasion. Naala was so warm, so soft and some nights she would pull him close, her lips pressed on his neck and her breath brushing against his skin. He would get so lost in the moment and all he could think of was being one with her, in the truest sense.

He couldn't.

She was not his wife, not yet. She was Naala. A Descendant. Her honour was far greater than anything he had ever come across. He may be no Madi, but even a swindler like him could understand that.

'Will you marry me?' he whispered, not for the first time. He had taken to asking her every morning as she slept. Some days he came dangerously close to asking her when she was awake. A foolish notion. What marriage could he give her now? What ceremony? With her family snatched from her and his family ... Eni shook the thoughts out of his head.

He needed to walk.

*

He passed through the palace gates and was struck by the bitter scent of smoke that clung to the depleted city. A herald to the new regime.

Akunna had managed to flee the city of Nri, taking with him a significant portion of the city's wealth. Neither was there any sign of his accomplice, Agymah. Eni ground his teeth at the thought of the demon. He had depleted the squalors, treating them like rats. They had learned that he was an Adze, a demon from the Kingdom of Wagadou. He spread the egbu illness through the city and created blood ties with the masses in the squalors under the guise of a cure. Blood ties that he then used to transform them into the bụrụ-ọnụ. Eni wanted to leave every day to find the man that had stolen so many souls. Yet, he couldn't leave Naala's side. Not with everything so *new*.

The Obis had elected Arinze as their new leader. Unlike his unsuccessful predecessors, Eze Arinze had not snatched power. He had accepted it, reluctantly at that, much like the old ways where the people elected their most worthy leader. Eni wrinkled his brow. Would it be enough? Nri might have been repaired, its cracks and ụlọs reconstructed by Naala and Madi, but it wasn't the same. There were cracks that the eyes couldn't see. Cracks that would crumble the city.

Eni could feel the thirst brewing within the squalors. The common folk had been hit hard by the events that had washed over the city. They had been flung to the frontline while the nobles hid behind their high walls. Eni had a feeling they would all pay for that soon.

The only bright spot he could detect was the Descendants of the First. Naala, Sinai, Madi and Ina. The quartet had sparked something within the people ... an unbridled reverence; some even bowed low in their presence, whispering the names of the old gods under their breath. It unsettled the noble class, and yet they too were plagued with fear.

Eni didn't like it. The rising tension that tugged him to and fro. It spoke of unseen dangers. It spoke of loss. *As soon as Ina is fit to travel, we leave.* They needed to put some distance between them and the city of Nri.

Eni heart thudded at the sight of the ulo. It hadn't been his intention to return here. He wanted nothing more than to turn around and leave but memories held him steady in place. The sand bricks at the foot of the ulo that he had broken his toe against as a child. The straw from the hay roof scattered on the ground by the high winds that he used to collect. It seemed so much smaller than he had remembered.

'Afam?' a voice sounded behind him. He knew it immediately though it was raspier than he remembered. No doubt from years spent hollering. He had to stop himself from doubling over when he turned to face her. She was so *old*. Her hair was grey now, plaited into a cone braid and fraying on the sides; her smoky brown skin had leathered with age. The only feature that had been left untouched were her dark piercing eyes. The eyes that she had passed on to him.

'Afam? What are you doing here.'

'I'm not Afam,' he murmured. He remembered the name distantly; his brother nearly 20 years his senior. His chest hollowed.

The woman squinted at him and drew closer. 'Emeka?' she said, and Eni clenched his jaw, blinking back at her as he steadied his breathing.

'Emenike,' he said eventually. 'You named me Emenike.'

She nodded back at him. 'Yes, yes, Emenike, is that not what I said?'

He regarded her for a moment. 'You can call me Eni,' he said coolly, his body stiff as the woman smiled at him.

'Eni.' She nodded slowly as she feasted on his attire. 'Kai, look at you, *Eh-ni!* You look so fine,' she said, drawing closer to him and tugging at his akwete cloth.

He flinched at her touch but he didn't back away. Her emotions scattered around in the air. They engulfed him as she stepped closer. His pulse quickened and his throat dried as her insatiable desire for wealth that she had never known surged through him. A hunger for something she couldn't pin down. He was struck with another sensation flowing within her. It gripped him coldly: fear. An old forgotten fear that blossomed as he watched over her. She lowered her eyes and stepped back.

'Is my father here also?' he asked, his mouth dry; he didn't know what to do with his hands.

'He passed in the plague.' His mother grunted before looking back at him. 'So what are you now, eh? You're more than a servant, that's for sure. *A specialist?*'

'I'm ...' Eni started but he found that he didn't have an answer to that question. He stopped speaking and scrunched his face exasperatedly before letting out a short laugh. 'I need to be going,' he said as her eyebrows pulled together. He didn't wait for her answer.

Eni stormed through the squalors blindly. What had he hoped to gain from that? His palms moistened and he couldn't hear anything over his pounding head. Nothing. Fool. He was a—

'Sorry,' Eni mumbled as he bumped into someone. The bald man sneered back at him wordlessly as shadows danced on his face.

'No trouble at all,' Agymah said, revealing his razor-sharp teeth.

Eni's body tensed but by then it was too late.

CHAPTER 54
THE WHITE RAM

City of Nri

Red. That was all Eni could see. Though he'd been sucked into the air, he couldn't seem to breathe. His fingers clawed at his throat as he struggled, fruitlessly, against the invisible demon.

A sharp pain exploded against his shoulder blade and he scrambled up from the ground, spluttering as he tried to steady himself. Eni was no longer in the squalors. He knew this place. He stumbled over to the silvery liquid running smoothly through the ọnụ ụzọ. He was in the cave.

'It has a charm to it, don't you think?' Agymah said.

Eni lunged for him. 'You will die today!' he cursed, clutching at the demon's neck. He gripped it and squeezed with all his might before falling forward, clutching at nothing but air.

'I will?' his voice sounded through the cave, 'how fortuitous.' His cackle echoed through the air.

Eni shifted around. His eyes peeled for any sign of movement.

'Emenike,' a familiar voice sounded.

No.

A cold sweat formed on Eni's back but he turned all the same to face the Isi, shimmering in the ọnụ ụzọ, her pale skin glowing unnaturally with the silver light.

'You …' he said '… you *lied* to me. You had me sending those people to their *deaths*.' The words tumbled out before he could think. He was so used to managing other people's emotions that he was too often helpless with his own. They were foreign, consuming and *difficult*. His eyes pricked but he sniffed the sensation away. Tensing his jaw and as he brought his brows down sternly, he said, 'You will pay dearly for that.'

'Emenike, you are troubled, I see, but you don't mean that.'

'You lied to me.'

'What is a lie between you and I?' the Isi said, almost smiling, but the grin soon died on her cold lips. 'So is it the truth that you seek?'

'That's all I want now,' he said. Eni was tired of living in the shadows. He wanted to stand *by* Naala and for that he needed to come out into the light. He resolved to talk to her today about *everything*. About his mother. About the Isi: the woman who'd raised him, the woman who'd confined him to the shadows. He would tell her about his *ability*.

That one would be hard.

He did not talk about that. The Isi may have her assumptions, but nothing she had garnered had ever come from his lips. He used to talk about it, when he had been a boy. He would tell people what they wanted, what they were feeling, and they hated him for it. Who was this boy who exposed them of their hidden truths and desires? It had lost him friends. It had lost business for his parents. It was why they had sent him away.

'Very well,' the Isi said. 'Come closer.'

He looked at the silver screen with one eyebrow raised. Did she think him a fool?

'You always were a stubborn child.'

'You poisoned me.'

'But did you die?'

'You tried to kill me!'

'If I had tried, you wouldn't be here,' she said. 'This petulance is beneath you, Emenike. If you do not wish to know the truth about what you are, then just say that and let it be.'

A chill crept up Eni's back. He should walk away. He knew he should walk away.

The truth about what you are. The Isi's voice echoed through his chest and he drew closer to the ọnụ ụzọ. Red mist filled the centre of the structure, melting away the Isi's shimmering form. Eni blinked as an image of himself formed, as though the ọnụ ụzọ was nothing more than a looking glass. Only, he wasn't *himself.*

His eyes were dusted with red mist and he drew his hand out to touch the ọnụ ụzọ. He had to touch it. He had to know. When his hand touched the surface a sensation erupted from the tip of his fingers and spread to the rest of his body.

'The will of the people,' he said, though he didn't understand where the words had come from.

When he pulled away from the ọnụ ụzọ, mist crept up his right arm and formed a band around his eyes just as he had seen. He gasped when it enveloped him. It was intoxicating. He could see everything, feel everything. A rich, dark feeling that sank into him. A glorious rage, a succulent force that rippled through him intently, he wanted more, he needed more until—

Naala.

Eni blinked furiously as he backed away.

'What-what was that?' he heaved.

'You,' the Isi said; her violet eyes were brighter than he had ever seen it. 'Now look down at your hand.'

Eni frowned when he saw that he was holding the eziokwu scroll. Eni's stomach dropped at the sight of it.

'No,' he said, his eyes filling with tears as he clenched the Isi's blood-red scroll in his hands. The scroll she used to write down her findings on the Descendants. It would take blood from her if what she wrote was false, and it would ink her words in gold when she wrote the truth.

'Read it,' she demanded.

Eni's hand trembled as he obeyed.

Emenike – Born in the Umuihi Nkebi within the City of Nri. Born from Enyinnaya, a Descendant of the Third man and Kasemobi, a Descendant of the First woman. Blood marked to receive Amadioha, the white ram, the god of justice, the author of thunder and lightning.

Eni's eyes blurred as he stared at the page. Amadioha. The god who started the war. The god who destroyed the world. The god who Naala must stop.

Naala.

A bolt of lightning tore out of his hand, splitting the scroll into two. He dropped the charred parchment to the ground.

'No,' he choked.

'Yes,' the Isi replied. 'Emenike, the Earth Mother created an ingenious system – there's no denying that – but who rules it? Happenstance? Random acts that we remain at the mercy of? Why? Why? When we have you? When justice can right these wrongs, when you can give us the freedom to reign and control what happens to us.'

'I won't.'

Naala.

'You will, for that is who you are, the will of the people, and this is what we want.'

'I'm not him,' he said.

Naala.

'Don't be naive,' the Isi said. 'After all, it was you who summoned me.'

'I didn't,' Eni said, taking a step back as the Isi regarded him bemused. 'T-the world is supposed to be balanced; the Earth Mother will bring that back.'

'But you don't believe that, do you?'

'I do. I choose to believe it. I choose *her.*'

'Really? Then what are you doing here?' the Isi said as curls of red mist escaped through the ọnụ ụzọ and swirled around his body. He could feel his skin prick as it slithered around him.

'Agymah brought me here.'

'And who commands him?' the Isi asked and Eni's gut churned.

'I have nothing to do with that demon,' Eni spat as the red mist danced about him. It filtered through his garments until it began to pull at a weight. He spun out of its grasp but it was too late. The necklace embedded with the Mother's Crystals hung, entwined in ropes of red mist. How did it get here? Was it in his garments? Eni didn't have any of those answers but he did know that he couldn't leave without it. He sprang at the necklace but it moved quicker than light.

It sank into the ọnụ ụzọ. Eni plunged his hand through the portal but it tore through the Isi's image as though it were made out of smoke. He roared out in frustration.

'Settle down, Emenike,' the Isi said coolly as she watched over him. 'This was no mistake. Nothing is *happening* to you. You are the designer of your own fate. You and you alone.'

'You took them,' he said weakly. 'I didn't give ... I'm not him. I'm not Amadioha.' He threw his head back and howled to the heavens. Cursing at whoever allowed him to believe that life could offer him anything other than a life in the shadows. He felt the lightning crash through him and thunder laced his roar. The electrifying white light slashed through the silver water until the cave was pitch black.

'No,' was all he could manage as he lay on the ground with nothing but the echoes of the Isi's words to keep him company.

CHAPTER 55
HOPE IN THE FLOWER DUNES

City of Nri

Sinai and Naala sat in silence as they watched the crimson flame tree rustle before them. Brightly coloured petals were scattered across the Nzuzo gardens, coating it with a blanket of reds and browns.

'You were right. There *is* beauty in this palace,' Naala said, as she threw a smile at Sinai. 'I was so close to whacking you when you told me that.'

'Oh, I knew.' Sinai grinned wearily as she sat back on the tree trunk that Naala had fashioned into a seat. The Nzuzo garden was the perfect haven. They could hide from the glares, the whispers and, worse still, the *bows* that followed them down the halls of the palace.

In a moment Sinai had gone from the ostracised efuola to a beloved, and at times feared, goddess. Neither of those titles felt right to her. It didn't take long for her to seek out an escape.

That wasn't new for her – she glanced over at Naala – only this time, she was no longer alone. It felt good.

'The palace is a strange place,' Sinai said. 'It's always been strange and now everyone seems so at ease ... and yet ...'

'It feels like there's worse to come,' Naala said as Sinai nodded, biting her lip.

'I don't want to sound ungrateful,' Sinai started. 'I'm glad that we didn't destroy the Kingdom – very glad – but we also lost.' Her stomach tightened every time she thought of the crystals. How could they lose them … all of them? Again? Sinai felt like a fraud. Worse than a fraud. She felt like a failure.

'This kingdom lives to see another day.' Naala shrugged. 'Sounds like a win to me.'

'But we don't have the crystals.'

'We'll find them.'

Sinai mused, biting her lip. 'We still don't know where the Agymah is or the pit of Eriri Uhie. We need to—'

'—find the crystals,' Naala turned to Sinai patiently. 'We just need to find crystals.'

'Yes,' Sinai said slowly, 'we need to find the crystals.' Her stomach tightened again. 'How, though? We have no map. No true way to find them. We …' Sinai stopped as Naala chuckled beside her and heat rose to her cheeks. 'It's not a laughing matter.'

'Where is the girl who tamed the Aido-Hwedo? Who cleansed Anyanyu's flames? I like that girl. I miss her; she didn't whine so much,' Naala teased.

'She saw what she was up against and ran away,' Sinai grumbled.

'Well get her back, we need her. We need to work this out.' Naala shrugged. 'What else is there?'

'You once said that every time we try to fix things, they get worse. Well, maybe you were right,' Sinai said as Naala frowned. 'We tried to save the world from Dogbari and we ended up unleashing a pit of Eriri Uhie. We tried to save the city and we ended up losing the Mother's Crystals.'

'We saved Dogbari. We saved a lot of people who had been cursed. Ina should have perished but she survived. My sister nearly died but now she's safe enough to complain tirelessly – and now we have more days, more days to work all this out.'

Sinai's chest squeezed almost painfully. She sprang her head up at Naala and allowed herself to smile as she swallowed the lump forming in her throat. 'Sister?' she said, nudging Naala slightly as the girl shrugged.

'I mean it's quite obvious, is it not?' Naala replied with a grin.

In a sudden flurry, the petals on the ground lifted in unison and began to dance in the air.

'It makes no sense.' Naala turned to watch the dancing leaves. 'It makes no sense why we form these bonds. We lose people like that,' she said, snapping her fingers. 'We're wired to be selfish, to preserve ourselves and yet we form bonds that are designed to break us. Designed to make us value something more than we value ourselves,' Naala mused before turning to Sinai brightly, 'but I think this is how we actually survive. That is what keeps us going, and that is why we have to keep trying even in the face of all those troubles you mentioned; we have to push through it.'

'You're—' Sinai started but Naala's attention had shifted elsewhere. Sinai frowned as she followed Naala's gaze to the dancing petals. They had started to form a structure, a series of curves that folded smoothly over one another; smaller leaves dusted over the structure so that it began to resemble mountains of red dust.

'Why are you doing this?' Sinai asked as Naala turned to her, puzzled.

'I thought you were doing it,' Naala said as she rose from her seat and walked over to the structure, peering at it curiously.

'I'm not,' Sinai insisted as she followed the mystified girl.

'Is this …?' Naala muttered. 'Isn't this the Sand Dunes of Namibia?' Naala asked curiously.

'You know this place?' Sinai said.

'Yes, I think I've seen sculptures of it,' Naala said and a shiver ran through Sinai's spine as she drew closer. The tiniest glints sparkled within the flower structure and something magical began to stir within Sinai's spirit.

'This is where the crystal is,' Sinai whispered. 'This is where we start.' She stepped forward.

'What?' Naala retorted. 'How do you know? Because the flowers told you?'

'Yes,' Sinai replied, engrossed, as the flowers formed an image of Meekulu Kaurandua's face. 'Because the flowers told me,' she said with a smile.

The End.

*Naala and Sinai will return in Book 3 of
The Return Of The Earth Mother series.*

ACKNOWLEDGEMENTS

I want to take a moment to thank you, my dear reader. Thank you for picking my book out of thousands of others and continuing with me on this journey through Nri.

This book was undoubtedly the hardest thing I have ever written. I drafted, re-drafted, cut 40 thousand words, then re-drafted again, then again, cut out another 20 thousand words, all in a matter of months. Notwithstanding the efforts I took to try and remain sane(ish) in the middle of a global pandemic, civil rights movement and a generally rubbish time. Interestingly, that arduous process resulted in the best thing I have ever written, and I couldn't have gotten here without the help of some truly amazing people.

Thank you to my wonderful Amar, Simi and AJ, for reading the early messes of my manuscript, sitting me down to go over pages of your invaluable notes, and enduring my sulky unappreciative responses. Thank you to my mum and dad for the abundant encouragement you've showered me with and for never forgetting to express how deeply you resonated with the more profound, and often overlooked, messages embedded within this story. I can't tell you what that meant to me. Thank you, Ade, for listening to my endless queries about the plot and for pointing out typos over my shoulder whenever you got the chance. Thank you, Mariam, for sending over inspirational videos and constantly reminding me of the beauty of a lengthy editorial process when all I could see was annoyance and shame.

Thank you, Alice, for the brilliant work you've put in at Onwe to help see this book hit the shelves. Thank you, Donna, for being an excellent and patient editor. Thank you, Lian, for writing, *Across the Nightingale Floor*, a book I read in school and undoubtedly influenced my work now. Thank you for, in turn, reading my book and providing invaluable advice and feedback. Every time I think deeply about the fact that you have read(and liked!) my work, it blows my mind.

Thank you to Chloe, Kaylynn and Dorothy, the brilliant authors who took the time to read early (typo-riddled) versions of my book. Thank you to my fantastic translators Aunty Chi Chi, Aunty Chioma, Uncle Adedeji and Eunice, for ensuring I didn't blunder up any words in our beautiful languages.

Finally, to all the fantastic people who have sent me lovely messages detailing how much this Daughters of Nri meant to you, I say thank you with all of my heart. I am so grateful to have met every one of you. It is a great honour to have you read my work and an even greater one to know that it resonated with you. Thank you.

DICTIONARY OF WORDS

Word (Pronounciation)
Language
Meaning

Abara (Ahh-baa-rah)
Igbo
A double-edged sword, originally used by the Ika people of Delta State, Nigeria

Abumoonu (Ah-boo-moon-u)
Igbo
Cursed

Achicha Ede (Ahh-Chi-Cheh Eh-day)
Igbo
A native Igbo dish consisting mainly of dried Cocoyam, mgbụmgbụ, and palm oil

Adze (Ads)
Ewe
A vampiric being in Ewe folklore, located in Togo and Ghana

Agbaya (Ahg-bah-yah)
Yoruba
An older person, who despite his age, is considered useless

Aido-Hwedo (Ahh-kwa)
Fon
The rainbow serpent from Fon mythology

Ákúkó-álá (Ahh-kwu-co Ah-la)
Igbo
A form of storytelling in Igbo culture in the form of anecdotes about past events

Akwa (Ahh-kwa)
Igbo
Nest

Akwete (Ak-wet-tay)
Igbo
A unique handwoven fabric of Igbo women of Akwete in Abia State, Nigeria. Akwete cloth weaving is said to be as old as the Igbo nation.

Akwụna (Ahh-kwu-nah)
Igbo
Prostitute

Ala (Ahh-la)
Igbo
Earth Goddess; female diety of the earth, fertility, creativity and morality

Àlà (Ay-la)
Igbo
Earth

Amadioha (Am-ahh-dee-owm-ha)
Igbo
God of justice; Metaphysically, Amadioha represents the collective will of the people; he speaks and strikes through thunder

Amaghị (Ama-yee)
Igbo
Mysterious; unknown

Amoosu (Am-oh-sue)
Igbo
Witch

Amụrụ ha abụọ (Am-oh-roh ah abohr)
Igbo
Born From Both

Anụ ofia (An-yoh-f-yah)
Igbo
Curse word; wild animal

Anwu (An-who)
Igbo
Sun

Anyanwu (An-yahn-woe)
Igbo
Anyanwu is an Igbo solar deity. The direct translation is "eye of the sun"

Aturu (Ah-two-rue)
Igbo
Sheep; Followers

Biloko (Bee-low-ko)
Mongo-Nkundo
A bloodthirsty, blood-red fey. These gnome-sized hunters stalk the wildest depths warm jungles and orginate from Congo

Bụrụ ọnụ (Boh-roh oh-noh)
Igbo
Cursed Ones

Chi (Ch-ee)
Igbo
Chi, the spirit believed to inhabit each individual; soul

Chínēkè (Chee-nay-kay)
Igbo
God

Edemede (Eh-de-meh-de)
Igbo
Awakening

Efe-efe (Eh-fay Eh-fay)
Igbo
Flying

Efere (Eh-fair-reh)
Igbo
Plate

Efuola (Eh-fu-oh-lah)
Nsinri
Illegitimate

Egbu (Ehg-bu)
Igbo
Kill

Ẹka (Eh-kah)
Igbo
Cave

Erhọ (Eh-roh)
Igbo
The polished and dry bark of the natural wetland flax plant of the Niger Delta region traditionally called erhọ; used for making the traditional fibre rope

Eriri Uhie (Eh-ri-ri Ou-he)
Igbo
High

Eziokwu (Eh-zyo-kwo)
Igbo
Fungi

ɛyɛ sɛ wo yɛ (Ey-yeh sow-we yeh)
Twi
I demand it

Gele (Ge-lay)
Yoruba
A head tie is a women's cloth head scarf that is commonly worn in many parts of West Africa and Southern Africa

Ibu (E-bu)
Igbo
Cargo

Icheku (E-che-ku)
Igbo
African velvet tamarind is the fruit of a native West African tree called Dialium Guineense. Commonly known as "Licky Licky"

Idemili (E-day-mili)
Igbo
The River Goddess Idemili (literally means Pillar of Water) is regarded as the goddess of all water bodies

Idu (E-du)
Igbo
Settlement

Igodo (E-goh-do)
Igbo
Key

Ihunaya (E-who-an-yah)
Igbo
Love

Ike Obi (E-keh Oh-bee)
Igbo
Heart Power

Ikenga (Ee-ken-gah)
Igbo
Literal meaning "place of strength"; a horned deity; personal god of human endeavor, achievement, success, and victor

Iko (Ee-ko)
Igbo
Cup

Ikuku (Ee-ku-ku)
Igbo
Air

Ikusa (Ee-ku-sah)
Igbo
Break

Imeda (Ee-me-dah)
Igbo
Weaken

Isi Agwọ Ahụ (E-si Ahg-wo Ah-ho)
Igbo
The Head of the Snake

Itucha (E-too-chah)
Igbo
Salve; ointment

Izu (E-zu)
Igbo
Week

Jikọọ (Jee-koo)
Igbo
Connect

Kedu (Keh-du)
Igbo
What?

Kpọ (Po)
Igbo
Explosion

Kpofuo (Po-phuoh)
Igbo
Explosion

Lolo (Louw-louw)
Igbo
Lady; revered woman

Mami wata (Mah-me woh-ta)
Pidgin
Water spirit; mermaid

Mba (Mm-bah)
Igbo

No

Mgbanwe (Mm-ng-ban-way)

Igbo

Change

Mgbapu (Mm-ng-bah-pu)

Igbo

Going away; leaving; running away

Mmiri (Mm-ee-ree)

Igbo

Water

Mmo (Mm-moh)

Igbo

Spirit

Ndewo (Nn-de-oh)

Igbo

Greeting; welcome

Nakombse

Gur

A noble class in the ancient kingdom of Mossi (modern day Burkina Faso) who claimed the right to rule

Ncoh

pidgin

Is that so?

Ndụ (Nn-du)

Igbo

Life

Ngwa (Nn-gwah)

Igbo

Quick

Njem (Nn-jem)

Igbo

Journey

Nkebi (Nn-keb-ee)

Igbo

Section
Nkịta Ọhịa (Nn-keeta O-high-yah)
Igbo
Section

Nna (Nn-na)
Igbo
Father

Nnunu (Nn-nu-nu)
Igbo
Bird

Nsibidi (Nn-si-bee-dee)
Igbo
Ancient igbo written script

Nwanne-nwanyi (Nn-wan-nay- Nn-wan-ye)
Igbo
Sister

Nzuzuo (Nn-zuh-zwo)
Nsinri
Secret

Oba Akwụkwọ (Oh-bah Akwu-kwo)
Igbo
Place of Books; Library

Ọbara (Oh-bah-rah)
Igbo
Blood

Obi (Oh-bee)
Igbo
An aristocratic title, meaning either elder in the first instance or chief in the second; also symbollically meaning heart

Ofo (Oh-for)
Igbo
A staff carried by selected Igbo elder men

Ogene (O-ge-ne)
Igbo
An Igbo musical instrument instrument, which is a large metal bell

Ọgụgụ (O-gu-gu)
Igbo
Reading

Ọgwụ (Og-wu)
Igbo
Medicine

Ọja flute (o-jah)
Igbo
A traditional Igbo music instrument made of carved wood. They instrumentalist uses the fingers and leaps to manipulate the sounds.

Okike (Oh-ki-ki)
Igbo
Creation

Ọkụ (O-ku)
Igbo
Fire

Ọmuti (O-moh-tea)
Yoruba
Drunkard

Ọnụ ụzọ (Onour uh-zoh)
Igbo
Entrance; portal

Ọnwa (Oh-wah)
Igbo
Moonlight

Ọnwu (Oh-wu)
Igbo
Death

Onyeisi (On-yay-see)
Igbo
Boss

Oroma (Oh-ro-ma)
Igbo
Orange

Ọnye Nyocha (On-yay Ny-oh-cha)
Igbo
Reporter; someone who reports; spy

Otomy (Oh-toh-me)
Nsinri
Atoms; miniscule particles

Ozo (Oh-zoh)
Igbo
Sir; revered man

Rie (Ree)
Igbo
Eat

Udo (Ou-doe)
Igbo
Peace

Udu (Ou-du)
Igbo
A West African drum instrument in the form of a clay plot

Ụlọ (O-Loh)
Igbo
House

Urukpuru (Uo-rook-pu-ru)
Igbo
Cloudy

Zobo (Zo-bo)

Igbo

A cold, refreshing hibiscus drink